Being an author has al
dream. But it was only v
during her final year at
soon she wanted that dr
got serious about her writing, and now she writes the kind of books she wants to see in the world, featuring people who look like her, for a living. When she's not writing she's spending time with her husband and dogs in Cape Town, South Africa. She admits that this is a perfect life, and is grateful for it.

Brenda Harlen is a former attorney who once had the privilege of appearing before the Supreme Court of Canada. The practice of law taught her a lot about the world and reinforced her determination to become a writer—because in fiction, she could promise a happy ending! Now she is an award-winning, RITA® Award-nominated national bestselling author of more than thirty titles for Mills & Boon. You can keep up-to-date with Brenda on Facebook and Twitter, or through her website, brendaharlen.com

Also by Therese Beharrie

Tempted by the Billionaire Next Door
Surprise Baby, Second Chance
Her Festive Flirtation
Island Fling with the Tycoon

Conveniently Wed, Royally Bound

United by Their Royal Baby
Falling for His Convenient Queen

Billionaires for Heiresses

Second Chance with Her Billionaire
From Heiress to Mum

Also by Brenda Harlen

The Sheriff's Nine-Month Surprise
Her Seven-Day Fiancé
Six Weeks to Catch a Cowboy
Claiming the Cowboy's Heart
Double Duty for the Cowboy
One Night with the Cowboy
Baby Talk & Wedding Bells
The Last Single Garrett
Maverick Christmas Surprise
Bring Me a Maverick for Christmas!
The Maverick's Midnight Proposal

HER TWIN BABY SECRET

THERESE BEHARRIE

A CHANCE FOR THE RANCHER

BRENDA HARLEN

MILLS & BOON

First Published in Great Britain 2020
by Mills & Boon, an imprint of HarperCollinsPublishers,
1 London Bridge Street, London, SE1 9GF

ISBN: 978-0-263-27868-2

0220

HER TWIN BABY SECRET

THERESE BEHARRIE

For Grant,
who would pretend to be in a fake relationship
with me so I could save face in a heartbeat.
If we weren't already married, I mean. I love you.

For the online friends
who've become my community.
I didn't ever think you could exist,
but I'm so grateful you do.

PROLOGUE

ALEXA MOORE HAD never thought the pressure her parents had put on her her entire life would result in this. She barely contained the squeal of excitement tickling her throat.

Her father was sitting beside her in the car, her mother at the back. Both were staring at their phones. They were either checking their emails, replying to emails, or writing their own emails. Leighton and Karla Moore were simple in that way. Work came first; everything else, second. They'd reconciled having a family in light of those priorities by treating their children as though they were work. That was why Alexa and her younger brother by a year, Lee, were raised to function much as their parents did: work was the most important thing. Being Leighton and Karla's children, they had to work harder than anyone else.

Who needed a loving, emotionally supportive family anyway?

But that wasn't for today. Today was for happiness and new beginnings. She wasn't stubborn enough not to acknowledge her parents' contribution to this moment. It was part of why she'd brought them with her. They were the ones who had suggested—instructed—her to start working as soon as she turned sixteen. They'd told her to give them half of what she earned, and because she was their child she'd asked them to help her invest the other half. On her graduation from her Honours degree in business, they'd gifted her with a policy they'd taken out with that money. It had been an impressive nest egg. And it had kept growing while she attended culinary school.

She'd got a bursary to study at Cape Town's Culinary Institute. She was lucky. If she hadn't, she would have had to use that nest egg and she wouldn't be able to move forward with her dream. Her parents had paid for her studies in business on the condition that she got distinctions for all her subjects. She had, though not easily, because she knew she'd already disappointed them by not taking the mathematics bursary an elite tertiary faculty had offered.

But her dream was her dream. A business degree helped her get to that dream—and helped her please her parents more than culinary school had. Their disappointment was worth it for this moment though. She had no student loans, four years of business knowledge, two years of culinary knowledge, and two years' experience in the industry. She was finally ready. This was the last step.

She pulled up in front of the property, letting out a happy sigh before she got out of the car. The brick façade of the building was as appealing as it had been the first time she'd seen it. As the first time it had encouraged her to take a chance on it.

'This is it.'

She clasped her fingers together behind her back to keep from fidgeting.

'This?'

'Yes.' She straightened her spine at the disapproval in her father's voice. 'It's an up-and-coming neighbourhood.'

'It looks unsafe, Lex,' Karla said.

'Oh, it's fine.' She waved a hand. 'You know how Cape Town city centre is. The fanciest road is right next to the dodgiest one. Besides, there are so many people around.'

As if proving it, a group of young people walked past them. They were most likely students; not exactly her target clientele. But everyone had to start somewhere, and students meant lecturers and parents and more mature people who would come to the classy joint in the dingy neighbourhood for the feel of it. She jiggled her shoulders.

'I'm going to call it In the Rough, because this place is a diamond in the rough.' She grinned. 'It's going to be—'

'Lee, darling!'

The world either slowed at her mother's exclamation, or Alexa's heart was pumping alarmingly fast. Why was her brother here? How much of what she'd said had he heard? Would he use it against her?

'What are you doing here?' she asked, her voice cool, a reaction to mitigate the heated emotions those questions had evoked. She would not show them that vulnerability. 'I didn't tell you about this.'

'Dad did,' Lee said, taking their father's hand in a quick shake. 'He told me about a week ago you were planning on showing them a property. Gave me the address and everything, so I could check it out myself.'

'Why would you want to?'

'I can't check on what my big sister is doing with her life?'

No, she wanted to answer. She would have, if their parents weren't there—they would disapprove. Somehow, after years of trying and failing to obtain their approval, she still wanted it. After years of her brother using that desire as a weapon to compete with her, she was still offering it to him.

'To be fair, I'm not doing this with my life yet.' She was trying to be civil, like she always did. Because she was still trying to be a decent person with Lee, too. When would she learn her lesson when it came to her family? 'I wanted Mom and Dad to see this place before I put in an offer.'

'I know.'

'Did you want to see it, too?'

'Oh, I already have.'

She frowned. 'Why?'

'Because I made an offer.' He shoved his hands into

his pockets, his smile catlike. 'The owner accepted it this morning. This place is going to be mine.'

There was a stunned silence. Her parents broke it by asking Lee why he'd bought the place. Bits and pieces of his answer floated across to her. He wanted to secure the place as a surprise for Alexa. It was a smart business decision to invest in property, particularly in a neighbourhood that was fast becoming one to watch. If he and Alexa worked together, there was less chance of failure. The Moores could become a powerhouse in the hospitality industry.

Lies. Lies, all of it.

Lee spoke to them as fluently as he did his other languages. His linguistic skills were as impressive as her mathematical skills. He knew five of South Africa's eleven official languages; he also knew how to fool their parents. They thought he was a good, supportive brother when in reality, he was a master manipulator. All for the sake of winning a competition he'd made up in his head where they were the only competitors and he the only willing participant.

'Alexa,' Karla called. 'You're daydreaming, darling.'

She blinked. 'Sorry.'

'Did you hear what your brother did?'

'Yes.'

'Aren't you glad?'

'Why would I be glad?'

Her mother exchanged a look with her father. Leighton took the baton.

'Lee's made the smart decision here. It's not a buyer's market at the moment, so you might not have got the property. He has more capital, and more clout, so he had a better chance of being successful in the purchase.'

'He didn't know about the property before you told him,' she said numbly. 'And he only has more capital because he's been working longer.' In the business sector, which was more lucrative. Even her nest egg couldn't beat that. 'The owner said she hadn't had much interest in the six months the property's been on the market.'

'She did sound thrilled with my offer.'

She turned at the satisfaction in Lee's voice. When she saw it reflected on his face, her heart broke. This didn't feel like the other times. When he'd race to the dinner table, turn back to her and say, 'I win!' though he'd been the only one running. Or when he would bring a test home from school, announcing that he'd beat Alexa's mark from the year before.

This was more malicious. It was…uglier. And it proved that she would always be a target Lee would shoot at, no matter what the cost.

Unless she did something about it.

'I hope you find a tenant soon, Lee.'

'Wait!' he said when she started walking to her car. 'I thought you'd rent it?'

'So you can pop in whenever you want? Make your presence known in my business? Pull the rug out from under me when I think I'm safe?' She shook her head. 'I appreciate the offer, but you'll have to find someone else.'

'Alexa, you're being foolish.'

'No, Dad, I'm being realistic. But this is a great neighbourhood.' Her voice cracked, echoing her heart. 'He'll find someone to rent from him soon enough.'

'Darling, your brother only wants to help.'

She took a deep breath before offering her mother a smile. 'I know.' Even after he'd punctured a hole in her dreams and her parents were defending him, she couldn't be blunt. 'I can't take his help or I wouldn't be making the Moore name proud, would I? It's all about achieving things we can be proud of. I can't be proud of this.'

Another breath.

'You should go to the restaurant I booked for us tonight

with Lee. He deserves it.' She smiled at her family, well aware that it didn't reach her eyes. 'I hope you enjoy the food.'

She got into her car and drove away, leaving her heart and her dreams shattered behind her.

CHAPTER ONE

Four years later

'OH,' ALEXA SAID FLATLY. 'It's you.'

Benjamin Foster couldn't help the laugh that rumbled in his chest. 'Yes, it's me.'

Alexa Moore, owner of the elite Infinity restaurant, and the woman who probably hated him more than anyone else in the world, glowered.

'You need to stop following me.'

'I'm not following you,' he denied.

'Are you sure? You seem to be everywhere I am.'

'Because we're in the same business.'

Her eyes stopped scanning the room and settled on him. Sharpened. 'You're here to offer Cherise de Bruyn a job.'

He tilted his head. 'How did you know?'

'You think I didn't hear about Victor Fourie being poached from In the Rough?' She smiled, but it wasn't friendly. 'It's terrible when karma does her thing, isn't it?'

'I'm not sure why she would get involved.'

She gave him a look. He allowed himself a small smile.

'Fine, I do know.' A few seconds passed. Something cleared in his brain. 'You're here to offer Cherise a job, too.'

She responded by ignoring him. He shouldn't have wanted to smile. It seemed rude to since he was the reason she had to offer Cherise a job. She hadn't confirmed that was why she was there, but he was fairly certain. When the thought of being rude did nothing to deter his amusement—

apparently what his presence did to her tickled his funny bone—he turned to the barperson and ordered a drink.

'Can I get you one?'

'I don't want to owe you one, so no, thank you.'

He *tsk*ed. 'That's not very mature, Alexa.'

'Maturity is for the weak,' she muttered under her breath.

He didn't bother hiding his grin this time, but paid for his drink before he replied. 'I don't agree with that.'

'Why would you, Benjamin?' she said with a sigh. 'I said it. On principle, you can't agree with me lest *you* seem weak.'

'"Lest"?'

'It means to avoid the risk of.'

'I know what it means. I'm wondering why you said it.'

She sighed again, as though he were chopping up the last of her patience. Which was probably true. They'd known one another for eight years now. Or perhaps it would be better to say they'd known about one another for eight years. They didn't know one another, not by a long shot. They had only gone to the Culinary Institute together, the current venue of their meeting, and met on and off in the six years after that.

Whenever they did, they rubbed each other up the wrong way. It caused a friction so intense that sometimes Benjamin struggled to figure out how he felt about her. On the one hand, she never backed down, said interesting things like *lest*, and made him laugh. On the other hand, she was his greatest competition.

Who could be friendly with the competition?

Infinity was rated highly on all the important websites. He often heard whispers of the patrons of his own restaurant comparing In the Rough's food or ambience to Infinity's. It wasn't uncommon for patrons to do so; comments like that were part of the business. But her restaurant was the one he heard mentioned most frequently. It was also the one they preferred most frequently.

'Really?' she asked when he leaned against the bar. 'In this spacious, beautiful, but most importantly *spacious* place, you couldn't find someone else to bother?'

'Bothering you is more fun.'

Her reply came in the form of a glare. He smiled back, sipped from his drink, and didn't move. He did watch though.

She was right—the venue was gorgeous. It was nestled in the valley of one of the many vineyards in Stellenbosch. Bright green fields stretched out in front of them courtesy of an all-glass wall. The room they were in, usually a dining hall, had been transformed for the sake of the graduation. Chairs were set out in rows, a small stage had been erected on one side, and the opposite side housed the bar they were at. On the other side of the glass wall, accessed through a door on the side, were tables and chairs under tall trees.

He remembered sitting there many a lunch time when he'd been at the Institute. Hell, he remembered watching Alexa glower at him from inside the dining hall much in the same way she was doing now. He'd known even then that she was dangerous. How, he wasn't sure.

'What the hell is he doing here?'

The words weren't meant for him, but he heard them. When he followed her gaze, he saw the cause. Her brother, his business partner, was there. Benjamin didn't know why. Securing a head chef was more in line with Benjamin's responsibilities. But their partnership had evolved in the last four years, and their roles weren't what they initially were when they started working together.

Back then, Benjamin was the head chef and Lee's management company dealt with the running of the restaurant. Benjamin had since taken over some of those responsibilities, which was hard to do without a head chef. It meant that

Benjamin's time was still needed in the kitchen. For three glorious months after Victor Fourie had been persuaded to work for In the Rough, Benjamin had been able to explore more of the management side of things. As it turned out, he enjoyed running a restaurant more than spending all his time in the kitchen.

But Lee had been acting strangely when it came to this head chef thing. With Victor Fourie, Lee had actively encouraged Benjamin to go after the man even though he knew Victor worked for Alexa. It had started out harmlessly enough. They'd been out for drinks one night, discussing work, when the chef walked into the bar. It had seemed like a perfectly fair move to ask him to join them. After that night, Lee had told him to get Victor to take over some of Benjamin's responsibilities. Since it would take an immense amount of pressure off Benjamin, he'd done it, though he hadn't understood Lee's insistence. Now Lee was here…

'Ben!' Lee said when he saw them. His eyes flickered to his sister. Something Benjamin didn't like shimmered there. 'Fancy seeing you here.'

'Is it?' Benjamin asked, taking Lee's hand. 'I told you I was coming.'

'He has to pretend it's a surprise in front of me,' Alexa said, her voice emotionless.

He'd only ever heard her speak that way with her brother. He would have thought, after his and Alexa's antagonistic history, she would have aimed that tone at him, too. But when she spoke to him, her voice was icy, or annoyed, or full of emotion, none of which he could read. He found he preferred it.

'If he doesn't,' she continued, 'it would be clear that he's really here because of me.'

'Not everything I do is because of you, Alexa.' Lee said it smoothly, but Benjamin could feel the resentment.

'I wish that were true.'

Lee didn't acknowledge that Alexa had spoken. 'What I am surprised about is finding you two together.'

'Why?' Benjamin asked.

'Don't you hate one another?'

He looked at Alexa; Alexa looked at him. For a beat, they said nothing. Her expression changed then, going from icy cool to warm. His heart thundered in response to her hazel eyes opening. They grew lighter when they did, so that he could see the green flecks in the light brown. In a way no grown man should experience, Benjamin's knees went weak.

Her eyebrow quirked, as if she knew, though there was no possible way she could. But the show of sassiness pulled the side of her face higher, softening a defined cheekbone. It was an extraordinary juxtaposition to the other side of her face, which was untouched by the expression. It was still hard lines and sharp angles. That had never applied to her lips though, one side of which was now quirked up—much like her brow—in amusement. At him. He was amusing her.

Because he was admiring her full lips that looked as soft as dough. An interesting comparison, though not surprising since he regularly dealt with dough. What *was* surprising was that he wanted to mould that dough as he did in the kitchen. But with his lips instead of his hands, though he could imagine brushing a thumb over those soft creases…

He took a long drag from his drink, severely disappointed that it wasn't alcohol. He could have done with the shock, the burn of downing a whiskey. But no, he'd decided he shouldn't drink because he wanted a clear head when he spoke to Cherise.

How was this clear?

'Well, Lee,' Alexa said, her voice as smooth as the brandy he'd longed for. Or had he thought of whiskey? 'You know what they say: hate and love are two sides of the same coin.'

Lee's head dropped. 'What are you saying?'

'You don't know?' She turned to Benjamin. 'You kept your word. How lovely of you.'

Benjamin didn't know what was going on, but he understood he shouldn't say anything.

'There's no way you and Ben are dating.'

'You're entitled to believe what you want to, Lee. We don't owe you explanations.'

'You're dating her?' Lee asked Benjamin now. 'No. Of course not. You would have told me.'

'I asked him not to. Apparently his loyalties are divided now.' She wrinkled her nose. 'I shouldn't have said that. It was insensitive.'

She grabbed Benjamin's hand. Good thing he was still numb from shock, or he might have felt that explosion of warmth from the contact.

'I'm sorry, Ben.'

Their eyes met again. Nothing he could read on her face gave him any clues to her feelings. No plea that he play along; no acknowledgement that this was strange. Or maybe there were clues, but he couldn't recognise them.

Then she smiled at him. Her mouth widened, revealing strikingly straight white teeth. Those lips curved up, softening all the lines and angles of her face. Even her gaze warmed, though he had no idea why or how. It was a genuine smile that both stunned and enthralled him. He couldn't look away.

'Oh, you *are* together.' Lee's voice penetrated the fog in his brain. 'Wow. I can already see the headline in *Cape Town Culinary*: "Rival restaurant owners fall in love".' He paused. 'Maybe we should get the photographer to take a picture of you two now for the article? I'll call her over.'

Both of them wrenched their gazes away from one another to stare at Lee.

CHAPTER TWO

'I'D RATHER NOT,' Alexa said when she recovered from the shock. She set the water she'd been drinking on the bar, slid off the stool. 'If you'll excuse me, I think some fresh air would do me good.'

She looked at neither of them. Not the man who'd broken her heart too many times for her to count; not the man who'd helped her brother do it. Though now, of course, she was pretending that he was her boyfriend. She alone, because Benjamin had not once said a word about the elaborate tale she'd woven. He would now, of course. As soon as she was out of the way, he'd tell Lee that she was lying and they'd laugh at her.

Nausea welled up inside her. She hoped it didn't mean she'd throw up. She could already imagine Lee's questions: *Rough night last night, sis? Or are you pregnant?* He would laugh, she wouldn't, and he'd know something was up. The last thing she needed was her brother discovering her secret.

She soothed the panic the idea evoked by reminding herself that Lee's presence in the last four years had generally made her queasy. That could be the answer now, too. The thought calmed her. Remembering she'd been feeling surprisingly good these last months helped, too. She took a breath, exhaled slowly. She was one week away from entering her second trimester. Once she got there, she'd tell her parents, and there would be no chance Lee could tell them for her.

It might have been a little paranoid—but then, it might not. She had a brother who was intent on ruining her life after all. Telling their parents she was pregnant before she could was exactly the kind of thing he'd do. She wouldn't get the chance to tell them the story she'd practised since she'd decided to do something about her need for a family. Not the broken one she currently had, but a whole one. A safe one. A family she could actually trust.

As usual, the thought sent vibrations through her. Pain, disappointment prickled her skin. She stopped walking, bracing herself against a tree as she caught the breath her emotions stole. She didn't get the chance to.

'You haven't seen me in months and this is how you treat me?'

She closed her eyes, put all her defences in place, and turned. 'I thought you'd get the message.'

'What message?'

'I don't want to see you, Lee,' she told him. 'I don't want you in my life.'

Something almost imperceptible passed over his face. 'We're family. You have no choice.'

'I'm aware that we're family.' She took a deep breath. 'That's the only reason we've seen one another at all in the last four years. Mom and Dad have birthdays, and there are special days, like Christmas and…' She broke off. She didn't have to explain anything to him. 'Anyway, we have to see one another at those occasions. But not outside of them.'

'All this because I bought a building you wanted?'

'You know it wasn't only a building,' she snapped. Pulled it back. But it was hard to contain. It sat in her chest like a swarm of angry bees, waiting to be let out. She could *not* let it out. 'You've insisted on making this about you and me, but really it's about you. It's always been. I want to live my life without you. You can't seem to live yours without me.'

He smirked. 'You're putting an awful lot of importance on yourself.'

'No, you are.'

She meant to stride past him, but his hand caught her wrist.

'I assume you're here for a new head chef. What happens if you don't get one, Lex?' he asked softly. 'You can't keep running Infinity and its kitchen. You must be spreading yourself thin since your last chef left.'

'He didn't leave. You stole him. You and Benjamin stole him.'

'Which makes me wonder how your romance bloomed?' Lee's lips curved into a smile that broke her heart. Because it was mean, and so unlike that of the brother she'd once thought she had. 'Were you looking for revenge? Maybe you thought you could make him fall in love with you, then break his heart? Or maybe use your body to—'

'Lee.'

The voice was deep with unbridled emotion. Both she and Lee looked in the direction it came from. Benjamin stood there, watching them with a glower she'd never seen on him before. He was usually effortlessly charming, which had been one of the reasons she didn't like him. No one could be that charming, certainly not *effortlessly*. Her conclusion had been that he was a demon, or some kind of magical being sent there to test her patience. The test was going smoothly. Her results were not as positive.

His disapproval should have been aimed at her then, considering their history of battling against one another. But it wasn't. It was aimed at Lee. A thrill went through her before she stomped it down viciously. She did a few more jumps on it for good measure.

'Ben,' Lee said with a smile. He tended to reserve the vicious side of his temperament for her. 'Didn't see you there.'

'I thought as much. I doubt you'd be talking to Alexa that way if you did.'

Benjamin's eyes met hers. She wasn't sure how she knew

it, but he was asking her if she was okay. She angled her head. He looked back at Lee.

'You should probably get someone to help you if that's your perception of relationships.' He held a hand out to her. It took her a moment to realise he meant for her to take it. As if someone else were in her body, she did. 'Even so, I have to say I'm not thrilled with your implication. Alexa and I are in a healthy relationship. Neither of us is using the other. Unless there's something you want to tell me, Lex?'

Oh. He was keeping the pretence going.

Oh.

She shook her head.

'If I say something corny like "I'm using you for your addictive kisses", would you be mad?' he asked.

There it was, that effortless charm. It was kind of nice when it was being used for good. To help her instead of annoy her.

'You probably shouldn't say it, to be safe.'

He laughed. For a moment, it was just the two of them, amused at one another. A part of her wiggled with glee; another part told her to take a step back. This was confusing, and happening too fast. She wasn't even sure what 'this' was.

'Seriously?' Genuine confusion lit Lee's face. 'I thought this, you two, were a joke.'

'You were accusing Alexa of those things earlier and you thought this was a joke?' Benjamin's voice had switched from charm to ice.

Alexa cleared her throat. She didn't want this turning into a full-on brawl. Even if the prospect of seeing Lee punched brought her more joy than it should have. She was strangely certain that would be the outcome if she didn't intervene.

'Ben and I agreed to keep business and our personal

lives separate,' she told Lee. 'That's why no one knew about our relationship until today.'

'And you told *me*?' Lee asked. 'Now I know you two are lying.'

'You don't have to believe us, Lee.'

But she really wanted him to. Maybe that was why she went along with what Benjamin said next.

'He doesn't have to believe us, but why don't we show him why he should?'

When he looked at her, asked her permission with his eyes, she nodded. Told herself wanting to make Lee believe her was why she'd went along with what Benjamin did next. But all of that dissipated when he kissed her.

He'd never wanted to punch someone as much as he'd wanted to punch his business partner in the last few minutes. He wasn't sure if it was because Lee was acting almost unrecognisably, or if his instincts were tingling because he *did* recognise the way Lee was acting. It was the same way people in his past had acted. They'd need something from him, then act surprised, attacked, victimised when he asked them if they were taking advantage of his desire to help.

His instincts could also have been tingling because despite his past, he still wanted to help someone who needed him. It was clear Alexa did. It was his weakness, helping people. Not when the help was appreciated; only when the help was taken advantage of. He didn't know where Alexa fitted into that. It didn't keep him from kissing her though.

Not his best decision, though his lips disagreed. They heartily approved of the softness of Alexa's lips pressed against them. She smelled of something sweet and light; reminded him of walking through a garden at the beginning of spring. It felt as though he'd been drawn into that scene when her mouth began to move against his. His body felt lighter, as it often did after a long, dull winter and the sun made its comeback. He could easily imagine the two of them in that garden, surrounded by flowers, overcome with the joy and happiness a new season tended to bring.

The taste of her brought him sharply back into his body.

He hadn't intended on *really* kissing her. A quick meeting of lips was enough to convince her brother they were together—people who didn't like one another didn't kiss at all. He assumed. Before he started to kiss this woman he supposedly didn't like.

There was no time to think of it since his tongue had somehow disobeyed his desire to keep things simple. Instead, it had slipped between Alexa's lips, plunging them both into complicated.

But damn, if complicated didn't feel *good.* She was sweet, spicy, exactly as her personality dictated. The tangling of their tongues sent pulses through his body, settling in places that made him both uncomfortable and desperate. He used it as an excuse to rest a hand on the small of her back, pressing her against him. She gave a little gasp into his mouth as her body moulded against his, but she didn't pull away. She did the opposite in fact, reaching her arms around his neck and pulling herself higher so their bodies were aligned at a more pleasurable height.

It was that thought that had him pulling away. He wouldn't embarrass himself in public. More importantly, he couldn't embarrass Alexa. Both would happen if they didn't pull themselves together.

She didn't protest, lowering herself to her feet again, her gaze avoiding his. But then she shook her head and looked at him. Curiosity and desire were fierce in her expression, but it was the confusion that did him in.

Was it brought on by this little charade they were performing? Or was she surprised at the intensity of their kisses?

'Happy?' she asked.

He almost answered before he realised she wasn't talking to him. Good thing his brain had started working in time. He would have said something he couldn't take back if he answered. Something in the vicinity of a *yes and no* and maybe a few other statements.

Lee was watching them with a frown.

'You two really are together.'

'So you keep saying.'

'I mean it this time,' Lee said. His next words were directed at Benjamin. 'You've complicated things.'

No kidding. 'You didn't know about us for months.' *Because there was nothing to know.* 'We'll be fine.'

'I'm sure Cherise de Bruyn agrees.'

Benjamin thought that was a strange thing to say until he saw the jerk of Lee's head to the side. Cherise stood with her fellow graduates, watching the three of them with a bemused smile on her face. Considering he'd spoken to her first thing when he arrived, he was sure Alexa had, too. Now Cherise was watching the two people competing for her to work for them kiss, and was probably wondering what the hell would happen next.

To be fair, so was he.

CHAPTER THREE

ALEXA PAUSED AT her front door, wondering why she was doing what she was doing. No answer she came up with made her feel better about doing it, so she simply unlocked the door. She stepped aside to let Benjamin pass her, then closed it and resisted—barely—leaning her forehead against it. Alexa couldn't give in to her impulses any more. They were what had got her into trouble in the first place. If she hadn't pretended Benjamin was her boyfriend, she wouldn't be letting him into her home now to discuss the way forward.

It seemed particularly cruel that she had to do that here. Her home was *her* space. It was where she recovered from long, rough days. It was where she cried when the pressure of running a business got to her. It was where she remembered her complicated feelings when her sous chef had brought in her new baby.

Kenya had come in to show the baby around and had brought her mother, too. There had been so much love between the three of them. Alexa had watched it, her heart breaking and filling at the same time. When Kenya had handed her the child, that breaking stopped. She'd remembered all those times she'd thought family couldn't only mean competition and neglect. She hadn't seen examples otherwise, but she'd hoped. Then, between her studies, work, and her brother ruining her dreams, she'd forgotten that hope. Until she'd seen Kenya and her family. Until she'd held that baby.

She'd remembered that, once upon a time, her dreams

had included having a family. A warm, happy family with people who loved and respected one another. She thought about how she had no one to go home to at night. How the idea of dating and trusting someone so she could have someone to go home to made her feel ill. A new idea had popped into her head then. One year later, whoops, she was pregnant and there was no going back.

It wasn't so much *whoops* as going through vigorous fertility treatments and being artificially inseminated twice. But *whoops* was what she planned to tell her parents. Rather their disappointment that she hadn't been careful than tell them she didn't want anyone in her life who could hurt her the way they had.

She was clearly in a very healthy mental space.

'Nice place,' Benjamin said, breaking into her thoughts.

'Thanks.'

It was more invasive than she'd anticipated, having him look at her stuff. But they needed privacy, her place was the closest, and it was better to be here than at Infinity. There was more of her there, and with their baggage, it had felt wrong to take him there.

It wasn't that she wasn't proud of her home. Everything in it had been put there for a reason. The beige sofas were comfortable and expensive, the first items she'd bought for the flat. The restaurant had still been a baby, so it had taken most of her disposable income to buy them. She had slept on them for four months. They weren't as comfortable as a bed, but then, she hadn't been sleeping much anyway. She had been fuelled by the desire to succeed, and three to four hours of sleep were more than enough in those days.

The coffee table had come next, then the dining room set, both made from the most gorgeous stained wood. The fluffy carpet had been an indulgence considering she still hadn't had a bed, but filling the open-plan lounge and dining-room had been more important to her. It had made the flat feel like a home.

Her priorities had then shifted to her bedroom, which took her six months to complete. Last was her kitchen, separated from the dining room by half-wall, half-glass, with an opening on the right. The style somehow managed to give the impression of being open-plan, but offered privacy, too. She hadn't had the money to do what she wanted in the kitchen for the longest time, which was why she'd left it for last. Besides, she had everything she wanted at her restaurant, and that was enough.

After a year and a half, her kitchen was exactly what she had imagined it would be. Her appliances were top-of-the-range. Shelves were strategically placed all over the room; spices near the stove, fresh herbs near the window. Cupboards were filled with the best quality ingredients, and close to where they were needed. She'd added colour with fake plants, because her energy was mostly focused on keeping the herbs alive and there was too much competition for the light. And her utensils! Those were colourful, too, though pastel, which made her feel classy and grown-up. Heaven only knew why.

'I didn't expect it to be quite this…warm.'

She threw her handbag onto the sofa, shrugged off her coat. 'Because I'm so cold-hearted, you mean?'

'Not at all.'

'Then what did you mean?'

'It's just…' He looked around, as if to confirm what he was about to say. 'It really is lovely. Everything fits. It's like you selected each thing on purpose.'

'You didn't?' she asked. 'In your own home?'

'I don't have my own home.'

'What do you mean?'

'I live with my parents.'

She stared at him. She didn't know how long it was until his lip curled.

'You have an opinion on that?'

'No,' she replied. 'I don't.'

'You have an opinion on everything. Also, your face is saying something different.'

'You're right. I do have an opinion. But I don't want to share it.'

It was pure stubbornness, since sharing her opinion would have been the perfect segue into the questions she had. Why was he, a successful adult, still living with his parents? She knew he was successful because In the Rough was her main rival, according to reviews and social media, and she was pretty damn successful, despite the forces working against her.

It still smarted that they were succeeding with a restaurant that had been meant to be hers. The location, the property, the name—Lee had stolen it all from her. Then he'd gone and recruited Benjamin to work with him. Lee could have chosen *anyone* else. Actually, she was sure that Lee had specifically chosen Benjamin because the man annoyed her so much, though she wasn't sure how Lee would know that. Either way, Benjamin annoyed her more now that he was in cahoots with her brother. At least before, he'd annoyed her on his own merits.

He'd singled her out their first day at the Institute. She had no idea why, since she minded her own business. For some inexplicable reason, he'd decided she was partly *his* business, and he began to compete with her. She'd instantly recoiled; she had enough competition in life. She hadn't cut Lee out of her life and minimised her contact with her parents, only to replace them with a negligible man-child.

Now she had to work with the man-child.

'Would you like some alcohol?' she asked after a deep sigh.

His eyes flickered with amusement, contrasting the tighter lines on his face. ‘Anything you want to give me is fine.’

She bit her tongue before she could reply. She hadn’t thought of anything to reply with, but her tongue was often quicker than her brain. She didn’t want to take the chance of saying something inappropriate. Such as how what she wanted to give him was another kiss to see if the spark she’d felt was a fluke…

She poured him a generous glass of whiskey from a bottle that was still three quarters full and settled on water and peppermint for herself.

‘You’re not having any?’ he asked, accepting the glass from her.

She leaned back against the counter on the opposite side of the kitchen. ‘I’m on an alcohol fast.’

‘Why?’

She rolled her eyes. ‘Does it matter?’

‘You’re annoyed because I asked?’

‘Yes, actually. It’s rude.’

Plus she didn’t have a good answer for him. She hadn’t anticipated him asking why she was fasting from alcohol. She should have known he wouldn’t be polite and leave it at that though.

‘Sorry.’ His lips twitched. ‘So…’

He didn’t say anything more. She didn’t speak either. The silence stretched between them like a cat in the sun. Then, as a cat would, it stared Alexa in the eyes, unblinking, until she sighed.

‘This is what dating you is like?’ She didn’t wait for an answer. ‘How disturbing.’

How she knew exactly what to say to get under his skin was what was really disturbing.

But then, disturbing seemed to be the theme of the night.

What with the fake relationship, the kiss, being in Alexa's home. He'd offended her by noting that her flat was homey, but he couldn't help but be honest. She'd done an amazing job turning what would have been a trendy, but not particularly special place into something he could imagine coming home to.

Well, not him, exactly. He had his own home. With his parents. Which she had an opinion on, but wouldn't tell him about because she was stubborn. He couldn't be upset by it since he was stubborn, too. If she'd asked why he still lived with his parents he wouldn't have told her.

Not that any of it was important now.

'Cherise saw us.'

'I know.' She drained her glass. Her gaze rested on his, before it rose to his face. Something about it made his body feel more aware. 'Would you like some more?'

He glanced at the glass. Empty. Strange. He didn't remember drinking from it. Except for that one time when he'd taken a long, deep gulp and—

Ah, yes. He remembered now.

'No, thank you.' Probably best with all the disturbing stuff happening.

'Tea, then? I'm making myself some.'

'Anything to avoid having a straight conversation with me?'

'What is this we're having, then?' she asked, filling the kettle with water. She took out two mugs, despite the fact that he hadn't answered her. 'A skew conversation? Diagonal?'

'Funny lady.'

Amusement flickered in her eyes. 'I try.'

'To annoy me, yes,' he muttered.

The amused light danced in her eyes again. He felt an answering light in his chest. He didn't care for it. It made him think the tables had turned.

'I know we have to talk about this.' She took out ginger from the fridge, sliced up some pieces and threw it in one cup. She looked over at him. 'Tea? Coffee?'

'Coffee. Please,' he added as an afterthought.

She began to make his coffee, expression pensive. 'I suppose I wanted to make the conversation easier. Less awkward. A discussion over hot drinks seemed like something that would help with that.'

His mother would like her, he thought before he could stop himself. Usually, he was more careful when it came to comparisons between his mother and people he wasn't related to. Hell, people he was related to, too. It tended to evoke protective feelings in him when he did. He blamed it on the fact that he felt protective of his mother, so when he recognised something akin to her in someone else, those feelings bled over. It had too often in the past, and he'd been hurt because of it. Which should have made him more careful. It usually did. Except now, apparently.

'How did I manage to upset you with that?' she asked, more resigned than curious.

'You didn't.' A lie. Or half-lie. He'd upset himself, but because of something she'd said.

Her eyes narrowed, but she finished his coffee, slid it over the counter towards him. She finished her own drink with a teaspoon of honey, then leaned back against the counter as she had with her water.

'Okay, so let's talk straight.' She bit her lip, then straightened her shoulders. 'I'm sorry for pretending you're my boyfriend. It was an impulse.'

'Why did you?'

She tilted her head, as if considering his question. Or perhaps considering whether she'd answer it.

'My brother is a jerk.'

He stared.

'You can't possibly not have noticed,' she replied at the

look. 'He's entitled, and competitive, and generally unkind. I wanted to push him off a cliff. Since literally doing so would send me to prison, I settled for figuratively. You were the figurative.'

He took a minute to process that.

'He's normally a decent guy.'

'Maybe to you. But since you said normally, I think you recognised that he wasn't decent today.' She paused, her lips pursing. 'He normally isn't decent with me.'

Lee's behaviour today didn't encourage him to disagree with her. So he didn't.

'It's weird that you pretended *I* was your boyfriend. You hate me.'

'You were the closest person,' she said coolly, not denying his statement. 'Also, you're his business partner. Best cliff.' She shrugged.

He took a steadying breath. He didn't like being used. He'd had too many instances of it in his life. His last girlfriend, his father's colleague, his cousin. Those were but a few, but they were the most recent. Remembering them had him steeling himself against Alexa's charm—or whatever it was that kept him standing there.

'I don't like being used.'

'I'm sorry.' Her voice and expression were sincere. 'I'm sorry for putting you in a position to be used. For using you.'

It was that sincerity that had him saying, 'Apology accepted,' when he wasn't entirely sure he meant it.

'Thank you.' There was a brief pause. 'So maybe now you can explain why you decided to go along with the charade. Maybe you can apologise for that kiss, too.'

CHAPTER FOUR

THE EXPRESSION ON his face was comical. But, since she'd asked him a serious question, one she would very much have liked an answer for, she decided not to give in to the smile. To wait.

His expression became more comical. His mouth contracted and expanded, as if he were mouthing what he wanted to say, but not quite. Emotions danced in his eyes, though she couldn't put her finger on what they were. But really, it was that tick near his nose, which she'd never before seen, that amused her the most.

Still, she didn't smile.

'I thought… I mean, he was… I wanted to…'

His stammers made resisting the smile harder. It was strange. She had never before spoken with him long enough to have to resist any of her emotions. Usually, those emotions ranged from irritated to downright angry. Amusement generally didn't feature; not unless it was tainted with satisfaction. This wasn't. This was simply…amusement.

An alarm went off in her head.

'You wanted to *what*?' she asked, her words sharp, marching to that alarm.

He cleared his throat and met her eyes. His expression was now serious.

'I wanted Lee to stop acting like a jerk.'

'Well.' It was all she said for a while. 'You succeeded, just for a moment.'

'But at what cost?'

His eyes bored into hers, and her face began to heat.

Was he asking how she'd felt about that kiss? If he was, he'd have his answer in her blush.

Because it had embarrassed her, she assured herself. Her fingers lifted and slipped under the neckline of her dress. She lifted it, let it fall, sending air down her body, which had suddenly become clammy. For some reason, her skin was itchy, too. It was exactly how she felt on a summer's day in the kitchen. Hot and sticky, but satisfied at what she was cooking up.

Wait—satisfied? Where had that come from? What was happening to her?

Embarrassment, an inner voice offered again. She clung to it. Ignored the fact that her memories of that kiss, of how she'd felt much as she did now while he'd been kissing her, were vehemently disagreeing.

She took a deliberate sip of her tea. She'd put enough ginger in it that the flavour burned her throat. She relished it. Then met his eyes.

'A high cost,' she told him. 'It means Cherise thinks we're dating.'

He was watching her closely. She hoped to heaven he hadn't developed the ability to see into her head. 'And now she's confused about our opposing offers.'

'I tried to tell her the same thing we told Lee,' she said with a sigh. 'The whole "we're dating, but we're keeping our personal and professional lives separate" thing. I don't know if she bought it. She's certainly confused by it.'

'Me, too, to be honest with you.'

He gestured, asking if she'd like to have a seat in the lounge. She would have, desperately, since her body was aching from a day of standing. Her baby apparently didn't like that kind of strenuous activity. But it felt too intimate, sitting with him on the sofas she'd bought and slept on for months. A twinge in her back urged her to reconsider, and she spent hopelessly too long trying to decide. In the end, she strode past him without answering, as though it had been her idea all along.

Man, pregnancy was making her *stubborn.*

It was definitely the pregnancy. She didn't possess a stubborn bone in her body normally.

She sank into the sofa as soon as she sat down, a sigh leaving her lips immediately. His brows were raised when she looked at him.

'Why didn't you say something?'

'About what?'

'Needing to sit down.'

'I didn't need to.'

'So what you did now wasn't you finally relaxing and your body thanking you for it?'

'I have no idea what you're talking about.'

He shook his head, but the sides of his mouth were quirked. 'Stubborn isn't an appealing quality.'

'I don't care if you find me appealing.' She didn't give herself a chance to figure out why that felt like a lie. 'Besides, it's been a long day.'

'You get stubborn after a long day?'

'That's what I said, yes.'

'Is it because you're tired?' He was outright smiling now. Taunting her, really. 'Or is it a physical symptom? Aching legs, sore back, stubborn personality?'

'Yes.' It wasn't an answer, but it was all he'd get. 'Now—what are we going to do about Cherise?'

The smile faded, but the twinkle in his eyes didn't. He was sitting beneath the light fixture, which could account for that twinkle. But it didn't; she'd seen that twinkle before. It appeared whenever he was amused with her. It was frustrating to know. More frustrating was how attractive that amusement made him.

It danced in his brown eyes, crinkled the skin around them. That forced his cheeks up, which spread his full lips—lips she now knew had objectively impressive skills. None of that factored into how the angles of his face were affected. Warming them, softening them; perhaps a combination of the two. Either way, it dimmed his arrogance, that self-assured *I know I'm successful and handsome* edge of his. That edge was as devastating as it was irritating, particularly as it always seemed to be directed at her.

'What were you planning on doing about Cherise before all this happened?'

She snorted. 'Wouldn't you like to know?'

'Yes,' he deadpanned. 'That's why I asked.'

'You asked so you could outdo whatever I planned to do.'

'I wouldn't dream of it.'

'Like you wouldn't dream of stealing my head chef? Who was already working for me, I might add. Happily. For months.'

'That can't be true if he left,' Benjamin pointed out softly. 'It didn't take me much to convince him either.'

'Are you defending *stealing* my chef?'

'I didn't steal him. I...gave him another option.'

'You stole him,' she said flatly. 'Probably at the behest of my brother, because, as I mentioned before, he's a jerk.'

He hesitated, which gave her the answer. And disappointed her, strangely. Why, she wasn't sure. It might have been because he'd defended her in front of her brother and hadn't freaked out completely when she'd pretended he was her boyfriend. But one day's experience couldn't erase years of experience to the contrary. That experience had taught her that Benjamin Foster could be just as much of a jerk as her brother.

'I think you're on the right track though,' she powered on. If she did, it would help get him out of her house and she'd finally be able to rest. 'We do what we intended to do and let her make the decision as she would have without this complication.'

'We're not continuing the charade?'

She thought about it. 'We have two options, I suppose. One is that we do, but only verbally. If she asks, we'll talk about one another lovingly. Affectionately. Then, in a few months, we break up.'

'And the other option?'

'Tell her the truth. We were playing a joke on Lee.'

He went quiet for a few seconds. 'But if Lee finds out, we both look foolish. We'll have to answer why we were so...' he hesitated '...*invested* in proving we were together.'

'There's that,' she said slowly. She didn't want him to know she'd thought about that, too. Not to mention she hated the idea of Lee discovering the truth. He'd take such pleasure in it. He'd probably hold it over her head every time she'd have the misfortune of seeing him. 'There's also the implication that we're friends. Why would we play a joke on Lee if we weren't?'

'You're worried about people thinking we're friends, but not that we're in a relationship?'

'Well, yeah. At least there's a physical aspect to a relationship. People would think I was distracted from your personality because you look the way you do.'

He frowned. She could almost see his brain malfunctioning. Mostly because she was pretty sure that was what was happening to hers.

'Is that a compliment?'

'No,' she answered immediately.

But it was. She couldn't figure out why she'd said it.

She vowed there and then never to admit she found him attractive again. She wouldn't even *think* about his broad shoulders and full lips. He certainly wouldn't kiss her again either, so she'd have no reason to. And if she did think it—and he did kiss her—she'd remind herself there were high stakes involved.

She laid a hand on her belly, feeling the slight curve. At

this stage it could have been a good, generous meal as much as a baby, which amused her. She stroked her thumb over the curve, mentally assuring her child that she'd protect it. She paused when she saw him watching her.

What was it about being in his presence that made her lower her guard?

She moved her hand.

'Fine. We'll pretend to be together,' he said curtly. 'But only because Lee deserves to think it, after how he treated you.' He paused, as though something had just occurred to him. The frown deepened. He was scowling when he continued. 'We'll do whatever we intended to do with Cherise. I'll keep talk of our relationship with your brother to the minimum. We should both do that, to whoever we meet.' He downed the rest of his coffee and set the cup on the table. Stood. 'And in a few months, our fake relationship will end. It'll be as clean as this situation allows.'

'Er...yeah, sure.'

She set her own mug down, confused by the change in his temperament. But that was the least of her problems. She'd just realised her pregnancy wouldn't be a secret for much longer. People would have questions about the paternity of her baby. If she said it was Benjamin, she would be dragging him down an even more convoluted path. If she said it was some random guy as she'd planned to, people would do the calculations and accuse her of cheating on Benjamin.

Oh, no.

She really should have thought about this earlier.

'Benjamin, I think we need to talk about—'

'We've talked about everything already, haven't we?' he interrupted. His eyes were sharp, and she almost shivered from the intensity of them. So she just nodded.

'Great, then we don't have to see one another again for a while.'

'Okay.' Numbly, she followed him to the door.

'Thanks for the drinks.'

'Okay.'

'Good luck with Cherise.'

'Thanks.'

And then he was gone, leaving her to think about the extent of the mess she'd created that day.

The resolution he and Alexa had come to regarding their fake relationship went up in flames the moment he walked into In the Rough the next morning.

'You're dating my sister?' Lee asked, sitting arms folded at a stool in front of the bar. Apparently, he'd been waiting. 'What the hell, man? Do you have no boundaries?'

It wasn't early in the morning. In the Rough only opened from lunchtime, so generally he worked from home for a couple of hours when he woke up, then made his way to the restaurant at about nine. His staff would start trickling in then, too, most of them there by ten, and then it would be a bustle of activity until they closed at eleven at night. This morning, he'd been particularly grateful for the quiet so he could figure out what the hell had happened the night before.

One moment he'd been deciding whether to let Alexa's backhanded compliment slide, the next he was watching her stroke her stomach and his gut had clenched with need. It made no sense, but that gesture had seemed somewhat protective. It reminded him of the times he'd seen pregnant women do the same thing. Though Alexa probably wasn't pregnant, it had made him think about a life he'd never wanted. He was too busy taking care of his parents to even consider it.

Not that he minded; not in the least. His mother was lovely. Sharp and charming and the kind of mother who made sacrifices for her children. Except there were no children, only him. And that sharpness and charm and kindness didn't negate the strain of her illness.

They'd had no idea what caused it for a long time. His mother had been his father's admin help at the panel-beaters' company his father owned and ran. For ten years, almost, until she'd started complaining about the pain right after she'd had Benjamin. Aches that felt like they were all over, restricting her movement, making simple tasks hard to carry out. Doctors had prescribed ibuprofen, diagnosed her with the flu, told her she'd strained a muscle, or pushed too hard, or that she needed to take a break.

But even when she took a break, the pain would continue. Sometimes, if she stayed in bed and rested, it would make it worse. The doctors maintained they could find nothing wrong. It was the eighth doctor she'd gone to in four years who had diagnosed her with fibromyalgia.

His life hadn't changed dramatically, or at all, with that diagnosis. His father had simply sat him down and explained as best he could to a four-year-old that his mom was sick. Frank Foster had told Benjamin to try not to bother his mother as much when she was in bed. Maybe Benjamin could even help out a little more at home. He hadn't known the difference between that and what he'd done before, except now it came with the weight of verbal responsibility.

But she was his mother, and he wanted her to be happy. As he grew older, he thought having him couldn't have helped with his mom's pain. Because she'd made sacrifices for him at the cost of her own health, physical and mental, he would do the same for her. So he had. For the past twenty-odd years he had helped his parents. Now he cared for his parents. There wasn't really room for him to consider caring for anyone else in that situation either.

That pulse of need he'd felt with Alexa the night before? A fluke. There was nothing more to it. And he didn't engage with it any more because something more significant had occurred to him when he'd been talking with Alexa.

Now might be the time to confirm it.

'Did you hear me?' Lee demanded.

But maybe not before he'd had another cup of coffee.

'Mia,' he said to the tall woman behind the counter. 'Is the machine on?'

'You know it,' she replied with a sympathetic grin. It made him realise she'd heard what Lee had said. 'The usual?'

He unclenched his jaw slowly. 'No. Double espresso, please.' Her brows lifted, but she only nodded. He looked at Lee. 'Can you wait for me in the office? I'll be there in a second.'

'Mia, could you please add another cappuccino to that?' Lee said. 'And bring it to Ben's office when it's ready?' He shook his head. 'Or have someone else bring it. Sorry. It slipped my mind.'

Her smile didn't waver, but something on Mia's face tightened. It probably wasn't because Lee had been referring to her disability—the limp that Benjamin hadn't once asked about because it was none of his business—but because Lee had done so poorly. Benjamin wouldn't have expected it from him; Lee handled most things smoothly. Then again, he hadn't expected Lee to be a jerk to his own sister, so maybe he didn't know his business partner as well as he thought.

'Yeah, sure,' Mia said.

'Thank you.'

Lee gestured for Benjamin to lead the way. After one last glance at Mia to make sure she was okay, Benjamin walked away from the enticing smell of coffee to his office. It was a simple room. Not very big, but there was enough space for his desk and cabinet, and the large windows gave it an airy feel. Unfortunately, those windows looked out onto a car park with a busy Cape Town road just behind it. But that was the price he paid to be in a central location.

At least, that was what Lee had told him when he'd been courting Benjamin. Over the years, Benjamin had begun to believe him. Was he a fool to do so?

'This isn't your only business,' Benjamin noted, taking off his jacket and slinging it over the chair. 'Surely you have better things to do than to wait for me to talk about something that isn't business.'

'Except this affects our business,' Lee said with none of the charm, the ease Benjamin had once been privy to. 'Honestly, Ben. There are millions of women in South Africa, but you decide to sleep with my sister?'

'Watch it,' Benjamin growled, though he had no reason to defend Alexa. Apart from their fictional relationship. Which was not, as the title stated, real.

'She's already changed you,' Lee replied with a shake of his head. 'You weren't foolish before yesterday. Hell, the last time we spoke, you knew how important getting Cherise de Bruyn to work with us was. But now you're letting your head be messed around by your—'

'Be careful about what you say next.'

Lee's jaw tightened. 'This isn't going to work.'

'What isn't?' he asked coolly, leaning back in his chair. 'This partnership? Or my relationship with your sister?'

Lee opened and closed his mouth several times before he said, 'The relationship.'

'That hardly seems like any of your business.'

'It's literally my business.'

'No, my relationship has nothing to do with this business.' He paused when one of his waiters brought in their coffees. 'Alexa and I have been able to keep our relationship under wraps for months. It hasn't affected the way I've run things around here.'

'And yet here you are, snapping at me.'

'Because for some reason, when it comes to your sister, you change, too, Lee.' He downed the espresso. When it seared his stomach, he remembered he'd forgotten to eat breakfast. 'I don't like the way you treat her. I don't like the way you treat me when it comes to her.'

It was a warning.

'I thought this wouldn't happen.'

'What does that mean?'

'I thought working with someone who competed with my sister meant *I'd* be working with someone who competed with my sister.'

And there it was. Confirmation of his suspicions. When he told Alexa he wanted to continue the charade because of how Lee treated her, he realised there was more to it. It was because of how Lee had treated him, too. Lee had used him. Much as so many other people in his life had.

'My relationship with your sister doesn't have to affect the way we do things around here,' he said coldly. 'It won't for me. I'm perfectly capable of working with you and dating your sister. Since you two don't have a relationship, it shouldn't matter to you anyway.'

Lee's face was tight. Benjamin couldn't read what caused that tightness, or what was behind it. All he could see was a complicated mess of emotions. Since he had enough of those himself, especially after Lee's little bombshell, he didn't need to figure Lee's feelings out.

'We won't let your involvement with my sister affect the business.'

Benjamin gave a tight nod.

'What about our friendship?'

Benjamin didn't know how to answer that. He didn't trust Lee any more. How could they still be friends?

'See?' Lee said. 'You're already treating me differently.'

'I've explained why.'

He'd use Lee's treatment of Alexa as the scapegoat here.

He was sure she wouldn't mind. They were in this together after all.

Lee exhaled harshly. 'Fine. We'll just pretend you're not dating my sister.'

'What?'

His mother stood in the doorway, eyes impossibly wide.

'You're dating Benjamin Foster?'

Alexa's feet stopped working. That meant she was standing in the doorway of her office, frozen by both the words and the stare of accusation from Kenya.

'Who told you that?'

'You should have.'

'How did you find out?'

'A friend of mine was at Cherise's graduation yesterday.' Kenya leaned back in Alexa's chair. 'She asked me why I didn't tell her. Apparently, you and Benjamin were hot and heavy yesterday and it was the talk of everyone there. *And I didn't know.*'

'It hasn't been going on for very long,' she grumbled. *Like, less than twenty-four hours.* 'Besides, I didn't want people to know. It's new.'

And fake.

'Am I still people, Alexa?'

The question was serious enough to make Alexa blink. When she recovered from the shock, Kenya was watching her, waiting for an answer.

'I... I didn't tell anyone.'

Kenya stood, nodding slowly as she did. 'Yeah, why would you tell anyone? Least of all someone you've worked with for four years. Least of all someone who considers you a friend. Clearly that doesn't apply to how you consider me, does it?'

It would be so easy to get through this. If Alexa told Kenya the relationship was fake, contrived when she'd been desperate and in a panic to get away from her brother, Kenya wouldn't be upset with her.

She opened her mouth, but nothing came out. Not a single word.

What would happen if she told Kenya the truth? She'd look like a fool, for one. But Kenya might tell her friend, who might tell their friend, and before she knew it both her and Benjamin's reputations would be ruined. Not to mention that her brother would find out. And she couldn't face Lee's smirk when he heard she'd made up the entire thing for his sake.

'You can't even dispute it,' Kenya said, hurt thick in her voice. She strode past Alexa. Alexa wanted to say something, but her phone rang before she could. Picking up the landline, she barked, 'Yes?'

'Benjamin Foster's on the line for you,' came the voice of one of her waiters.

She bit back a sigh. 'Put him through.'

'Alexa?'

His deep voice was even more disturbing over the phone. Now she had to imagine his face. And for some reason it came without the arrogance that usually put her off.

'You called for me, didn't you?'

'Yes, I did, darling.'

'Darling? Really?' She looked behind her to ensure no one was there. 'You realise we're on the phone, right? No one else can hear what we're saying.'

'I'm here with my mother.'

'Your mother?'

'She'd like to meet you.'

'She'd like to… Wait, I'm missing something, aren't I?'

'Yes.'

It was the first time she felt as though he was answering her properly.

'Are you free for dinner tonight?'

'I'm not, actually. I'm working. As are you, considering we run restaurants.'

'I'm sure you can take an evening off for this *very important date.*'

She rolled her eyes. Belatedly, she realised he couldn't see her. She let the disappointment pass through her.

'Look, Benjamin, I don't know what's going on, but there's no way I'm going to meet your mother.'

'She would like to meet you.'

She could hear he was clenching his teeth.

'Is she giving you a hard time, Benny? Let me talk to her.' There was a short pause where Alexa could swear she heard Benjamin apologise. 'Alexa? This is Nina, Benjamin's mother.'

She closed her eyes. 'Hi, Nina.'

'Is it possible for us to meet?'

'Mrs Foster.' Alexa cleared her throat. 'I, um, I'm not sure.'

'Be sure, dear.' There was admonishment there, but Mrs Foster spoke again so quickly Alexa barely had time to process it. 'This evening might be too soon, considering your commitments. How about tomorrow evening? Could you arrange for someone to take care of things then?'

'I…um… I…don't know…'

'I just wouldn't want to meet you at your restaurant, dear.' Mrs Foster gave a sparkling laugh. 'You'd have to come out and speak to me in front of your employees and… Well, I don't need to tell you how awkward that might end up being.'

'No,' Alexa said numbly. 'You don't.'

'So it's settled, then! I'll see you tomorrow.'

'I… Yes, you will.' She cleared her throat. 'Could you please put Benjamin back on the phone?'

'Of course.'

There was another pause, then a, 'Yeah.'

'I have an hour for lunch today and clearly we need to talk. Can you meet me at St George's Mall at one?'

'Yes.'

'It wasn't a real question, but I'm glad you agreed. It makes things easier.'

CHAPTER FIVE

'What were you *thinking*?'

It was the first thing Alexa said when she saw him. A bit rude, in his opinion, but he allowed it because she'd made a good impression on his mother. Nina had murmured her approval and patted his cheek in affection. All this came after she'd read him the Riot Act for keeping his relationship a secret.

'Hello, Alexa,' he said calmly. 'Would you like to have a seat at one of the coffee shops? It is lunch, after all. And I haven't had breakfast. A busy morning,' he added, taking her elbow lightly and steering her through the crowds of people milling about. 'What with speaking to your brother about our fake relationship, having my mother find out about it, and then, of course, my actual business, which is open, but why would they need the manager and acting head chef there for the lunchtime rush?'

'I have responsibilities, too.'

'And yet here we are, gallivanting in the middle of the day.'

'It's not gallivanting.'

But she said it under her breath. He took it as agreement. How could he not?

St George's Mall had once been a busy street in Cape Town, but it had been reimagined for pedestrians. Now people walked through the bricked area lined with green trees and yellow umbrellas without the bother of traffic. There were three men playing drums a little way away from them, a boy who couldn't be older than nine dancing to the beat. Tourists browsed through the stands selling jewellery and African-inspired crafts. Residents walked with purpose to get to where they needed to be, or stopped at one of the cafes to grab something to eat. Police presence was heavy, but quaint, since they monitored the area on horses.

It was one of his favourite places, just fifteen minutes away from his restaurant. It screamed with the vibrancy of Cape Town, which was one reason he loved his city. He wasn't sure why Alexa had suggested it, since it was further away for her than for him. Could she have been considering him? Or was she merely trying to minimise the chances of someone she knew seeing them together?

He would have related to that, except his mother already knew, so his father would, too, and they were the main people he cared about. It was too late for keeping secrets for him.

'Hey,' she said, snapping her fingers. 'Can we sit here? Or should I ask another time?'

'Sorry,' he muttered, and gestured for her to sit.

They took a few minutes to look at the menu. At least, he did. She'd glanced at hers quickly, then set it down and was now watching him.

'You must be thinking it's a pity you don't have X-ray vision with how you're staring at me.'

'Hadn't considered it before, actually. Just like I hadn't considered having to talk to your mother and be manoeuvred—quite expertly, I might add—into having dinner with your family.' She slapped her hand against her leg under the table. *'I'm not even your girlfriend.'*

He exhaled, hoping the nervous energy in his body would escape from his lungs. No such luck. It stayed in his chest, bouncing around as though it were being chased by a happy puppy.

'Let's get something to drink.'

'Why would you let your mother think we're in a relationship?' she asked, ignoring him. 'This turns something that could easily be solved into something so much more—'

'Alexa,' he interrupted, his voice slicing through her panic. 'Let's get something to drink. We can talk about it afterwards.'

Her jaw locked, but she nodded. The waiter came over. He ordered sparkling water—he needed a break from the coffee. It was probably the cause of the nervous energy. Probably—and Alexa got rooibos tea. When the waiter left, Alexa stared wordlessly at him. To emphasise her displeasure, she folded her arms and leaned back.

He took a deep breath.

'My mother being under the impression we're together wasn't my fault,' he said slowly. 'Lee ambushed me this morning—' that was more aggressive than what Lee had done; or maybe not '—and when he was talking about the relationship, my mother walked in. I'd forgotten some papers at home and she thought I might need them.'

He could hardly be upset with her for being sweet.

'Anyway, she found out, and since I've never told her about any of my relationships, she kind of latched on to the information. I couldn't tell her it was a lie without…' He grasped on to the first thing he could think of. 'Without your brother overhearing it.'

'Couldn't you have told her when he left?'

'No.' Anger made the word choppy. 'She was excited. I couldn't disappoint her.'

'People survive disappointing their parents.'

The words were so unexpected, so cool, his anger fizzled.

'Is that what happened to you?'

'It doesn't matter.' Her features softened, but the lines around her mouth were still tense. 'What's going to happen when she finds out we're not really together, Benjamin? You don't think she's going to be disappointed then?

You don't think she's going to hate knowing that you lied to her? That you don't have a girlfriend?' She blushed. 'I mean, I'm assuming. I don't care about your romantic—'

'Of course I don't have a girlfriend,' he said, affronted. 'Do you think I'd be pretending to be your boyfriend if I did? Do you think so poorly of me?'

She stilled, though her eyes, big and bright, remained steady. 'You want me to say no, but experience has taught me I can't say that without reservation.'

He had no reply to that. What could he say? But it left a bitter taste in his mouth that she thought that of him. He didn't deserve it. The only thing he'd done that was morally ambiguous was offer her chef a job at In the Rough. Even then he'd done things above board. Victor Fourie had accepted Benjamin's offer without a comment about what he'd left behind. In the same way he'd left In the Rough behind when he'd moved on a couple of months ago.

Then again, he could see why she'd have that opinion of him. He worked with her brother, a man she had no relationship with. A man who treated her poorly, and apparently went out of his way to do so. Lee had used Benjamin to that end, too, and he'd unwittingly become a tool to hurt Alexa with. Frankly, he was still working out how he felt about it. Especially since he'd considered Lee a friend until all this had happened.

His fake relationship had thrown everything into upheaval. Including his relationship with his mother. He wasn't proud of it, but he couldn't bear to break his mother's heart. Up until today, he hadn't even known his mother wanted him to be in a relationship. But the happiness in her voice as she questioned him about his girlfriend—his first, according to her—told him otherwise.

He couldn't tell her it was all fake. He loved her too much. And yeah, maybe he'd get over disappointing her. But in that moment, it hadn't even occurred to him.

The waiter interrupted his thoughts, and when the man walked away, he sighed.

'I'm sorry. About my mother. I wasn't thinking. Or I wasn't thinking properly.'

She held the mug in her hands as if to warm herself, though it was a typical summer's day.

'I've been there,' she murmured. Then she set the mug down and took her head in her hands instead. 'I was there—yesterday. Because of my stupid brother, I caused this mess and—'

She hiccupped. An actual hiccup that was most likely the precursor to a sob. His hand shot out of its own volition, grasping her arm and squeezing in comfort. A hand left her head and rested on his hand.

And just like that, he knew he was in trouble.

Of course, he'd known that before. The entire thing with Alexa was, as she said, a mess. But before, he'd still had some control over his actions. He wasn't helping her because she needed help. Well, not *only* because she needed help. He also wanted to help her with his own free will. The moment she showed him vulnerability, though, that free will had waved goodbye and jumped on the nearest plane to anywhere but his mind. Because now he wanted to help her because she *really* needed help. She was distraught, and things needed to be fixed, and he was the ultimate help when things needed to be fixed.

He'd done it with his mother and father for most of his life, more so as an adult. He'd done it with his last girlfriend. His cousins. Friends. And he would do it now, with Alexa.

He curled his free hand into a fist.

She was *crying*. In public. In front of him. Because she was pregnant and because she had to tell him the truth. It was terrifying.

She pulled away from his touch, comforting—disturbingly so—as it was, and reached into her bag for a tissue. She found one, mopped herself up, and sternly told her hormones she wouldn't stand for tears again. When she was certain they'd got the picture, she downed the rest of her tea, lukewarm now, because of the tears, and looked at him.

His expression was inscrutable. She didn't know if that made her feel better or worse. But she couldn't rely on him to make herself feel better. So she took a deep breath, held it for a few seconds, then let it out. It was shaky at best; hitched at worse. She did it again, and again, until it came smoothly. Then she said, 'I'm pregnant.'

He stared at her.

She cleared her throat. 'So, you see, you have to tell your mother the truth or she'll think the baby's yours and things will get more complicated.'

He still stared at her.

'I wouldn't have told you if I didn't have to. I went over it in my head a million times last night, and again, after that phone call with your mother.'

He didn't say a word. She pursed her lips when they started to shake.

No, she told the tears that were threatening. *I had you under control. You can't disobey me.*

'I didn't want you to know,' she said, thinking that speaking would distract her. 'I didn't want *anyone* to know until I had no choice but to tell them. No one knows besides you. Because somehow, my decision is now going to reflect on you.'

He kept staring, but his mouth had opened. She had to wait a while longer before he said anything.

'You're pregnant?'

She nodded.

'We have to tell people the truth.'

She clenched her teeth when the statement brought a

fresh wave of heat to her eyes. She would *not* cry in front of him. Not again.

'Okay.' Her voice broke as she said it. Damn it.

'They'll think the baby's mine, Alexa,' Benjamin said, his voice pleading. 'My mother and your brother and everyone else. We can't just break up then.'

'Why not?' she asked desperately. 'Who cares what they think?'

'I do.' His face was stern. 'It'll be my reputation on the line.'

'It doesn't have to be,' she said, desperation once again taking the wheel. 'You can tell them I cheated on you.'

'What?'

'Make me the bad guy.' She hated the thought of it, but it was her only option.

'You'd rather have everyone think you cheated than tell the truth?'

'I don't care what everyone thinks,' she said heatedly. 'If Lee finds out I made this up because of him…' She met his gaze. 'He took my property and my restaurant years ago and he had no reason to. If I give him this, it'll fuel him for years.'

'What do you mean, your property? Your *restaurant*?'

She scoffed. 'Please don't pretend you don't know what Lee did. It's an insult to you and me both.'

'I have no idea what you're talking about.'

He seemed genuinely confused. Though that could have as easily come from the news that she was pregnant as from this. She sighed.

'I found the building for In the Rough. Came up with the name, too, because of the neighbourhood. I was determined to turn that place—*my* place—into a diamond.' The memory of it curved her lips. 'I went through hundreds of listings to find it, and I was so excited because it was *finally* time. I'd spent eight years working towards that moment, and finally…' She trailed off when a wave of sadness crashed over her. 'Anyway, I was supposed to take my parents to see it. I mean, I did take my parents to see it. But I made the mistake of telling them where it was when I scheduled the event with them a week before. We always had to make plans in advance with them.'

She shook off the resentment that she'd had to schedule the meeting with her parents in the first place. Second, but not by much, was that they'd told Lee.

'They told Lee, and he bought it out from under me. He offered to rent it to me. I declined. He would have never allowed me to do what I wanted to do.' She waved a hand. She wasn't sure what it was meant to signify. 'And then I heard you two had become partners. It made sense. If my brother was the devil, I suppose I considered you a demon. My dreams had turned into my own personal hell.'

It was as funny as it was heartbreaking. She was sure the small smile she hadn't been able to resist conveyed both.

'I knew none of that.'

'Would it have changed anything if you had?' she asked, wanting to know.

A complicated array of emotions danced across his face. She supposed she could understand it. It was a good business decision to be a partner with Lee. He came with property, a smart name, business knowledge, and experience. He also came with baggage: her. She had no idea whether Benjamin cared about that, but what she'd told him now didn't reflect well on Lee regardless. Unless he shared Lee's opinion of her, and her brother's lack of scruples, in which case it wouldn't change anything.

But he wouldn't look this tortured if things hadn't changed for him, would he? Or was she grasping at straws, desperate for someone, anyone, to finally be on her side instead of Lee's?

'It's smart to be in business with Lee,' came the careful answer. 'He's a good businessperson.'

'You still think so after what I told you?'

The stare flickered. 'He's been good to me.'

She licked her bottom lip before drawing it between her teeth. Then she nodded. 'I suppose that's fair.'

Disappointing, but fair. But it helped sharpen her idea of him. She'd been faltering on what she thought of him because he hadn't deliberately set out to hurt her with the restaurant. But after what had happened with her chef, and now, with his opinion of Lee remaining unchanged… It was best if she didn't think he was someone he wasn't.

'If we tell my brother the truth, he'll use it against you, too,' she said.

His lips parted, as if he hadn't considered it. Or maybe he didn't believe it was possible.

'It's too complicated to continue this lie, Alexa.'

She exhaled. 'Okay.' It was time to leave. She needed to recover from all this in private. She needed to prepare, too. 'Give me a few days. It shouldn't make a difference for you, but it'll help me figure some things out.'

He gave a slow nod. 'Then I guess I'll tell my mother.'

'Let me.' She had no idea why she said it, but it was too late to take it back. 'I'll come to dinner tomorrow. I'll tell her I dragged you into this and that you were being the perfect gentleman. I'll explain to her what happened with my brother, and how you couldn't come clean with him near by. We'll make you come out of this smelling of roses.'

'Why?'

'It's the least I can do after the trouble I caused.' She took out money and tossed it on the table. 'Call Infinity with the details about tomorrow.'

She hoped he couldn't see her shaking as she walked away.

CHAPTER SIX

He offered to pick up Alexa at her flat. Partly because his mother had taught him to be a gentleman, and partly because he felt bad about the way things had gone the day before. He blamed it on his shock. She was *pregnant*, and he was the only person who knew. It seemed significant. It shouldn't have. She hadn't told him because she wanted him to know, but because it made their lie infinitely more complicated. Though he wanted to help her, he couldn't see how to. And he'd disappointed her because of it. But rather her than his mother.

Nina's reaction to the news that he was in a relationship had been surprising. After her shock and the millions of questions that had come with it, she told him how happy she was that he was dating.

'You're always taking care of us, Benny,' she'd said. 'I was worried it stopped you from living your life. But now you have someone!' She had clasped her hands in glee. 'I can't tell you how much I've wanted this to happen.'

He could only imagine how she'd react if she thought he was having a baby. He was worried enough about telling her the truth.

He took a shaky breath and rang Alexa's doorbell. Tried to keep his jaw from dropping when she opened the door almost immediately.

She wore a light pink dress, cinched below her breasts and falling softly over her stomach. He thought it might be a wrap-around dress considering how the material crossed over her body, parting in a slight V at her legs, ending in two different lengths. The V revealed two gorgeous legs, toned, sliding down into heels that matched the exact shade of the dress. There was another V, though he kept himself from looking at that too closely, since it appeared at her chest.

He *had* looked closely enough to notice that her breasts had become fuller with pregnancy.

Not that he had anything to compare them to. He hadn't looked at her breasts before. He'd simply...noticed they were there. She was an attractive woman, and, since he was attracted to attractive women, he'd noticed. And now he noticed that her breasts were fuller. It was all scientific. There was nothing more to it.

He noticed the style of her dress was somehow both highlighting her pregnancy and hiding it. Or did he only think that now because he knew she was pregnant? She wasn't showing apart from the fuller breasts and the slightest curve of her stomach. The dress flattered her body shape, which even before pregnancy had been a glorious mixture of full curves and lean muscle.

She'd always dressed for her body. Sometimes in dresses that made her look demure and saintly; other times in skirts and shirts that made him think she wanted to torment every person in the room around her. Though this dress seemed to fit with her general style—flattering, understated, seductive—at the same time it somehow didn't. It was warmer, softer, though he'd bite his own tongue off before admitting it.

'Are you going to say hello or keep staring?'

He instantly blinked, as if his body was trying to tell her he wasn't staring. But that was undermined by the blush he could feel heating his face. It got hotter when he realised he hadn't looked at her face since she opened the door. If he had, he wouldn't have spent such a long time contemplating her dress or her style, but trying to get his breath back.

She'd left her hair loose. He couldn't remember ever seeing it that way before. It was long, wavy, flowing past her shoulders and stopping halfway to her elbows. She'd parted it so that most of the thick locks had settled on the right side of her face. The rich brown of it bled into the lighter brown of her skin, as if folding dark chocolate into milk chocolate for a deliciously sinful dessert. Just at the beginning stages, before they mixed and created a brown that was more like his own skin tone.

Her lips were painted the same colour as her dress, her checks dusted with some of that colour, too. Her eyes, which were watching him speculatively, were somehow more pronounced, more emotive than usual. He guessed that also had something to do with make-up.

'Keep staring, then,' she answered for him. 'Okay.' She reached behind the door to somewhere he couldn't see, bringing a coat back, which she handed to him. 'Could you at least make yourself useful, please?'

He took the coat without a word, stepping back when she closed the door behind her. Then she looked at him.

'Honestly, Benjamin, this is an overreaction, surely.'

'No.'

'No, it's not an overreaction?' she asked. He nodded. 'You've seen me dressed up before. Mixers at the Institute. Graduation. Ours and Cherise's.'

'Not like this.'

'This is because I'm pregnant and I didn't feel good in anything else.' She straightened her shoulders. 'I know it's probably more formal than tonight required. It's just… The shop assistant told me it suited me.' She lifted a shoulder, though it wasn't as careless as he was sure she intended. It was defensive. 'I thought the dress deserved more effort from other parts of me.'

'Your hair's loose.'

'It has been before.'

'I've never seen it loose before.'

She frowned. 'Well, it's not my preference.'

'I know. That's wearing your hair in a bun.'

'I… Yes.'

She lifted a hand, tucked some hair behind her ear.

'A ponytail would probably be your next option.'

Her lips parted.

'Either on top of your head, when you're working, or at your nape, when you're dressing up.' He had no idea why he was doing this. It felt as if he was seducing her. But surely seduction couldn't happen without him intending it? He kept talking. 'Sometimes you plait your hair in two, then twirl the plaits around your head and pin them like a crown.'

Breath shuddered from between her lips. He swore he heard her swallow. Then she said, 'Only in the kitchen.'

He lifted a hand, pausing before he could do what he wanted. 'Can I touch it?'

'Can you…? My hair?' she asked, her eyes dipping to where his hand hovered above the strands on her shoulder. He nodded. 'Okay.'

'You're sure?'

'Yes.'

She sounded annoyed that he'd clarified. It made him smile. So did the strands of her hair, which were curly and soft and just a little wet.

'I like it like this.'

'In that case, I'll wear it this way more often,' she said dryly. 'It's incredibly practical for someone who owns a restaurant.'

He laughed. Gave in to the urge to tuck her hair behind her ear as he'd seen her do earlier. 'I wouldn't say no.'

She exhaled. 'What are you doing, Benjamin?'

He dropped his hand, looked at her face. 'I don't know.'

'You do know.'

'No, I don't.' He smiled. Almost as soon as he did, the smile vanished. 'Except for right now. Right now, I'm contemplating how to get you to kiss me again. I'd say it's an appropriate response to how incredible you look.' He shook his head. 'I was staring earlier because I didn't have anything to say. You're so beautiful. And so is this dress…and your hair, your face…' He shook his head again. Offered her a wry, possibly apologetic smile. 'I'm sorry. I think the last couple of days have officially caught up with me.'

Her expression was unreadable, but she said, 'It's been a rough couple of days.'

'Yeah.'

'Because of me.' She paused. 'I'm sorry.'

'You don't have to apologise. You already have, anyway.'

'Right.' She leaned back against her door, which he realised only now she hadn't moved away from. 'This hasn't been easy for me either.'

'I know.'

'A large part of it is because you get on my nerves. A lot,' she added when he frowned.

'That seems uncalled for, considering I just gave you a bunch of compliments.'

'You want acknowledgement for that?'

'A thank you would be nice,' he muttered.

'You're right.'

'Sorry—could you say that again?' He patted his pocket, looking for his phone. 'I want to record it for posterity.'

'This, for example, is extremely annoying. But at the same time, I can't stop thinking about the kiss we had the other day.'

He stilled.

'Which gets on my nerves, too. An interesting conundrum. Am I annoyed because I'm attracted to you? Am I annoyed because you annoy me but I'm still attracted to you?' She exhaled. It sounded frustrated. 'I don't have answers, but I keep asking these questions. Then, of course, you do something decent, like pretend to be my boyfriend even though you have no reason or incentive to. You stand up for me in front of my brother, which I found disturbingly hot. In the same breath, you act stupidly, and tell your mother—your *mother*—that I'm your girlfriend. Which, tonight, we have to rectify.'

She shook her head.

'Honestly, Benjamin, these last few days have been the most frustratingly complicated of my life, and I'm an entrepreneur with a crappy family. And I'm *pregnant*, about to become a single mother. Complicated is the air I breathe. But you make things…' She trailed off with a little laugh. 'And still, I want to kiss you, too.'

It took him an embarrassingly long time to process everything she said. By the time he got to the end of it, the part where she wanted to kiss him, his jaw dropped. Trying to maintain his dignity, he shook his head.

'I don't need someone to kiss me out of charity. Especially not someone who thinks I'm annoying.' The more he spoke, the more indignant he felt. 'I'm only annoying because you're annoyed with everyone. Don't deny it,' he said when she opened her mouth. 'It was like that at the Institute. You had so many people trying to be your friend and you'd brush them aside. Draw into yourself. It's like no one was ever good enough for you.'

She tilted her head, the muscles in her jaw tightening and relaxing, one eyebrow raised. 'You're upset—and lashing out—because I called you annoying?'

'I'm not…' He clenched his teeth. 'This is exactly what I'm talking about.'

'Oh—was this you trying to be my friend? Is this me drawing into myself?'

'You know what?' he said, shrugging his shoulders in an attempt to shrug off the irritation. 'I don't need to do this.'

'No, you don't,' she agreed. 'You should have just kissed me like I asked you to and neither of us would be annoyed now.'

'When did you ask me to kiss you?'

She narrowed her eyes. 'You think I told you I've been thinking about our kiss for the fun of it? That I'm attracted to you because I was ranting?' She snorted. 'You spend an eternity staring at me, telling me you're trying to get me to kiss you, and when I give you permission—'

'That was *not* permission.'

'Yes, it was. I said, and I quote—'

'Shut up.'

'Excuse me?'

'You gave me permission?'

'I did. But if you think you can—'

This time, he shut her up by kissing her.

Apparently, he did think he could. And she wasn't mad about it.

Not about the way his lips pressed against hers with a force that had her pushing back against her front door. Not about the fact that they'd had a ridiculous argument that culminated in this kiss in the passageway of her flat. She had no idea what her neighbours thought. She liked the idea of them cheering her on. It wasn't what she'd be doing if someone was arguing near her flat, but she was uptight like that. Her neighbours generally seemed cool.

None of that mattered now, of course. Benjamin had teased her lips open—it hadn't taken much cajoling—and now their tongues were entwined, moving around one another like two loose strands of a rope longing to be tied. She blamed the inelegance of it on the passion. Their argument had fuelled it, though she suspected it was always there between them, simply because of who they were. She couldn't fault it when it created a hunger that could be sated like this. With his lips moving against her, allowing gooseflesh to take the place of her skin. With his tongue, sending heat to places in her body that had been cool for longer than she could remember.

As if he had heard her, Benjamin's hands began to move. They'd been on her waist, keeping her in place, she suspected. But now they skimmed the sides of her breasts, running along her neck, angling her head so he could kiss her more deeply. The throaty moan that he got in response was a soundtrack for his journey back down, although now he lingered exactly where she needed him to. His touch was gentle at her waist, his thumbs brushing her belly. She gasped. It was intimate, him touching her stomach like that. It felt as if he was claiming her. Her baby.

And that was more intense than when he reached her hips and pulled her against him, bringing the most aching part of her to where she needed him.

But that wasn't true any more. The most aching part of her was her heart now, his innocent caress of her stomach awakening things that she'd forced to sleep years ago. When he pulled back, she offered him a small smile of reassurance. It was okay, him kissing her. She was okay. She wasn't being threatened by the loneliness that always followed her. She wasn't overcome by the enormity of her decision to have a baby alone.

After the thing with Kenya and her baby had happened, Alexa had thought more seriously about having her own. She'd done so with her head *and* her heart. Her head had told her that she was thirty years old, and her ability to become a mother wouldn't always be as simple as it was now. It told her that her business was steady enough for her to take maternity leave, and that when she came back she'd be stronger for having had her baby. If her business took a knock, she was still only thirty, and she'd work her tail off—with even more incentive than usual—to make sure it was back on track.

Her heart had told her that she was ready. She'd spent her entire life examining what she shouldn't be as a mother; who she shouldn't be as a parent. She was ready to finally have the family of her dreams. Where support, love, inclusion were the norm. She wouldn't push her child to breaking point, or create an environment where her child felt they needed to compete for her love. No, she would create warmth and happiness. A home, as she'd done with her flat.

But that was before she'd lost her head chef. Now her business didn't seem nearly as stable as it had been before. And that was before this kiss with Benjamin. Suddenly she was thinking about whether she was robbing her child of having someone else to love them. If she was robbing herself of sharing the miracle of the life growing inside her; or the tenderness Benjamin had shown her.

'Hey,' he said softly, his thumb brushing over her cheek. 'It couldn't have been that bad.'

'What? No.' She shook her head. 'It's not—it wasn't bad.' She gave him that smile again. 'We should probably get to dinner.'

'Alexa—'

'I'm fine, Benjamin. I promise.' But she wasn't. She was promising a lie. 'We're fine, too.' That one she meant.

Because in her head, this would be the last kiss. Tonight would be the last night they spent together. Soon people would know their relationship was fake, a joke. Lee would know—but she would survive it. She would go on to court Cherise de Bruyn and focus on getting the chef, as she should have from the beginning. No one would distract her. Not even Benjamin.

At least that way, though her heart seemed to be unsure of her decisions, her head wouldn't be.

CHAPTER SEVEN

'REALLY, MOM?' SAID Benjamin when they walked in. 'You haven't even said hello but already you have baby videos out?' His mother gave him a bright smile in return, and he couldn't even be mad. He rolled his eyes though. Looked at Alexa. 'Go ahead. Clearly my mother would like to start the evening with embarrassment.'

Alexa walked past him, wearing a smile more genuine than the last few she'd given him. He didn't know if he was relieved or annoyed. Neither. Both.

'I'm going to be very disappointed if there are no videos of him running around naked,' Alexa said. 'It's the only level of embarrassment I'll accept.'

'Well, then, you're in luck,' Nina Foster said with a smile.

'It's lovely to meet you, Mrs Foster.' Alexa held out a hand.

'I've already told you my name is Nina.' His mother ignored Alexa's hand, instead pulling her in for a hug. Alexa accepted with a small laugh. Benjamin released a breath he didn't realise he'd been holding. When his mother pulled back, she said, 'You can call me Aunty Nina, dear.'

At that, Alexa grinned. 'Perfect.'

'I take it Dad's in the kitchen,' Benjamin said to distract himself from the troubling warmth in his chest.

'Yes. He's almost done though. That man loves to cook.' Nina aimed that at Alexa. 'It's where Benny gets his talent.'

'In that case, I'm looking forward to dinner.' Alexa turned to Benjamin. 'Should I hang this up, or can I drape it over a chair?'

'Oh, I've got it.'

He took the coat, went to his bedroom and hung it on a hanger from his own cupboard. It was the least he could do, considering the coat had been collateral damage in their make-out session, when he'd tossed it on the floor. He wouldn't have bothered doing anything with her coat otherwise.

His mother would have scolded him, but only after he'd already set the guest's coat down somewhere innocuous. It was the approach he took with most of his clothing, as evidenced by the tornado that had gone off in his room. His parents refused to go in there. Since he helped with the household expenses, they had a *you're an adult, you deserve your privacy* policy. Except he didn't think they meant privacy in the form of someone—including, on particularly bad days, him—being unable to find anything inside the room.

He took another look at things, winced. It would be better if Alexa—

'Is this your room?'

He turned quickly, blocking the doorway with his body. She was a little further down the passage, so she hadn't seen anything. Yet. He would keep it that way.

'Er…no. I mean, yes.' He closed the door behind him. 'It's where I…do things.'

'Things?'

'Sleep.'

'Hmm.'

'Dress.'

'Okay.' She narrowed her eyes. 'Why don't you want me to see it?'

It was obviously too much to hope that she would be polite and ignore his reluctance. But no, not Alexa. She was too straightforward, too unapologetic to allow something like politeness to get in the way of information she wanted.

'It's untidy.'

She waved a hand. 'So was mine the other day.'

'*That* was untidy?' He rolled his eyes. 'Honestly, I have no idea what that word means with some people. My mother says exactly the same thing and the place is spotless.' He paused. 'I'm willing to bet she told you our place is untidy right now. And I know for a fact she spent the entire day supervising our cleaner.'

'I wouldn't take that bet.' She lifted her nose in the air before she grinned. 'Because she just did.'

He chuckled, but stopped when she took a step forward. 'I'm not like you or my mother.'

'What does that mean?'

'When I say something's untidy, I mean it.'

'Well, so do I. I have certain standards, same as in the restaurant. If I say it's untidy, it doesn't suit those standards.' Her gaze sharpened. 'I've never been to yours. Are you saying you keep a sloppy house?'

'Of course not,' he said, offended. 'I have high standards, too.' But he winced. 'That doesn't necessarily translate to my room.'

'So what you're saying is you live in a pigsty.'

'I would not say that.'

'Let me see it, then.' She folded her arms, baiting him.

Damn her.

'I'd rather not. Did my mother send you here?' he asked without waiting to hear her reply. 'I was barely gone for a minute.'

'No. I asked to use the bathroom. What with this situation happening…' She gestured to her stomach.

'You *told* her?'

'That I needed to go to the bathroom because I'm pregnant?' She pulled a face. 'Of course not. Why would I?'

'Oh.' He winced. 'I'm sorry. That was an overreaction.'

She rolled her eyes. 'The bathroom?'

'That one.' He pointed to the room across the hallway.

'Thank you,' Alexa said, and walked into it.

Benjamin stood there for a beat, feeling foolish as his heart rate went back to normal. He shook his head. He needed to put this lie behind him. It was making him skittish. But when he went back to the living room to do just that, his mother was sitting with her hands interlocked over her stomach. Her eyes were closed, and to someone who didn't know her, it would seem as if she was napping. To someone who did know her…

'Mom,' he said, lowering himself in front of her. 'Why didn't you tell me you weren't feeling well?'

She opened her eyes, the tight lines of pain in the creases around them confirming his suspicion. 'I'm fine. Stop fussing.'

'Do we have to do this every time? It's been decades.'

'Exactly. Decades and I still have to tell you I'm fine.'

'But you're not fine. You're in pain.'

'Just a little, from the excitement of the day.'

'Mom…' He trailed off, sighed. 'I wish you'd told me. We could have cancelled. You could have got some rest and not put so much pressure on yourself.'

'And miss the chance to meet Alexa?'

'Mom, Alexa's not—' He broke off. Mostly because he couldn't tell her the truth when she was like this. 'Alexa's not going anywhere,' he finished lamely. 'I'd have brought her the moment you felt better.'

'Would you have?' his mother asked, her eyes tired but sharp. 'I didn't even know about her until yesterday. You never tell us about your dating life. I assumed she's your first proper girlfriend, but I don't even know if that's true.'

'It's because—'

'I had to force you to bring her here,' she interrupted him. Her eyes were flashing now, pain mingled in with the anger. 'And she's pregnant, Benny. *Pregnant*. You hid that from us.'

'What? Oh, no, Mom. She's not—'

'Your bedroom isn't that far away, Benjamin.'

She'd heard them. Damn it. Why hadn't he thought about that?

'We can talk about it when you feel better. Let me help you to bed now.'

'No.' Nina straightened, though he could see she was doing her best not to wince. 'I want to have dinner with you and get to know that woman who's going to be in our lives from now on.'

'She's not…'

He broke off, his mind spinning with how to tell her the truth. Through it, he heard the memory of Alexa's voice asking him why he hadn't told his mother when she'd first overheard him. He should have. But he was caught by that excitement on her face, and he couldn't bear to disappoint her.

He was as much to blame for the situation they were in as Alexa was, he realised. At least this situation. And now, his mother was in pain because of him. Because of his lies.

He exhaled. 'Mom, Alexa's baby… It's not mine.'

She was intruding. She'd known it the moment she'd seen Benjamin crouching in front of his mother. When she'd heard them talk, the conversation so personal she'd had to rest a hand on her chest because her heart felt as if it was breaking, she told herself to walk away. Except she couldn't. She was too riveted by this tender side of a man she'd once called a demon.

She'd felt that tenderness during their kiss. It was what had turned the moment from a purely physical one into something emotional. So she shouldn't have been surprised that he had the capacity to be tender. But seeing it up close and personal, especially after *feeling* it up close and personal? It felt as if someone had walked into her body, gathered her emotions together and tossed them in the air like confetti at a wedding.

She was scrambling to get them back together again when his mother had told him she knew about the baby. Then he confessed it wasn't his, and said nothing about their fake relationship. She'd given him a moment to continue, to tell his mother *why* the baby wasn't his. He hadn't. He merely watched his mother gasp, lift a hand to her mouth, his face crumbling.

So Alexa threw the emotions she had just collected to the ground, and stomped over them to help Benjamin.

'Ben,' she said softly. He looked at her, his eyes ravaged with sadness. 'Let me.'

'We need to—'

'No, *I* need to.' She sent him one look to tell him to shut up, then looked at his mother. 'Benjamin isn't the father of my baby. He's just a decent man who…is decent.' She offered him a smile before sitting on the sofa opposite Nina.

'Mrs Foster… Aunty Nina… I found out I was pregnant pretty quickly. After about two weeks. Benjamin and I hadn't started dating yet, and, well… I got myself into a situation.'

She was keeping as far to the truth as possible. The fertility treatments meant she had found out she was pregnant early. When she had, she'd refused to come in to monitor the pregnancy as her specialist had advised. She wanted to have a normal pregnancy as far as possible. Since it had started out in an unusual way, monitoring things had overwhelmed her.

She also hadn't been fake dating Benjamin then.

'I didn't want to tell him when he asked me out because he seemed like a good guy. For once, I wanted a good guy in my life. I didn't tell him for the longest time. It was wrong, and selfish, and it hurt both you and him. For that, I will never forgive myself.'

She swallowed when her eyes began to prickle. Pressed a hand to her stomach because she felt alone in this deeply personal and strangely true tale she was telling Benjamin's mother. It comforted her, which sent another wave of prickling over her eyes, and she took her time before she continued.

'He hasn't known I'm pregnant very long. I think he was still deciding what to do when you found out about me. It put him in an impossible situation. He didn't want you to be disappointed, but bringing me here tonight makes it seem like he wants me and the baby, and he isn't there yet. He didn't tell you about me because he didn't want that, for either of us,' she said with a lift of her hand.

There was a long silence. Alexa didn't know if someone was waiting for her to speak, or if she was waiting for someone to speak. Eventually, Nina broke the silence.

'Knowing all this, you're still here?'

'It's an impossible situation,' she said with a small smile. 'But it's our normal. So...*normally*... I thought meeting his mother was important.'

There was another long silence. This time, Benjamin broke it.

'I'm sorry, Mom. It was never my intention to...to disappoint you.'

His mother heaved out a sigh. 'You haven't disappointed me. In fact, your behaviour with Alexa... I'd like to think *I* raised you to be someone who doesn't judge people by actions you don't agree with.'

'If it were really you,' Benjamin said slyly, 'you wouldn't judge me for my recent actions.'

Alexa bit her lip, but stopped trying to hide her smile when Nina laughed.

'You're too charming for your own good, boy.'

'I've always thought so, too,' Alexa agreed.

'Thank you,' Benjamin replied with a grin.

Nina gave them an amused look. Then she sobered. 'My son clearly cares about you, Alexa. That's enough for me.'

Alexa nodded, pressure she didn't realise was there releasing inside her. 'Thank you.'

Nina shook her head. 'I'm actually rooting for this to work out. Because at this pace, that baby of yours might be my only chance at a grandchild.'

They didn't have time to reply, as a tall man with a shock of grey hair walked into the room.

'Benjie, boy.' In the man's grin, Alexa saw Benjamin.

'Hi, Dad.'

Benjamin's father looked at their faces, frowned. 'What did I miss?'

CHAPTER EIGHT

'THIS ISN'T MY PLACE,' Alexa said, as if only now noticing he hadn't taken her back to her flat. Which was surprising, as they hadn't spoken since they'd left his house, so she hadn't been distracted. In fact, she'd been staring out of the window the entire time.

'No, it's not.'

He didn't say anything else as he drove along the gravel road that led into the quarry. Handy, because if he had, he wouldn't have heard her small gasp when he parked. He couldn't deny that part of why he'd brought her was the wow factor. The quarry was spectacular at night; on a summer's night, even more so. There was no cool breeze to chill them, no dew glazing the grass that stretched out in front of the car park. The sky was clear, the full moon illuminating things enough that he didn't have to get out his phone's torch to guide them to the water.

And really, it was the water that was the star of the quarry. It was nestled in the hollow of the rocks, stretching out in inky darkness. The moon was reflected in it, the stars, too, and it made him wonder if perhaps this was all a little too romantic. But he wanted quiet, and the quarry was quiet. He went to the back of his car, and got out the camping chairs he kept there.

'You prepared for this?' she asked when she got out of the car. 'Were you intending on bringing me here?'

'No.' He carried the chairs to his usual spot beneath the tree at the edge of the water. When he heard her behind him he said, 'I keep these in my car.'

'For this reason?'

'Exactly.'

'You bring ladies out here a lot, then?' She gave him a sly look as she lowered herself into the chair. Then she frowned. 'You'd better be prepared to help me out of this chair. It's low, and being pregnant means I have zero control over my balance.'

'So what you're saying is that I could leave you here and you'd have to stay in the chair for ever?'

'Yes,' she replied, voice dry as a badly made cake. 'That's exactly what I'm saying.'

'Good to know.' He paused. 'Better watch your attitude.'

'You know what? I don't even need your help. The grass looks pretty soft. I can tilt to the side, break my fall with my hand, and figure it out from there.'

'The grass is lower than the chair.'

'I said I'd figure it out.'

He couldn't help his laugh, though he tried to be respectful and kept it quick and low—until she joined in, which he hadn't expected. It was strange to be laughing with her, but he suspected they were relieving the tension of the night. There'd been an undercurrent during the entire meal. He didn't blame his mother for being reserved—both Alexa's news and her pain had probably occupied her mind and her body—but it meant that he'd overcompensated. The result was a strained meal where everyone pretended nothing was wrong and it was…draining.

When they stopped laughing, they lapsed into an easy silence; another surprise. But honestly, he was grateful for it. It gave him a moment to gather his thoughts, prepare his words.

'Thank you.'

'For what?'

'What you had to do with my mom. You made a difficult situation easier.'

She sighed. 'I lied.'

'Did you?'

She frowned. 'You mean, besides the fact that I kept our fake relationship going?'

'Yes, actually.'

It took some time for her to understand.

'Oh, you want to know if the stuff I said about the father of the baby's true.'

He did. But now that she said it, he felt as if he was asking too much. Maybe if he was honest with her, too…

'Look, I know I said the lies had to end. But…' He trailed off, sighed. 'At some point tonight I realised it worked for me to be in a fake relationship, too. It made my mother happy. Maybe I knew it would and that's why I let her think we were together in the first place.' It was something he'd have to think about. 'Your pregnancy complicated things, and I got scared. But your explanation made sense. Hell, it somehow made both of us look good.'

She looked at the water. 'I wouldn't say that.'

'I would.' He let it sit for a moment. 'I realised tonight the only people whose opinions I care about are my parents. So, we can keep this going for as long as we both want to.'

'You're not afraid of disappointing your mother when it ends?'

He heaved out a breath. 'I can't see an outcome that won't hurt her. I'd rather she think I tried and it didn't work out than know I lied to her.'

'Sneaky,' she commented.

'You're one to talk.'

She laughed. 'Touché.' There was a beat. 'Thank you.'

'This isn't only for you.'

For once, he believed it. He wasn't doing this only to help her. It helped him and his family, too. It might have been strained at dinner this evening, but there'd also been light. That light had been because of Alexa. Because of what she represented to his parents.

A future that didn't only involve taking care of them.

He'd sacrifice his reputation for his parents' peace of mind.

'I know,' she said softly. 'Still. Thank you.' Silence danced between them for a few minutes. 'To answer your earlier question, I don't know what kind of guy got me pregnant.'

His brain took a moment to shift gears. 'You don't know…if he's a good guy?'

'I don't know who he is.'

'Oh.'

Sure. That was fine. She was allowed her sexual freedom. If she didn't know who she'd slept with, that was her business. Except…

No, no exceptions. He wouldn't be a judgemental jerk.

'I was waiting,' she said into the silence, 'for some kind of bigoted statement about my sex life.'

'I wouldn't dare.'

She laughed lightly. 'You were basically biting your tongue.'

'It isn't my business.'

'No, it's not.' Her laughter faded. 'Which makes why I'm telling you I was artificially inseminated by donor sperm puzzling.'

'You were artificially inseminated?' he repeated dumbly.

'Yep.' She unclasped the hands that had been locked around her knee. 'I wanted to have a baby and the available men were… Well, I suppose there were none. Whom I trusted anyway.'

'You have no male friends?'

'I don't have any…' She broke off. 'I don't have that many friends. Besides, could you imagine me asking a friend to be the father of my child?' She shuddered. 'That would be asking for trouble. Involvement. People don't tend to keep their word, so the promise that they would never encroach on the way I raised a child would be gone pretty quickly, I bet. Especially if the baby looked like the friend.'

He thought about it. 'Alternatively, you could have gone through this *with* someone. You wouldn't have to make decisions alone. You'd have support.'

'Spoken like a man who's had support his entire life.'

'Is that a criticism?'

'Not a criticism. An observation.'

'In return, then, I observe that you don't trust people.'

'An accurate observation. Trusting people isn't worth a damn.'

He tried to formulate an answer, but found himself at a loss for words. Not emotion though. He felt sorry that she'd lived a life that encouraged her to think this way. There was some rage, too, because it seemed completely unfair that he'd had parents who'd loved him and taught him the value of leaning on family and she hadn't. Or maybe it wasn't so much rage as it was guilt, because he had something she didn't.

'Don't feel sorry for me.'

'I'm not.'

'Your mother wouldn't like you lying to me.'

His face twisted. 'Are you really using my mother to make me feel guilty about this?'

'Yes. I am a smart woman who uses the tools at her disposal.'

He chuckled softly. 'Can't argue with that.'

'Finally, you learn.'

She settled back in the chair, resting her hands on her belly. It had the same protective tint as the way she'd rubbed her stomach that night in her flat. Now he knew she'd done it because she was pregnant. What he didn't know was why *he'd* done it. Why, when they'd kissed, he'd grazed her stomach and felt a rush of protectiveness he didn't know existed inside him. Need had joined so quickly and intensely that he'd had to pull back from their kiss to deal with it. To try and deny it, as he'd done the first time he'd felt that need.

'I don't feel sorry,' he said slowly, 'I feel sad.'

She didn't answer, tilting her head from side to side.

'What?' he asked.

'I'm trying to figure out whether sad is worse.'

'And?'

She looked over, eyes shining with emotion he couldn't read but knew meant something. 'It isn't.'

Without thinking about it, he reached out a hand. She stared at it, at him, looked down, then slowly took his hand. He wanted to stand up and shout for joy. He wanted to thank her for letting him in. He wanted to pull her into his arms and kiss her. Sate the heat the contact sent through his body. Instead, he squeezed and let the quiet of the evening settle over them.

It surprised him by settling the twisting of his stomach, too. He was used to the twisting, since it came whenever his mother was in pain.

When he was young, he had thought he could do something about it. His mother would be in bed, curled up to favour whichever side of her was aching more, and he'd bring her tea. Make her food. Offer to run a bath for her, or cuddle her until she felt better. She'd never accept, and she'd apologise afterwards. She'd tell him the version of her who was in pain wasn't really *her*.

Throughout her illness, she'd tried to separate the person who was in pain and the one who wasn't. Which he understood. Her illness had been relatively unknown in South Africa when she'd been diagnosed, and even the dialogue with her doctors had separated those identities. But he knew, even as a kid, that the same mother who couldn't move some days was the mother who would spend hours reading to him. Or taking him to some exciting place he wanted to see. Or answering all his questions with patience and honesty. As he grew older, he realised his mother had separated who she was because she saw her body as her enemy during her flare-ups. It was separate for her; it was separate *from* her. It was betraying her.

He'd wanted to help her because he wanted her to remember he loved all of her, even if she couldn't do it herself. It was a big burden for a kid to undertake, even though he hadn't completely understood it. And it had evolved as he got older. Now, he tried to nudge instead of directly say. He tried to support instead of fix. It was navigating a minefield—a stubborn minefield—but since there weren't any explosions, at least not yet, Benjamin thought he was doing pretty okay. As long as he was there, he would keep doing okay.

'Is your mom going to be all right?'

He frowned, trying to remember if he'd spoken out loud and the question had been provoked. He was sure he hadn't, which meant Alexa was simply curious. He sighed in relief.

'Yeah, she'll be fine.'

'Is she unwell?'

He took a breath. 'She has something called fibromyalgia. It's a—'

'I know what it is.' At his surprised look, she rolled her eyes. 'People are more open about chronic illnesses these days.'

'But… I mean, it's not something you just know.'

'I didn't,' she agreed. 'Until I went to look it up after seeing an acquaintance talk about it online.'

He kept his mouth shut because if he didn't he was sure he'd make inelegant grunts she'd make fun of.

'It sounds tough,' she said softly. 'Living your life in pain the whole time. I can't imagine.' There was a short pause. 'I *can* imagine how hard it must have been for you.'

He gave her a sharp look, dropping her hand in the process. She didn't seem fazed, only folding her hands over her stomach again.

'What do you mean?' he asked.

'Well, you're the kind of person who agrees to be in a fake relationship with his mortal enemy because you were feeling protective. At least, I guess that was how you were feeling? Maybe it was indignant at how Lee dared to act towards me. I can't tell with you.' She shrugged. 'Regardless, you're someone who does things when other people seem vulnerable. I'm guessing you see your mother's pain as her being vulnerable, which makes you want to do something. Except you can't, because it's *her* pain.'

It was remarkably astute. Uncomfortably astute. Which was why he said, 'No.'

The corners of her lips twitched. 'Hmm…'

'It's been fine for me.'

'Okay.'

'She's the one in pain.'

'Sure.'

'Is it hard for me to see her that way? Sure. But is it worse for me? No.'

'That's not what I said though. I know it's worse for her. Of course it is.' She paused. 'I might be off base here, what with having a messed-up family situation myself, but I don't think it would be easy for me to see someone I care about in pain.'

'It's…not.'

'I don't doubt it.' There was a long pause as the words washed over them. 'It's not an excuse for you not to pick up after yourself though. How do you even find anything in your room? It looks like the aftermath of a police search.'

As soon as the surprise faded—though he should have known she'd look—he started laughing. 'It's organised chaos.'

'Rubbish!'

'It's not rubbish.'

'You're telling me you know where every T-shirt is placed? Every shirt? Pants?'

'Exactly.'

'So if I hid something in there you'd find it?'

'Did you hide something in my room?'

She gave him a sly look. 'Maybe.'

'Alexa,' he nearly growled.

'What?' She blinked at him innocently. 'You said it's organised chaos. I'd just like to prove, once and for all, on behalf of everyone who's been sceptical about organised chaos, that that's nonsense.'

'You're trying to trap me on behalf of an entire group of people?'

'Sometimes your actions have to be bigger than yourself.'

He shook his head, but even his disbelief couldn't overshadow his amusement. Then he thought of something.

'How did you know I'd say organised chaos though?'

'Please. I've spent years trying to avoid interacting with you. It hasn't worked—' she sent him an accusatory look '—but at least I got to know who you are.'

He sighed. 'What did you hide in my room?'

'A handkerchief.'

'You carry a handkerchief?'

'Yes.' She sniffed. 'It's for the essential oils I carry in my purse, too. In case I have an overbearing bout of nausea.'

'Efficient.'

'Thanks.'

'Can you at least tell me what the handkerchief looks like?'

'Pink. Like my dress.'

'That should make it easier to find.'

'It'll be a breeze. You know where everything is, remember?'

She patted his hand, winked at his glare, and he turned away before he could smile again.

He couldn't say whether it was the teasing that soothed him, but the anxiety in his body had stopped humming. Except it couldn't be the teasing. She'd done plenty of that before, though it had lost its snarkiness at some point over the last few days.

As he thought about it, he realised it was that she understood. His position in his family had always made him feel alone, and finally he didn't feel that way any more.

He let it wash over him. Didn't even question that Alexa had been the one to make him feel that way—or what it meant. Still, he couldn't let her get the upper hand.

'So,' he said casually, 'are we going to talk about that kiss?'

'What kiss?'

He snorted. 'There's no way you don't—'

'What kiss, Benjamin?'

At her tone, he looked over. Saw her determination. It made him laugh, which turned the determination into a glare. Satisfied that he'd won, he stood and offered a hand to help her up.

CHAPTER NINE

ALEXA WALKED INTO the restaurant and saw him immediately.

'You've got to be kidding me,' she muttered, pausing.

It had been a few days since she and Benjamin had had *that* moment. It wasn't a defined moment. She couldn't say—oh, this thing happened and things have changed. Besides the kisses. And the fact that she thought he might be nice, despite the whole stealing-her-chef thing. Or how kind he was with his parents; how eager he was to please them. All she knew for sure was that at some point at the quarry, things had shifted. She needed time to sort through it, and she had other things to do first.

Such as secure her chef before she went on maternity leave.

There was time. She was days away from entering her second trimester, so she had about six months. That was what she told herself logically. In reality, she was freaking out. Hiring a new chef was a nightmare. She knew because she'd done so months before and it had all gone to hell anyway. So she needed time to find the right person, make sure they worked well with the rest of her team. Train them to work for Infinity, with her and with Kenya. She had to be there to observe and make sure everything would go smoothly when she was away.

She only had six months to do so.

No wonder she had indigestion.

That could have been her pregnancy, too, but she had a feeling being stressed about the new chef didn't help. Or being at odds with Kenya, who'd stubbornly refused to talk about anything other than work in the last week. Usually, Kenya was a champagne bottle, shaken and uncorked and overflowing with personal anecdotes. Now she was a bottle of wine; one that was aging and still and not overflowing with anything.

It was hard for Alexa to believe she missed all of Kenya's energy and her much too personal stories about her life. But she did. And now she had to deal with realising she missed the connection of it, too, and think about how to fix it, and about why Kenya was really so mad at her. She did *not* need to face Benjamin and his kissable lips today.

She marched over to the table.

'You're stealing my appointments with Cherise now, too?'

He looked up, smiled at her, and did it all so slowly that it felt as though someone had pushed a button for that to happen. Her heart did a little skip at that face; her mind recognised that his surprise, his pleasure at seeing her were genuine.

'Hey!' He stood. 'You have an appointment with Cherise, too?'

'Too?' She looked at the table. There were only two seats. 'How can we both have an appointment with her?'

He shrugged. 'She called me the day before yesterday to ask me if I could meet her here.' He gestured at the restaurant. It was perfectly nice with black and white décor, some greenery courtesy of plants, and the faint smell of fish because of its position near the water of the V&A Waterfront. 'Said it would be a nice neutral space.'

Alexa huffed out a breath. 'Yeah, because that's what I told her. After I called her the day before yesterday to ask for this meeting.'

He blinked. 'You called Cherise after we spent the night together?'

'I'm not sure I'd describe dinner with your family as us spending the night together, but yes, I did.' She straightened her spine. 'You said we should continue with our plans as usual.'

'Yeah, but I didn't expect—'

He frowned. Shoved his hands into his pockets. Suddenly she noticed that he was wearing a shirt. She'd seen him in one before, but now he looked…different. His shoulders were broad, chest defined, the material clinging to all of it. She half expected him to move and tear through a perfectly good piece of clothing.

Why was a part of her cheering for that to happen?

'I guess she wanted to speak with both of us at the same time.'

'I did,' Cherise said from beside them. Alexa nearly jumped out of her skin.

'How long have you been there?'

'Just arrived,' Cherise replied. 'Sorry to spring this on you.' She narrowed her eyes. 'Although I was sure I wouldn't actually be able to do that, since you two are dating.'

There was a beat as Alexa realised she was going to have to pretend again. Fortunately, Benjamin spoke before she could say anything.

'We keep our personal and professional lives separate.' He smiled, oozing charm. Alexa nearly slipped on the puddle of it before she realised this was what he did. He charmed people. But *not* her. Especially not if she continued ignoring the fact that they'd kissed. 'Thought it for the best, considering we're in the same business.'

'I imagine that must help. Or make things more complicated, if you're meeting up like this.'

'It doesn't happen as often as you'd think,' Alexa answered Cherise. Cherise gave her a rueful smile.

'I thought it might be easier to discuss this together.' She paused. 'In hindsight, I suppose I was using your relationship to make things easier for myself. I wouldn't have to have two meetings about possibly the same thing. I'm blurring things for you,' she added with a frown.

'Don't worry about it,' Benjamin said smoothly. 'We're mature enough to handle it.'

He sent Alexa a look as if to say *I'm mature enough.* It took all of Alexa's willpower not to roll her eyes at him, or stick out her tongue. Or do anything really that would undermine her maturity. She could be mature.

'Should we get someone to add a chair to this table?' Alexa asked coolly. Maturely. She gestured to a waiter. 'I booked a two-seater.'

'This is the table I booked, actually,' Benjamin said, also gesturing to the waiter. When he looked at Alexa, she pulled a face. *This is you being mature?*

'Oh, I booked a table for three,' Cherise interjected. 'I just saw you two here and came directly to speak to you. I'll have the waiter take us.'

Soon they were sitting together and ordering drinks.

'So,' Cherise started, 'I know whatever either of you wanted to say to me today probably isn't going to work out because the other crashed the lunch.'

She and Benjamin exchanged a look. They hadn't *crashed* the lunch. Cherise had invited Benjamin to an appointment Alexa and she had agreed on. If anything, Cherise had done the crashing. By proxy.

Acid pushed up in Alexa's chest. She'd done a lot of research to find Cherise. Her first step had been to call her old mentor at the restaurant she'd worked at after the Institute. He'd recommended two people, one of whom was studying at the same institute she'd studied at—Cherise—the other of whom was still working for him, but was looking for something more, more urgently than what he could offer.

It had taken her a while to find out that Cherise wasn't

studying at the Institute as a newbie who wanted to learn everything she could. No, Cherise had worked under the best chefs, her old mentor included, for almost a decade, and had decided to formalise her knowledge by getting an official qualification. She was interested in something new, which, after speaking with some of the people Cherise had worked with, including the instructors they had in common, Alexa was eager to offer.

Except now it seemed Cherise wasn't going to be that good a match after all.

'I thought I'd say some things to both of you instead,' Cherise said. 'One: I would be happy to work with either of you. I'm looking for something different to what I've done in the past, which tended to lean towards more traditional fine dining. Nothing wrong with it,' she added quickly, 'but I'd like to do something more creative than cauliflower purée. I'm eager to explore that creativity, and I believe your restaurants, both younger, trendier places, would give me the space to do that.'

Alexa rubbed the burning in her chest thoughtfully. It wasn't subsiding, though her doubts about Cherise were. Perhaps that was enough for now.

'Two: I have no idea which one of you I'd like to work for.' Cherise gave them a small smile. 'I've dined at both your restaurants. Both of them were amazing experiences, and each of your spaces I respond to. Yours is more traditional, with the wood and the partitions between each side of the restaurant,' she said to Benjamin, 'but there's something about it that makes me nostalgic. Yet I love how modern Infinity is,' Cherise continued, speaking to Alexa now. 'It's sleek, and so not where I'd expect to be served fine dining.'

'Thank you…?'

Cherise laughed. 'It's a compliment,' she assured Alexa. 'You've brought a younger crowd in by modernising your place, and I respect someone who can instil respect for good food in a generation that fast food was basically designed for.'

'Well, then, thank you,' Alexa said more firmly.

'The conclusion I've come to is that it will depend on who I get along with the best. The only way I can know that is to spend more time with you both.'

'Of course,' Alexa said. 'You can come to the restaurant any time you'd like. I can show you around, have you speak with some of my staff. I'm sure Benjamin would allow that, too.'

'Sure.'

'And I'd love that. But I was thinking of something a little different.'

'What?'

She wrinkled her nose. 'School.'

'Why do I feel like we were being interviewed?' Benjamin asked minutes after Cherise had left the restaurant.

'Not were,' Alexa corrected. 'Are. We now have to take a three-day course at the Institute. Which I don't mind per se, it's just…' Her voice faded and she let out a huge sigh.

'Everything okay?'

'Fine.'

But she dropped her head onto a hand she'd rested on the table.

If his instincts hadn't already been tingling from that sigh, this would have done them in. In fact, it felt as though an alarm was going off in his head. It dimmed the sound of the inner voice warning him not to get involved. Things were already almost impracticably complicated between them; he didn't need to further complicate that by getting involved with her issues.

Except she looked so fragile, sitting there with her hand on her head. It was so different to how she usually seemed—abrasive, bull-headed, *strong*—that he had to fight harder than he would have liked not to ask. And then he found himself fighting against *that* because he did want to ask. Hell, he even wanted to make it better. Which was exactly how things usually went wrong. People would take advantage of his tendency to take over. After he'd had a 'friend' do it recently, he'd learnt his lesson.

He eyed Alexa.

'You okay?' he asked anyway, because he was a fool who hadn't learnt a thing.

'I've already said I'm fine,' she said, but there was no heat in the words. If she were feeling herself, there definitely would have been heat in the words.

'It's just that—' he tried not to show his surprise that she'd continued '—this is turning out to be a lot harder than I thought it would be. Everything is,' she said in an uncharacteristically small voice as she lifted her head. 'I wanted to get Cherise to work for me so I could go on maternity leave without worrying I was ruining my restaurant by having a baby. Leaving it vulnerable in some way. Maybe even to you and Lee. Now I have to do this course with you.' She looked up at him. Her eyes were gleaming, but sharp. 'No offence.'

He wondered if he should dignify that with a response.

'Why can't anything be simple?' she whispered now. 'Why can't I have a family that doesn't suck? Why couldn't my chef have stayed on so that I wouldn't have this stress during my pregnancy? Why couldn't...?'

She exhaled. Waved a hand.

'I'm fine.'

'Clearly.'

She gave him a dark look. He preferred it to the sadness.

'I can't help you with—'

'Any of it,' she interrupted. 'You can't help me with any of it. But I appreciate the effort.'

'I wasn't going to say that.'

'Oh, I know,' she said, straightening now. She took a deep sip of water, but kept her gaze on him. 'I know what you were going to say, Benjamin. It was going to be about what you could help me with. You might even have been considering stepping out of this race with Cherise because things would be easier for me then.'

'I wasn't—'

She cut him off with a single raised eyebrow. And because, of course, he *was*.

'Where would it leave you, Benjamin?' she asked softly. 'You'd have to look for another chef. You'd have to answer to my brother. You're clearly letting your personal feelings override how you feel professionally.'

'There are no personal feelings.'

She looked at him strangely. The confusion cleared in seconds.

'Oh, no, I don't mean *for* me. Of course not.' There was a beat. 'I meant you're letting your desire to fix things for people cloud your professional opinion. Which should be that you should do that three-day course and fight to have her work for you.'

She grabbed her purse, threw some notes onto the table. 'That's what I'll be doing.'

Then she was gone.

He sat, bemused, until the waiter came to the table, saw the money Alexa had left, and asked if he wanted the bill. He said yes, stuffed her notes in his wallet, and paid with his card. Then he walked. Not to his car, where he probably should have gone. He had work to do.

But his thoughts demanded that he pay them heed, and he couldn't do that when he was driving, or working. So he walked. Away from the bustle of the Waterfront, where tourists shopped and locals ate. Down, past the docks, until he was simply walking along the edge of the Waterfront, waves splashing against the rocks beyond the railing.

The conversation he'd had with Alexa…

Well, he couldn't exactly call it a conversation. More a monologue, with the occasional pauses. He couldn't be upset with her though; she was right. There'd been a moment, and not a brief one, where he'd thought about giving up the fight for Cherise.

A lot about that bothered him. The first was, simply, that it was stupid. He'd spent a long time trying to find her. Speaking with his contacts at restaurants she'd worked in and at the Institute. Making sure she had the skills a chef in his kitchen would need.

He'd started out as the head chef, back when Lee had reached out to him years ago. Though that was tainted now with the knowledge that Lee had done it to get back at Alexa, Benjamin could still recognise his luck. Because Lee had been the one to help him make the transition once he'd discovered his passion went beyond the kitchen.

Since Lee had multiple businesses, he couldn't invest much time in the restaurant. So when Benjamin had decided to switch gears and spoken to Lee about his desire to branch out, Lee had offered to train him. For two years, they'd done just that. This was the first year he'd taken on the responsibility fully, and he wanted to make Lee proud. Hell, he wanted to make himself proud. Giving away his chance because he wanted to help out a woman who didn't need his help was definitely stupid.

The second thing that bothered him about wanting to was that she'd seen through him. She had the uncanny ability to do so, which she'd displayed at lunch today and at the quarry the other night. He could blame the ability on the fact that she didn't seem to want his help. Despite what he'd first thought about her, Alexa wasn't using him. If she was, she would have said it by now. She was disturbingly honest like that.

Which was why he couldn't be dishonest with himself when it came to her. She didn't see through him because she didn't want his help. Well, not only because of that. It was also because she knew him, could see him, and he didn't like it.

He had a persona to maintain. An important one. The moment his parents realised he felt responsible for looking after them, they'd stop him from doing so. The moment his mother saw that he'd seen another future for himself because of the fake relationship with Alexa, she'd do anything she could for him to have it.

But he couldn't have it. It wasn't compatible with living at home, helping his father around the house, spending time with his mother. If Alexa saw through him, she might see the things he didn't want anyone knowing, too. What if she mentioned it to his mother? To his father? And just because she wasn't using him now didn't mean she never would. Look at what his friends had done. His cousins.

They pretended to spend time with him, be his friend, but they only wanted things. Money, free food, help with an event. It was predictable in its consistency. As predictable as his ability to fall for it. Because they needed him.

He had reasons to stay away from Alexa. To not give in to the pull he felt between them. Good reasons. Professional *and* personal reasons. He only had one reason to see her: he had to get Cherise to work for him.

One more reason, a voice in his head reminded him. He almost groaned.

Yes, he had one more reason to see her. He was also supposed to be in a relationship with her.

CHAPTER TEN

A FORTNIGHT LATER Alexa arrived at the Institute early, ready to get the first day of the course over with. Perhaps not a winning attitude, but the best one she could muster under the circumstances. She'd been to the doctor the day before for her thirteen-week appointment. Apparently, she'd been blessed with twins.

It did not seem like a blessing at that moment.

She'd known it was a possibility, of course. She'd read many articles about fertility treatments; her doctor had pretty much repeated the information to her verbatim. But she hadn't once considered that *she'd* have twins. Twins weren't for someone who needed to find a chef for her business so it wouldn't fail or be vulnerable to attacks by a sibling or for someone who didn't know how to raise one child, let alone two. *Two!* What had she done to deserve this?

Well, a voice in her brain said, quite reasonably, *you're at odds with your family. You're pretending to date a man and lying to the people you care about. Your only friend isn't talking to you because of the lie, and you refuse to tell her the truth. You also haven't told her you're pregnant—with twins—and you've pushed away anyone who could possibly come to care about you.*

It was a long list of her flaws. Surprisingly long, considering her own head had provided them. Although that the list was there at all wasn't a surprise. She wasn't perfect. The fact that she was prickly, bull-headed, and stubborn wasn't news. But since those characteristics had helped her survive her family and build her business, she could see the good in them, too.

So maybe twins were her punishment for her irreverence.

Not that her children were a punishment. Of course not.

'Sorry,' she murmured to them. 'I'm just surprised. And worried. What if I'm not a good mother to you? There are two of you now, so I'll be screwing up twice as much.'

She let out a huge breath, and sipped the herbal tea she'd bought before she'd left for the Institute. The warmth of it gave her some much-needed comfort. The rap on her window did not—nor did seeing who it was.

She opened the window. 'I'll be sending you my hospital bills.'

Benjamin gave her a half-smile, almost as if he expected her to give him a hard time. Almost as if he liked it. 'For what?'

'My heart attack.'

She grabbed her things, closed the window, and got out of the car. He hadn't moved far away, so when she turned, she found herself in his bubble. His musky scent didn't make her nauseous, as she'd expected it to, since it was in the window of her morning illness time. Maybe because her other body parts had woken up and decided to respond to it.

When she'd read that pregnancy would make her more… sensitive, she'd laughed. She hadn't been sensitive to anyone in such a long time. She couldn't even remember who the last person she'd been sensitive to was. And yet what she was feeling now was anything but amusement. She was incredibly aware of the smell of him. Incredibly aware of his body only centimetres from hers.

He looked delicious in his black T-shirt and jeans; his standard outfit in the kitchen, even when they'd been studying. Again, she noticed his shoulders, his chest. His body was muscular and strong and she wondered what it would be like if he scooped her into his arms. Would she feel light, even now, pregnant with twins? Would she be annoyed that he'd dare do it?

Or would she be amused, attracted? A playful combination of both that would have her inching forward to kiss him…?

'Oh,' she said, and leaned back against the car.

'Are you okay?' he asked, moving even closer.

'Yeah. You're just…um…awfully close.'

He looked down, seemingly only noticing it now. His lips curved into a smile that had her heart racing. Not because it was sexy and sly. Of course not. It was because she knew what that slyness meant.

'Are you having a tough time because I'm close to you, Alexa?'

Oh, no. He was speaking in a low voice that was even more seductive than the smile.

'No.' She cleared her throat when the word came out huskily. 'I'm having a hard time because I'm pregnant. I need air and space and…stuff,' she finished lamely.

It was a pity. He'd believed her until she'd said that. Now he was smirking, which was quite annoying. But it gave her an idea.

'It's probably good that I'm close to you though. I'm so dizzy.'

She braced herself, then rested her head on his chest. The bracing didn't help. Not when his arms automatically went around her, holding her tighter against him. His heart thudded against her cheek, her own heart echoing. She closed her eyes as she realised her mistake.

'It's okay,' he said softly. 'I've got you.'

The words had a lump growing in her throat. She looked up, defiantly, she thought, because she didn't need him to *have* her. But she completely melted at his expression. It was soft and concerned and protective. Then he ran the back of his finger over her cheek, his gaze slipping to her lips, and she was melting, all right, but for the wrong reasons.

'I should…sit down.'

'Yeah,' he said shakily, stepping away.

He'd been as affected as she had.

She wrapped her hands around her cup. How was she still holding it? How hadn't she dumped it all over Benjamin? She began to walk over the strip of stones that separated the car park and the grass. They settled on the bench under a large tree metres away, and she sighed at the view of the vineyard. Bright green and dark green with the brown of the sand stretching out in front of them. At the very end of the vineyard rose a mountain; tall and solid, it enclosed the area and made everything seem private. With the quiet of the early morning settling over them, Alexa realised she hadn't come early to get the day over with as much as she'd come for this.

She could remember the days she'd done the same thing when she'd been studying. She'd still been living at home, paying her parents for the pleasure with the little she earned working part-time as a kitchen hand. She couldn't wait to escape to this beautiful place every weekday. Away from the attention her parents had lavished on her about her goals in life. Goals that weren't aligned with the ones they'd had for her life, which was why they had kept pushing.

Pushing and pushing, until she had been sure she would fall over from the stress of it.

'Is it better now?'

'Hmm?' She looked over at him. Blinked. 'Oh, the dizziness? Yes. Tons.'

He smiled, but apparently knew better than to comment. 'What distracted you just now?'

'I used to love coming here early. It's so beautiful, and

peaceful.' She exhaled, forcing out the bad memories that came with the good ones.

'It really is something,' he agreed. Except he was looking at her. Intensely.

She cleared her throat. 'Is…um…is this why you're here so early?'

'You know what they say. Early bird gets the best view.'

'And maybe the station third from the front.' She laughed at his expression. 'We all know that one's the best.'

'Not true. Station seven is.'

'Station seven's left stove plate can't simmer.'

He laughed. 'How do you know this place so well?'

'You mean, how is it that you can't fool me?' She gave him an amused look. 'I pay attention.'

'Yeah,' he said softly. 'You do.'

Somehow, she didn't think he was referring to the stove. She sipped her tea instead of asking him, and nearly spat it out again when he said, 'You've grown.'

Swallowing it back down proved challenging.

'What do you mean?'

'Your stomach is bigger,' he said quickly. Which, of course, she'd known, but it was worth asking the question for that look of panic on his face. She hid her smile with another sip of tea.

'Yes. This happens when you're expecting.'

'It's only been two weeks. Is it supposed to grow so quickly?'

She laughed lightly. 'I hope so. But my doctor is happy with everything. I saw her yesterday. I guess growing fast is what happens when you're expecting two.'

Maybe a part of her had known he would react this way. Multiple blinks, mouth opening and closing, every muscle she could see frozen. He was in shock, and it felt like a vindication of her own reaction. It even made her want to laugh at her own reaction, which was probably as comical as his. No—most likely more. She was the one carrying the twins.

'Two? As in twins?'

She merely raised her brows in answer.

'Of course it's twins. Two are twins.' He stood, began to pace. 'You're sure?'

Though she hadn't quite anticipated *this* reaction, she nodded, eager to see where it would go.

'Man. Twins? *Twins.*' His long legs easily strode back and forth over the distance in front of the bench. 'I can't believe you're having two.'

'I couldn't either,' she said slowly, 'and I'll actually be the one giving birth to them. Raising them.'

It took him a few moments, but he seemed to understand the implication. He stopped, gave her a sheepish smile.

'Sorry. I guess for a moment there I was...' He broke off, confusion crossing his face. 'I don't know what I was doing.'

'Maybe you imagined what it would be like if we really were dating,' she offered. 'Think about it. You started dating a woman who was pregnant, something you didn't sign up for, but you're too good a guy to let that keep you from developing a relationship with her. So, hey, maybe you can be a father to one kid if you liked one another enough. But two?' She gave a slight shake of the head. 'That would freak anyone out.'

'Even you?'

She laughed. It sounded a little deranged even to her own ears. Not that that kept her from answering.

'I always wanted a family. A good one, I mean. I realised about a year ago that I could only create that for myself. I couldn't rely on my own family for that.' She stared at that green in the distance, letting herself speak. She needed to say it out loud. 'I thought someday I'd have another. I'd teach them to cherish one another. To be each other's best friend, not competition. Not like my relationship with Lee. They would be different, how I dreamt siblings would be—always there for each other, so they would always know love.'

She rested her hands on her stomach. On the two lives growing there.

'But I would have time between them. Two right away? It's scary. What if I'm not cut out for this?'

She exhaled sharply; shook her head sharply. Now wasn't the time to have a breakdown. She'd only found out about the twins the day before, and clearly she needed to process. But she wouldn't do it now, in front of him. Well, *more* in front of him than she already had done. She wouldn't say anything about her fear of her restaurant failing. Or failing the people who relied on her there. Less because she felt it—although she did—and more because she knew he'd feel sorry for her. Based on his expression now, he already did. And her pregnancy didn't even involve him.

She inhaled now. Offered him a smile. 'But no, I'm not freaking out.'

He smiled back, because she was vulnerability wrapped up in fire and he wanted to burn himself so badly. He couldn't help it. The combination of her traits—traits that were polar opposites in everyone but her, that made her who she was—was so appealing. Fascinating. Intriguing.

Even as he thought it, he shook his head. How could he find her appealing? Fascinating? Intriguing? He'd just thought—seconds ago—that she was vulnerable. Vulnerability meant she would need someone. It put her in the perfect position to use someone. And that someone couldn't be him.

Mainly because something inside him, *everything* inside him, wanted it to be him.

He'd been trained for this, hadn't he? He'd spent years

managing his mother's vulnerabilities. Not that they needed to be managed, he thought with a frown. His mother's pain wasn't a problem he needed to solve; he knew that. It was just… He'd had to manage his reaction to it. He had to be the person she needed during her bad times, which meant he couldn't take over and demand she do what he wanted her to, no matter how strong the urge. He had to support her without overwhelming her. It was the hardest thing he'd ever done. But he'd done it. He was good at it. Maybe that was why he was so attracted to Alexa—he could be good at managing himself with her, too.

'Good thing,' he replied, unwilling, or maybe unable, to dive into the mess of his thoughts. 'If you were freaking out about it, I wouldn't be able to reassure you.'

She gave him a bland look. He chuckled.

'There's nothing wrong with accepting reassurance.'

'But I don't need to,' she said, voice full of emotion, though she was desperately trying to control it, 'because I'm not freaking out.'

'A logical reaction to your news.'

'Hmm.'

'Not freaking out. Who would freak out, finding out they were going to have two children when they were expecting one?' He sat down beside her. 'I'm going to be honest with you: you don't have to worry about being a bad mother. There's no way.'

He wanted to reach out and take her hand, but it felt too intimate. Then he did it anyway, because his gut told him to and he wasn't going to think about where that gut feeling was coming from.

'It's okay to feel jolted by this. I think anyone would. But your reaction now doesn't mean you'll be a bad mother.'

'I didn't think…' She broke off. Looked at him. 'I did.'

He smiled. 'I know. But you're strong-minded. Kind when it counts. Resilient. You'll get through having two.'

'You sound sure about that.'

'I am. You've built a restaurant from the ground up, Alexa. It's successful because of you. Surely raising two kids can't be much harder.'

He winked at her, and she smiled despite the emotion running wild over her face. Then it disappeared.

'What did I say?'

'Nothing. You were doing a perfectly adequate job of comforting me.'

He chuckled. 'As long as it was adequate.'

'Thank you.'

She squeezed his hand. Then, without warning, she leaned forward and kissed him. It was over before he could react, the only evidence it had happened the tingling at his lips.

She stood. 'You can't see that I'm pregnant, can you? I mean, I know *you* can, but as someone who didn't know?'

He opened his mouth. Closed it. Lowered his eyes because what else could he do? He tried to focus on her question. What had she asked him? Oh, yes, her clothes.

She was wearing… He didn't quite know what. It was a brightly coloured piece of material that was draped over her front from left to right. It did wonders for her cleavage, and he had to wrench his gaze away to answer her question. The material hung loosely over her stomach, and, paired with her tights and trainers, made her look both chic and comfortable. And not pregnant.

'You can't tell. It's loose enough that if I didn't know you were pregnant, I'd think…'

He broke off, but it was too late.

'You'd think what?'

He shook his head.

'You'd better say it, Foster.'

He shook his head again, this time more vehemently.

'You're saying that if people didn't know I was pregnant they'd think I was putting on weight?'

'I did *not* say that.'

'Only because you thought better of it.'

But her chest was shaking, and soon, sound joined.

'You think this is funny?' he asked.

'*You're* funny.'

'Wow. Thanks.'

She shrugged. Patted him on the shoulder. 'I appreciate that you wanted to preserve my feelings. But honestly, I don't care what people think of my body. As long as I feel good and everything works like it's supposed to, weight isn't important to me.'

He opened his mouth, then closed it when he realised he had nothing to add to that. It was a healthy way to think of the body, and, because he knew how prevalent weight-watching was in their culture, very enlightened.

'Yeah,' he said. 'You don't have to worry about being a mother, Alexa. You'll do fine.'

Her surprised look made the compliment well worth it.

CHAPTER ELEVEN

HE'D BEEN COOKING his entire life. It started because he wanted to be exactly like his father when he was younger. It continued because he wanted to make his parents' lives easier after his mother's diagnosis. She couldn't work at his father's business for periods of time, and during those periods his father had been overwhelmed at work. At least until he realised a temp could solve his problems. In any case, Benjamin had taken the opportunity before his father had realised that to make himself useful in the kitchen at home.

He hadn't known much at that point, and dinner had often been some form of a sandwich. Then he'd moved on to pasta, which had seemed doable for a boy under ten. He began to study his father more seriously, helping with the harder tasks. By the time he was a teenager, he could fry a steak with the best of them. Soon after, he was adding sauces and presenting meals he saw on the cooking shows he'd come to love. When he had to decide what he wanted to do with his life, it seemed natural to go into professional cooking.

Except he didn't get into culinary school the first year. Or the second, or third. Competition was steep, and he had nothing to give him an edge. He spent the years he wasn't cooking getting a degree in financial management, thinking he could at least help his father out if he couldn't have his dream. When he graduated, he'd pretty much given up on the Institute. Until his parents sat him down and told him he deserved to give it one more try if it truly was what he wanted to do with his life.

He spent the two years after that in kitchens of different restaurants, wherever would have him. Sometimes he got work as a kitchen assistant; sometimes he washed the dishes. But he always, always tried to learn from those in charge. And eventually, the fourth time he applied, he got into the Institute.

And not once in all that time, and during all those experiences, had he thought baking was for him.

Today proved that.

'I didn't realise the course was going to be about decorating,' he said casually.

Cherise was beside him, putting buttercream into several separate bowls so she could colour them for her rainbow cake.

'Yeah,' she said, 'I thought it would be fun. And, since it's the Institute's only short course, it worked.' She looked at him. 'Are you having trouble?'

'Not at all.'

He'd already coloured his buttercream, which he knew would be the easiest part of his day. He hadn't done anything more than that because it would have entailed showing his weaknesses, and he preferred not to parade those if he could help it.

Cherise smiled. 'This isn't a test to see whether you can decorate a cake. I'm aware you probably don't need those skills at the restaurant.'

He took a beat, then realised it was best to be honest. 'It's not that I don't need the skills. It's that I don't have them, no matter how hard I try.'

Her smile widened. 'Well, then, today should be fun for you.'

'Not sure that's the word I'd use.'

She laughed and her focus went back to her cake. He sighed and did the same with his. But not before he sneaked a look at Alexa, who stood on the other side of Cherise. She was already on the second layer of her cake, and looked as comfortable with the task as she did with any other. It was part of the problem he'd had with her when they were studying together. Nothing seemed to faze her. No task, no matter how ridiculous, pulled the rug out from under her.

Back then, he hadn't appreciated how easily she found everything. It had simply seemed unfair that she would have skill with everything in the kitchen. Now, at least, he could admire that skill. Except he saw that Cherise was admiring it, too.

It frustrated him, almost as much as it had in the past—except now feelings were creeping in.

He tried to tell himself he was just a sucker who couldn't resist someone who needed his help. It was clear Alexa did, even if she didn't think so. And he could easily be like her brother, using his vulnerabilities, his desires, to get what she wanted.

A voice in his head told him he had it all wrong. He didn't listen, instead focusing on getting his cake decorated as best he could. It took much more concentration and precision than he would have liked, but when he was done, he was proud of what he'd created.

'Nice job,' Cherise commented.

'Thanks.' He wiped his forehead with an arm. 'It was hard work.'

She laughed. 'Worth it though, don't you think, Alexa?'

Alexa peered past Cherise, appraising his cake before looking at him. 'It looks good.'

That's it. That's all she said. There was no judgement, no praise. Just an honest statement and yet somehow, it made him mad. He was sure she'd decorated her cake with a fraction of the effort he had put into his own. And now she had the cheek to tell him his looked good?

He wasn't being logical. A part of him recognised it. But he leaned into the irrationality of his thoughts, letting it fuel him for the rest of the day. He worked through lunch, though he knew it was silly, considering he was there to get to know Cherise. As far as he could tell, though, it seemed as if Cherise was more interested in chatting with him during their working sessions. Alexa was oddly quiet, though when he glanced out of the window during lunch, he saw her and Cherise laughing about something.

He gritted his teeth, did what he had to do, and at the earliest moment he could he walked out of the doors. Seconds later, footsteps followed him.

'Hey,' Alexa said. 'Wait up.'

He kept walking.

'Benjamin,' she said, her voice exasperated. 'I'm pregnant. There are two people growing inside me. Please don't make me run after you.'

That forced him to slow down, but he didn't stop. He was afraid of what would happen if he stopped. He was well aware he was in a mood. He also knew his mood was tied up in her, in both good and bad ways, except he couldn't discern between the two at the moment. It didn't bode well for their conversation. So when she caught up with him, he decided to stay quiet.

'Cherise wanted to know what's wrong with you.' Alexa rubbed her stomach. 'She asked me like she expected me to know. But I didn't know, and I had to pretend to, because we're together and when you're in a mood, apparently, I need to be able to explain that.'

'What did you say?' he couldn't help but ask.

'That you're competitive. And a perfectionist. When you put the two together, it can be a damning combination.'

'So you bad-mouthed me.'

'Not entirely,' she said easily, ignoring his bad temper. 'I also said it makes you a hell of an entrepreneur. You want to give your patrons the best. It makes you serious, disagreeable perhaps, but it also makes you one of the best people she could work for.'

He took several moments to reply. Even then, he could only manage a, 'Why?'

'Because it's true.' She shrugged. 'Because I don't blame you for a being a good chef and leader.'

He narrowed his eyes. 'Sounds like you're implying something.'

'Why would I?' she asked sarcastically. 'It's not like I gave you a compliment, spoke highly and fairly about you to a potential employee, and you're choosing to focus on the negative in all that.'

All fair points and, consistent with his mood, that annoyed him. He bit down on his tongue. After a few seconds, she sighed.

'Look, I get that you're in competition mode, or whatever, but I'm not going to keep defending you for acting boorish. If you want Cherise to get to know you, you should show her who you are. Unless, of course, you *are* boorish, and the man who was kind to me this morning and this entire time actually doesn't exist.'

She sounded tired, defeated, and his heart turned. But he couldn't tell her that he was going through something. How could he? He didn't understand it himself. It had to do with her, and with him not trusting himself around her, and that sounded like...like admitting that he was still the same fool who had let the people in his past take advantage of him.

'Yeah, I thought I might have been fooling myself,' she said softly. She closed her eyes before he could see any emotion. When she opened them again, they were unreadable. 'Cherise asked if we'd be interested in having a drink with her after work. I said yes, but now I'm not so sure.'

She turned on her heel. It took him a beat before he could move after her.

'You're not going to go?'

'No, I'm going.' She didn't stop walking when he fell into step beside her. 'I'm just not speaking for you. If you want to go, you can tell her yourself.'

It took him all of the way back to Cherise to decide that he would be going, too. In the mood he was in, heaven had better help him.

'You're not drinking?'

'Oh. Um…no.' Alexa had prepared for this in the car. But there was something about actually being asked about her pregnancy, even indirectly, that made her freeze up. Probably the fact that she had to lie. 'I'm driving.'

'One drink wouldn't hurt,' Cherise said kindly.

There was nothing Alexa wanted less than kindness at that moment.

'She's a lightweight,' Benjamin cut in. 'One drink and she's about as tipsy as I am after four. So, to answer your question—one drink *would* hurt.'

If she went by Benjamin's tone, it wasn't kindness that inspired his words. But it wasn't malice either, and he was saving her from having to think about a more intricate lie. She gave him a half-smile in thanks, but looked away before she could see whether he smiled back. He was acting weird, and she didn't want to be hurt by whatever mood he was in.

Because you're already hurt.

No, she told the inner voice. She wasn't hurt by Benjamin's attitude. So what if he was acting like the old Benjamin? The one who was reluctant and competitive and reminded her more of her brother than of the person she was beginning to think of as more than an acquaintance?

If anything, the problem was that she had begun to think of him in a friendly manner. He wasn't her friend—she wouldn't make that mistake—but she'd confided in him and kissed him. No wonder she was feeling a little out of sorts now that he was acting like someone she hadn't confided in or kissed. She should have anticipated it, and she hadn't, and that was partly why she was feeling this way.

Benjamin had always been so competitive in class. She hadn't known him before, so she'd assumed he was just a competitive person. Working with her brother, stealing her head chef… Those things seemed to prove it. Then he'd pretended to be her boyfriend in front of Lee. She'd seen him with his mother, he'd offered to give her Cherise… Those things didn't seem like a person who was inherently competitive, but simply someone who liked competition.

There was nothing wrong with that. Hell, she was even willing to be in the competition with him. But that was before today had happened. Before she'd seen him watching her as she worked and she could all but feel the frustration radiating off him. He glanced at her so many times that she knew he was comparing. It was common sense as much as it was experience; she'd spent her entire childhood knowing what that comparison looked like. Lee had done it to her. And she had no desire, none, to be a basis of comparison again.

That was what this empty feeling in her chest was. Annoyance that Benjamin saw her as someone to beat. Someone to be better than. She didn't think better or worse had anything to do with Cherise's choice; it would be the person Cherise got along with best. Except it was clear Benjamin didn't see it that way. So she was annoyed. Maybe a little disappointed. But that was it.

'He's right,' she said with a quick smile. 'I've never been able to hold my alcohol well.'

'Fortunately we don't have that in common,' Cherise said, lifting the glass the bartender set in front of her. She downed it, hissing as she slammed the glass back on the counter. 'I can drink with the best of them.' She grinned. 'I probably shouldn't tell potential employers that.'

'Why not?' Benjamin asked. 'It's not likely we wouldn't find out.'

'I don't intend on drinking on the job. Or coming in hungover.'

'The longer you spend working with us, the higher the possibility of a fun night out. Or some kind of event.' Benjamin shrugged. 'We would have found out during the second or third drinking game of the night.'

'You play drinking games with your staff?'

Benjamin raised his glass and tilted it to her. 'We're not of the belief that there should be all work and no play.'

'That happens at Infinity, too, Alexa?'

'Oh, no,' Alexa said with a shake of her head. 'I let my employees have their fun on their own time. Making sure they have that time is more of a priority to me.'

'What about team morale?' Benjamin asked her.

'Created through good pay cheques and a healthy working environment.' She waited a beat. 'In the Rough should try it.'

'Ooh,' Cherise said with a smile. 'Harsh.'

'And probably undeserved.' Alexa smiled back, but didn't look at Benjamin.

'Probably?' he said.

She directed the smile at him, but it wasn't genuine. Nor was the teasing tone of his voice.

'You guys are really cute together,' Cherise said. 'You've never thought about one big business?'

'Oh, no,' she said at the same time Benjamin chuckled with a shake of his head.

'Why not?' Cherise asked. 'You're both skilled. Can you imagine what you could create together?'

'You're only saying this because we're both so wonderful and you'd rather not choose,' Alexa teased, trying to ease the tension that was settling in her stomach. 'If we joined forces you would be our second in command, and you're drunk on the prospect of such power.'

'Well, you're not wrong.'

They laughed. The tension unfurled. Then there was a tap on the microphone. They turned to a small stage at the opposite end of the room as a tall woman with tattoos up and down her arms cleared her throat.

'Thank you all for coming to Wild Acorn tonight.'

There were cheers from who Alexa assumed were regulars. They sat at a table in the front, all still fairly formally dressed as though they'd come straight from work. She could see that happening. The bar was down a quiet road in Somerset West near the Institute, and they'd followed Cherise to get there. There was no way they would have found it by themselves, and yet it seemed popular.

'As most of you know, tonight is karaoke night—' she paused for another round of cheers '—and for those of you who don't, I thought I'd go over the rules.'

'There are rules for karaoke?' Alexa said under her breath.

'One,' the lady continued, seemingly answering Alexa, 'you have to take this seriously. No making anyone uncomfortable with a bad rendition of some famous ballad.' There was a beat. 'Just kidding! The only rule is that you have fun. Sing from the heart, dance if you will, and the best performer tonight has their tab taken care of.'

'Nice prize,' Benjamin commented. He looked at Cherise. 'Did you bring us here thinking you could make us sing?'

His smile faded when she answered, 'Hoping to.' She looked from Benjamin to Alexa. 'Who's going to go first?'

CHAPTER TWELVE

'I FEEL LIKE I shouldn't be watching this.' He was about to reply, but Cherise's voiced cracked on a high note and he winced instead. Alexa looked at him with a wrinkled nose. 'Yeah, we definitely shouldn't be watching this.'

'It's a bar. Where are we going to go?'

'You're saying we're trapped.' She took a long sip from her drink, studying Cherise as she executed some dance moves. 'I didn't think we would see how Cherise responds in a disaster at such an early stage.'

'And she responds—' he waited for Cherise to finish moonwalking '—poorly, apparently.'

Alexa gave a laugh. It wasn't the first time she'd done it that evening, but it sounded like her first genuine one. He couldn't be critical of it, of her, when he knew he was the reason she wasn't enjoying herself. And he felt terrible because of it.

With each sip of alcohol, he'd gained clarity. By the end of his second glass, he'd realised he was conflating his insecurities about trusting himself with his insecurities about trusting Alexa. He didn't know if she was fooling him; he didn't know if he could trust his gut when it told him she wasn't. His third glass told him he had been a jerk today, trying to figure it out. He started ordering water instead of alcohol, and was now wondering what the best way was to apologise.

'Look, Alexa—'

'Your turn!' she exclaimed, cutting him off.

He narrowed his eyes. 'I didn't say I was going to go up there.'

'You didn't say you weren't either.' She lifted a shoulder. 'I'm not the one asking you to go on stage.'

She tilted her head, gesturing to Cherise, who was eagerly waving at them.

'That wave could be for you, too.'

'It could,' she acknowledged, 'but since you're volunteering…'

'I'm not—'

In a movement quicker than he could have defended himself against, she stuck a hand underneath his arm and poked his armpit. Hard. The result was both surprise and amusement—he'd always been ticklish there. It was also a hand which popped into the sky, making it seem as though he were volunteering.

'Clever.' He stood, walked until he was so close to her he could smell the mint on her breath from her virgin mojito. 'But I'm clever, too.'

She tilted her head up, her eyes cool. 'Not everything is a competition.'

'No, it's not.' He lowered slightly, bringing their faces close. 'This isn't me competing. It's getting revenge.'

'Revenge?'

'You're going to do this with me.'

She smiled. It was mocking and unconcerned and—though he had no idea how or why—incredibly sexy.

'Oh, no, Benjamin, I will not be doing this with you.'

'Except—' he lifted a hand and tucked a stray curl behind her ear '—you are. Otherwise this would seem like a seduction to anyone looking.'

She pressed up on her toes, bringing their faces closer. 'Isn't it?'

'No.' It was though. And somehow he was being seduced, too. 'It's a request to do a duet.'

'I'm not doing a duet.'

'Not even for your fake boyfriend?'

Her lips parted. He brushed a thumb over it. When hot air touched his skin, he inhaled sharply. Then exhaled, because it felt as though he'd inhaled a copious amount of desire for her, too. His brain scrambled trying to remember what he'd intended when he stood up. To make it seem as if he was asking her to join him? To touch her and remind himself that she was the person she seemed to be, independent and not manipulative and certainly not who his fears made her out to be?

She took his hand, pulled it away from her face. 'This isn't going to happen.' The statement was ambiguous enough that it made him wonder what she was talking about until she clarified. 'I'm not making a fool of myself up there.'

He swallowed. Right. Of course she was talking about the singing and not…whatever had just happened.

'It'll be fun.'

'How?'

'We'll sing together. We'll both sing poorly together, I mean.'

'Yet another reason not to do it.'

'We're not auditioning for a singing competition,' he said, frustrated now. 'We're only singing.'

'No, I meant that if you sing badly, I refuse to sing with you.' She stood, emptying her glass as she did. 'I will not let my perfect soprano be tarnished by you.'

He couldn't even argue with that since he'd said he sang poorly. Then he realised she was moving to the stage, and he blinked. Why had she been arguing with him if she intended on singing? Was he really that awful that she didn't want to be on stage with him?

Yes, probably, he thought, sitting back down and offering Cherise a weak smile when she joined him. He'd been terrible to Alexa all day—save for that morning. But that morning had felt as though they were in a bubble, and once things had got real, the bubble had popped and he…

He'd fallen hard to the ground while Alexa somehow stayed afloat, looking down at him in pity. Disappointment. Could he even blame her?

'I thought you were going to go up with her.'

'Me, too.'

'Your seduction didn't work?' Cherise gave him a sly grin. He smiled back weakly.

'Apparently not. I'm going to have to work on it.'

'Probably,' she said, bringing her beer to her lips. 'She doesn't seem like the type of person to fall for the usual stuff. She's tougher, but that kind of makes it mean more, in my opinion.'

He thought about it as he turned to the stage, watching as Alexa waited for the music to play. A couple of guys in the front were eyeing her in appreciation, and he had the absurd urge to get up and shield her from their view. But that made no sense, the desire less so, and instead he kept looking at Alexa.

She looked comfortable there, her clothing still strange, still chic. She'd tied her hair up again, but it was higher than it had been in the morning, piled onto the top of her head as if she'd put it there and forgotten about it. The waves refused to be tamed that way, though, and they fell over her forehead, created the shortest and strangest fringe he'd ever seen. It was also the cutest. Hell, she was cute. And sexy, and enticing, and he was pretty sure he had a problem.

Then she started to sing and he stopped thinking about that altogether.

Her voice was smooth and clear. Perfectly pitched on the higher notes; soulfully deep on the lower notes. She swayed in time to the beat, slowly, smiling when the lyrics were saucy or snarky.

'You've got to be kidding me,' Cherise said somewhere halfway into the song. 'She sings like it's what she does for a living.'

He agreed, but he was too enamoured to respond. He couldn't take his eyes off her, his ears thanked him profusely, and his mind was incredibly glad he hadn't spoiled this with his own voice, which was comparable to a cat's on a good day. When she was done, the entire room exploded with applause. Everyone was looking at her in appreciation now. She smiled brightly, happily, and he couldn't quite believe she was the same woman who could skin him and lay the spoils on the floor as she walked over them.

Damn if that brightness, that happiness didn't draw him in as much as her sharp wit.

'Stop looking at me like that,' Alexa said as soon as Cherise got into the taxi she'd called. Cherise was having her brother use her spare key to pick up her car, since she wasn't in any condition to drive. 'It's unnerving.'

'I just… I can't believe you've been hiding that voice away.'

'I wasn't hiding it away.' She hoped to heaven her skin wasn't glowing at the compliment the way her stupid heart was. 'It's never come up. Why would I bring it up?'

'Because it sounded like *that*?' He gestured with a thumb to the bar behind them. 'I'm still trying to figure out how you managed to do that.'

'Easy. I opened my mouth, and instead of speaking, I sang.'

'Like an angel.' She laughed. 'I'm not even mad you're being snarky,' he said, his voice filled with wonder. 'You should be singing.'

'Do you know,' she said after a moment, 'I'm really good at maths? I scored in the top five per cent of the province in my final year of school. I had a couple of bursaries to study maths that were generous.'

She didn't mention that her parents had applied for all those bursaries. They'd been so disappointed when she'd chosen not to take any of them that they hadn't even cared that she'd chosen business management instead. Well, they had cared. If they hadn't, she would have gone to culinary school from the beginning.

'Congratulations?' Benjamin's voice interrupted her thoughts.

She laughed. 'My point is that just because I'm good at something doesn't mean I want to do it for a living. I love what I do. I love the challenge of running a restaurant. I love working with my chefs to make efficient meals that are delicious and new and…' She broke off, feeling heat spread over her cheeks. 'Anyway. I won't be leaving to sing any time soon.'

'A pity,' he said with a small smile. 'But I suppose, since you're good at running a business, too, the world isn't completely missing out on your talents.'

Somehow, it didn't feel like a compliment.

'I should get going. The ride back home is long.'

'Yeah.'

But he didn't let her pass him, and, since he was standing in front of her, she kind of needed him to.

'Benjamin—'

'Is there anything you aren't good at?'

And there it was.

There isn't one thing you're bad at. Nothing. You do everything well. It's annoying.

Exhausting, too, she'd wanted to tell her brother. She wouldn't call it lucky that she was good at the things her parents thought she should be good at. It was half luck, half hard work, and all exhaustion. Her parents had come to expect her to be good at everything, so she didn't think she could fail. If she did, they would care for her even less than they already did. As a kid, she couldn't bear the thought of it.

That was the one thing she wasn't good at: accepting that her family wasn't what she wanted them to be. She tried and tried to make her parents proud, but nothing she did would ever be enough. She had tried with Lee, too, because he was the only one who would understand how their parents' pressure could become unbearable. But he'd had no interest. For every outreached hand was a slap in the form of a record she'd set that he'd broken, or a mark of hers that he'd beaten. When he'd bought the building out from under her she'd finally decided to stop reaching out her hand, and hoped it would mean no more slapping.

Except it still came. And apparently through proxies now, too.

'I should really get home.'

She moved past him but he caught her wrist. She looked at him.

'You're not going to answer?'

'What would you like me to say?' She was proud of the stiffness in her voice. It meant the thickness in her throat hadn't tainted her speaking. 'Yes, I'm good at everything. Except making rational decisions, like when I pretended you were my boyfriend. If I hadn't, we wouldn't be in this position. I wouldn't be in this position.'

He frowned, and let go of her arm. 'I'm sorry. I didn't mean to…' He exhaled. 'I'm sorry,' he said again.

'Okay.' She swallowed. 'Now can I leave?'

CHAPTER THIRTEEN

He wanted to say sorry. For acting like a jerk the day before; for making those assumptions the night before. He arrived at the Institute early in the hope of finding a moment to talk with her again before the course started. No such luck. Which wasn't a problem—until the start of the class came and both Alexa and Cherise weren't there. Cherise rushed in ten minutes late, looking like hell.

'Sorry,' she muttered. 'My car broke down on the way. And I probably drank too much last night, made a fool of myself, and I promise you it won't happen again.'

'Sorry to hear about the car,' he said. 'About last night… You don't have to apologise. You're not working for us yet.'

'But I would like to, and I seem to have handed you reasons not to hire me.'

He smiled. 'It's nice to know you actually want this.'

'I really do.' She smiled, but it faded almost immediately. 'Although I think I spoilt my chances with Alexa. I'm pretty sure I'm the reason she's sick.'

'She's sick?'

'Yeah.' She gave him a strange look. 'She didn't tell you?'

'No.' When he realised why she was so surprised, he cleared his throat. 'We're supposed to have a date after this today. I think maybe she didn't want to tell me in case I cancelled.'

'Oh, that's so sweet,' Cherise said. 'You guys are cute.'

'Thanks.'

They fell into silence as the instructor began to guide them in a brand-new decorating nightmare. He couldn't really focus. He was too busy thinking about Alexa. He stumbled his way through the class, but that was pretty usual for him. He did notice that Cherise's hangover, and the rough morning she'd had, hadn't affected her concentration. She did the work perfectly, patiently, without one mistake. Which told him she wouldn't bring personal problems into the workplace. He was almost thankful for the night they'd had before.

She seemed forgiving of his lack of decorating skills, and by the end of it he knew their one-on-one time had done wonders for their professional working relationship. He even suspected that he might have had an edge over Alexa. It made him feel guilty. Not that he had any reason to feel guilty. He hadn't orchestrated her sickness, had he? He hadn't done anything so that he could spend time with Cherise while Alexa stayed home, sick, probably unable to breathe, her nose blocked, chest phlegmy…

He grunted, got into his car, and started it. Then he grunted again, because he already knew where he was going to, even before he started driving to the pharmacy. When he got there, he started grabbing things that usually helped him when he was feeling under the weather. He walked past an aisle, paused, looked down it. Saw a bunch of pregnancy and maternity things. Vitamins, baby bottles. He looked at the things in his hands. She probably couldn't use any of this, being pregnant. He went back to the pharmacist, and got fewer things. Bought ingredients to make some good chicken soup. Some fresh bread, too.

None of that made it easier when he was finally in front of her door. He felt as though he was intruding on her space. She obviously didn't want him to know she was sick, or she would have told him. Now he was pitching up at her door, assuming that she wanted to see him? Especially after how he'd treated her the day before?

He took a deep breath and was brutally honest with himself. He'd told himself guilt was the reason he was there. Maybe it was, but not only because he got to spend time with Cherise when Alexa couldn't. No, it was redemption. For how he had treated her the day before. To ease his conscience, or to make it up to her, he didn't know. Either way, he was there, and he was going to make sure she knew he wasn't all bad.

He knocked on the door. Again when he heard nothing inside. A long while later, he heard some shuffling. Then the door opened. He almost dropped everything in his hands.

'You're, um…you're…' He cleared his throat. He couldn't…point out what the problem was without telling her that he had looked at her chest. But not pointing it out meant he studiously had to avoid looking down. He gritted his teeth, then thought it might look intimidating and offered her a smile. 'You're okay,' he finished lamely.

She folded her arms. Doing so should have covered the flesh spilling out of the top of the loose nightgown she wore. Instead, because of the sheer generosity of her breasts, the movement pushed them together instead.

'What are you doing here?'

'I heard you're sick.'

'Yes.'

He frowned. 'I was sorry to hear that.'

'Thank you.'

He gestured to the bags in his hands. 'Do you think I could come in?'

'Why?'

'I…' Was he really this bad at showing he cared about something? 'I thought I'd make you some soup.'

She studied him, expression unreadable, though there were dark rings around her eyes. Seconds later, as if she knew he'd seen it, she sagged against the doorframe. 'It's a bad bout of nausea. I thought because things weren't so bad in my first trimester—' She shrugged. 'Apparently my babies hate me.'

'They don't hate you,' he said automatically.

'I appreciate that.' She exhaled slowly. 'You can come in. But you can't cook anything. I'm pretty sure I'd throw up if you did.' She cast a look at him. 'That's not a reflection on your cooking or anything.'

'Thanks,' he said dryly.

He followed her inside, closing the door behind him. He wasn't sure what to do now that his grand plan wouldn't work. Plus, seeing her like this was a distraction. She'd gone back to the sofa, curled up and closed her eyes, as if he weren't in her space. And he shouldn't have been.

There wasn't much he could do about morning sickness. With a cold or flu he could ply her with medication, encourage her to sleep. But constant nausea? Enough that she couldn't come in to work? What was he supposed to do about that?

Since she wasn't looking, he asked the internet that question. Then he wandered into her kitchen, set down the things he'd bought, and looked in her cupboards. They were meticulously packed. He couldn't see what order they were in, but they were definitely in order. Same with the fridge. He tried not to disturb anything as he looked for what the internet suggested. Minutes later, he walked into the kitchen, set the tea on the coffee table and crouched down in front of her.

'Alexa?' She opened one eye. Somehow, she managed a glare with it. He resisted his smile. 'Have you eaten anything today?'

'Some toast this morning.'

'This morning?'

'I haven't really had the energy for much.'

'Okay.' He frowned. 'Well, the internet said something bland would do you good.'

'Sounds amazing.'

He chuckled softly. 'How about some brown rice? Plain avocado? Or toast with peanut butter and banana? Broth?'

Her other eye opened. 'Sounds like you're trying to get nutrients into me.'

'They said it would be best if what you ate had nutrients in it.'

'They?'

He scratched the back of his head when his skin began to prickle with heat. 'The internet.'

'You went on the internet for this?'

'Did any of what I offered sound appealing to you?' he asked instead of answering.

'The toast,' she replied after a moment. 'It's not the most appealing, but it's the easiest option, which we'll both be grateful for if I end up throwing it up.'

He appreciated her logic, but he would actually feel better if he could put some more effort into whatever he made her. To assuage the guilt, he told himself. For redemption, he added. Not because he cared enough to put more effort into it.

'On it. Also, I made you some ginger tea.'

'Did the internet tell you to do that?' She was teasing him, giving him a small smile to show it.

He offered her a hand. 'If you want me to help you sit up, you won't get the answer to that.'

'It would almost be worth it.'

But she took his hand and he helped her up. Her colour didn't look good, but that made sense since she was nauseous and hadn't eaten since the morning. He handed her the tea. Her fingers brushed his as she did, and for some bizarre reason a shiver went through him. Bizarre, because things were weird with them, and she was sick, and the only reason he was in her flat was because he felt guilty. He shouldn't feel attraction in this moment—or whatever it was that caused that shiver. It also had nothing to do with her cleavage, impressive and visible as it was. It was simply her, and how much she intrigued and confused him.

He exhaled, leaving her to the tea as he went to make her toast. It was quick work. When he handed it to her, he thought he'd head back to the kitchen, start making a broth even though she didn't seem to want it. But she said, 'Wait.'

He turned. 'Yeah?'

'You didn't make yourself anything?'

His mouth curved. 'Did I make myself some peanut butter and banana toast as well? No. Surprisingly.'

'No need to be smug about your ability to eat something other than this.' But her eyes were warm. 'Thank you.'

'You don't have to thank me.'

'Why not?'

She tore a small piece off the toast and put it into her mouth, looking at him expectantly.

'Oh…er… It wasn't a big deal.'

She chewed and finished. Swallowed. 'It is to me.'

There was a brief moment where they stared at one another before he realised he'd better look away if he wanted to keep his sanity. Although deep down he knew it wasn't his sanity he was worried about.

'Will you sit down?' she asked, looking down now, too.

'Do you want me to?'

'I wouldn't have asked if I didn't want you to.'

'Good point.' He smiled at the dry tone. 'I'll just grab myself something to drink.'

'Yeah, of course. Anything in the fridge is yours.'

He went to the kitchen, got himself a sparkling water, and went back to the lounge. It didn't even occur to him to dawdle, or delay long enough that she would be done with her meal. The opposite, in fact. He wanted to sit with her, talk to her, and he didn't know what it meant.

Or he did, but he preferred not to think about it.

When he got back, he saw her toast looked the same as it had when he left.

'Feel sick?'

'Not at the moment. I'm waiting to see how my stomach's going to react to it.' She took a slice of banana off the toast and ate it. 'It seems cruel to me that someone who enjoys food as much as I do can't eat it.'

'But it hasn't been like this your entire pregnancy, you said?'

'No, it hasn't. I have been nauseous, but it's been pretty consistently in the mornings before work and the evenings after. I thought I was lucky.' She groaned. 'Turns out my body was lulling me into a false sense of security.'

'How has today been different?'

'You mean apart from the waves of nausea all day?' She tore off another piece of toast, but didn't eat it. Instead, she patted the seat next to her. He didn't even hesitate. Just obeyed. 'I've been throwing up more, though that seems consistent with being nauseous more, doesn't it? I've also been a little dizzier, but that could be because I haven't been eating.'

'You should have been.'

'I know,' she agreed, easily enough that he knew she wasn't feeling herself. 'But it seemed like a lot of energy to go to the kitchen and get something to eat when I could lie here.'

He studied her. Took a long drink of his water to make sure he really wanted to say what he thought he wanted to say. Sighed.

'Look, you can argue with me when you have energy for it later, okay?'

Her eyebrows rose. 'A promising start to a conversation.'

'It's concern.' He paused. 'You have to look after yourself, Alexa. That's how you're looking after your babies right now. By looking after yourself.'

Her hand went to her belly, before she brought it back to the toast. She put a piece in her mouth, then opened her palm as if to agree with him. Something in the gesture made her seem so vulnerable, he wanted to pull her into his arms and comfort her. Hell, there was a part of him that wanted to do that regardless of the vulnerability.

He settled for edging closer to her.

She deserved to have people to care about her. She deserved that she care about herself, which he thought she might struggle with. He had no proof, and he wouldn't dare ask, since he was already pushing his luck with their current conversation. But something about Alexa made him think that she put others ahead of herself. Even with her pregnancy. She was trying so hard to make things with Cherise work. Not for herself, he thought, but for her restaurant.

Part of that was because Lee had taught her she couldn't let her guard down. And yes, when he'd offered Victor Fourie that job, he'd shown her that, too. Now she was terrified of going on leave because she thought it would put all she'd worked for in jeopardy.

Someone who'd grown up as she had would hate that idea. They'd hate that it might result in failure, too. He couldn't imagine how much that would mess with someone's mind. He could, however, see that he'd contributed to her fears. That his question the night before, about her being good at everything, would add to that pressure. Which would explain how tense she'd got.

He would apologise for it. Not now. Now he had a different mission.

'You're going to have to take care of yourself when they're here, too,' he said quietly. 'It's the most important thing, your health. Not only because they need you to be healthy to take care of them.'

'What else is there?'

'Your happiness. It's going to be important to them.

They'll want to see you living your life as you would have even if they weren't there. That means taking care of yourself, making sure you're as important in your life as they are.'

'You speak as if you know.'

'I…do.'

It felt a little like a betrayal, admitting that. But if he had to betray his mother—just a little—to make Alexa see she was as important as her children, then so be it. Hell, he reckoned his mother might even agree. She'd called him two days after that dinner with Alexa and told him she liked his new girlfriend.

'The baby situation is complicated,' Nina had said, 'but I can see why you couldn't move on without giving things with her a try. She's refreshing.'

'You're good at it,' Alexa said, piercing through the haze of memories.

'What?'

'Caring for people.'

The words hit him in the gut. 'I've had a lot of practice.'

'With your mom? Inference,' she said when he looked at her.

'I wouldn't say I took care of her.'

'I didn't say that you did. Only that you cared for her.'

He almost laughed at how she'd caught him out. He didn't because it wasn't funny.

'She needed a lot of support with the fibromyalgia.'

'Support can sometimes mean caring for them.'

'That's not what happened with my mom,' he said tersely.

'It was a compliment, Benjamin.' Her expression was a combination of bewilderment, kindness, and…hurt? Had he hurt her? But then she clarified. 'Speaking as someone who didn't have it all that much in her life, it's certainly a compliment.'

'I'm sorry.' He stared at the bottle in his hand. 'I seem to be apologising a lot to you these days.'

She shrugged. 'It's because I rub you up the wrong way. What?' she asked with a little laugh. 'You don't think I noticed? It's kind of hard not to.'

'To be fair, I think the reverse applies, too, and yet you don't seem to apologise nearly as often as I do.'

'I'm more irreverent.' She gave him a half-smile. 'I'm definitely less in touch with my emotions. I find them—' she wrinkled her nose '—inconvenient.'

He laughed, and some of the tension in his stomach dissipated. 'I'm not much more in touch with my emotions. They're inconvenient as hell, and it's easier to ignore them.'

'The apologies tell me you don't do the easier thing,' she pointed out. 'You might not be able to deal with them very well, but you feel them. It's more than I can say for myself.'

'And why's that?'

She heaved out a sigh. 'I don't know. No, no, I do,' she interrupted herself. 'Honestly, it's just… I guess ignoring them is what I'm used to. If I had felt every little thing when I was a kid, I wouldn't function nearly as well as I do today.'

She began to eat again, slowly, and he waited until she was done to ask the questions tumbling into his head. When she was done, she set down the remaining toast on the table. Then she moved closer to him. His heart thudded, but she didn't do anything else. Not one more thing, even though his body felt as if it was bracing for impact.

'Do you want to talk about it?' he asked hoarsely.

'I don't think so.' Her expression was uncertain when she met his eyes. 'Is that okay?'

'Of course. We don't have to talk about anything you don't want to.'

'I will, someday. It seems like a lot of effort to think about it now.'

She rested her head on his shoulder. He froze—but not

for long. Slowly, so he wouldn't spook her, he lifted his arm. She immediately snuggled into his chest.

It was a good thing he was sitting, or the way his knees had gone weak would have taken him to the ground.

'Tell me what your day was like?' she asked. 'Was Cherise as hungover as she should have been after last night?'

Somehow, he managed to laugh. But as he told her about his day, it felt more natural, them sitting like this, talking. He was honest about how things had gone with Cherise, and she didn't seem upset about it. She asked him questions, laughed at his description of how terribly he'd done. He kept talking when she shifted onto her side, curling into much the same position he'd found her in. Except now she was curled into his side, then lying with her head on his lap. When she faltered he lowered his voice but kept talking, since it seemed to soothe her.

She was fast asleep shortly after, but he didn't get up as he should have. He stroked her hair, which was messy and somehow beautiful. He brushed her skin, bronze and smooth. He sat there, her warmth comforting something inside him. Much too long later, he took the dishes to the kitchen and began making her something to eat for when she got up. When he was done with that, he let himself out, but not without one last look in her direction.

She looked so peaceful, lying under the blanket he'd covered her with. His heart did something in his chest. Lurched, turned over, filled—he wasn't sure of the description. He only knew that seeing her, speaking her with her, caring for her…

It had changed him. Something had changed between them, too. He wondered if she would acknowledge it. He wondered if he would.

CHAPTER FOURTEEN

SHE WAS FEELING better the next day. She hadn't thrown up the toast Benjamin made her, and she'd slept through the entire night. It didn't seem normal to feel better when the day before she'd basically been knocked out. She supposed that was pregnancy. Or she hoped it was. If it wasn't, everyone in class, including her, was going to get more than they'd bargained for.

She had a nice long shower, got dressed, and went to the kitchen. Everything was in its place; it was as if Benjamin hadn't been there. And maybe he hadn't been. It seemed consistent with the state she'd been in the day before. Maybe she'd conjured him up, and he hadn't been sweet and patient and caring. He hadn't made her laugh, held her, stayed with her until she'd fallen asleep.

Except when she opened her fridge she found a glass container with clear broth in it and a sticky note—she had no idea where he'd found one.

In case you're feeling up to it. B.

B. B was definitely Benjamin. She couldn't deny that he'd been there any more. Him leaving food for her meant she hadn't imagined he was sweet and patient and caring either. And if that was true, she had to believe that he'd made her laugh, held her, stayed with her as she'd fallen asleep. And he'd cooked. For her.

She took a long, deep breath as she removed the broth from the fridge and heated it up. But it didn't help, and she spent the entire time eating the flavourful liquid quietly sobbing. She was certain it was pregnancy hormones. Mostly. She supposed that was the problem.

But when was the last time someone in her life had checked on her when she was ill? When was the last time she'd let someone in her life do that?

Kenya would have, if Alexa let her. She had, once upon a time. When Kenya had started working at Infinity, something had clicked between them and they'd got along well. But Alexa had confined that relationship to the restaurant. She'd thought it best, easier, better for the restaurant. Now, after the entire Benjamin debacle, Alexa wondered if it was simply better for *her*. If she didn't go out with Kenya, she wouldn't risk getting hurt. Except by doing that, she'd hurt Kenya. And that, by some cruel twist of fate, had hurt her, too.

She thought about it the entire drive to the Institute. Once she got there, she made sure there wasn't a trace of her crying on her face. She had a feeling Benjamin would pounce on it if he saw it. Which turned out to be a fruitless concern anyway, since he wasn't there.

'He must have what you had,' Cherise said with a knowing look. Alexa murmured in agreement. She had no choice but to. She'd told Cherise she had a twenty-four-hour bug, which seemed like a half-truth. But she knew that what she had wasn't contagious. She also knew Benjamin well enough that she could piece together what had happened.

When he'd told her about his day the night before, he'd been excited, but restrained. That restraint had come through most strongly when he was relaying the more fun parts of the day, as if he'd felt bad. The fact that he wasn't here told her he did feel bad. It made her think the reason he was at her place last night had been because he'd felt bad, too.

She set it aside as she spent the day with Cherise. At one

point, her prospective chef pointed out something Alexa was doing poorly. Alexa thanked Cherise, adjusted, and realised that, while it had helped in some ways, it hadn't in others. So she coached Cherise through doing it her way, and Cherise was pleased with the ending.

'Maybe we can put it together and come up with a technique that could give us the best of both worlds.'

'Yeah, that would be great,' Cherise said with a bright smile.

She smiled back, and wondered if Benjamin had felt the same glow of appreciation at connecting with Cherise. Her heart skipped at the thought. Not at its content, but that she'd thought it at all. That she'd thought about him at all. It was dangerous; more so because the thoughts were accompanied by a soft, squishy feeling in her chest that she had no name for but made her feel warm and safe.

But how could she feel safe when even feeling that told her she was in danger? It was a conundrum, one she made no effort to clarify, even when she told herself to. She set it aside again, tried to focus on the day with Cherise. She felt worn at the end of it, her legs aching and her back, too, although it was much too early for her to be feeling that way. Then again, those were normal, non-pregnancy feelings after a long day. Today had seemed long, despite the fact that it was shorter than most days for her. Maybe being pregnant meant the length of what was long would change.

It didn't bode well for all she had to do before she went on maternity leave. Or should she even go on leave at all? She'd thought it would be a good idea to get to know her babies, but now it felt as if she was leaving her first baby, her restaurant, exposed. It was her responsibility to make sure it wasn't exposed. The fact that she hadn't meant that she'd...failed.

She drove home with that troubling thought racing in her mind. When she stopped, though, she didn't find herself at her home, but at In the Rough. It was the first time she'd been there since Lee had bought the building. She'd refused to go, on principle, despite her parents calling her stubborn. But the day that she'd wanted to show them her building, and they'd told Lee about it, had changed things for her. Their disappointment no longer hurt as much as it had. Or maybe it did hurt, but it didn't cripple her any more.

She still tried with them: a phone call every couple of weeks, a dinner once a month, telling them important news. But the truth was that she didn't want them in her life as much any more. Especially when they insisted on having Lee be part of the package.

Slowly, she climbed out of the car, staring up at the sign as she did. Black lettering flickered at her against the brick façade, courtesy of a faint white light outlining the letters. The front of the restaurant itself was all glass, allowing her to see the patrons laughing and enjoying themselves.

She took a breath and walked into the restaurant. She took in the dark wooden feel of the place, noted the red-haired barperson. It was a strange experience, seeing the place done, compared to the last time she'd been there. More so comparing it to the vision of what she'd had for the space. She'd executed the idea almost identically at Infinity, but she'd had to make adjustments because it didn't fit as well in her current space as it would have there.

The disappointment of it washed over her, and she took another breath, deeper this time, before she walked to the bar.

'Do you know where I can find Benjamin?'

The woman quirked her brow. 'Who are you?'

'Oh. I'm…er…'

She didn't know what Benjamin had told his people. Of course, she knew what Lee knew, but that didn't mean he'd announced it to his entire staff. If he hadn't, she didn't want to complicate things by telling his employee she was his girlfriend. But she also didn't want him to know she was there. He'd likely pull a runner, pretend he was really sick, and she couldn't tell him he was being a jerk.

'Is he here?'

'He might be.' She tilted her head. 'You look familiar.'

'I don't think so.'

'No, you do.' The woman came closer, limping slightly as she did. 'Have you been here before?'

'Definitely not.' She tried to cover it up when she realised how that sounded. 'I mean, I haven't had the chance.'

'You're missing out.'

She took a look at the full restaurant. It was barely six in the evening and already the vibe was jovial. The patrons were pretty much as she had imagined when she'd thought about the space. Benjamin had clearly turned it into *the* place though, since it was just about bouncing with energy.

She turned back to the barperson. 'Apparently so.'

'I think, considering it's you and considering you're my main competition, that's almost a compliment.'

She was rolling her eyes before she was even facing him fully.

'Hi.'

'Hi.'

She wasn't prepared for the way he leaned in to her, or the kiss he brushed on her cheek. It wasn't a sensual greeting in theory, but the heat of it seared through her body.

'You're feeling better?'

'Much.' She started to brush her hair off her forehead, but stopped. The movement would make her look nervous. She was already feeling it; she didn't have to look it. 'Thanks for leaving me that broth.'

'Was it good?'

'You know it was,' she said with a half-smile. 'Stop looking for compliments.'

'You gave me one now, I think,' he replied with a half-smile of his own. 'But I won't push you to see if you have any more.'

'Good. You might not like what you find.'

'Mia, could you have a whiskey and—' He looked at her expectantly.

'Oh. Water.'

'And a water sent to my office, please?'

'Sure.'

Mia waved them off, but not before Alexa saw the questioning look in her eyes. Alexa couldn't blame her. A random woman comes to the bar, asking about the boss without giving any reason, and moments later the boss appears and whisks said woman into his office? It looked dodgy, even to her, and *she* was the random woman.

'Please, sit,' Benjamin said when they walked into the small space of his office.

'Thanks.'

She took the seat opposite him. The space was confined, making it big enough only for his desk, two chairs, and a cabinet.

'If you get a smaller desk, have some floating shelves installed, you could create more space for yourself.'

'Why would I want to?' he asked dryly. 'I have everything I need.'

'You're right.'

Purposefully, she swung her handbag to her lap. It knocked a pile of books off his desk. She gave him a look, then bent to pick the books up and set them back where they were.

'Why would you need more space?'

'Fine, you've proved your point.'

He was chuckling when a young man, probably early twenties, knocked on the door and set their drinks in front of them.

'Anything else?' he asked, after Benjamin thanked him.

'We're good for now,' Benjamin replied, looking at her to confirm. She nodded. 'I'll call the kitchen if I need anything else.' He waited until the man left. 'You would have had a smaller desk and floating shelves, wouldn't you?'

'Yeah. I was going to do the shelves on that wall.' She pointed at one wall. 'Put the desk here.' She pointed at the opposite wall. 'I probably would have got some fancy desk, with three sections that were stacked on top of one another, so I could have options to stand and have plenty of space.' She shrugged. 'I didn't need to in the end, because my current office is huge.'

'Rub it in, won't you?' But his eyes were serious. 'You really wanted this, didn't you?'

'I was going to buy it,' she said in answer. 'I had plans for it.' She picked up her water and took a sip to quench her suddenly dry throat. 'It taught me to act first, dream later. An important lesson.'

There was a long silence. She resisted the urge to fidget during it.

'He just bought this from under you?' Benjamin asked.

'Yes.'

'Knowing you wanted it?'

'Yes.'

Another pause.

'Then he offered the space to me.'

'He's smart.'

Seconds passed.

'He was using me.'

'Weren't you using him, too?'

'I don't feel like it's the same.'

'Probably not,' she conceded. 'Don't look so sad.' Sadness wasn't quite the emotion in his expression, but she went with it because it also wasn't *not* sadness. 'It turned out well in the end.'

'Yeah, but it's still…' He offered her a small smile. 'It's

hard to wrap my head around. The man who gave me a chance did so by robbing you of something. I considered Lee to be a friend, and now I'm wondering whether I was a fool to do so.'

She thought about it. Sighed.

'This wasn't what I thought I'd be doing here, but okay.' She set her glass down. 'The Lee you know is the Lee you know. You've known him for years. You've worked with him. Have likely been through a lot with him. The way he's treated me doesn't change that.'

'It does though,' he said softly. 'He has the capacity to be cruel and—'

'Only with me,' she interrupted. 'It's part of why my parents could never understand why I had such a problem with him. They couldn't believe he was the person I was claiming he was, even though they created the environment that forced us to compete.'

'Forced…compete?' He leaned forward. 'What do you mean?'

She couldn't answer him. It would rip off the bandage that she had put over the wounds of her childhood. She'd spent her entire adult life trying to put, to keep, that bandage in place. She wouldn't remove it now because this man was asking her to.

'You, um… You don't look sick.'

He blinked. Seemingly acknowledged she didn't want to talk about it because he didn't press. Instead he leaned back in his chair.

'I am.' He gave a very fake cough.

She rolled her eyes, but smiled. 'You're obviously not. You didn't have to do that.'

'I didn't do anything.'

'Benjamin.'

He frowned. 'Fine. But I was only making sure the playing field was level.'

'Were you?' She bit her lip as she sat back. 'Was that what last night was, too? You were making sure things were level as you spent the night with me?'

'It wasn't quite spending the night,' he protested, colour lighting his cheeks.

'Of course not.' She didn't bother hiding her smile. 'But it was guilt, wasn't it? You felt guilty about getting a day with Cherise, and you came to look after me so you could tell yourself that you tried to make things better.'

'It wasn't exactly like that.'

She lifted her brows, waiting for him to tell her what it was like. He sighed impatiently.

'Maybe there was some guilt. But it was more because I wanted to apologise for being a brute the day before yesterday.'

'What was today, then?' she asked. 'Surely you made up for it last night? More than, even. You didn't have to do it.'

'It was fair.'

'It was stupid.'

'Can you just…?' He stopped, lowering his voice when the words came out loudly. 'Can you just say thank you?'

'No,' she said after a moment. 'I'm not going to thank you for feeling sorry for me.'

She stood, knocking over the books with her handbag again, this time unintentionally. With a sigh, she lowered to pick them up. Then found that she was stuck.

'Oh.'

'Oh.' He stood now, too. 'Oh, what?'

She tried with all her might to push up, but her balance was shot. It only ended up pushing her forward. She put a hand out in time to keep from knocking her head.

'Lex, are you okay? Are you in labour?'

'Of course I'm not in labour.' She scowled. 'I'm thirteen weeks pregnant. Of course I'm not in labour.'

'Okay.' He crouched down in front of her. 'Why are you not getting up, then?'

'Because—' she gritted her teeth '—I can't.'

'You can't get up?'

'Seems you need your core to stand up. Who knew?'

She could almost feel him laughing at her. She chose to ignore it. Largely because she really couldn't get up and the floor was surprisingly terrible to be on.

'Are you going to help me?'

'Yeah.' But she heard the click of a camera. Her head shot up.

'What did you do?'

'Nothing,' he said innocently, taking her under the arms and lifting her gently.

'Benjamin, if you took a photo of me struggling to get up, I swear I'll make you regret it.'

'Which is exactly why I need the photo. For protection.'

'Why do you need protection?'

'You're a voracious opponent.'

'Am I an opponent?' she asked lightly, though she didn't feel light. It had nothing to do with him taking a picture of her or getting stuck on the floor.

'I didn't mean it that way.'

'How did you mean it?'

'You're a sparring partner,' he said, shoving his hands into his jeans pockets. They were close enough that she could reach out and pull them out if she wanted to. 'We argue and debate. It's what we do.'

'Yeah, but all of that started because you saw me as an opponent *in that way*.' She lifted her head because, although it smarted, he was taller than her, and the lack of distance between them meant she had to. 'Something about me in class made you think of me as competition.'

'You were the best, Alexa.' He shrugged. 'People don't

compete against someone in the middle. They do so with the person at the top. And you were.'

Or they compete with the only person who's there, she thought, remembering all the years her parents had encouraged her and Lee to be better than those around them. Their words weren't only for her and Lee; *they* competed with those around them, too. Even with one another. It seemed to invigorate their marriage though, rather than cause the relationship to crumble. Sometimes Alexa wondered whether she was their child, since she was the only one in the family who hadn't been invigorated by competition. She was the odd one out. Lee had simply been following their parents' example.

It didn't make it right though. At least not for her.

'I should… I should go.'

'Alexa,' he said, reaching for her hand. She stilled when he threaded their fingers together. Let herself go to him when he pulled her in. 'I didn't mean to upset you.'

'I know.'

'But you're upset.'

She sighed. 'It's not you. Well, not you alone.' When he only looked at her, the heat of his hand pulsing into her body, landing at her heart, she sighed again. 'I spent my entire life being the person Lee had to beat. Not because I was the best, or at the top, but because I was there. My parents told us to be the best. We got rewarded with love or gifts if we were.' She closed her eyes. 'I don't… I don't want to live my entire life like that. That's why I cut Lee out of it. That's why I barely speak to my parents.'

She dropped her head. It found a soft landing, and she realised he'd moved closer so she could lean against his chest. As it had the night before, it comforted her.

'This entire thing with Cherise is a nightmare for me,' she whispered. 'I just want it to be over. And before you say it—no, it won't be if you step back.'

'It will.'

She looked up at him. 'No, it won't. If you don't fight fairly, I'll know. More significantly, Lee will know. And he'll stop at nothing to convince Cherise to work for In the Rough, which will put me right back in the position I was in in the first place.'

She lifted a free hand and set it on his chest. Curled her fingers.

'You'll know, too. You'll know that you sacrificed this for me. I don't want that.' She beat her fist lightly against his chest. 'I want you to think of what's best for you. Fighting for this is what's best for you,' she clarified when he frowned.

His hand lifted, curled over her fist. 'I thought you didn't want us to compete.'

'I don't. But I'm not naïve enough to believe I won't encounter competition in my life. In my business. Just…' She sighed. 'Just make it a good one so we can all move forward without this haunting us.'

For some reason, she slid an arm around his waist, rested her head against his chest again. Her other hand remained in his as if they were about to dance.

'I'll be fine without you helping me, Ben. I promise.'

CHAPTER FIFTEEN

He wanted to believe her. He really did. But how many times had his mother said she was fine, only for him to find her curled up in pain somewhere? He was tired of the people he cared about hurting. And damn it, he cared about Alexa. No matter how much he tried to use guilt, or logic, or whatever other reason he'd used in the last weeks as an excuse to see her and spend time with her. He cared about her. He wanted her to be okay. Whether that meant her health, or her restaurant.

He needed her to be okay.

The urgency of it was partly from an unknown source, partly from that caring. Hell, it was partly because she was standing in his arms, looking up at him with reassurance in her eyes. Her stomach was pressed into his, and the rounding of it—not much, but enough—sent a rush of protectiveness through him.

Feeling the rest of her body against his wasn't as harmless.

She wore another loose top, but it clung to her breasts if nothing else, as if as amazed by them as he was. He hadn't been as fascinated by this part of the body since he was a teenager discovering his sexuality. His conclusion then had been that their biological function was as important as their appearance. He'd clearly been desperate to separate himself from his physical feelings then, which was most likely a form of protection. If he wasn't into romantic relationships, he would still be able to help at home.

His opinion had somewhat changed over the years. Probably because he'd learnt how to balance things better. If he prioritised, he could enjoy his physical feelings, too. He didn't have to shun them.

Thank goodness, or he might not have appreciated Alexa's breasts in that moment. And appreciating it caused his breath to go from simply oxygenating his body to giving her a signal something had changed. Her eyes fluttered up; something on his face had them clouding with desire. Most likely his own desire, his more rapid breathing.

He could appreciate more than Alexa's breasts though. Those eyes, clouded as they were, made him feel as though he were sitting in front of a fire on a rainy day. When they sparred, her gaze handed him a glass of whiskey, warming him from the inside, too. Her lips parted, and he couldn't resist dipping his head—until he realised what he was about to do.

'I'd like to kiss you,' he whispered.

'Okay,' she whispered back. 'Do it.'

'I was asking.'

'Your hand has been pressed into the small of my back for the better part of five minutes. Seconds ago was the first time you used it to pull me in closer. Now you want to ask?'

'I did?' He had no recollection of it. 'I'm sorry. I should have—'

He broke off when she put a finger over his lips. 'You weren't doing it on purpose. I understood that. It was part of the reason I didn't knee you in the groin.'

He laughed. 'If I ever do anything that makes you uncomfortable on purpose, please feel free to do just that.'

'I didn't need your permission.' Her mouth curved up. 'But thank you, I suppose. Now, shall we get back to that kissing thing?'

He kissed her then, glad she wasn't playing games when his need seemed to consume him. He moaned in relief when their lips touched and he felt the softness of her. Their essences tangled, their souls embraced, and he would never get over the enormity of it—from just a kiss.

Her tongue slipped between his lips, and he opened for her as desire pulsed inside him. She tasted sweet—or was that the promise of her? The idea of what they could share if they ever allowed this feeling to become more than a stolen moment. It didn't matter. All that did was his heart thumping harder against his breastbone, almost as though it were hard work; almost as though there were water in his chest and his heart was thumping despite it.

If that meant he would drown, he didn't mind. He would be drowning in her. In that scent of lemon and mint that came from he had no idea where. But it radiated off her skin, from her lips, and he'd never been a lemon and mint man until now.

His fingers stroked the skin of her arms, aware of how lucky they were to touch her. He memorised the smoothness; the bump near her right elbow where something must have bitten her; the indentations below her left shoulder where she must have got her vaccinations. She shivered when he skimmed her collarbone, when his index fingers stroked her neck. He stored the knowledge away for the future, when he could seduce her more thoroughly, when his desk and his employees weren't in the way.

That didn't stop him from giving it his best effort now.

He cupped her face, angling her into a position that would deepen their kiss. He was rewarded with her hands clinging to his waist, before they drifted up and fisted his shirt. Then they were exploring his skin, flesh to flesh somehow. He didn't know how she'd managed to slip her hands under his clothing, but he was grateful for it. Even if it did mean he'd never be able to let another person touch him this way. He couldn't; not when she was claiming him. Not when he wanted to remember her touching him. To remember how his blood seemed to follow along beneath her strokes, pulsing with need and desire, showing him what it meant to be alive. To live.

How had he not known it before?

'You're very impressive,' she said, pulling back. Her cheeks were flushed, there was a dazed half-smile on her face, and her voice was hoarse. She was the most beguiling she'd ever been. 'I don't suppose you became this way in the last few weeks?'

'I'm not sure what you mean.'

'These muscles.' She scraped her nails lightly over his skin. There was no way it would mark him, but they might as well have with the little sparks going off everywhere she touched. 'They weren't always there.'

'No,' he said slowly. 'I don't think they were when I was born. But I was an impressive toddler.' He laughed when she pinched him. 'Hey, I was using your words.'

'And being obnoxious about it.'

'I didn't want you to think I'd changed.'

Her own laugh was softer than his. Perhaps even thoughtful. 'No, I don't think you have. Even though I seem to be hoping you had. That somehow you'd become this man I'm attracted to and maybe even like in the last few weeks.' She brought her hands out from under his shirt, straightening the material as she did. 'That was what I was implying with the muscles, by the way. I know they didn't suddenly appear. I think I only just noticed them.'

Just like I only just noticed you.

She didn't have to say it. Everything she'd already said implied it. But he wanted to tell her she was wrong. He had changed. He could no longer see Lee without thinking about how Lee had used him. More importantly, what Lee had done to her. He didn't think competing with Alexa was fun any more; didn't see it as harmless. With her, he let himself be himself. He showed her that he cared for her, despite his better judgement. He let himself take care of her, was honest with her. She hadn't used those vulnerabilities against him either.

Sure, he hadn't entirely opened up to her about how he felt about his family—but then, neither had she. They were still checking one another out, tentatively testing whether they could trust the other. He thought they were there now. And he wanted to open up to her, wanted to know more about her.

'Do you want to go out with me?' he asked, desperate to do just that. 'Tonight, I mean. Do you want to go out?'

Her lips twitched; light danced in her eyes. 'Are you sure you're feeling well enough?'

'I've made a surprising recovery.'

'Must have been the same twenty-four-hour bug I had.'

'Not quite the same,' he said with a small laugh.

'Hmm. That would be slightly puzzling.'

'Only slightly.'

'Maybe you've had an elixir.'

'I have.'

He moved closer, nuzzled her neck. She angled, giving him better access.

'What are you implying?'

'You're magical.'

She laughed. Patted his chest. 'That, I know.'

'I don't doubt it.' He nipped at her lips. Then, when it felt good, kissed her again, lingering. 'Is that a yes?'

'What was the question?' she asked, voice breathy.

He chuckled. 'Can I take you somewhere?'

'I would love that.'

'I know you like kissing me—' *she hoped* '—but taking me to Lovers Lane seems like overkill.'

Benjamin laughed as he pulled into a parking space at the edge of the road. All the parking spaces on Lovers Lane were at the edge of the road. Alexa wasn't a fan of it since the road was on a cliff, which meant the edge was more dangerous than most edges. But she wasn't going to protest when Benjamin had brought her to this—admittedly—romantic place.

She also wasn't going to move.

Except to eat this broth he'd made her.

But she'd do it very, *very* slowly.

'I wanted to bring you somewhere with a nice view.'

'The quarry was nice. It didn't have such a blatant name. It was safe, too.'

'I've already taken you there.'

It was sweet enough that she leaned forward so she could see the view past his head. It looked much like the night sky itself: dark, save for the lights twinkling back at her. Those lights weren't stars, but the city of Cape Town, and they weren't demure and subtle, but brash and bright. They stretched up until the base of Table Mountain, leaving the landmark to loom over them in darkness. If the lights spoke of the city's vibrancy, its life, then the mountain anchored it. Reminded her that people had families here, careers. Generations had become stronger, less broken, more whole.

'It is pretty nice,' she said on an exhale.

He smiled.

She didn't want to be caught in it, though it was too late to be coy. She'd already given up something of herself when she'd kissed him earlier. Or had he taken it? No, she thought. The permission she'd given him meant that she'd given it willingly. It made her uncomfortable to think she had, so she was trying to blame him.

Uncomfortable didn't feel like the right word though. It was more…like she was going into a battle for the survival of the universe and she had nothing but a sword. Perhaps not even that. Uncomfortable? Sure. Dangerous? Stupid? Completely and utterly irrational? Definitely.

She took a breath and reached into the brown bag for the broth.

'Thanks for swinging by my place to get this.'

'I could have made you a fresh batch.'

'Your kitchen was busy.' She opened the container and sighed at the aroma. 'Besides, I didn't want my first In the Rough meal to be broth.'

She closed her eyes at the first taste of it. It had been hours since she'd eaten, and because she was at the Institute, she'd settled for one slice of toast and a banana. She'd blamed it on her bug when Cherise had asked. She'd also stared longingly at the steak Cherise was eating. But there'd be plenty of steak in the future. For now, she had broth. Warm, delicious broth that wouldn't turn her stomach against her.

Was pregnancy simplifying her appetite? She hoped not.

'Technically it is your first meal from In the Rough,' he said.

'This doesn't count. It doesn't come from the restaurant.'

'Just its manager. Its once-upon-a-time head chef.'

'I forgot about that,' she said, sipping the soup. 'Did you tell me why you decided you didn't want to be head chef any more?'

'Probably not.' He paused. 'I'm happy to share. If you are.'

She frowned. 'What do you mean? I… Oh,' she said when he gestured to the brown bag that still had his food in it. 'Sorry. I got distracted.'

'Yes, I got that.' He was smiling when she handed him his food. He went to open it, but stopped himself. Opened a window instead. Looked at her. 'The smell probably wouldn't be good if you're nauseous.'

'No,' she murmured, touched. 'Thank you.'

'No problem.'

He opened her window, too, and only then dug into his

food. It was lasagne, and her mind salivated over it if not her stomach. She'd steered away from rich food the last three months, with good reason, but she missed the taste of pasta and red meat and bacon. Sighing a little, she took another spoonful of broth.

'I wanted a change,' he said between bites. 'And I thought I was capable of more than being in a kitchen. The idea of running the restaurant intrigued me.'

'Did it live up to your expectations?'

'It did.' His mouth lifted on one side. 'I think I lived up to its expectations, too.'

'If that's your way of giving yourself a compliment, you didn't have to. I could have told you that you were doing a good job.'

'But would you have?'

'Maybe. After some coercing.'

'Of what kind?' His voice had dropped seductively. He leaned closer, but she pulled back. 'What's wrong?'

'I can't kiss you when you're eating that.'

'Oh.' He frowned down at the food, as if it had betrayed him. As if he couldn't believe that it had. 'I wasn't thinking.'

'You were, but not with…' She broke off with a demure smile. 'I'm not going to be crass.' She patted his cheek. 'But yes, that would have been appropriate coercion.'

'Seems a little cruel to remind me when I can't do it.'

'I can be a little cruel sometimes.'

With a small smile that seemed to say *I know*—which pleased her more than offended her—he asked, 'Why did you stop being head chef?'

'I never was. Well,' she reconsidered, 'a lot of my responsibilities blurred the lines with the position, but I knew that I wanted to have other input than in the kitchen to make Infinity the best it could be. I also wanted the business to run independently of me. Or I guess I wanted to run independently of the business.'

'So you could have a life.'

'And maybe babies.'

'You thought about babies then?'

'I suppose I did, though it wasn't "oh, I should do this to have babies".' She set the spoon against the rim of the container. 'I knew I didn't want my life to look like my parents'. Mostly business,' she clarified when she realised he wouldn't know. 'They work a lot, enjoy it, barely spend time at home. I wanted to have more than that. I wanted to have a family. I forgot about it while I tried to get Infinity up and running. Then after an employee brought her kid to work, it hit me: I wanted a home life, too. With babies.'

'That's why your place is so homey.'

'You still sound surprised.'

'Not surprised—jealous. I would love to be so intentional about…everything.' He closed the container his food was in. 'I spent a lot of my time not doing what I wanted to do. When I got to do it, I realised it wasn't really what I wanted to do.'

'But you're there now, aren't you?' she asked. 'You like running the restaurant.'

'Yeah.'

'Great. So you got there in your professional life. Just figure out how to get there in your personal life.'

'Easier said than done.'

'Of course. But you're the only one who can do it.' She closed the container her own food was in and put it in the brown bag. Did the same for his when he handed it to her. 'You can live your life doing the easy thing and going with the flow. It'll take you where you need to be, but maybe there'll be more pit stops. Maybe it'll make you feel as if you should have done more. But—' she dragged the word out '—taking the harder route and doing things intentionally will help you feel proud. Things might still take a long time, but you'll appreciate the journey more.'

She shook her head, rolled her eyes. 'I know I sound silly.'

'You don't. It's…harder, with my mom.'

'How?'

'She needs me,' he said simply. 'If I'm not around, she'll push too hard. My father would be alone to help her with it. It's how our family is.'

'Would you move out if she didn't need you?'

'I… Yeah, maybe.' His lips pursed, then parted to let an exhale through. 'Probably. I'm over thirty,' he said with a quick laugh. 'I shouldn't be living with my parents any more.'

'That's why you're taking me to Lovers Lane instead of home. Not that you should take me home.' She closed her eyes. 'I didn't mean it that way.'

'I know. But maybe that's what you get for being a little cruel.'

He laughed when she punched him lightly in the shoulder. They sat in companionable silence until he said, 'It's cool. The way you've crafted your life. Not everyone can do that.'

She leaned back against the seat. 'I have my parents to thank for that, I guess. For all their faults, they were very clear about having a plan. It was a set plan for them—school, university, work—and they weren't thrilled that mine looked a little different. But I did have one. They just didn't see it.'

She'd faltered at the end, so she shouldn't have been surprised at the hand Benjamin reached out and took hers with. Not even the way he lifted her hand to kiss it should have surprised her. Maybe it was the warmth that spread through her body because of his actions that did. The way it settled in her chest, soothing the holes in her heart her parents had created with their rigidity.

'I'm sure they're proud of you.'

'Maybe.' She reclined the seat with her free hand. Settled both their hands on her stomach. 'I guess they are now. Though they would most likely prefer me to be a business mogul like Lee is. One successful business pales in comparison to that.'

'Which is what he intended,' Benjamin said softly. When she lifted her gaze to him, the edge of his mouth lifted. 'You've told me a lot. I can piece together the rest.'

'So it seems.' She ran the index finger of the hand that wasn't tangled with his over his skin. 'Lee's ambitious. Smart. I like to think those things were the primary motivations.'

'But you know they're not.'

She couldn't admit it out loud, so she hedged. 'Our parents taught us to be the best. I took that to mean people outside of our family. Lee took it to mean…me.' She swallowed. 'But it gave us both motivation, thinking that. If I'm part of it, it's only because of that.'

He tugged at her hand. Frowning, she looked at him. His face was serious, but other than that, she couldn't read his emotion.

'What?' she asked.

'Why are you protecting him?'

'I'm not…' She broke off at his look. 'I'm his sister. His older sister. That's what I'm supposed to do.'

'By that logic, he should be looking up to you, his older sister. Not competing with you so much you've lost your ability to trust people who care about you.'

The shock had her pulling her hand out of his, grabbing a hold of her stomach with both hands. She wasn't sure whether she thought she was protecting herself, or her children. Didn't know why she thought she had to do either.

'Lex—'

'No, give me a moment.' Purposefully, she leaned back against the chair, relaxed her body. She smoothed her clothing, took a couple of deep breaths, let her mind settle. When she was ready, or as ready as she would ever be, she nodded.

'You're right. I realise this. Which is why I've chosen not to have him in my life.'

'I'm sorry. I shouldn't have said that.'

'Stop apologising, Ben,' she said softly. 'You keep doing it.'

'Because I keep messing up.'

'Being honest, caring… That's not messing up.' She bit the inside of her lip at his expression. Tried to fix it. 'Don't get me wrong, it's very inconvenient. Especially when you're trying to avoid your issues. Don't you dare apologise!' she said when he opened his mouth.

He gave her a wry grin and she laughed.

'It's like a disease with you.'

'I can't help it.'

'Sure you can. Just stop doing it.'

'I've been doing it my entire life.'

'Why?'

He didn't reply immediately, his expression contorted in confusion. 'I don't actually know.' He tried to hide the panic that answer brought by giving her a smile. She wondered if he knew how horribly he was failing.

'Okay, we're going to play a game.'

'A game?'

'It's a distraction, Foster.'

'In that case, tell me,' Benjamin said with a smile. It was more genuine now.

'Well, I'm going to try to get you to apologise to me, and you're going to resist.'

'What are you going to do?'

'Nothing specific,' she replied nonchalantly. 'You know that game where, when you're on a road trip, you pick a colour and have to count the number of cars in that colour?'

'Yeah…'

'That's how it's going to be. When the opportunity arises.' She brought a finger under her nose, pretending to stifle a sneeze. 'Oh, my sinuses are acting up.'

'Should I close the windows?'

'Just a little.' She pretended to stop another sneeze. 'Do you have tissues or something here?'

'Yeah, I do,' he said, just as she knew he would.

He reached for the pack of tissues in his door, reached out to give it to her. She held out a hand, but moved it slightly when he tried to drop the tissues into it. The pack fell between the seats.

'Oh. Sorry about that. I thought…' He broke off when he saw her shaking her head. When he saw the smile on her face, too. 'You planned that?'

'Yes. And you failed. Terribly. In the first minute of the game.'

'But that wasn't fair!'

'All's fair in love and war.' When there was an awkward silence, she wrinkled her nose. 'This is war, in case you were wondering.'

'I wasn't.'

But, if she was being honest with herself, she was.

CHAPTER SIXTEEN

WHAT WAS THE SAYING? *Going to hell in a handbasket?* If so, that was exactly what was happening. The handbasket was filled with delicious food courtesy of Cherise, but the tying of the bow, the giving? That was all Lee.

'You invited your sister?' Benjamin hissed the moment he saw Alexa walk into the hotel ballroom.

Okay, not the moment he saw Alexa. The moment he saw Alexa he stopped, his brain stopped, and he was pretty sure his heart stopped. She looked…amazing. It was too inadequate a word, but he clung to it. The gown she wore was somewhere between coral and peach, the colour of it magnificent against the bronze of her skin. It was a halter-neck dress that clung to her chest, ending just below her breasts in a cinch, before flowing down over the rest of her. The material was pleated, and when she moved, it moved with her. When she was still, those pleats created the illusion of space. All for the benefit of hiding the bump he knew was growing by the day.

The reason he knew it was because he'd found a reason, every day since they'd been to Lovers Lane, to see her. He didn't once go to her restaurant—he worried that would be invading her personal space—but he visited her flat under the guise of bringing more food. He asked her to go out for tea under the pretence of picking her brains about something. It had been a week and a half of this, where he was clearly making up reasons to see her, but she never once called him out on it.

He told himself that if she'd wanted to, she would have.

She wasn't the kind of person not to. The fact that she wasn't saying anything told him she wanted to see him, too. As did the small, private smile she smiled every time she saw him.

The days she invited him in were the ones he liked best. Her flat was fast becoming his favourite place, in no small part because they could be whoever they wanted to be there. Turned out, they wanted to be friends. The kissing that happened quite frequently—and sometimes progressed to other things, but never far enough to undermine their friendship—was merely a bonus. But things were so easy between them when they were there. He told her about how he'd grown up trying to help his parents; she told him how she'd grown up trying to make hers proud. They comforted one another, teased one another, and, yes, kissed and touched, and it was all magnificent.

And it was going to end.

'I didn't invite her,' Lee said slowly. 'She wouldn't have come if she'd known the invitation was from me.'

Benjamin resisted grabbing the man at the front of his collar. 'What did you do?' he said through his teeth.

'Used the grapevine.' Lee smirked. 'It still works.'

It took Benjamin a long time to remember what he was like when he wasn't so damn angry. Not that anger was such a bad thing. It gave him a clarity he hadn't had before. Sure, some of that clarity was also because of his conversations with Alexa, but it was clarity nevertheless. And he knew exactly what he had to do.

'I quit.'

'What?'

'Resign, effective immediately.'

'You can't do that,' Lee spluttered. 'Your contract says you have to give me at least a month's notice.'

'Then you have it.'

'What the hell?' Lee's expression was stormy. 'This is

because of my sister, isn't it? She poached you.' He shook his head in disbelief. 'You let her? You let her because you're sleeping with her?'

'Lee,' he warned.

Lee took a breath, clearly trying to get hold of his emotions. 'You can't do this, man. We've been working together for years. I gave you a chance. You can't walk out on me.'

'I'm grateful for what you did for me.' And he meant it. But the weight that had lifted from his shoulders the moment he'd quit told him he'd needed to. 'Truly, I am. You're an incredible businessman. I've learnt a lot from you. I have no doubt I could have learnt more.'

'Then why are you leaving?'

'Because you used me to beat your sister.' Saying it out loud made Benjamin feel in control. As if finally, after all those people had used him, he'd regained what they'd taken from him. His pride, perhaps. Or perhaps it was that he was no longer scared of saying it. 'And you're malicious. To your own sister, who's done nothing but love you.'

'Is that what she told you?' Lee scoffed. 'She must be really good in…'

He broke off when Benjamin, quick as lightning, took his arm. 'I'm warning you about what you say next.'

Lee's chest heaved. 'Okay. I'm sorry.'

He let go. 'I appreciate that.'

'You're serious about this?'

'Deadly.' He straightened his tie. 'I respect who you are in business, but not as a man. I can't, knowing how you've treated the woman I… I love.'

He'd hesitated in speech, just as he had with his feelings. But he could see they'd been there long before the last month. The moment he'd seen her in that class, he'd tumbled. Knocked his head in the process, it seemed, because he went back to being a kid and tried to compete with her so she would notice him.

But she'd never allowed him close enough to see that she had noticed him; not in the way he'd intended. He'd reminded her of her brother, the man, he suspected, had hurt her most. She seemed to have some kind of resignation about who her parents were, but not with Lee. With Lee, she'd tried, and he'd brushed her away. When she let Benjamin in the last few weeks, he could see how much it hurt her—and how much he had hurt her, simply by acting like a teenage fool.

Now what he had seen, what she'd allowed him to see, convinced him that if he hadn't been a fool, he would have had these feelings aeons ago. She might not have iced him out, and he might have seen who she really was. That was who he was in love with. The woman who wasn't even a little cruel. Who was passionate and driven and who cared about people.

It was the biggest honour of his life that she'd chosen to open up to him. She'd let him see her vulnerable, and he hoped with all his might he'd done enough to show her she could be vulnerable with him. He knew she struggled with it, and if he had to be patient he would be, simply because she was worth it.

If he had to spend his entire lifetime proving that she could trust him, he would. Because he loved her. And she deserved it.

He had to tell her.

'Benjamin!'

The exclamation came from a short distance away. When he turned towards it, he saw Cherise.

'Thanks so much for coming,' she said, stopping in front of him. 'I thought I should show you what I can do, too, since I hope we can work together.'

It was what he'd wanted to hear most, once upon a time. Now, what he wanted to hear most was Alexa's voice, saying anything, really, but mostly talking about them sharing a future together. He turned, barely thinking about the fact that Cherise was there, waiting for an answer.

He didn't think about it at all when he saw Lee follow Alexa out of the ballroom.

The moment she saw him walking towards her she knew.

It was silly of her to think that she could walk into an event being catered by Cherise to get another opportunity to speak with her. To perhaps even see her in action. Alexa had found out about the charity event through an acquaintance, thought it would be harmless and beneficial, considering she hadn't heard from Cherise for over a week. When she saw Lee, it all fell into place: she hadn't heard from Cherise for a reason, she'd been set up, and she shouldn't have come.

She didn't give the gorgeous ballroom and its glistening lights and formal guests any more thought. She walked out, down the brick steps, past the fountain. She was on the small stretch of grass between the fountain and the car park when Lee caught up with her.

'Leaving so soon?'

She stopped. Closed her eyes. Turned to face him. 'Sorry I didn't stay for the *gotcha*. That's what you wanted to say, isn't it?'

'No one forced you to be here,' Lee said calmly. 'Although I'm surprised you didn't accompany Ben.' He pretended to think about it. 'Is it that he didn't tell you about this, or that you really are trying to keep your personal and professional lives separate?'

He hadn't told her, though she didn't need to tell Lee that. Nor did she have to figure out why Benjamin hadn't said anything. He was protecting her, or maybe himself, and though she understood it—he was so used to protecting the people in his life—it bothered her on a deep level. But that wasn't important now.

'Look, Lee, I don't want to stick around for the gloating, okay?'

'Not even your own?'

'What are you talking about?'

'Oh, you're going to pretend you didn't ask him to do it. That seems like an odd position, all things considered.'

'Tell me, or let me go,' she said sharply.

'Your boyfriend quit.'

'He what?'

His brows rose. 'Nice acting, Sis. Didn't know you had it in you.'

'He quit? Why?' She narrowed her eyes. 'What the hell did you do?'

'Absolutely nothing.' Though she could barely see it, she knew he was biting the inside of his lip. He used to do it when they were younger, on the side. 'He told me it's because of the way I've been treating you.'

She caught the swear word before it left her lips. Mentally, though, she let the curses fly. The idiot! It was fine if he kept things from her because he thought he was protecting her—okay, not fine, understandable—but this? This was stupid. This was his entire future. It was his life. And he was doing it for her! It seemed much too much for people who'd been close for less than two weeks. This felt more like a gesture; something someone did before proclaiming their love or something.

A thin thread of panic wove between the synapses in her brain. It threatened to overcome her, and for a second she thought she would fall over. But that would hurt her babies, and she had to be strong. She couldn't let them suffer for things she was responsible for.

She looked at her brother. Realised she needed to sort this out if she wanted to keep that promise to her kids.

'If I talk to him, convince him to go back to you, would you leave me alone?' She could already see, before he even said it, that he was going to make some stupid remark. 'I'm being serious. If I get Ben to go back to In the Rough, I don't want to see or hear from you again. Unless there's a family function, which, fortunately, doesn't happen often. But outside of that. No surprises. No manipulation. Nothing.'

'You really want that?'

He'd taken the stance of a victim, his voice hurt and surprised, as if he had no contribution to why she wanted this. It made her snap.

'What I want is to have a brother who doesn't make me feel as if I have to walk carefully everywhere I go in case he pulls the rug out from under me. I want to have a brother who doesn't *enjoy* pulling the rug out from under me. Who, when I fall, asks me why I'm on the ground. Who gets upset when I refuse his help.'

She'd never spent enough time with Lee to learn how his expressions revealed his emotions. Or maybe it was that the only expressions he wore around her were variations of smugness or satisfaction or a combination of the two. So she couldn't tell how he felt now, because none of that came through in his expression.

'I thought… This is what we do, Lex. We compete with one another. We make one another better.'

'What? That's what you think this is? No—*how* do you think that is what this is?' Her voice was high with disbelief. She didn't try to temper it. 'You competed with me, Lee. I *congratulated* you for beating my records, or scoring higher than me.'

'You were conceding.'

'Conceding…'

Now she recognised the look on Lee's face: bewilderment. He genuinely didn't understand why she was so upset. She nearly laughed. He was the least self-aware person she knew.

'I wasn't conceding. I was sincerely wishing you well because I was happy for you. At first. I could see competing with me made you happy and gave you purpose and I wanted you to have that.' She took a steadying breath. 'But you didn't want me to be happy. If you did, you would have supported me the way I supported you. You would have taken the hand I held out every time I asked you to go to a movie with me, or watch a show, or do whatever stupid things brothers and sisters do together. But you said no. Instead you tried to beat me at things that didn't even matter.'

She folded her arms, suddenly cold.

'And you tried to beat me at things that did matter, too.' She blinked when that made her want to cry. 'You bought the building I spent months trying to find. Months,' she said with a shake of her head. 'I did research into who I was buying the building from, into the neighbourhood, into how much it would cost to renovate, how long it would take. Then you swooped in and stole it. Just stole it.' She lifted a hand, dropped it. 'The only thing you knew about it was that I wanted it.'

'I… I didn't realise.'

'You didn't realise that you'd destroyed my dream?' she asked. 'Of both that restaurant and ever having a normal relationship with you?'

He didn't reply, though he ran his hand over his hair a few times, lips moving without sound. He looked at her, and if she wasn't so numb by the conversation, she would have been touched by the vulnerability she saw there.

But she was numb. She had to be. If she wasn't, the reminder of all the times she'd wanted to forge a relationship with her brother would have consumed her. The hope she'd once had was enmeshed in those memories. She'd desperately wanted to shield herself against her parents, had known that if Lee was behind the shield with her she could be stronger. *They* would be stronger together. Except

Lee chose to wield their parents' weapons against her, too, even when she'd surrendered.

She wasn't surrendering any more. It might have seemed as if she was by offering Lee Benjamin, but she knew she wasn't. She was lifting her shield, protecting herself once more. Because the only way she could truly do that against her brother was by coming to a truce with him. Which meant he needed to make the decision, too.

She could smell the faint smoke of guilt at using Benjamin as a pawn, but maybe he would understand. He might even be grateful that he wouldn't have to protect her any more.

'You don't, um…' Lee cleared his throat. 'You don't have to get Benjamin to work for me.'

She just studied him.

'I'll leave you alone. I didn't realise…' Now he shook his head. 'I'll leave you alone. I promise.'

She almost ran a hand over her stomach before she remembered Lee didn't know about her pregnancy. She settled for clasping her hands over the bag she'd brought with her.

'Thank you.'

Neither of them moved. But there was a movement behind Lee. Alexa's eyes automatically shifted to it, before she realised it was Benjamin. Her body wanted to sag against something, let it hold up her weight as she prepared for another conversation that would leave her raw. It was so different to how her body had responded to Benjamin in the last weeks. With relief, excitement, attraction, desire. She'd felt safer than at any other time in her life.

This interaction with Lee seemed to prove how much safety was an illusion.

CHAPTER SEVENTEEN

'ARE YOU OKAY?'

It was the first thing that came into his mind when he reached her, but he immediately realised it was a stupid question. Of course she wasn't okay. He could see it in her stance, in her eyes, in the brittle tone of her voice when she lied and told him she was. She looked broken, tired, and he hated the person who'd put that look on her face.

He turned to Lee. 'Leave.'

Lee looked at Alexa, then back at him. Uncharacteristically withdrawn, he nodded. After one last glance at Alexa, a parting of the lips that made it seem as though he wanted to say something, he turned around and walked away. Benjamin waited until he was out of sight, then turned.

'Come on, let's find somewhere to sit down.'

She didn't fight him on it, and his worry kicked up another notch. But he kept it inside long enough to find a bench. The restaurant was in a vineyard, much like most prestigious restaurants in Cape Town. But instead of looking out onto the vineyard, the restaurant looked out over the stretch of property on the opposite side of it. It was mostly grass and a long deck that went out into a pond. The pond was still, though Benjamin saw the occasional disturbance of water and the rings that resulted from that disturbance. He watched it for a long time, waiting for Alexa to recover from whatever had happened with Lee.

When he thought she might have, he asked, 'Did that go okay?'

'He agreed to leave me alone, so I guess so.'

'That's what you wanted?'

'I asked for it.'

But she didn't say it was what she wanted, and he had a feeling it wasn't. He wasn't sure if she knew that though, or if she needed to figure it out. He wasn't sure about his position in this either: Should he prod? Give her space? Point her in the right direction? None of the options seemed right. He didn't speak, crippled by the indecision.

'Did you quit your job?' she said into the silence.

'He told you?'

'Accused me,' she corrected. 'Apparently I've been using you to get to him.'

'Sounds diabolical.'

'You can't say I didn't warn you.' She opened her palms on her lap, looking at them, not him. He should have taken it as sign, prepared himself. Because he didn't, he was completely taken aback by her next words. 'I hope you didn't do this because of me.'

'No. Of course not.'

'You didn't quit because of me?'

'No.'

'Then why did you?'

'I…couldn't work with him any more. He got you here because he wanted to…' He broke off at her look. 'Fine, maybe it had something to do with you. But it wasn't *because* of you.'

She threaded her fingers together. 'You're going to regret it.' Her voice was neutral. 'You're going to blame me when you regret it.'

'I won't.'

'You will. Unless you can tell me you're leaving because of more than just me.'

'I…want to do my own thing.'

'Liar.'

'I'm not lying,' he snapped. Took a breath. 'I shouldn't have said that. It was—' he relaxed his jaw '—uncalled for.'

'It was, especially since it's the truth.'

'It's not fair,' he replied, barely retaining control over his anger. 'It was never fair of you to expect me to work with a man I don't respect any more.'

'You shouldn't have let the way he treated me affect your working relationship.'

'He used me to get to you.' He stood now. Walked away, trying to keep that control. Came back when it didn't help him have more of it. 'Do you know how many people have used me in my life? Too many,' he answered for her. 'It was worse that he did it to get to you. It was worse that he was still so terrible to you. How can you ask me to ignore it?'

'Because of this!' she exclaimed, shifting to the edge of the bench. 'You quit your job. The one you love, at the restaurant you built. Don't you see that? Don't you see you're going to lose everything you've worked for all because of me?' She dropped her head. 'One day you'll think I used you for this, too. I almost did.' Her voice was barely above a whisper. 'I told him that if I got you to work for him again, he had to leave me alone.'

He took the time he needed to work through that.

'Because you care,' he said, crouching down so he could see her face. 'You know what the restaurant means to me.'

'Maybe. Maybe I did it because it meant getting what I want.'

Her eyes, defiant, met his.

'You're saying this to hurt me,' he said, realising it. 'You're pushing me away.'

'Yes,' she whispered. 'You deserve more than me. You deserve someone who can care as much as you do. Selflessly. I… I can't.'

He froze. Slowly, he rose. He rubbed a hand over his face. 'Why not?'

'Can't you see?' She was sitting up, spine straight. It looked so out of place against the curved back of the bench. 'You're selfless. You protect the people you care about at all costs. Even if you're lying to them.'

He could hardly deny it when that was exactly what he'd done that day.

'I've been alone most of my life. I'm used to thinking about myself. More importantly—' she took a deep breath '—I can't trust someone who won't tell me the truth. And I can't keep worrying that I'm keeping you from doing what you want to do. But if I don't, you'll keep putting yourself last.'

'It's not… I'm not…' He exhaled. 'Why don't we talk about you being unable to accept when people try to care for you?'

She bit her lip. 'Okay. What about it would you like to discuss?'

It took him a moment to get over his surprise.

'Why?'

'Why can't I accept people caring for me?' she asked. He nodded. A short moment later, she continued. 'Because it goes away. In some shape or form, I'll discover I can't trust them. It goes away, Ben.' There was a quick inhale of air. When he moved to her, she held out a hand to stop him. Sniffed. 'No, I'm okay.' But two tears streamed down each of her cheeks. She wiped at them quickly. 'I don't want to go through that.'

'It doesn't just go away.' He went to sit next to her, as far away as the bench allowed so she had her space. 'I can't care one day and stop caring the other.'

'But you can *think* you care one day and realise you don't the other.'

'Has this happened to you?'

'No. I wouldn't let it.'

'You mean you haven't let anyone close enough to allow it to happen.'

She inclined her head in acknowledgement.

'That's not healthy.'

'It's safe.'

'Safe isn't going to give you happiness.'

'Are you speaking from experience?' she asked blandly. 'You're staying at home so you can be safe, so you can protect your mother and help your father. So you don't have to face your real feelings about your family.'

He stared at her. 'There are no feelings.'

'So you're happy?' she prodded. 'You're safe and happy, the ultimate juxtaposition, according to you?'

He stood again. 'This isn't fair.'

'It is, but you don't like it.' She stood now, too. 'Which is fine. You don't have to like it.'

'You're using this as an excuse to push me away.'

'I don't need an excuse. I've told you every reason we can't continue this.' She gestured between them.

'You're really that scared of trusting someone?' he asked. 'Is being alone better than taking a chance?'

She folded her arms, the line of her mouth flat. 'Yes. I've spent my life learning that lesson. I won't let anyone hurt me the way my family has.'

'Even if it means pushing away someone who—' he swallowed. Said it anyway. Because he was a fool '—loves you?'

She blinked. Again, and again, until her lashes were fluttering like the wings of a butterfly. He tried to give her a moment to process. He couldn't.

'I haven't once let you down, Alexa. I've been there for you since this entire thing with Lee started. I lied, yes, but I thought…' He shook his head. 'I wasn't doing it to hurt you. The very opposite, in fact.' He took a step closer. 'Trust me. Trust me because I love you, and I'll try to do better because I love you. Trust me because I've shown you that you can.'

She was shaking her head before he had finished speaking. 'You need to care about yourself, too, in order to love, Ben. I don't think you do.'

With that, she walked away.

It had not been a good week. Someone had forgotten to order the seafood for the restaurant on Monday. It meant that Alexa had to remove all relevant dishes from the menu, make thousands of apologies, and offer substitutes. Then, on Wednesday, someone had forgotten about the staff meeting, come in late, and the event that was being hosted that evening had a few hiccups because the meeting hadn't proceeded.

Everyone made mistakes. She tried to remember that on Friday evening, when she was dead on her feet and contemplating disciplinary action. It complicated things that she'd been the someone who'd forgetten and needed to be punished. Maybe she would get her staff to give her a roasting. Making fun of her would hopefully rebuild the morale that seemed to be lacking, too.

'Hey.' Kenya appeared in her doorway, leaning against the frame of it as though she'd always been there. She was holding two bottles of beer. 'I thought you could use one?'

'Thanks, but I can't drink it.'

Kenya's brow quirked. 'Since when are you this strict about alcohol on a Friday night?'

She couldn't be bothered to keep it a secret any more. She was almost sixteen weeks pregnant with twins, her body was becoming fuller by the day, her plan to have the restaurant secured before her maternity leave had imploded, and she was tired of keeping it all to herself. At least before, she'd had Benjamin to confide in. That was no longer an option. She tried not to listen to the crack of her heart at that thought.

'Since I got pregnant.'

'You're pregnant?' Kenya stepped inside the office, slammed the door, and then put both beers on Alexa's desk. 'Who do I have to kill?'

'Why are you killing someone?' Alexa asked with a laugh.

'Because they knocked you up! Unless…' She eyed Alexa suspiciously 'Did you want to be knocked up?'

'Yes.'

'Oh.' Kenya frowned. 'You trapped them.'

She chuckled again. 'I didn't trap anyone. I went to a sperm bank because your family made me remember how much I wanted my own. How soon I wanted it, too.' She shrugged and let out a small smile. 'Anyway, that's why I've been dressing like this. Trying to hide the bump.'

'I was wondering.' Kenya dropped into the chair on the visitor's side of Alexa's desk. She drank her beer. 'Honestly, I thought you were going through a boho chic period.'

'Seriously?'

'I didn't want to limit you with my expectations of who you are.' Kenya smiled, but it lacked its fire. Alexa found out why a couple of seconds later. 'Why didn't you tell me you were doing this? I could have come with you. Supported you. From what I know about the process, it isn't easy.'

'No, it isn't. And honestly? I could have used the support.' Her heart ached at the acknowledgement. 'But I'm an idiot.' She offered Kenya a small smile. 'I thought that if I let you in, you'd hurt me. I've got so used to doing things on my own, I thought I could do this.'

She wasn't talking about conceiving her children any more, and they both knew it.

'Why would you think that?' Kenya's voice was soft, and a little judgemental. Alexa smiled.

'It's what I'm used to,' she said. 'My family is messed up. And every time I thought something was going right, it was really…not.'

She should have explained it better, but it occurred to her that she hadn't told Kenya anything of her personal life. She knew that Kenya had three older brothers, seven nieces, one nephew and a daughter, and that motherhood had pushed her to finally get the therapy she thought she needed. Alexa knew all of that, but she hadn't told Kenya one thing about her family.

'It's a long story, and I should have told you more of it sooner,' she said softly.

Kenya didn't blink. 'You should have, yes.'

'I'm sorry. For all of it.'

'Good.' Kenya didn't look away as she drank from her beer. 'So, should we thank the pregnancy for this stupendous week, or the family?'

'Neither. Or maybe the family? I don't know.' It was the perfect opportunity to make things right with Kenya. Or at least to start to. 'I think it's mostly because of the fake boyfriend.'

'Explain.'

So she did. She told Kenya about her terrible brother, who'd inspired her to pretend her rival was her boyfriend. How Benjamin had gone along with it, even after he'd found out she was pregnant. She told Kenya about the twins—to which she got a colourful reply—and about how things had snowballed, but in a nice way, with Benjamin. And then how it had all melted, leaving her feeling as though she was drowning.

She ended on an apology, because she'd been a bad friend and a worse boss. She couldn't secure the restaurant before she was on maternity leave. She could probably still try, but time was running out and—

'Firstly,' Kenya interrupted, 'you've been a pretty terrible friend. There's no way you're worse as a boss.'

'Wow. Thanks.'

'Secondly,' Kenya continued with a grin, 'we haven't had a head chef for almost four months now. I know you've been picking up a lot of the slack, but that's because you didn't trust us—' she gave Alexa a look '—to help you with it. You don't have to kill yourself to find a replacement chef before you go on leave. If you do, great, and we'll help train them. If you don't, we'll survive.'

Kenya leaned forward and rested a hand on Alexa's.

'Babe, you've built a damn good team. You've also earned our loyalty. That includes helping out when things get rough.' She squeezed. 'It includes taking care of things while you have your babies. We could probably help you get ready for the babies, too.'

'Oh, that's not—' She cut herself off. 'Thank you,' she said instead. 'That means a lot.'

'Yeah, well, it should.' Kenya softened her words with a smile. 'You mean a lot to us.'

'And you mean a lot to me.'

Kenya blinked. Then took the last swig of her beer. 'Thanks. Now, let's go tell the people out there you're having two babies.'

'Oh. Oh, yeah. Okay.'

'It's been a rough week for all of us. This would help. But only if you want to do it.'

She thought about it for a long time. Then she nodded and stood up. 'Let's go.'

The reaction was more than she could have ever anticipated or expected. A stunned silence followed her words, but after that someone began to cheer. People came forward to congratulate her, offering her words of encouragement and advice, asking how they could help.

Alexa swallowed down her emotion many times in the next hour, her eyes prickling at the support she had no idea she'd already had. When she caught Kenya's eye later, she got a wink and a knowing look in return. It made the tears she was holding back run down her cheeks, and she was immediately handed tissues from three different directions. She laughed, waved off concern, pressed the tissue to her eyes. And in that moment she realised two things:

One, she'd spent so many years afraid of opening up and trusting people. Yet despite that, she'd found the very family she'd hoped for her entire life. And they trusted her, for whatever reason. Apparently, she'd earned it. Maybe it was time that she allowed herself to see they'd earned her trust, too.

Number two was more complicated. Because the entire time she'd experienced this emotional, overwhelming thing, she'd felt as though she were missing a limb. She didn't let herself think of it until she was alone that night in her flat. When she did, she didn't like that Benjamin had wedged himself so deeply in her mind that she couldn't go through her day without thinking about him. That she couldn't have important experiences without wanting him there. Without having him there.

She settled on the sofa, but it smelled like him, so she moved. It didn't make sense—he hadn't been there in over a week and her sofas were regularly cleaned.

Except it *did* make sense. She just didn't want to face it.

At some point during the night as she tossed and turned, she realised she already had. She knew exactly what the problem was: Benjamin hadn't wedged himself in her mind; he'd wedged himself into her heart.

CHAPTER EIGHTEEN

HE'D NEVER THOUGHT his dream job would become a nightmare. But it was. Working in a place he loved but had given up for—his darkest moments in the last week had made him think—nothing. He only had himself to blame. Alexa hadn't asked him to do this, neither had Lee. He'd done it because he'd thought he was being principled.

He *was* being principled. He couldn't work for a man like Lee. Someone whose cruelty would one day be turned on Benjamin or their staff. Benjamin would have left then anyway, so he'd just hurried along the inevitable by handing in his notice.

But principles didn't pay the bills, or help the mind when dreams were dashed. The euphoria he'd felt after saying he was leaving was well and truly gone. Now he only thought of his responsibilities, of what his parents would say when he finally told them what he'd done, and how Alexa had walked away from his proclamation of love.

A knock brought him out of his thoughts.

It was Saturday night after the restaurant had already closed and most of his staff had gone home. Lee's appearance in his doorway was perplexing for more than that reason though. The very fact that he was there after a week of radio silence was troubling. So was the fact that he'd knocked, which he never had, in all the years they'd worked together, done.

'Can I come in?'

Benjamin opened a hand, gesturing to the chair opposite him. He tried not to think about how Alexa had filled it almost three weeks before. Or anything else they'd done in the office.

'I'm surprised to see you here,' Benjamin said.

'I should have come earlier.'

'Should you have?'

Lee smiled at the casual comment. Or maybe not smiled, but Benjamin didn't think there was a description for Lee simply showing his teeth.

'Yes. We should have had a meeting to discuss the implications of your resignation and the transition plans. Have you told the staff yet?'

'No.'

'Great. We'll—'

'Lee,' Benjamin interjected. 'Did you really come here this time on a Saturday night to talk business?'

'No,' he said after a moment. He leaned forward, rested his arms on his knees. 'I'm here to apologise.'

'Apologise?'

'For setting this in motion.' Now he clasped his hands. 'I always knew you were ambitious, and that In the Rough wasn't where you'd end up. But… I sped it up, by acting like a complete jerk to Alexa. And to you. I'm sorry.'

Benjamin sat back and let his mind figure out what was happening and what he should say next. 'I appreciate that. I'm more concerned about whether you're extending that apology to Alexa.'

'No.' Lee looked down. 'She doesn't want to see me. I want to respect that.'

'I bet she'd want to see you if you're intending on apologising.'

'You think?'

'You spent your life torturing her. I think an apology would be a nice change of pace.'

Lee winced, but he straightened and ran a hand over

his face. 'I don't know how I didn't see how much I was hurting her.'

'We all have blind spots when it comes to family.'

It was one of the little nuggets of wisdom his brain had come up with at three or so in the morning some time in the past week.

'Yeah, but hurting her?' He shook his head. 'That's more than a blind spot. It's…' His voice faded, and for a while after, he didn't speak. 'It's not what a brother should do to his sister.'

'Agreed.'

Lee nodded. Got up. 'I don't have anything else to say right now.'

'You could talk about the transition.'

He laughed a little. 'That was me hedging so I wouldn't have to apologise.'

Benjamin chuckled, too. 'I've been there.'

Lee walked to the door but, before he left, turned back. 'We do have to talk about the transition.'

'I know.'

'Maybe we could talk about you buying this place from me.'

'What?'

'It's lost its appeal, now that I know what it did to Alexa.' He angled his head. 'This seems like a good way to restore balance.'

'You should sell it to her, then.'

'Are you kidding me? Her place is much more popular than this. It would be a downgrade.'

With a quick wink, Lee was gone.

He hadn't left things any worse than the way he'd found them. Not even his offer to sell the place to Benjamin had made much of an impact. Perhaps because Benjamin already knew the answer: he wanted In the Rough. He wanted to run the business himself, and do things the way he'd learnt to do them. He had no doubt he would make mistakes, but that was part of the package. He was very much looking forward to making mistakes, in fact.

So yeah, he'd been lying to himself when he said he didn't know why he'd decided to leave. He'd done that because he wanted something else. But he'd also done it because he was standing up to Lee—because he was standing up for Alexa. It smarted that she didn't want him to do that. It hurt that he'd offered and she'd rejected him. She couldn't see that he wanted to do this, that he needed to, so that he could make up for…

He paused. He didn't have to make up for anything. He'd already apologised to Alexa for what he'd done to her before he'd known her. He'd tried his best to show her none of that would happen again. Why had his brain automatically gone there, then? To make up for something, as if he were in the wrong?

Because he'd taken responsibility for her life in some ways, he realised. He thought he could make the hurt she'd been through better by protecting her. But she was right: the way he'd protected her was all wrong. He had done what he thought was best, knowing that she wouldn't appreciate it.

Did he always do that with her? With anyone? With his…with his mother?

Yes. He did. It was so clear to him that he could have been staring at its physical form right in front of him. But he didn't want to look at it by himself. He wanted to talk to Alexa. He wanted to share it with her; share everything with her. Because she was his friend, and because he loved her.

He was halfway to her place when he wondered whether it was a good idea. It was the middle of the night on a Saturday. Not to mention the fact that she clearly didn't consider him her friend. She certainly didn't love him. It took the rest of the journey there for him to realise he didn't do a good enough job of fighting for her. She might not love him, but he was sure she cared about him, and maybe they could still be friends. He'd take her friendship if he could have nothing else of her.

Then she opened her front door in her pyjamas. A cotton nightgown that dipped in the valley of her full breasts and caressed her growing stomach. He felt a lot of things in that moment. Protectiveness. Desire. Tenderness. Love. None of it inspired him to think of friendship, and he knew he'd made a mistake.

'I shouldn't have come.'

'You realised this because I opened the door?'

'Yes, actually. What were you thinking, coming to the door like this?'

'Excuse me?'

'You're wearing lingerie.'

'This is not lingerie,' she scoffed. 'It's an old cotton nightgown. My oldest, in fact, because it's the most stretched and none of the others fit me.' She frowned. 'You're one to talk.'

He looked down at his T-shirt and jeans. 'I'm perfectly respectable.'

'Except I can see your biceps and your chest muscles.'

'You can't see my chest muscles.'

'Your T-shirt is tight. I can imagine them.'

'You think I'm dressed inappropriately because of your *imagination*?'

She folded her arms. 'Isn't that what you were doing?'

'I… Well, no. Your breasts are right there.'

She looked down, as if seeing them for the first time. 'Oh. I guess this is not only stretchy around my waist.' She shrugged. 'It's not like you haven't seen this much of them before.'

He closed his eyes and prayed for patience. And maybe a douse of cold water. Maybe an ice bucket, because then he could stuff his heart that was beating with love and amusement for her in it, too.

'Do you want to come in?' she asked when he opened his eyes.

'Yes. No. Yes?' He honestly didn't know. 'I have stuff to say.'

'You don't know where you want to say them?'

'I…think I might get distracted inside.'

'Why?' She leaned against the frame. 'Never mind. It doesn't matter.' Folded her arms. 'Say the stuff.'

'You were right,' he blurted out, because he was avoiding her chest and her eyes and because it was bubbling up inside. 'I take responsibility when I don't have to. But I've been doing it my whole life. With my mom, I mean. She needed me, so I don't know if I didn't have to—'

'You didn't,' she interrupted. 'You chose to. Because she's your mother and you love her, and the way that you show you care is by helping. Doing. Protecting.'

He frowned. Her lips curved.

'Maybe I have some stuff to say, too. But please, continue.'

'Very gracious of you.' He cleared his throat. Tried to remember where he was. 'I blamed myself. For her being sick. I had no reason to. She never made me feel that way. But in my kid brain I thought that if I hadn't been there, hadn't been born, she wouldn't have got sick and—'

She'd moved forward, so when he stopped because of the pain, because he needed to, she took his hands. Slowly, she put them on the base of her waist. Cupped his face.

'Just look at me,' she said. 'Look at me and tell me what you need to say.'

She must have woven a spell on him because he said, 'I don't know why I blamed myself. Maybe because my father said we could make things easier for her. If we could make it easier, we could make it harder. Maybe I already had made it harder. Maybe I was the cause of it?'

'Oh, Ben,' she whispered, lowering her hands to his chest. 'She got sick when you were too young to understand it. Of course your father telling you to help her made you think you needed to because you contributed to it.'

'"Maybe", not "of course",' he replied, though he appreciated the understanding. 'But it happened. The responsibility of caring for her was heavy, but I got stronger. Too strong. I carried it even when she didn't want me to. She might not have wanted me to carry it at all.' He shrugged. 'I did the same with you.'

She sucked in her cheeks, releasing it before her mouth fully became a pout.

'Remember earlier, when I said I have some things to say, too?'

'You mean a few minutes ago? Yeah.'

She'd begun to walk her fingers up his chest. At his comment, she paused to pinch him.

'Okay, okay,' he said with a small laugh. 'No more wise-guy comments.'

'Good, because I need to be serious for a moment.' She took a breath: 'You need to learn how to balance it. Caring for someone, and protecting them so blindly that you do silly, unnecessary things.'

'I know. Lex—'

'Shh,' she said, putting a finger on his lips. 'I'm not done yet.'

He nodded for her to continue.

'I need to learn how to not push you away because I'm scared.' She knitted her brows. 'It might be easier for me because I'm tired of doing it. Protecting myself… It's so much work. It takes so much energy to keep up the shield and to be careful.' She leaned her head against his chest. 'And I'm tired of doing that and of being pregnant.' She lifted her head. 'Do you know how tiring it is to be pregnant? I still have five months to go. I can't do it all.'

He bit his lip to keep from laughing.

'Yeah, okay, laugh at the pregnant lady.'

'I'm not laughing at you,' he said, catching her hand and pressing it to his lips. 'I'm happy. It sounds like you're telling me you want me to do the protecting for you.'

'Did you hear nothing of what I just said?'

'Yeah, but I'm still me. I'm still going to want to protect you. But I'm going to try,' he said sincerely. 'It's not healthy. I know that. I know the situation at home with my family isn't healthy, too. It's…it's safe.'

'For them,' she said gently. 'For you, it's familiar. But it's hard. And every time you see your mother in pain, you'll think it's because of you.'

'I can't snap my fingers and have it disappear.'

'I know that. I'm not asking you to. But I am telling you to be intentional. If you want to be happy, you need to move away from safe. You need to stop taking responsibility for people and things that don't need you to do that for them. Or that, quite simply, aren't your responsibility.' She ran her hands up and down his arms. 'Your mother's illness isn't your fault. Nor is my pregnancy. Or my problems.'

He inhaled, then exhaled. Again, when the first time he did made him feel lighter. He hadn't realised until that night how much he'd blamed himself for a range of things. This conversation made him think that he'd gone along with Alexa's plan because he'd blamed himself in some way for how Lee had treated her. He wanted to make up for it, though he couldn't possibly do that when he wasn't the cause of the treatment.

He saw it now. And, as he told Alexa, it wouldn't immediately go away. Especially not with his mother, where things were more complicated. But he promised her he'd try, so he would.

'Does this mean you're not pushing me away any more?'

'What do you think?'

He smiled when she bumped her belly lightly against him, reminding him of how close they were.

'I need you to say it.'

She rolled her eyes. 'You're annoying.'

'But you love me.'

She hesitated, but her eyes were fierce and sure when she nodded. 'I do.'

Who knew such simple words could set off such intense emotion in him?

'I love you, too,' he said softly.

'I know. You've loved me from the day you first saw me.'

'An exaggeration, I think.'

'I could see it in the way you looked at me. You were such a sucker.'

They were still debating when she led him into her flat. Smiling, he closed the door.

EPILOGUE

Four years later

'Do you know what's worse than having twin toddlers?'

Benjamin didn't look over, too busy trying to get Tori, his daughter, off her brother. 'Tori, come on. You know you're bigger than Tavier.'

'Don't you dare get off your brother because you feel sorry for him,' Alexa said, kneeling on the sofa and looking over its back at them. 'He needs to learn.'

'You're encouraging this?' Benjamin asked.

'He loves it.'

Tavier gave a giggle just then. Benjamin threw up his hands. 'Honestly. I was trying to help you.'

Tavier grinned, and pulled his sister's hair. She responded by sitting on him. All things considered, they were playing fair.

'You haven't answered my question.'

He went to join her on the sofa. 'I'm too tired to pretend to remember what you asked.'

'What's worse than having twin toddlers?'

'Is this a riddle?'

He pulled her against him. Because she'd been kneeling, she had no way of resisting. Not that she would have resisted, he knew. Their marriage was a lot of debating, teasing—she was still talking about how he'd never found her handkerchief in his room—but none of it had to do with touching.

'It's not a riddle,' she said.

'A puzzle, then?'

'Same thing.'

'I don't think so.'

'Ben,' she said, taking his face in her hands. She did it whenever she was being serious with him. After four years together, two of them in marriage, it had happened all of four times. So he knew she was serious.

'What's worse than twin toddlers?' he repeated. 'I'm not sure. Our restaurants failing.'

'Our restaurants aren't failing.'

Of course they weren't, but he'd needed to say it because he needed to get over that fear. It was still there, though he'd been running In the Rough for three years now. It was still competing with Infinity, but somehow that competition didn't matter, since they were both doing what they loved. They both seemed to be good at it, too.

Of course they weren't failing.

'I give up.'

'So easily.'

'Baby.'

'Fine. What's worse than twin toddlers…is another baby.'

He blinked. 'I'm not sure I follow.'

'I'm pregnant, dummy.'

'You're…' He trailed off. Looked at the twins. 'But they're only three.'

'They'll be four when the baby gets here.'

'You're sure?'

'I'm pretty good at maths,' she said, rolling her eyes.

Now he rolled his. 'No. I meant, are you sure you're pregnant?'

'Doctor's results came back this morning.'

Because he had no words, he drew her in, holding her so damn tightly. Their lives together had been tough. Their family situations weren't easy. His father had passed away round about the same time he'd got the restaurant, but his mother had refused to live with him and Alexa. She'd found herself an assisted care facility, visited them occasionally, and Benjamin had had a tough time accepting that. Alexa had, a year after Lee had promised not to contact her, agreed to see him. It had taken them a lot of work to get to where they were now: Lee's monthly visits.

But all of that had been okay because they'd had one another. Their family, their kids… It was a life he'd never imagined. It was better than anything Alexa had imagined, she'd told him one night after the twins were born and they were staring at them.

'I can't believe they're yours.'

'Ours,' Alexa had replied, gripping his hand. 'You were here through everything, and you know you love them as much as I do. They're ours.'

She'd changed his life. And now she was doing it again.

'You're the best thing that ever happened to me,' he whispered.

'Wait until we're outnumbered before you say that.'

But she was smiling when he pulled away.

'We're having another baby,' he said.

'We are.' She leaned forward and kissed him. 'I love you.'

'I love you.'

A vase crashed as the twins rolled against the table. He and Alexa both jumped up, but the vase had been on the kitchen table, and the twins had knocked the coffee table, which had then knocked the vase to the ground in the kitchen, away from them. Their children were unharmed. The vase? Not so much. Tori and Tavier stared at them with wide eyes.

'I guess this means they love us, too,' Alexa said when they each had a twin in their arms.

'What a life.'

'What a life,' she repeated, and kissed him again.

* * * * *

A CHANCE FOR THE RANCHER

BRENDA HARLEN

This one is for Cheryl Paterson—
an amazing mum, extraordinary teacher,
fabulous friend and the most kick-ass woman
I’ve ever had the privilege to know. XO

Chapter One

Watching for the arrival of the veterinarian, Patrick Stafford exhaled a relieved breath when he finally spotted a vehicle coming down the long driveway. He didn't recognize either the mud-splattered pickup that parked beside the barn or the woman who exited the vehicle, and the rancher felt a brief twinge of disappointment that his injured horse would have to wait a while longer to be tended. But as a man who appreciated women, his interest was immediately piqued.

She was tall and slender, wearing a sheepskin-lined leather jacket unzipped over a plaid flannel shirt tucked into slim-fitting jeans with a wide brown belt around her waist and well-worn cowboy boots on her feet. Which only meant she was dressed like most of the other women who lived on the ranches that dotted the countryside of Haven, Nevada, and didn't begin to explain why he found himself so drawn to her.

He continued his perusal anyway: long brown hair that was tied away from her face in a neat braid that fell to the middle of her back. As she drew nearer, he realized that her hair wasn't actually brown but auburn, and that it shone with hints of bronze and copper in the afternoon sun. Her eyes were the color of dark chocolate and fringed by long lashes. Her mouth was unsmiling but temptingly shaped. And as his gaze lingered on her lips for just a moment, Patrick realized it had been a long time since he'd kissed a woman—or even wanted to.

He pushed the wayward thought aside to focus on his visitor. "Can I help you?"

"Actually, I'm here to help you." Now her lips curved into a smile and she proffered a hand. "Dr. Langley."

He shook it automatically, noting the long, slender (and ringless!) fingers, neatly trimmed, unpainted nails and firm grip. "Patrick Stafford," he replied automatically. Then her words registered, and he frowned. "You're not Dr. Langley."

"Well, I don't carry a copy of my diploma with me, but I can show you my driver's license," she offered, shifting the backpack he hadn't noticed was on her shoulder so that he could now see the patch bearing the letter *V* superimposed on the staff of Asclepius—the immediately recognizable symbol of her profession.

Apparently she was *a* vet, but he still felt confident in asserting, "I remember Dr. Langley from his visits to Crooked Creek Ranch when I was a kid, and you're definitely not him."

"That would have been my father," she said. "Dr. *Bruce* Langley. I'm Dr. *Brooke* Langley."

Which made sense, as the other Dr. Langley had been older, with salt-and-pepper hair and a stocky build that promised he was capable of handling the ranch animals that were the foundation of his rural practice.

"Where's Ranger?" she asked.

"I might not have been clear when I called," he said now. "But Ranger is a twelve-hundred-pound stallion and rather ornery right now."

"This isn't my first rodeo," she assured him. "It's also not the first time I've been out here to tend to one of Gus Sterling's animals."

"They aren't his animals anymore," he pointed out. "They're mine."

"Right now, I'm more interested in Ranger's injury than in who's paying the bill, but if you want to wait for my father—who's currently tied up out at Whispering Pines helping to birth a breech foal—that's entirely up to you."

Her response didn't eliminate all his doubts, but he decided that if Gus had trusted her with his horses then Patrick could, too. He slid open the barn door and gestured for her to enter.

The heels of her boots clicked on concrete as she made her way down the center aisle to the stallion's stall, but it was the subtle sway of her hips and sweet curve of her derriere that held Patrick's attention. And though he regretted the circumstances that had required him to contact the veterinarian office, he wasn't sorry that Dr. Brooke Langley had answered his call.

Haven wasn't so small that everyone knew everyone else, but there were usually only two or three degrees of separation between one person and the next. As he'd already mentioned to Brooke, he remembered her father from his visits to Crooked Creek Ranch, but he had no memory of her. And though she must have attended the same high school he did—because there was only one in Haven—he drew a blank there, too.

But Ranger seemed to know her, and Patrick was reassured by the animal's acknowledgment of her presence. The stallion's long nose appeared over the door of his enclosure as she approached and actually seemed to nod, as if in greeting.

Brooke lifted a hand to rub the horse's cheek, and Ranger whinnied softly.

Patrick stood back, both mesmerized by the wordless interaction and a little terrified for the woman who boldly opened the gate and stepped inside the stall. He'd guess that she was about five feet eight inches tall, but next to the horse, she looked small.

And breakable.

Of course, anyone who'd spent any amount of time around horses had to respect the powerful strength of an animal whose muscular legs and flashing hooves could do serious damage, even inadvertently. But Brooke didn't hesitate to enter the enclosure, and Ranger didn't shy away from her presence. And somehow, her quiet confidence only added to her allure.

"How are you doing, Ranger?"

Her tone was quiet, soothing, but the hands stroking the animal were steady and sure. Everything she said and did seemed to reassure the animal that she was in charge. Her quiet murmuring trailed off when she crouched down far enough to examine the wound. After a moment's hesitation, she resumed her monologue and continued her study.

When she rose up again and turned to Patrick, her voice was as hard as her gaze. "He's cut all the way through the coronary band. How did this happen?"

"I don't know," he admitted. "I put the horses out in the paddock this morning but somehow Ranger got out and—"

"Somehow?" she interjected.

"I thought I latched the gate, but when I went back to check on the horses, it was swinging free."

"Is Ranger the only one who got out?"

"No, but he's the only one who got hurt."

"I'm going to need more light," she said, reaching over the door for Ranger's halter and lead rope.

It was a testament to Ranger's training—and reassuring to Patrick—that the animal didn't balk in any way as she secured the halter and led him to the cross-tie area, where textured rubber mats provided stable footing for both the animal and the vet, and additional lighting illuminated the area even in the dark of night.

He watched as she opened her pack and began rifling through the contents. "He was favoring his right foreleg when I found him."

"No wonder." She unwrapped a syringe, slid the

point of the needle into the vial and measured out the medication.

"This is a tetanus antitoxin," she told Patrick. "He's also going to need a shot of penicillin to combat any infection. Then I'm going to flush the wound and pack it with ichthammol ointment."

"What can I do?" he asked, feeling responsible and guilty and wanting to help.

"You know how to make coffee?" she asked.

He almost breathed a sigh of relief that she'd assigned him a task he could handle. He nodded. "What do you take in it?"

"Black is fine."

"Coming right up," he promised.

While Patrick was gone, Brooke took her time tending to Ranger's injury. She knew the stallion had to be in pain, but at least he seemed to understand that she was there to help. Though initially agitated and skittish—as any wounded creature would be—he stoically endured her ministrations.

In her experience, most animals tolerated necessary treatment if they were given an opportunity to understand that the hands poking and prodding wanted to heal. Sure, she'd endured occasional kicks and nips—and once even a nasty headbutt from a nanny goat that resulted in a concussion—but the veterinarian-patient relationship was generally one of mutual respect and understanding. And if she was ever in doubt, she sedated the animal in the interest of their mutual safety.

She wasn't worried about Ranger. Though pain could

make any man or beast unpredictable, he was a gentle soul. She suspected he was also confused by the change in his circumstances, as evidenced by the departure of the ranch's former owner and the arrival of Patrick Stafford in his stead, and her heart went out to the animal.

"I can't believe Gus left you behind," she lamented aloud. "But maybe there aren't a lot of places to stable a horse in a retirement community in Arizona. And a horse born and bred in Nevada probably wouldn't like Arizona much, anyway."

She'd heard rumors about the old rancher selling, but it was only when she'd turned into the gravel drive and saw the freshly painted barn bearing the new logo of Silver Star Ranch that she realized they were true. A couple of rough years had resulted in the Sterling Ranch teetering on the edge of bankruptcy and one more would have pushed it over, so she could hardly blame Gus for looking for a way out.

But she did blame him for selling to Patrick Stafford—and she definitely blamed the new owner for the horse's nasty injury. The man obviously knew nothing about ranching and even less about caring for the animals that had apparently been entrusted to him as part of the deal.

A deal that would turn the failing ranch into a tourist attraction.

A dude ranch, for Christ's sake.

As if she needed any more proof that Patrick Stafford was just a bored rich guy playing at being a cowboy and opening his doors to other bored rich guys who wanted to do the same thing.

It was only too bad he didn't appear to have the soft,

pale body of a man who'd spent his life behind a desk and under artificial light. Instead, he was tall with broad shoulders and lean hips, looking very much like the rancher he was pretending to be.

And if the checkered shirt with the polo pony embroidered on the chest pocket and distressed designer-label jeans detracted a little from the authenticity of the cowboy image, he was handsome enough to compensate, with sun-bleached sandy-brown hair, tanned skin, surprisingly green eyes, a straight nose, thin lips and a strong jaw shadowed with stubble. But aside from his hard body and striking good looks, he possessed an aura of confidence that added to his overall appeal.

Of course, Patrick Stafford had probably been born with swagger. Certainly he'd had it even in high school. Though she hadn't known him back then, she'd known who he was, because his mother was a Blake and the Blakes were the wealthiest family in Haven, Nevada. And Blake Mining was the town's single biggest employer—which made her wonder why he'd chosen to leave the family business to embark on this new venture. Not that she was going to ask. After all, his rationale had nothing to do with her reason for being at his ranch.

And though Brooke wasn't ordinarily the type of woman who got all tongue-tied or weak-kneed in the presence of a handsome man, she'd definitely felt a quiver of something low in her belly when Patrick looked at her. It had been a long time since she'd experienced such an immediate attraction to a man—eight years, in fact—and she was unnerved by her response to this man now. Thankfully, she was a lot older and wiser than she'd been eight years earlier, and she had a much better understanding of what was at stake.

So she pushed her personal observations of the rancher aside to focus on her task. When she was done, Ranger gently bumped her shoulder with his nose, as if to say *thank you.*

She rubbed her palm over his cheek. "You're very welcome. But try to remember—as tempting as unlatched gates might be, it's not safe to wander off on your own."

He blew out a breath, as if to sigh, and she smiled.

"Do you always talk to your patients?" Patrick asked curiously.

Brooke hadn't heard him return and started now at the sound of his voice, but she responded to the question without missing a beat.

"Always," she confirmed. "I mean, I'm no Doctor Dolittle, but I believe the animals understand my tone and intent if not the actual words."

"Ranger certainly seems to," he acknowledged. Then, offering the mug he carried, he added, "Your coffee."

"Oh, um, thanks."

She took the mug and lifted it to her lips. It was strong and hot, just the way she liked it, though she hadn't wanted the drink so much as she'd wanted him not hovering while she tended to the injured horse.

"I was wondering about something you said earlier," he commented now.

"I said a lot of things—and held a lot more back," she admitted.

He smiled, and *damn* if that smile didn't do funny things to her insides.

Older and wiser, she reminded herself.

And with so much more to lose.

"You said that you were more interested in Ranger than the man paying the bill," he said, as if to prod her memory.

"You're still going to get a bill," she promised.

"I would expect so," he said. "But are you at least a little bit interested?"

She frowned as she took another sip of coffee. "What?"

"Being 'more interested' in Ranger suggests you're still interested in me. Doesn't it?" he asked hopefully.

"I'm definitely interested in being paid," she told him. "But Larissa—the clinic manager—will send you the bill."

"You're sidestepping my question," he noted.

"Actually, I'm waiting for you to stop talking so I can give you instructions for Ranger's follow-up care."

He inclined his head, a silent invitation to her to continue.

"His dressing will need to be changed daily until the wound is healed," she told him. "Do you have any ichthammol ointment?"

"I'm not sure," he said.

"I'll leave some and add it to the bill," she decided.

"What about changing the dressing? Will you come back to do that?" he asked.

She shook her head. "That shouldn't be necessary."

"Let me rephrase," he said. "Can *you please* come back to do that?"

She was surprised by the request. "Do you have any

idea what it will cost to have me come back out here to change a bandage?"

"I don't care what it costs," he told her.

Of course he didn't.

And because he didn't, she shrugged. "In that case, I'll see you tomorrow."

"Thanks." His quick smile conveyed relief and gratitude. "And how about tonight?"

"He'll be fine tonight," she assured him.

"I wasn't asking for Ranger," he said. "I was asking if *I* could see you tonight."

"No."

"Just for a drink," he cajoled.

Then he smiled again—this time a deliberately slow and sensual curve of his lips that had undoubtedly melted the resistance of many other women. Thankfully, experience had immunized Brooke against such obvious ploys.

She hoped.

"Or dinner, if you prefer," he said, when she didn't immediately respond.

"No and no," she replied, wondering how it was possible that he didn't already have a date lined up. Because it wasn't only a Friday—it was Valentine's Day.

Not that the occasion was a big deal to Brooke. It didn't matter to her that she wouldn't get chocolates or flowers, because she would be spending the night with the most important guy in her life.

"Tomorrow, then?" he suggested as an alternative.

She was flattered. And flustered.

But definitely *not* interested.

She shook her head. "No."

Still, he wasn't dissuaded. "Are you seeing someone?"

"How is that any of your business?"

"I'm curious about my competition," he said.

"There's no competition," she told him. "I'm not dating anyone right now and I'm not interested in dating anyone, especially not a pretend cowboy who doesn't have the sense to latch a paddock gate."

"Ouch," he said, feigning hurt.

Or maybe his pride really was wounded.

She didn't imagine a man as handsome and wealthy as Patrick Stafford heard the word *no* very often.

And perhaps her response had been a little harsh, not to mention unprofessional.

Yes, it frustrated her that an innocent animal had paid the price for his mistake, and it annoyed her that even now he didn't seem to realize there could be lasting repercussions for Ranger as a result of the injury. But she knew as well as anyone that busy people sometimes missed little details.

An unlatched gate.

A loose stirrup.

An expired condom.

Each one had repercussions.

"I'm sorry," she said. "That was uncalled for and possibly unfair."

"If you were really sorry, you'd offer to buy me a drink," he said, adding a wink for good measure.

She was grateful he'd accepted her apology—and irritated by his inability to take a hint.

"I'm not going to do that," she said. "But I will give you the ichthammol ointment at cost."

"Of course, I have no idea what 'cost' is," he acknowledged.

"About thirty percent less than you'd pay at the feed store," she told him, as she returned her equipment to her pack and zipped it up.

"A bargain," he decided. "Maybe I could put those savings toward a meal at The Home Station with you."

"You really don't understand the word *no*, do you?"

"I understand the word," he assured her. "I just thought, since it's getting close to dinnertime and we both have to eat, we might as well eat together."

She glanced at her watch. "Actually, it *is* almost dinnertime, which means that I just might make it home in time to eat with Brendan for a change."

He frowned at that. "Who's Brendan?"

"My seven-year-old son."

Chapter Two

Well, *that* was an unexpected revelation.

Patrick took a mental step back. He didn't realize he'd taken an actual physical step, too, until she called attention to his instinctive reaction.

"Yeah, that's the usual response from guys like you," she said.

"What response? And what do you mean—guys like me?"

"The retreat," she said, answering only his first question.

He frowned. "What are you talking about?"

"You literally took a step back, as if the responsibilities of parenting might be contagious."

"I did not," he denied. Except he realized that he was

standing a little farther away from her now. "Or if I did, I didn't mean anything by it."

"It doesn't matter," she said dismissively. "At least now we both know where the other one stands."

"And where is it that you think I stand?"

"As far away from any potential complications as you can possibly get."

He wished he could deny it—or at least point out that she didn't know him or anything about him. But while he often used flattery and charm to convey his interest in a woman, he tried to always be honest, too. Although he'd dated a lot of different women in his thirty-two years, the one thing those women all had in common was that they were no more interested in a long-term relationship than he was. And even if he did meet someone who might make him reconsider, the ranch was his priority now and for the foreseeable future.

He didn't have the time or—to be perfectly honest—any interest in a committed relationship. And he sure as hell wasn't looking to be a stand-in father to someone else's kid, because that was a scenario that *screamed* "complication" to him.

And while Brooke Langley might be the sexiest female to cross his path in months, she wasn't what he wanted. Even if the pressure behind his zipper suggested otherwise.

"I was just...surprised," he finally responded. "And now I'm curious... Is your son's father from around here?" he asked, wondering if the man might be someone he knew.

"Brendan doesn't have a father."

His brows lifted at that.

"The man who contributed to his DNA has no interest in being a dad," she explained. "He made that perfectly clear when I told him I was pregnant."

"I'm sorry," he said automatically.

"There's no reason to be," she told him. "He got his freedom and I got Brendan. And since my work is finished here, I really do want to get home to him now."

"But you'll be back tomorrow?" he said, not really a question so much as a reminder.

"I'll be back tomorrow," she confirmed.

He nodded, already looking forward to seeing her again.

As much as she loved her job, Brooke always looked forward to the end of the day because she loved coming home to her little boy even more. From the very first moment he was placed in her arms, her heart had filled with so much love, she'd been certain it would burst right out of her chest.

It wasn't always easy being a single mom, but she never regretted her decision to keep her baby. Of course, she was fortunate to have the unwavering support of her parents—and the luxury of living with Brendan in the apartment above their detached garage. The space was a little on the small side, but plenty big enough for the two of them, with two bedrooms, a four-piece bath, a decent-size family room and a modest kitchen with a breakfast bar.

The kitchen was the focus of her thoughts now, as she tried to remember what ingredients she had to put together for a meal. She was pretty sure there was ground beef in the freezer, and tacos weren't only quick and easy, they were one of Brendan's favorites.

She thought wistfully, for just a moment, about Patrick's invitation to dinner. It would be nice to go out to a restaurant where someone else prepared the food and cleaned up afterward. Of course, if that was really what she wanted, she could take Brendan out to eat at Diggers' tonight. The occasional treat at the popular bar and grill was within her budget even if a meal at The Home Station was not.

She pulled into the driveway beside her parents' house and parked in her usual spot in front of the garage. But she headed to the main house rather than her own apartment, knowing her son would be there. His school bus stopped in front of the house and, when he got off it at the end of the day, he knew to go see Gramma if his mom's truck wasn't in the driveway.

Brooke entered her childhood home through the side door and sat on the bench in the mudroom to remove her boots and hang her coat before stepping into the kitchen, where her mother was at the stove, stirring something in a pan. Though Sandra Langley had recently celebrated her sixtieth birthday, she still looked like the bride she'd been in the photos taken on her wedding day. There were some discernible changes, of course, the most obvious being that she wore her hair much shorter now, in a chin-length bob. But the shiny auburn tresses were the same color they'd been back then (thanks to a little assistance from Wendy at the Clip 'N' Curl), and her dark brown eyes still sparkled with humor.

"Mmm," Brooke said, sniffing the air as she crossed the room to kiss her mother's cheek. "Something smells good."

"It doesn't smell like much of anything yet," Sandra remarked. "I'm only browning ground beef."

"Well, it smells good to me," she insisted.

"You worked through lunch again, didn't you?"

"The clinic was packed," she said.

"You need to eat," her mom admonished. "How can you take care of the animals if you don't take care of yourself?"

"I do eat," she said. "In fact, I'll eat whatever you're cooking, if we're invited to stay for dinner."

"Tacos," Sandra said. "And of course you're welcome to stay."

She grinned. "Were the tacos Brendan's suggestion?"

"He did mention that he hadn't had them in *for-ev-er.*" Her mother stretched out the word to emphasize it the way Brooke was sure her son had done.

"Which is why I'd planned to make them for him when we got home," she said.

"Now you don't have to," Sandra told her.

"You spoil us," Brooke said.

Her mom smiled. "It's a mother's prerogative to spoil her kids—and grandkids. And since your father isn't home yet, having the two of you here for dinner means I won't have to eat alone."

"Is Dad still at Whispering Pines?"

Sandra shook her head. "He was on his way home when he got a call from Frieda Zimmerman asking him to stop by and take a look at Cupcake."

Brooke huffed out a breath. "She came into the clinic with Cupcake today. I gave the cat a thorough exam and assured Mrs. Zimmerman there was nothing wrong with her pet aside from the fact that she's fourteen years old."

"And for all of the fourteen years that Frieda's had the cat, she's been taking her to your dad for care," her mom pointed out.

"Sometimes I wonder if inviting me to help out in his practice has been any help to Dad at all."

"Of course it has," Sandra assured her. "And your dad is so proud and excited to work with you."

"Unfortunately, his clients are a little less enthusiastic when I show up instead."

"Why do I get the feeling you're talking about someone other than Frieda Zimmerman?"

"I'll fill you in on all the details after I hear about Brendan's Valentine's Day party at school. Where is he?"

"In your dad's office, doing his homework."

"He loves sitting in Grandpa's big chair," Brooke acknowledged.

"I think he loves spinning in Grandpa's big chair," her mother said, smiling. "Just like you used to do when you were a kid."

Brooke leaned in and gave her mom a hug, then went to find her son.

As she made her way down the hall, she found herself reflecting again on her good fortune. She knew there was no way she could do what she did without the support of her family—especially her mother. Sandra had been there not only to offer support and advice throughout

Brooke's pregnancy, but she'd given up her part-time job as a vet tech after Brendan was born so that she could take care of her grandson while Brooke finished college.

Though Brendan was in school full-time now, Brooke found that she relied on her mother just as much now for support and advice. She had friends in town, of course, but motherhood, school and then work had caused their paths to diverge long ago. As a result, her mom was probably her closest friend and confidante.

Pausing outside the door of her dad's office, she peeked in to confirm that Brendan was in the big leather chair, spinning, his hands catching and releasing the edge of the desktop as leverage to keep the chair turning.

She stepped into the open doorway and fisted her hands on her hips.

It took three more complete circles before Brendan noticed her, but when he did, he immediately grabbed hold of the desk with both hands to stop his momentum. He cast his eyes down, his cheeks flushed with guilt—or maybe it was excitement that was responsible for the color.

"What does Gramma say to you about spinning in Grandpa's chair?" she asked him.

"Not to let Grandpa catch me doing it," he said.

"Oh, really?" Brooke had to press her lips together to hold back her smile.

When she was a kid, she'd been told—firmly and repeatedly—not to do it, but apparently there were different rules for grandchildren.

"Or you could *not* spin in the chair. Then you wouldn't have to worry about getting caught," she pointed out to him.

"But it's fun to spin," he said and tipped his head back to smile at her, showing off the gap between his teeth where he'd recently lost both his central incisors.

He'd been sad when the first one started to loosen, until he learned that he could leave his tooth under his pillow and the tooth fairy would exchange it for money. Since then, there had been a few times that she'd caught him trying to wiggle teeth that weren't loose. *Just checking* was always his ready excuse.

"How come you're late today?" he asked her now.

She lifted a hand to ruffle his shaggy mop of hair. "I had to stop by Mr. Sterling's ranch to check on an injured horse."

"Did you make him better?" Brendan asked.

With both a mother and grandfather in the business of caring for animals, it probably wasn't surprising that he was so instinctively kindhearted and empathetic. Or that he'd announced, shortly after his seventh birthday, his intention to be the next Dr. B. Langley.

Brooke knew it was likely he'd change his mind a dozen times before he went to college, but it pleased her to know that, at least right now, her little boy looked up to her and wanted to follow in her footsteps.

"I gave him some medicine and bandaged his wound, but it's going to take a little time before he's all better," she said, mentally crossing her fingers that the stallion would make a full and complete recovery. "How was your party?"

"It was great," he said. "I got a valentine from everyone in my class—and *two* from Livia and Ruby. Do you want to see them?"

"Of course I want to see them."

He reached into his backpack and pulled out a brown paper bag labeled with his name in carefully printed letters and decorated all over with glittery pink and red hearts. He turned the bag upside down over the desk to dump out the contents.

"That's a lot of valentines," Brooke said, biting her lip to keep from smiling.

"I know," he gleefully agreed and proceeded to go through the pile, one by one, reading the traditional catchphrases or silly jokes printed on each of the cards and then telling her who it was from. Thankfully there were only eighteen kids in his second-grade class.

When he was done and the valentines were all stuffed back in the bag, she noticed the page of math problems on the desk. "Miss Karen gave you homework today?"

"Yeah." He made a face. "Math."

"I thought you liked math." She propped a hip against the corner of the desk.

"But this is *bo-or-ring*," he said, drawing out the word for emphasis.

She glanced at the half-completed worksheet. "It might be boring but knowing how to count money is important."

"I know how to count money."

"Do you? Because you circled the two quarters as representing fifty cents."

"Two quarters is fifty cents," he said confidently.

"But that's not the only grouping of coins that adds up to fifty cents," she pointed out. "And the instructions say to circle *all the groups* of coins that add up to the total amount given."

Brendan studied the problem for a moment, then drew a second circle around the picture of five dimes and a third around the image showing a quarter with two dimes and five pennies.

"Good job," she told him. "Now I'm going to let you finish that up while I help Gramma get dinner ready."

"Are we staying for dinner?" he asked hopefully.

"That's the plan."

"Yes!" He added a fist pump for good measure. "Gramma's making tacos."

"I know," she said.

"I *love* tacos."

"I know that, too," she said and dropped a kiss on the top of his head before heading back to the kitchen.

As she passed the dining room, she spotted the vase of long-stemmed red roses set on top of a crocheted doily in the center of the antique table.

The first year her parents were married, Bruce had apparently bought a single red rose for Sandra, to symbolize their first Valentine's Day as husband and wife. The second year he'd bought two roses, then continued to add to the number each successive year, so Brooke didn't need to count the gorgeous red blooms to know there were thirty-seven stuffed into the vase this year.

It was a lovely tradition and reassured her that happily-ever-afters were possible, even if the prospect of her own continued to be elusive. Not that she was actually looking for one right now, because she had different priorities as a working single mom. But maybe…someday.

"So tell me about your day," Sandra urged, after Brooke had washed up and began grating the block of cheddar she'd taken out of the fridge.

"You mean the part where I had my credentials questioned at the Silver Star?"

Her mother frowned. "Who would dare question your credentials?"

"The new owner."

"Patrick Stafford bought Gus's place, didn't he?"

Brooke nodded. "Though I have to wonder why. The man obviously doesn't know the first thing about taking care of animals."

"He must know something," Sandra said. "After all, his family was raising cattle on Crooked Creek long before gold and silver were discovered in the hills."

"Well, he didn't know to make sure the paddock gate was latched, and his horses got out and one of them was injured."

Her mom winced in sympathy. "How bad was it?"

Because her mother had been a vet's wife for thirty-seven years and worked as a vet tech in her husband's clinic for a lot of that time, Brooke didn't hesitate to share the details of her assessment and treatment of the stallion.

"At least Patrick had the good sense to call someone qualified to provide medical attention," Sandra remarked.

"He thought he was calling Dad," Brooke reminded her.

"Did you take care of the injury?"

She nodded.

"So now he knows he can call you instead." Her mother's eyes took on a speculative gleam. "Or maybe he'll call you even if he doesn't need help with a sick or injured animal."

"Don't go there," Brooke urged.

"Why not? He's handsome, charming and—"

"And he's well aware of his own attributes," she interjected.

"Ahh," her mom said, understanding. "He already hit on you, didn't he?"

"Yeah, but it wasn't too hard to shut him down," Brooke said, as she dumped the grated cheese into a bowl. "All it took was mention of my seven-year-old son."

And though she hadn't been the least bit surprised by Patrick's instinctive reaction, she had been the teensiest bit disappointed. And that reaction *had* surprised her.

"There's no doubt how much you love Brendan, but you've got to stop using him as a shield," Sandra admonished.

Brooke frowned at that. "How is being up-front about my status as a single mother using my child as a shield?"

"Maybe it's more like a sword," her mom decided. "A preemptive attack against any expression of interest."

"If a guy's interest can be struck down that easily, he's not someone I want to be with."

"That's probably a fair point," Sandra allowed. "But one of these days you're going to meet someone who isn't so easily dissuaded."

"I hope I do," she said.

But she already knew that Patrick Stafford wasn't that man.

So why was she looking forward to seeing him again?

Chapter Three

Patrick had gone off to college with the security of knowing there would be a job for him at Blake Mining as soon as he graduated. He'd never anticipated that, after only six years—and five different jobs—he'd feel trapped within the walls of his executive office. Or that he'd impulsively decide to walk away from the family business and buy a failing cattle ranch.

But that was what he'd done and, for the past four months, he'd lived and breathed the Silver Star. He'd known what changes and improvements he'd wanted to make, and he'd spent a lot of hours and even more money making them. He was determined to ensure the ranch was a success, to prove—to himself as much as his parents—that he could make it on his own in the real world. During that time, he'd been too busy to venture into town looking for female companionship—and likely too exhausted to do anything if he'd found it.

But he was starting to feel pretty good about the progress he'd made, pleased with the way everything was finally starting to come together. Or he had been until Dr. Brooke Langley called him a pretend cowboy and blamed him for Ranger's injury.

And *damn it*, she was right. If he'd latched the gate properly, the horses wouldn't have been running wild and the stallion wouldn't have been hurt. But her blunt assessment didn't just add to the weight of guilt he was already feeling; it rekindled his own doubts, further fueled by the incessant questions and criticisms of his parents, who were none too happy about his decision to leave Blake Mining and "play at being a rancher."

Maybe he was making a mistake. Maybe he would someday regret putting so much time and effort into the ranch. But that day wasn't today, and he'd come too far to back down now. He wasn't just invested but committed, and wouldn't the sexy vet be surprised to hear him confess that?

Except that he had to stop thinking of Brooke as the sexy vet and start remembering that she was a woman with serious responsibilities. A sexy single mom.

A mom he'd like to—

Whoa!

He immediately put a tight rein on *that* wayward thought.

No way was he going there.

Instead, he decided to go into town to grab a bite,

maybe have a couple of drinks, and clear all thoughts of the lovely Brooke Langley from his mind.

He wasn't looking for company when he took a seat at the bar at Diggers' Bar & Grill. And if he'd realized it was February 14, he likely wouldn't have ventured into town. But since he was here—and hungry—he ordered a draft and a pound of hot wings.

He'd taken the first sip of his beer when a curvy blonde hopped up onto the stool beside him and nudged her shoulder against his. "Hey there, handsome."

"Trinity, hi." He'd met the dental hygienist at a Fourth of July barbecue hosted by mutual friends a few years back, and they'd immediately hit it off. They'd had some good times together before going their separate ways, and when their paths had crossed again several months later, they'd enjoyed getting reacquainted.

They'd repeated the same song and dance a few more times after that, though the last time he'd seen her, she'd told him that she was dating somebody and thought he might be *the one*. Though Patrick wasn't sure he believed in such things, he'd been happy for Trinity and wished her the best.

He glanced past her now, looking for the man who'd been her constant companion in recent months. "Where's Christopher?"

Her easy smile wavered. "We broke up three weeks ago."

"I'm sorry." His response was both automatic and sincere.

"Me, too. It sucks to be alone on Valentine's Day."

Skylar Gilmore, working the bar, set Patrick's order

of wings down, then asked Trinity, "What can I get you?"

"Hendrick's gin and tonic with two lime wedges and half a twist of lemon."

The order didn't surprise Patrick—Trinity had always been high-maintenance, but he suspected that behind Sky's smile, the bartender was rolling her eyes.

"You can add that to my tab," Patrick said, when Sky set the G&T in front of Trinity.

The bartender nodded.

"Thanks, but I'm not the type of woman to go home with a man just because he buys me a drink—you'll have to share some of those wings, too," Trinity said with a wink.

"I'm happy to share." He nudged the plate toward her. "But I'm not looking to take anyone home tonight."

Trinity seemed puzzled by his response. "Nobody goes to a bar on Valentine's Day because they want to be alone."

"To be honest, I didn't even realize it was Valentine's Day until I got here and saw the Sweetheart Specials on the menu," he told her.

She selected a wing from his plate, bit into it. "So how are things at the Silver Star?"

"Pretty good," he said, because he was trying to forget about Ranger's injury and he definitely didn't want to discuss it with Trinity. She was firmly in his parents' camp, disapproving of his decision to walk away from a lucrative office job to live the life of a cowboy.

"You don't think you're going to miss working at Blake Mining with your family?" she pressed.

"I'm looking forward to the challenge of something different," he said. Because he'd never admit to anyone, except maybe his sisters, that he'd been looking for a way out for the past couple of years—and he was so glad to have finally found it.

"Is that why you're done with me?" she asked.

"You were done with me first," he reminded her. "As soon as you met Christopher."

"Because he told me he was looking to settle down and start a family," she said. "At least you were always honest about what you wanted and didn't want."

"And what I want hasn't changed."

"But what I want has—at least for tonight." She dropped the chicken wing bone in the bowl and lifted her hand to her mouth to lick sauce off her thumb. Then she drew it into her mouth, holding his gaze as she sucked on the digit.

It was a deliberately provocative action and one that would likely have piqued his interest at any other point in time. But tonight…nothing.

Because tonight he couldn't stop thinking about Brooke.

When Brooke woke up Saturday morning, she found Brendan already settled in front of the television with a bowl of cold cereal in his lap. She marveled over the ability of his internal alarm clock to unerringly shift between weekdays and weekends. Monday through Friday, it was a struggle to wake him in the morning. But on Saturdays, her son was always out of bed at the crack of dawn to watch his favorite cartoons on TV.

It was a routine she was happy to share with him whenever she had a Saturday off from the clinic. And since today was one of those days, Brooke got herself a bowl of Frosted Flakes, poured milk over her cereal and carried her breakfast to the living room to sit on the sofa beside her son. But as she chewed, she had the feeling there was something else she was supposed to be doing.

Or maybe she was just anticipating, because even when she wasn't scheduled to work at the clinic, there was always the possibility that she'd get called in to deal with an emergency—or called out to one of the local ranches, as had happened yesterday. And though the calendar was blank—save for the notation to check on Ranger sometime later in the day—and her phone remained silent, she couldn't shake the feeling.

When she and Brendan were both finished eating, she set their empty bowls aside. He snuggled closer to her side then and tipped his head back to smile at her.

Being a mom wasn't always easy, but it was always worthwhile. Sure, it might be nice to have a partner to share her life, but she'd rather be alone than with a man who couldn't understand and respect that her son had to be her number one priority right now.

She rarely wasted any time thinking about Brendan's father anymore, because the boy she'd fallen in love with in her second year of vet school had stopped being relevant to her a long time ago. But every once in a while—or when someone else brought up the subject (and, yes, that was another strike against Patrick Stafford)—she found herself wondering how any man could walk away from his child. But for the most part, she focused her attention and efforts on being the best mom she could be, so that Brendan wouldn't think about the fact that he didn't have a dad—and wouldn't feel as if he was missing out even if he did think about it.

Brooke knew her son had a couple of friends at school who also lived with only one parent, so his situation wasn't really unique. Except that each of Mason's and Felipe's living arrangements had changed after their respective parents divorced, and each of the boys still had both parents in their lives. So she had no doubt the day would come when Brendan asked why he didn't spend weekends with his dad like Mason and Felipe did with theirs. She just didn't know how she'd answer when it did.

"Did you finish your math homework last night?" she asked, when a commercial flashed across the screen.

He nodded. "Uh-huh."

"Did you double-check your answers?"

He nodded again.

"Did you leave it on Grandpa's desk?"

He threw his head back and slapped a hand against his forehead—a dramatic confirmation that, yes, he'd done that, too.

She chuckled. "We'll make sure we get it back before Monday."

"Maybe we can go get it after this show," he suggested.

"Are you worried we might forget about it?"

"No," he admitted. "I was hoping Grandpa would make pancakes."

"You just had breakfast," she reminded him.

"We could have pancakes for lunch."

"I could have made you pancakes if you'd really wanted pancakes," she said.

"Yeah, but Grandpa's pancakes are better."

She chuckled softly and hugged him close. "You're nothing if not honest, aren't you?"

"You told me I should always tell the truth."

"I did and you should," she agreed.

"So can we go to Gramma and Grandpa's?" he asked hopefully.

"Actually, I thought you might want to come to the Silver Star with me today."

"What's that?"

"It's the new name of Mr. Sterling's ranch."

"Why's it got a new name?" Brendan asked.

"Because Mr. Sterling sold the ranch to Mr. Stafford and moved to Glendale, Arizona."

"How come?"

She didn't think it was an appropriate time to get into a detailed discussion about economic downturns or retirement-age ranchers opting to sell off their properties because their kids had no interest in carrying on the family tradition. Instead she only said, "He wanted to move to a warmer climate."

"Why's it warmer in Arizona?"

"Because it's farther south and closer to the equator." She reached for the world atlas on the bottom shelf of the coffee table.

Brendan rolled his eyes. "You know you can get maps on the iPad, don't you?"

"Yes, I know," she confirmed. "But I want you to learn that you can find information in books, too."

"Why?"

"In case the internet blows up."

His eyes grew wide, conveying horror at the very thought. "Could that really happen?"

"Probably not," she acknowledged, opening the book and flipping through the pages until she found the double-spread illustration of the United States. "But we do sometimes lose our Wi-Fi connection."

"And that sucks," he said.

"That's the great thing about books—they don't need Wi-Fi." She tapped the page, drawing his attention to the map. "Do you know where we live?"

He immediately pointed to Nevada.

"That's right. But Haven is in northern Nevada," she said and nudged his finger closer to the state's top boundary. "And this—" she guided his finger down to Arizona "—is where Mr. Sterling lives now."

"That doesn't seem so far," Brendan decided.

"Scale can be hard to understand," she acknowledged. "Do you remember how long it took us to get to Disneyland last year?"

He nodded. *"For-ev-er."*

She smiled. "I'm sure it felt like forever, but it was actually about ten hours, split over two days. And this—" she pointed to Anaheim on the map "—is where Disneyland is."

His brow furrowed as he tried to equate the distance on the map with the hours in the car. "So Arizona is really, really far away," he realized.

"It is," she confirmed.

"Is that why he left his horses? Because they wouldn't want to be stuck in a trailer for a long trip like that."

She was always impressed by her son's innate understanding of and natural empathy toward animals, and she was both pleased and proud to know that he wasn't just a great kid but a compassionate human being. "That's probably one of the reasons," she agreed. "So do you want to go see the horses with me?"

Brooke ignored the echo of her mother's admonishment in her head. Because she knew that her motivation for inviting Brendan was that he enjoyed tagging along on official vet visits, just as she'd enjoyed tagging along with her father when she was a similar age.

She absolutely was not using her son as a shield—though she acknowledged, if only to herself, that she wouldn't object if Brendan provided a bit of a buffer. Because being in close proximity to Patrick Stafford made her tingle in places she hadn't thought were capable of tingling anymore.

"Would we go before or after Tanner's birthday party?" Brendan asked her now.

Birthday party?

And suddenly she remembered what she'd forgotten…

When Brooke pulled up at the Silver Star after dropping Brendan at Adventure Village for the birthday party, there were two vehicles in the driveway ahead of her. One was the same black F-150 that she recognized from the previous day; the other was an unfamiliar pale blue Land Rover.

Apparently the ranch's new owner had company, she mused, as she parked her dark green pickup behind Patrick's truck. Before she could speculate any further, the front door of the house opened and he stepped out onto the porch.

For a brief moment, she thought maybe he'd been waiting and watching for her. Then she realized he wasn't alone and probably wasn't even aware of her arrival, as his arm was slung casually across the shoulders of a gorgeous blonde who tipped her head back and laughed at whatever he said to her.

Well, it certainly hadn't taken him long to bounce back from her rejection the day before. Which proved that she'd pegged him right from the beginning and that her long-dormant hormones had come out of hibernation at the wrong time and for the absolute wrong guy.

She climbed out of her truck as the other woman gave Patrick a quick hug, then skipped down the steps. She wore a long black coat unbuttoned over a short scarlet-red dress paired with knee-high boots with chunky heels. Not just gorgeous but stylish, Brooke noted.

The blonde opened the driver's-side door of her vehicle, but before getting in, she called out to Patrick over the roof: "By the way, I left a toothbrush in the bathroom. Don't you dare throw it out."

If Brooke had any doubts about the woman's reason for being at the ranch, that parting remark answered them. Obviously she'd spent the night and expected to be back for a repeat performance.

Patrick didn't respond to his departing guest's comment, but he watched as the SUV zipped down the driveway and disappeared from sight before he moved off the porch.

"I didn't expect you'd be here this early," he said, falling into step with Brooke as she made her way toward the barn.

"I didn't think it was particularly early, but I'm sorry if I showed up at an inopportune time," she said.

He pulled open the barn door. "Why would you think it's an inopportune time?"

She gestured to the driveway, though the blonde and her Land Rover were long gone.

"Oh, you don't have to worry about Jenna," he said dismissively. "She has a habit of overstaying her welcome, but she's mostly harmless."

Brooke was so stunned by his callous remark, it took her a moment to come up with a reply. "If that's a recurring problem, maybe you should consider sleeping at her place," she suggested coolly, as she made her way to Ranger's stall. "That way you could leave whenever you wanted."

It was an effort to bank down on her irritation so the horse wouldn't pick up on her mood, but she managed to do so and turned her attention to the stallion. Using her voice and her touch to remind him of her presence and her purpose, she opened the gate and stepped inside his enclosure with his halter and lead in hand.

She was pleased—and maybe a little surprised—to discover that Ranger's stall had been freshly mucked out. Either Patrick hadn't spent all morning lounging in bed with his companion or he'd hired someone to perform basic chores. Considering his willingness to pay the cost of a site visit for her to change Ranger's dressing, she suspected it was probably the latter. Either way, it reassured her that—the stallion's injury notwithstanding—the animals at the Silver Star were being cared for.

"What are you talking about?" Patrick asked now, sounding sincerely baffled.

She glanced at him as she led Ranger to the treatment area.

The rancher was standing with his arms folded, a scowl furrowing his brow.

"I was just providing a solution to your girlfriend dilemma."

"Girlfriend?" he echoed blankly.

"I'm sorry—does that word carry too much meaning for you?" she asked, as she secured the stallion's ties. "I wasn't sure how else to refer to the woman who made a point of mentioning that she'd left her toothbrush in your bathroom."

He shook his head. "Not *my* bathroom. The guest bathroom."

"Oh, well, that's completely different, then," she remarked dryly.

Patrick no longer seemed confused. Now he looked amused. "I think you've misread the situation."

"It's really none of my business," she acknowledged. "My only purpose here is to take care of your horse. If you want to watch and learn, I'd be happy to explain what I'm doing. If you don't, please stop talking so I can give Ranger my complete attention."

He stopped talking, but he didn't leave, as she'd hoped he might do, and she felt his gaze on her the whole time.

When she'd completed her task and returned the horse to its stall, she took a small apple out of her pocket and offered it to the stallion—a reward for his good behavior. Ranger gently plucked the fruit from her hand and crunched down on the treat.

With a last pat on his cheek, Brooke turned around and found herself face-to-face with Patrick again.

"You misread the situation," he said, picking up the conversation where they'd left off.

"It's none of my business," she said again.

"True," he acknowledged. "But Jenna isn't my girlfriend. She's my sister."

"Your…sister?" she echoed, suddenly feeling foolish.

Because replaying his comment in her mind now, she realized the words that sounded like a callous dismissal of a lover could also be—and apparently were—the lighthearted teasing of a sibling.

"I have two of them," he told her. "Jenna's the youngest. She was at dinner with her boyfriend last night when he got called into work."

"On Valentine's Day?"

"Nate works at a tech company that does a lot of government work, and a break-in at the office meant that everyone had to go in. Anyway, that's how Jenna ended up at Diggers' after she finished the romantic dinner for two by herself and, because she didn't want to go home to an empty apartment, she decided to come back here."

"Oh."

"You could apologize now," he suggested.

"I apologize for jumping to conclusions," she said,

not just sincerely regretful but embarrassed by her uncharacteristically emotional reaction to the situation.

"And for impugning my character?"

"Actually, you should be flattered I imagined you could ever get a woman as gorgeous as your sister."

He chuckled at that, but his expression quickly turned serious again. "You don't have a very favorable opinion of me, do you?"

"I don't know you."

"And yet you were quick to assume that, only hours after you'd turned down my invitation for drinks and/or dinner yesterday, I'd go out and pick up another woman."

She shrugged. "There was no reason why you shouldn't."

"You're right," he acknowledged. "And the truth is, I did go out last night…but you're the reason I came home alone. Because the whole time I was at the bar, I couldn't stop thinking about you."

"I have a child," she reminded him.

"Yeah, you mentioned that," he said.

But this time, instead of moving away, he moved closer.

"And I have no interest in being the next notch on your bedpost," she said, determined to firmly establish the boundaries between them.

"I bought a new bed when I moved in here—there are no notches. In fact, there aren't even posts."

"I think you missed my point."

"It might not be what either of us expected, but there's definite chemistry between us," he said and lifted a hand to lightly stroke her cheek with the backs of his knuckles.

It was a gentle touch, but there was something so sensual about the caress that she found herself wondering how his hands might feel on other parts of her body.

On *every* part of her body.

And the wondering made her blood heat and her heart pound.

She swallowed. "I don't believe in chemistry."

"No?" His lips curved in a knowing smile. "Then explain to me why I can see the pulse point at the base of your jaw racing."

"Because you're crowding me, and I don't like to be crowded."

He immediately took a step back, giving her the space she'd claimed she wanted.

But then he asked, "How about being kissed?" And the low timbre of his voice was every bit as seductive as his touch. "Do you like being kissed?"

How could she answer that question when she could hardly remember how it felt to be kissed?

Oh, she got lots of kisses from her little boy, and she loved every one of them—even the wet and sticky ones. She also regularly exchanged pecks on the cheek with her parents. But she honestly couldn't recall when she'd last been kissed by a man.

And with Patrick's lips so temptingly close, she realized that she desperately wanted to answer his question.

Whether yes or no, she wanted to know how it felt to be kissed by this man. She wanted to know the taste of his lips and the touch of his hands. And even though she knew it might turn out to be a very big mistake, the wanting was suddenly stronger than her determination to resist.

"I'll let you know," she said and breached the short distance between them to press her mouth against his.

Chapter Four

Brooke's impulsive action had been fueled by curiosity. Would his kiss curl her toes inside her boots? Would it make her blood race through her veins? Would she feel the flutter of wings in her belly as butterflies soared?

Or would the experience be a disappointment, her excited anticipation unfulfilled?

It had been a long time since she'd experienced feelings of physical attraction—and even longer since she'd felt anything as immediate and intense as what she'd felt the first time she came face-to-face with Patrick Stafford less than twenty-four hours earlier.

And now she was kissing this man she'd only just met, and she was not disappointed.

Not just kissing him but pressing herself against him,

desperate to get closer. Apparently that was what eight years of abstinence did to a woman.

Or maybe it really was the inexplicable chemistry he'd mentioned that was responsible for her actions. She'd tried to ignore the tension between them, refusing to acknowledge that there even was an attraction. And while she couldn't deny that her pulse accelerated whenever he was near and she had to lock her knees so they didn't tremble, she'd mostly managed to ignore her body's instinctive response to his nearness.

Until he'd been too close for her to ignore.

Too close to resist.

But in the first moment that their mouths met, Brooke realized that she'd made a tactical mistake. Because in that first moment, a blast of unexpected heat flooded her system, melting her bones, making her weak.

Making her want.

She curled her fingers into his jacket, holding on to him as the intensity of the need shook her to the core. And that was before his tongue slid between her lips, stroking the inside of her mouth, stoking the fire that burned in her belly and spread through her veins. Before his hands slid up her back, drawing her still closer to the solid strength of his body.

Even through the layers of clothing and outerwear between them, she felt her breasts rub against the hard wall of his chest, her nipples tightening into hard buds that ached to be acknowledged.

Touched.

Tasted.

She could all too easily envision his dark head bent

over her breast, his mouth closing around the turgid peak, and the explicit and arousing image nearly made her gasp.

It *did* make her pull away, in a determined effort to regain control of her runaway hormones.

Patrick seemed to need a minute, too, before he asked, “Is that a ‘yes’?”

It took Brooke a moment longer to realize he was still waiting for a response to his earlier question. A question she could barely remember.

“Do you like kissing?” he prompted.

She pressed her tingling lips together. “It seems that I do,” she finally responded, keeping her tone light so he wouldn’t guess his kiss had set off a maelstrom inside her.

His smile was more than a little smug as he reached for her again, but she took a quick step back this time and held up a hand.

“You just admitted that you like kissing,” he pointed out. “And I really want to kiss you again.”

Brooke was flattered by his interest, but she was also wary. One kiss had been enough to nearly wipe her mind clean of all rational thought, unleashing such a surge of desire through her system that she could focus on nothing else. And she needed to focus.

She was a woman with obligations and responsibilities of a kind he didn’t want to know. So she couldn’t allow herself to get caught up in the heat of the moment, because she knew she’d end up getting burned.

“I also like Sweet Caroline’s Twelve-Layer Chocolate Bliss," she said lightly. "But I know I can't have it every day."

"I'm flattered that you equated kissing me with the best chocolate cake in the county, but I have to disagree with your premise on two grounds," he said. "First, a small piece of Chocolate Bliss every day wouldn't do any harm. In fact, it's widely believed that an occasional indulgence curtails the impulse to binge. Second, kissing—even *not* in moderation—isn't harmful to your health, and studies have shown that people who share kisses every day live longer and happier lives."

She narrowed her gaze. "You just made that up."

"Even if I did, I bet I could find such a study."

"And probably also a study that proves the opposite," she argued.

"You're a cynic, I see," he said, sounding amused.

"A realist," she countered.

"Science has proved that the endorphins released during sexual activity are natural mood boosters and stress relievers," he said.

"Well, aren't you just a font of self-serving information? But as much as I appreciate the chemistry lesson, I'm a single mom," she reminded him. "I have neither the time for nor any interest in having an affair."

"I think you're interested, but there's something holding you back. Tell me what it is, what you're afraid of."

"I'm not afraid of anything except my own bad judgment when it comes to the male species," she said. "So while I did enjoy our kiss, it won't happen again."

"That's too bad." He sounded sincerely regretful. "Because I think we'd be really good together."

He might be right, but she knew from experience that the temporary pleasure wouldn't be worth the heartache that followed. "I have no doubt you could sell that line to any number of women, but I'm not buying."

"Could I at least buy you a cup of coffee?" he suggested as an alternative. "A fresh pot just finished brewing when you pulled up."

As much as she wanted to make her escape, she needed to reestablish the professional boundaries of their relationship and decided that a discussion of neutral topics over a cup of coffee might help do that.

"Coffee sounds good," she decided and followed him out of the heated barn and into the frigid outdoors.

She detoured to her truck, to set her backpack inside, then fell into step with him again as he headed toward the main house.

Inside, he shrugged out of his leather jacket and hung it on a hook, then held out a hand for hers, hanging it beside his own.

"Don't worry about your boots," he said, when she started to reach down.

Since he obviously wasn't worried about his, she followed him into the kitchen.

She briefly wondered if she was crossing a line by entering his home, but immediately dismissed the concern. In rural practice, it was common for clients to become friends. She'd certainly never questioned the lines when she had a cup of tea with Stasia Krecji or accepted a bag of homemade lemon cranberry muffins from Betty Andersen. But she'd also never kissed Stasia or Betty, so maybe it was the lingering effects of the lip-lock she'd shared with Patrick Stafford that was causing her to question the placement of the lines now.

Maybe? her conscience mocked.

Brooke ignored the nagging voice to focus on her surroundings.

When she'd learned that the new owner of Gus Sterling's property intended to turn it into a dude ranch, she'd wondered about the changes that might be made to the homestead. Some of those changes—such as the new logo on the barn and the upgraded fencing around the paddocks—had been immediately evident when she'd pulled into the driveway the day before. But the two-story log home appeared unaltered from the outside.

Looking around the kitchen now, she was pleased to see that Gus's natural-stained maple cabinets remained, though the scarred and chipped laminate countertops had been replaced by dark granite. An island had been installed where the former owner's pedestal table and chairs had previously sat, and the high-end appliances were obviously new.

Patrick opened a cupboard beside the coffee maker and retrieved two mugs, then filled both with coffee and handed one to Brooke.

"Have a seat," he invited, gesturing to the four stools lined up at the island.

She accepted the mug and sat.

Patrick remained standing on the other side of the island, facing her.

"Do you cook?" she asked, eyeing the six-burner cooktop and double ovens. "Or are you planning to hire someone to prepare meals for your guests?"

"I suspect paying guests will expect a little more variety and substance than I can manage, so I'll hire someone," he said.

"If you don't mind my asking, what made you decide to walk away from an executive position at Blake Mining to take on something like this?"

It was a question Patrick had been asked by more than a few people after he'd tendered his resignation, and one he still wasn't entirely sure how to answer.

"I wanted a change," he replied, because it was true if not the whole truth.

"So you're just a spoiled little rich boy playing at being a rancher?" she mused, the teasing tone taking the sting out of her words.

"I can't deny the spoiled or rich part," he said. "But I'm neither little nor a boy."

"Spoiled big rich man, then," she noted.

"And I'm not playing at anything. This ranch isn't a whim or a hobby, though my parents have occasionally labeled it as both," he acknowledged. "It's my new life."

"What was wrong with your old life?" she asked curiously.

"Too much money and too little responsibility."

"Said no one ever," Brooke chimed in.

"I know it sounds strange," he admitted. "And maybe there will come a day that I want to go back to Blake Mining, where I'm expected to occupy a chair at board meetings but not actually have an opinion about anything—or worse, dare to express it."

"Was it really so bad?"

"Probably not," he allowed. "But the more time I spent there, the more I realized that I didn't want to spend the rest of my life there."

"But why a dude ranch?" she wondered.

"It's a vacation ranch," he said. "And truthfully, the idea wasn't even mine. It kind of came out of the blue as a result of me being late for the bachelor party of one of my college friends. When I explained that I'd been helping my grandfather brand the new calves at Crooked Creek, my buddies all started ribbing me about playing cowboy. So of course I said they only wished they had the same opportunity to escape their boring corporate jobs every once in a while, which led to a surprisingly coherent and meaningful conversation about the conflict between making a living and having a life.

"Anyway, it was Josh who said that when it was time for his bachelor party, instead of getting drunk and losing his money in Vegas, he wanted us all to go to a dude ranch."

"You bought Gus Sterling's ranch in order to host your buddy's bachelor party?" she asked incredulously.

He chuckled. "No. Josh wasn't even dating anyone at the time, so his bachelor party wasn't—and isn't—anywhere on the horizon. But his comment did get me thinking. After all, I knew a little bit about ranching, a little bit more about business, and I had available funds to invest in a new venture." He shrugged. "So when I heard that Gus was looking to sell, I took it as a sign that the time was right to pursue a career change."

"I would expect someone who buys a ranch to know more than a little bit about ranching," she noted.

"I knew enough to keep on Levi and Dean to look after the cattle."

She nodded, obviously recognizing the names of Gus Sterling's longtime ranch hands.

"They have more than forty combined years of experience and have probably forgotten more about cattle than I could ever hope to know," he continued.

"What would you have done if they'd wanted to move on when Gus sold?" Brooke asked.

"I probably would have considered selling the herd," he admitted. "Except that a cattle ranch without cattle isn't likely to draw many visitors."

"Not likely," she agreed.

"But Gus had good stock that I felt confident would do well with guests of various levels of experience and could be used for ranch work as well as on trails and for riding lessons. Which is one of the reasons I felt so awful when I realized Ranger was injured," he confided to her now.

"I know I gave you a hard time about the unlatched gate, but the truth is, coronary band injuries are quite common and can have any number of causes."

He nodded. "But I also know his injury is more severe than is common."

"He's going to need some time to heal," she said.

"And the attentive care of a good vet," he added.

"In coordination with the farrier," she said. "Gavin Torres is out of town this weekend, but he promised to stop by on Monday to check on Ranger and assess long-term options."

"You think there's going to be permanent damage," he realized.

"Damage to the coronary band usually results in slow and abnormal hoof growth, but it doesn't necessarily affect the animal's mobility or utility. Once it's healed, Gavin will be able to determine the best method to support the hoof during regrowth and give your stallion the best chance for a complete recovery."

Before his mind could wander too far down that dark path, she shifted the conversation again.

"It takes a lot of courage to step outside your comfort zone and try something new," she said. "And I really hope the ranch works out for you."

"Thanks. Of course, I do have a job waiting for me at Blake Mining if it doesn't," he pointed out.

"And now I'm a little less impressed," she said, but tempered the words with a smile.

"What about you?" he asked. "What made you want to become a vet?"

"I'm not sure," she admitted. "I only know that it's what I always wanted to do, and I feel grateful every day that I'm lucky enough to do it."

"I'm sure achieving your goal had more to do with hard work than good luck."

"There was a lot of hard work," she agreed.

"So maybe it's time to let yourself have a little bit of fun," he suggested.

"Is *fun* supposed to be some kind of code for *sex*?" she asked dubiously.

"Sex *is* fun if you do it right," he said.

She shook her head. "Unfortunately, I'm too busy with real responsibilities to have time for a fling with a pretend cowboy."

When he'd decided to make a drastic career change, he'd known that he'd need to prove himself, so he wasn't offended by her characterization. He was more than a little disappointed, though, by her determination to fight the obvious chemistry between them. "That is unfortunate," he agreed.

"And speaking of time—" Brooke glanced at the watch on her wrist "—I need to go if I'm not going to be late picking up Brendan."

She lifted her mug to her lips to swallow the last mouthful of coffee, then set the cup down again and pushed her stool away from the counter.

"Where is he?" Patrick asked.

"A birthday party for one of his classmates."

He didn't try to persuade her to stay even a little while longer. Though he might not have the same type of responsibilities, he understood and respected her priorities.

"I'll walk you out," he said.

After he'd done so, Patrick stood on the driveway and watched Brooke's truck grow smaller and smaller until it finally disappeared from his sight, with only one thought in his mind: he never should have kissed her.

Although technically she'd kissed him, he'd practically goaded her into it.

He'd been wondering about the taste of her sweetly curved lips since their first meeting, but instead of satisfying his curiosity, the feel of her mouth against his had only stoked his desire.

A desire that he suspected no other woman could satisfy.

He wasn't accustomed to being preoccupied by any one woman—especially a woman who'd made it clear that she wasn't interested.

Except that her enthusiastic participation in their kiss proved her claim of disinterest was a lie.

Brooke Langley *was* interested, even if she didn't want to be.

And he knew exactly how that felt.

Because she might be the hottest woman he'd met in a long time, but she wasn't at all his type. Not because he didn't like long-legged redheads, but because he didn't like complications.

So why, even knowing about her child, couldn't he get her out of his mind? What was it about her that appealed to him? Was it the challenge she presented? Was he so accustomed to getting what he wanted that he didn't know how to accept rejection?

Or was it simply that the kiss had affected him more deeply than he wanted to admit?

Because, really, that was all it had been—a simple kiss.

Except that there was nothing simple about the way she'd felt when she was in his arms.

Brendan apparently had a great time at Tanner's birthday party, and he talked nonstop the whole way home about everything the party guests had done at

Adventure Village—"we played three games of laser tag *and* got four tokens for the video games"—the cake Tanner's mom had made—"it had, like, six layers, and each one was a different color"—and all the goodies in his loot bag—"a yo-yo and a super bouncy ball and a slinky and stickers and bubble gum and a *gi-normous* lollipop."

Brooke was glad for his incessant chatter because it meant she wasn't expected to contribute much to the conversation. An occasional murmur of agreement or expression of awe was enough to keep her son talking, if not quite enough to alleviate her feelings of guilt.

And she did feel guilty. Not just because her son was only getting a fraction of her attention or even because she'd kissed Patrick, but because—more than an hour and a half later—she couldn't stop thinking about the kiss.

She never should have let it happen, because now that they'd shared one kiss, she wanted more. Not just more kisses but more of everything that came after the kissing.

For the better part of eight years, she hadn't regretted not having a man in her life. She certainly hadn't felt as if she was missing out on anything, because she had her little boy and he made her life complete so that she didn't need anything or anyone else. Or so she'd believed.

But now, after sharing only one kiss with Patrick, she found herself suddenly feeling a little less satisfied with her life. A little less complete. And she couldn't help but wonder: What was it about the man that urged her to step outside her comfort zone? What was it about him that made her want more?

He'd asked what she was afraid of, and she'd told him she wasn't afraid. But it was a lie. She was terrified of the way she felt when she was near him. The way her blood pulsed and her knees quivered; the way her blood heated and her body yearned.

She'd felt a similarly intense desire once before—eight years earlier. She'd fallen hard and fast for Xander Davis, and had her heart broken into a million little pieces as a result. Still, she'd never wished she could go back or change a single thing about their brief and passionate relationship, because it had resulted in Brendan—and her son was truly her biggest accomplishment and her greatest joy.

But her relationship with Xander had also taught her some important lessons: that passion was fleeting, romantic love was an illusion and her judgment was hopelessly flawed when her hormones were engaged. So the fact that she'd responded to Patrick as immediately and intensely as she'd responded to Xander was a great big and wildly waving red flag.

She wasn't afraid of what might happen if she fell into bed with the wrong man, but she was afraid of what might happen if she fell in love with the wrong man again. And Patrick Stafford was, by his own admission, the wrong man.

Having an affair with him would be reckless and irresponsible. (And, if his kiss was any kind of indicator, an incredible and exquisite pleasure.)

So it was a good thing that Brooke was too level-headed and responsible to let herself get carried away by her own wanton desires again.

But when she went to bed later that night, her lips were still tingling from the aftereffects of his kiss.

Chapter Five

The following morning, Brooke and Brendan walked over to the main house for breakfast, her son having convinced his grandfather to make banana-chocolate-chip pancakes. Not that he'd required much convincing. Bruce absolutely doted on his only grandson and was always happy to indulge his requests.

In addition to the towering stack of pancakes, there was a platter of bacon and sausage and, while her dad was scrambling eggs—because apparently it wasn't breakfast without eggs, too—Brooke poured coffee and juice and set the table. She sometimes enlisted Brendan to help with the latter task, but as soon as they'd walked through the door, his grandmother had ushered him upstairs to go through a box of old toys that she'd found in the attic.

"Remind me again why I thought it was a good idea to move out," Brooke said, as she stole a sausage link from the platter.

"You said you needed to stand on your own two feet so that Brendan would learn to do the same," Bruce said. "And you were right."

"Of course, I'm standing on my own two feet only three hundred feet away most of the time," she acknowledged. "And in your kitchen the rest of the time."

Her dad chuckled. "You know we don't mind. In fact, it's nice for your mom and me to have other people around the table. After almost thirty-eight years of marriage, we run out of things to talk about sometimes."

"I know that's not true," Brooke said. "You guys are an amazing example of what a marriage should be, even after almost thirty-eight years."

"There is no *should*," Bruce said. "Every marriage is as different as the people in it. But I know I got lucky, not just with my wife but the kids we had together."

"Especially me, right?" Brooke teased. "Because I'm your favorite."

"You're my favorite daughter," her dad confirmed.

It was a familiar exchange between them, and Brooke was smiling as she began folding napkins for the table. But her mind started to wander, and she didn't realize her dad had spoken again until she heard her name.

"I'm sorry—did you say something else?"

"Nothing important," Bruce said, scraping the eggs out of the pan and into a bowl.

Brooke finished with the napkins, then retrieved the butter and syrup from the fridge.

"Is everything okay?" her dad asked. "You seem a little distracted this morning."

"Just thinking about the day ahead," she said.

It wasn't a lie, because she had been thinking about her impending trip to the Silver Star—and seeing Patrick again. And trying to get a grip on the array of emotions that churned inside her. Because thinking about the upcoming visit made her stomach knot with excitement and apprehension.

She had no doubt the kiss she'd shared with Patrick had meant more to her than it had to him, and undoubtedly more than it should. Especially because he wasn't interested in a woman with a child.

Except that he hadn't kissed her like a man who wasn't interested.

But maybe, in the heat of the moment, he'd forgotten her single-mom status. If so, she could hardly fault him, as her son had been the furthest thing from Brooke's mind at the time, too. In any event, she was glad that Brendan had decided he wanted to visit the ranch with her today. There was no way either she or Patrick would be able to forget her maternal responsibilities when Brendan was right there.

Bruce called his wife and grandson to breakfast before he asked Brooke, "What are your plans today?"

"Aside from a quick trip to the Silver Star, I'm hoping to do a whole lot of nothing."

Her dad frowned. "Are you really going to go out there just to change Ranger's dressing every day?"

"As long as that's what the client wants and he's willing to pay for my time," she confirmed.

When everyone was seated at the table with their plates loaded up with food, conversation shifted to what was on her parents' agenda for the day.

"We're heading out to the flea market," Sandra said.

Brooke wrinkled her nose. "I've never understood your fascination with flea markets."

In her opinion, they were too crowded and noisy and musty smelling, but her mother's eyes always lit up just like Brendan's did when he was in front of a candy counter.

"One woman's trash is another woman's treasure," Sandra said, paraphrasing.

"The 'another woman' being your mother," Bruce chimed in, with a wink.

"So it would seem," Brooke agreed.

"I'll have you know that your apartment was primarily furnished with flea-market finds," her mother pointed out.

Brooke knew it was true. Luckily Sandra had a knack for spotting quality materials and workmanship, even when buried beneath layers of cheap paint and unidentifiable grime. She also had the patience to strip and sand and restore, after which the finished product usually bore little resemblance to what she'd brought home from the market. Most recently she'd found an oversize coffee table that she was repurposing for Brendan's wooden train set.

"Can I go to the flea market, too?" Brendan asked hopefully, no doubt thinking about the bins of secondhand toys and boxes of comic books that he could sift through, because Gramma always let him choose one to bring home. On a recent trip he'd found a rare Batman comic for only twenty-five cents and now imagined himself to be a treasure hunter like his grandmother.

"Of course," Sandra replied.

At the same time Brooke said, "You wanted to go to the Silver Star with me today."

"Oh, right," he said, but he no longer sounded as happy about that plan as he'd been earlier.

"And if we're not there too long, maybe we can stop at Adventure Village for a game of mini golf," Brooke suggested, sweetening her offer.

"Yay!" he agreed, with decidedly more enthusiasm this time. "Or maybe laser tag?"

She had no objection to Brendan playing laser tag with his friends, but the high-energy game with loud music and flashing lights was not really her idea of a good time.

"You played three games of laser tag yesterday," she reminded him. "So your options are mini golf or home."

"Mini golf," he immediately agreed.

When everyone had finished eating, Bruce shooed his wife and daughter out of the kitchen so that he and Brendan could do the tidying up.

"Is there any particular reason you don't want Brendan to come to the flea market with us?" Sandra asked, when they were settled in the living room with their refilled mugs of coffee.

"It's not that I didn't want him to go with you but that I wanted him with me," Brooke clarified. "He was at Tanner's birthday party for most of the day yesterday, and I kind of missed hanging out with him."

"Are you sure that's all it is?" her mom pressed. "Your desire for Brendan's company has nothing to do with the fact that you're going to see Patrick Stafford today?"

It was both a blessing and a curse that her mother could read her so easily, Brooke mused, as she sipped her coffee and considered a response to the question.

"Maybe not nothing," she allowed.

Sandra's brow furrowed. "I know I was teasing you about him being a handsome man, but if he's said or done anything to make you feel at all uncomfortable about being alone—"

"No." Brooke shook her head, eager to reassure her mother. "It's just...you were right. He is handsome and charming, and maybe I'm not as immune as I want to believe. So, yes, having Brendan there will serve as a reminder *to me* about what can happen when a woman lets herself fall under the spell of a handsome and charming man."

"Okay," her mom said. "Because we could send your father to the Silver Star to tend to the horse and you and Brendan could come with me."

"Thanks, but no," Brooke said, aware that her reason for turning down the offer had little to do with her dislike of the flea market and a lot to do with a certain sexy rancher.

Though he would never admit it to anyone else, Patrick was watching for Brooke's arrival. Sure, he was sitting in front of his computer in the den, pretending to review the website design samples his cousin Devin had sent to him, but he was too distracted by thoughts of the sexy vet to note subtle differences in background colors and font styles, never mind form an opinion about them.

As much as he was looking forward to seeing Brooke again, he knew it would be a mistake to pursue a personal relationship with her. As she'd pointed out, she was too busy with real responsibilities to indulge in an affair with a pretend cowboy, and he wasn't in a position to offer her anything more. All things considered, the smart move would be to take a step back.

Of course, as soon as he saw her truck pull into the driveway, he pushed his chair away from the desk and went to put on his coat and boots so that he could meet her by the barn.

His lips automatically curved when she stepped out of the vehicle. Then he heard the back door open and shifted his gaze in time to see a little boy hop out. Her son, he guessed, his surprise yielding to amusement as he realized she'd likely brought the kid to act as a barrier between them, to ensure there would be no more earth-tilting kisses like the one they'd shared the day before.

And while he was admittedly a little disappointed, he was also encouraged, because she wouldn't have felt the need for a safeguard unless she'd been as affected by their kiss as he was.

"Good afternoon, Mr. Stafford," she said by way of greeting.

"Dr. Langley." He matched her formality with his response, then turned his attention to the boy who'd taken position by his mother's side. The top of the kid's head, covered in a red knit pom-pom cap, was level with her breasts, so Patrick estimated his height at around four feet. He was wearing a puffy royal blue ski jacket over jeans with cowboy boots on his feet. His hair—what was visible beneath the edges of his hat—was sandy brown and his eyes were dark blue and wide with curiosity.

"I'm guessing this is your son," he said to Brooke.

She nodded. "This is Brendan."

"Hello, Brendan," Patrick said and offered his hand for the boy to shake. "I'm Patrick."

"It's nice to meet you, Mr. Stafford," the boy politely replied.

"Mr. Stafford is my father," he said. "Patrick is fine,"

"My mom says using titles is a sign of respect," Brendan told him.

"Well, I would never want to disagree with your mom," Patrick said, fighting against the smile that wanted to curve his lips. "But maybe we can come up with an alternative that doesn't make me feel so old."

"How about Mr. Patrick?" Brendan suggested. "That's what we call the teachers at school."

His brows rose. "You call all your teachers Mr. Patrick?"

The boy giggled in response to Patrick's feigned misunderstanding. "My teacher is Miss Karen, the librarian is Mrs. Donna and the gym teacher is Mr. Grant," he explained.

"Ah." Patrick nodded his understanding, then looked at Brooke. "What do you think, Dr. Langley?"

"I think Mr. Patrick is acceptable," she agreed, then turned to her son again. "But the most important thing to remember is that you're not to bother Mr. Patrick while we're here."

"I won't," Brendan promised, as he followed his mother into the barn.

Brooke retrieved the stallion's halter and lead rope from the hook beside his door and stepped into the stall.

"He's big," Brendan said, taking an instinctive step back when the stallion exited the enclosure.

"He is big," Patrick confirmed. "And incredibly strong. That's why it's important to keep a safe distance."

"It's hard to examine an animal from a safe distance," the boy said matter-of-factly. "But I know to always approach a horse from the side to avoid his blind spots and to talk to him so he knows I'm there. My mom gives me the same lecture every time we visit one of the local ranches."

"How often is that?" Patrick asked.

"Almost every weekend, and some other days when I'm not at school. But if Mom knows she's gonna be a long time—or if she's gonna be doing something she doesn't want me to see—she makes me stay with Gramma."

"You don't like staying with Gramma?"

He shrugged. "I don't mind, but I'd rather help with the animals. I'm gonna be the third Dr. B. Langley when I grow up."

"It's good to have goals," Patrick remarked, impressed by the child's confidence.

"Mom says I'll prob'ly change my mind a dozen times before I go to college, but she knew she wanted to be a vet when she was my age, so I don't think I will."

"Some people do change their minds a dozen times—or more," Patrick said. "Look at me, for example. I went to college to get a business degree, but now I'm a rancher."

"So why didn't I see any cows when we drove in?" Brendan asked.

"Because they're in their winter pasture."

"What about other horses?"

"They're in the paddock behind the barn."

"Can I go see them?"

"Brendan, I told you not to bother Mr. Stafford," Brooke interjected before Patrick could respond.

"Mr. *Patrick*," her son reminded her.

"And he's not bothering me," Patrick said. "If I had somewhere else to be, I'd be there. Since I don't, I'm happy to take Brendan to see the other horses, if it's okay with you."

"It's okay with me." Then to Brendan, she said, "But remember the rules."

"I *always* remember the rules," he said, with an exaggerated eye roll.

"What are the rules?" Patrick asked, as they exited the barn and headed toward the paddock.

"Respect the animals and their space, do what she tells me when she tells me, and don't touch anything without permission."

"Those sound like reasonable rules," he said.

"Yeah," Brendan agreed. "But why does she have to remind me *Every. Single. Time?*"

"I'd guess it's because she wants to make sure you're safe," Patrick said. And though it really was just a guess, it made sense to him.

Apparently Brendan thought so, too, because he nodded.

Then he spotted the horses, and his big blue eyes suddenly got even bigger. "Wow. You sure do have a lot of horses."

"Twelve, including Ranger," he said. "But there are only nine out here now, because Levi and Dean—they're my ranch hands—each took a mount to ride out and check on the cattle."

When they reached the fence, the boy climbed up on the lowest rail and leaned his arms over the top. "What are their names?" he asked.

"The white one with the black spots is Pongo—"

"Like the dalmatian in the movie?"

"I don't know," Patrick admitted. "He already had his name when I got him, but I think that's a pretty good guess." Then he proceeded to point out and name the rest of the group. "The cream-colored one with the white mane and tail is Biscuit, the dark dappled gray is Stormy, the lighter gray is Cloudy, the pair of reddish bays with the black socks are Joe and Jackson, the paint—that's the brown one with big white splotches—is Picasso, the big black one is Midnight and her filly is Blue."

"Blue?" Brendan echoed quizzically.

Patrick shrugged. "Again, she had the name when I got her."

"So what is a dude ranch?" the boy asked.

"Where'd you hear that term?"

"My mom told my gramma that you're turning Mr. Sterling's property into a dude ranch."

"Actually, it's the Silver Star Vacation Ranch," he said.

"What's a vacation ranch?" Brendan asked.

"It's where people go to learn about and help with the daily operations of a ranch."

The boy's brow wrinkled. "That doesn't sound much like a vacation."

"Maybe not to you and me," he acknowledged. "But for those who live in crowded cities, it's an opportunity to escape the noise and traffic and experience a simpler lifestyle."

"I'd rather go to Disneyland," Brendan said.

Patrick chuckled at that. "I think I probably would, too, but other people like the idea of trail rides, fishing trips and cooking under the stars. And for younger guests, there will be riding lessons and other activities."

An admittedly vague description, but he hadn't yet figured out exactly what those other activities might be.

"You should also teach them how to take care of a horse," Brendan suggested. "Grandpa says it's important to repay a horse for letting you ride with proper care."

"That's a good point," Patrick said. "I'll add it to my list."

"Junior rodeo events are fun, too. At cowboy camp last summer, we learned how to rope a steer—well, it was actually a hay bale with fake horns," he admitted. "But it was still fun."

"What else did you do?"

"I won the ribbon for mutton busting," the boy said proudly. "And that was a real mutton."

"Maybe I should hire you as a junior consultant,"

Patrick mused, making a mental note to look into the cost of acquiring and caring for a couple of sheep.

"You mean like a job? That would be so cool!" Brendan said excitedly. "Would I get paid?"

"Maybe we should ask your mom what she thinks before we discuss those kinds of details."

"She'll think it's okay," the boy said confidently. "'Cause she knows you've got more money than brains."

Chapter Six

Please let the earth open up and swallow me now, Brooke thought, as she heard the words come out of her son's mouth.

Unfortunately, the universe didn't comply with her request, forcing her to chastise him for repeating what he'd obviously overheard of a private conversation.

"Brendan Langley, that was a completely inappropriate thing to say."

"But that's what you told Grandpa," Brendan said.

Because her son was nothing if not honest.

And still, the ground remained solid beneath her feet.

"I'm sure you must have misheard," she said.

"No, I didn't," Brendan insisted, shaking his head for emphasis.

She slid a glance toward Patrick, trying to gauge

his reaction to Brendan's remark—or rather his repetition of her remark. The corners of the rancher's mouth twitched as he fought against a smile. Apparently he thought it was funny to watch her try to talk herself out of the corner she'd been boxed into.

"And even if you think that's what you heard," she continued to address her son, "you need to understand that some adult conversations aren't meant for your ears—or to be repeated."

"Does that mean I won't get paid?" Brendan directed this question to Patrick.

"Paid for what?" she asked, obviously having arrived on the scene after that part of the conversation.

"We can discuss that later," the rancher said. "How's Ranger?"

"It's only been a couple days," Brooke reminded him. "But at this point, there are no red flags."

"Coronet injuries are tricky," Brendan said solemnly. "If they don't heal prop'ly, they can cause perm'nent figurement or lameness."

"*Dis*figurement," Brooke corrected automatically.

"That's why I've chosen to pay someone with special expertise to care for Ranger rather than risk further damage," Patrick said to Brendan.

"That seems pretty smart to me," the boy decided, then turned to the horses again.

Brooke took a couple of steps back, away from the fence, and gestured with a jerk of her chin—a silent request for Patrick to follow.

"I owe you an apology," she said, when she was confident that they were out of earshot of her son. "And I am sorry."

"Sorry you said it or sorry your son repeated it?"

She just shook her head. "You're never going to let me forget this, are you?"

"I don't know… Never is a long time," he said. "And it's entirely possible that I do have more money than brains, but that's only because I'm unbelievably rich."

"And unbelievably humble," she remarked dryly.

He grinned. "But I was smart enough to get you to come back to my ranch."

"To take care of your horse."

"That was one reason," he acknowledged. "Another was that I really wanted another look at you."

She lifted a brow. "Are you flirting with me?"

"I'm trying," he admitted. "But flirting, not unlike sex, is an activity that's much more enjoyable with a partner."

"Well, I wish you luck finding one," she said.

"I'm looking at the one I want," he told her.

Her gaze skittered away.

"And I think you want me, too. That's why you brought your son with you today, to ensure there wouldn't be a repeat of what happened yesterday."

"What happened yesterday?" she asked, adopting a casual tone so that he wouldn't suspect how much she'd been affected by the kiss they'd shared.

But the slow curve of his lips warned that he wasn't fooled for a second. "Yesterday you plastered yourself against me and shoved your tongue down my throat."

"I did not," she denied hotly. "And it was *your* tongue that made first contact."

"Apparently you *do* remember what happened yesterday," he mused.

"It doesn't matter," she said. "Because what happened yesterday isn't going to happen again."

But it was a bold statement set on a shaky foundation, and they both knew it.

Sarah's Jeep pulled into the driveway as Brooke was buckling Brendan into his booster seat. Two minutes earlier, he'd wished he could talk the sexy vet into staying a while longer. Now he was glad she was on her way so that he wouldn't have to introduce the two women.

The older of his two sisters, Sarah had always had an uncanny ability to know when he was interested in a female, and she'd exploited that talent mercilessly over the years. No doubt she would only have to glance between Patrick and Brooke to know he was hot for the vet, and then she'd subject Brooke to a million questions.

"What are you doing here?" Patrick asked, when Sarah climbed out of her Jeep.

"It's good to see you, too, big brother," she said.

"I am happy to see you," he told her. "I'm just surprised because I thought you were in Vegas for the weekend."

"I got back this morning."

"And rushed over here because you missed me?"

"Because I heard that Ranger was hurt," his sister clarified.

"How could you possibly have heard that?" he wondered aloud. The only person he'd told about the horse's injury was his grandfather, in the hope that he would have been available to come out to take a look at the stallion. Unfortunately, one of Jesse Blake's own horses at Crooked Creek Ranch had been ready to foal for the first time and he hadn't been willing to leave her. Instead, he'd suggested that Patrick call Dr. Langley.

No doubt his grandfather had been referring to Bruce, but Patrick wasn't at all disappointed to find his beautiful daughter on his doorstep instead. "Gramps told Spencer, who of course told Kenzie, who asked me how the stallion was doing when I ran into her at The Daily Grind," Sarah said, explaining the source of her knowledge to him now. Spencer being their cousin and Kenzie his wife, who lived with their kids in the main house at Crooked Creek Ranch, where Gramps resided in the old bunkhouse.

"And you came right away to put your secret veterinarian skills to work?" Patrick teased his sister.

She punched him in the shoulder—playfully but not exactly lightly. "Maybe I did think I might be able to do something to help."

"There's not," he told her. "It's a coronary band injury that the vet has examined and treated."

"Is Ranger going to be okay?" she asked, sincerely concerned about the animal's welfare.

"Fingers crossed," he said. "But if you wanted to do something more..."

"Of course I do," she immediately replied.

"Great. You can make lunch."

Not surprisingly, his sister rolled her eyes at that suggestion. "You still haven't hired a cook?"

"I didn't see any point in hiring a cook before I had guests to feed."

"The point is that you'd have someone to make lunch for you rather than trying to manipulate your sister."

"That is a good point," he acknowledged. "But it seems kind of indulgent to have someone around to prepare meals only for me."

"It's not as if you can't afford it," she said.

"You'd think so, but most of my money has been invested in the property you're standing on."

Her eyes grew wide. "And you claim you're not a gambler."

"I know most of the family doesn't approve of what I'm doing here, but I thought you and Jenna would at least pretend to be supportive."

"You know we've always had your back," Sarah said.

And he did know it. As much as he'd always looked out for his sisters, they'd done the same for him. Gramps had dubbed them The Three Musketeers from an early age because they'd always had an "all for one and one for all" philosophy. Of course they'd had to rely on one another, as they'd often been left to their own devices while their parents spent most of their waking hours at Blake Mining, diligently adding to the family fortune.

Poor little rich kids.

"But having your back doesn't mean we don't worry about you," Sarah said to him now.

"You're worried because I chose to walk away from Blake Mining?" he guessed.

She shrugged. "You are a little young to be going through a midlife crisis."

"It's a simple career change, not a midlife crisis," he assured her.

"It's a big gamble," she said again.

"Speaking of which, how was Vegas?" he asked.

She let him get away with shifting the topic of conversation—at least for now.

"It was okay," she replied, with a half-hearted shrug.

"Did you lose all your money on the roulette wheel?"

"Blackjack," she told him.

"So what prompted this impulsive trip?" he asked.

"I didn't want to be stuck here, alone, on Valentine's Day," she admitted.

"Was it better to be alone in Vegas?" he asked. Then another thought occurred to him. "Or maybe you weren't alone—in which case, you can spare me the details."

"I wasn't alone," she said. "I went with a friend who was getting over a recent breakup and who decided that hooking up with a random guy was a better idea than hanging out with her also single friend."

"That sucks," he said.

She shrugged again. "It wasn't the worst Valentine's Day ever."

"I've never understood why there's so much focus put on a made-up holiday."

"If you think about it, all holidays are made up," she said.

"But only Valentine's Day was a conspiracy between the florists and candy makers who wanted an excuse to jack up the prices of their wares."

"So who did you buy flowers and chocolates for this year?" Sarah asked.

"No one." In fact, the date might have slipped right past without him even realizing it if he hadn't gone into town that night.

"Hmm… I thought you might have celebrated the occasion with Trinity, considering that she broke up with Christopher a few weeks back," Sarah said.

"We did have a drink at Diggers' Friday night."

"Which was Valentine's Day," she reminded him.

"Right."

"And after the drink?" she prompted.

"There was no 'after,' just a drink," he told her.

"Hmm…" she said again, somehow making the single syllable sound as if it was filled with meaning.

"So who is she?" Sarah pressed, when he didn't respond to her musing.

"Who is who?" he asked.

"The woman who inspired you to turn down a sure thing like Trinity?"

"Isn't it possible that I just wasn't in the mood for a hookup?" he countered.

"Possible," she allowed. "But not probable. I'm guessing it's the redhead who was getting into her truck as I drove up."

Yep, there were those uncanny instincts again.

"She must be someone special," Sarah continued. "Because you don't usually allow your…female companions… to hang around so late the next day."

"Brooke didn't spend the night," he said.

She nodded. "I should have realized. You're usually in a much better mood the morning after."

"Why are you here again?" he asked.

"I came to check on Ranger," she said. "And…I'm bored."

"You could get a job," he suggested.

"I have a job—Associate Director of Occupational Safety and Health at Blake Mining."

He snorted. "You have a paycheck."

"Yep," she agreed. "And one that I happily spend as fast as I earn it."

"Don't you want to actually do something with your life?" he asked, genuinely concerned that she was aimlessly going through the motions with little regard for her own happiness. Not unlike he'd done for far too long.

"Like what? Open a dude ranch?" Her skeptical tone left him in no doubt about what she thought of that idea.

"The Silver Star is a vacation ranch," he corrected automatically.

"Po-tay-to, po-tah-to," she said.

"And you know, maybe that's not such a bad idea," he decided.

"What?"

"You working here."

She waved her hands in front of her, clearly dismissing his suggestion. "Oh, no," she said. "You're *not* roping me into participating in this questionable venture."

"You're a people person, Sarah. You shouldn't be stuck in an office reading reports all day." Though his intention had been to turn the topic of conversation away from the sexy vet—and thank goodness Brendan had already been buckled into his booster seat, so his sister hadn't caught a glimpse of Brooke's son—his remark was nothing less than the truth. Sarah was good with people, sincere and empathetic, always willing to soothe and reassure others. Unlike Jenna, who liked to light the fuses and then sit back to watch the fireworks.

"We both know I'm only in my office a few hours a week," she said. "And you still haven't answered my question about your female visitor."

"Brooke is the vet who's been looking after Ranger's injury."

"What happened to Dr. Langley?"

"She's another Dr. Langley—his daughter, who works with him in his practice."

"This is all starting to make sense now," Sarah mused.

"What's starting to make sense?"

"When I saw Kenzie, I asked her about Buttercup's new foal, but apparently she hasn't had it yet, and Kenzie guessed it was going to be at least a few more days."

"And?" he prompted.

"Gramps has been a rancher his whole life. He's probably witnessed more livestock births than he can count."

"True," he acknowledged.

"So doesn't it seem a little strange that when you asked him to come out here to check on Ranger, he was too busy watching over an expectant mare who wasn't anywhere near ready to foal?"

"Obviously he misread the signs," he said, with a shrug.

"He didn't misread anything," Sarah denied. "He made an excuse about why he couldn't come out here so that you'd have to call the new vet."

Patrick couldn't imagine Jesse Blake going to such lengths in the vague hope of striking a romantic match for one of his grandchildren. "Our grandfather is hardly the type to play Cupid."

"I wouldn't have thought so, either," his sister agreed. "But he's had romance on his mind—and a definite spring in his step—since he's been dating Helen Powell."

He shuddered. "Aside from the fact that I don't want to think about Gramps and Helen, there's a major flaw in your theory."

"What's that?"

"There's no way Gramps could have known it would be Brooke who showed up instead of her dad."

"Sure there is. Gramps knows everyone in this town, and if he talked to someone who mentioned having a problem that required the vet, then he'd know the senior Dr. Langley would have been occupied and that another call to the clinic would result in his daughter coming out here," Sarah theorized.

The convoluted explanation left Patrick unconvinced.

But on the off chance that his sister was right, he'd have to talk to his grandfather about meddling in his personal life—and maybe say "thank you."

"I thought you might be waiting for Brendan to get home from school so you could bring him with you," Patrick remarked, when Brooke showed up at the Silver Star just before 4:00 p.m. the following day.

She shook her head. "I'd planned to be here around noon, but I got caught up at the Wallace farm, vaccinating the new kids." And then chatting with Howard

Wallace about his potential plans to expand his cheese offerings at the local farmers' market. As a result of that lengthy conversation, the vaccine cooler in the back of her truck now also contained samples of several new varieties that Howard had given her to try.

"I was riding fence with Levi and Dean and only got back a while ago myself, so I'm glad I didn't miss you," he said. "But if you ever do come by when I'm not around, feel free to do what you need to."

"I will," she assured him. "But I have no doubt you could handle Ranger's care yourself. It's not that complicated."

"But not my area of expertise, either," he told her.

"So what is your area of expertise?" she asked curiously.

"Market data analysis."

"A skill that will no doubt serve you well on trail rides and at cookouts," she remarked wryly.

"No doubt," he agreed with a grin.

When she'd finished with her task, instead of immediately packing up and heading out, she turned to him and said, "Can I ask you something?"

"As a matter of fact, I am free for dinner." He winked. "And breakfast."

"That's *not* what I wanted to know," she assured him.

"But still valuable information."

Though Brooke rolled her eyes, Patrick thought he saw a spark of amusement in their depths.

"Did you tell Brendan that you wanted him to be a consultant?" she asked him.

"Junior consultant," he clarified.

"Why?"

He shrugged. "It turns out he's got some pretty good ideas about the kinds of things kids might like to do when visiting a guest ranch, and since I didn't really have *any* ideas, it made sense. And I'm happy to pay for his time—unless you object to me spending time with your son?"

"You're not going to pay him," she said. "And I don't have any objections. I just want to be clear that spending time with Brendan isn't going to score any points with me."

"I'm not asking to spend time with him to score points with you," he said. "I happen to think he's a great kid."

"I didn't think you liked kids."

"I didn't think I did, either," he confided. "But it seems that I like Brendan. And I really like his mom."

"I'm flattered," she said. "But I'm not interested in having an affair, a fling or a one-night stand with you."

"I noticed you didn't dismiss the possibility of a relationship."

"I didn't think it was necessary, because everyone knows *you* don't do relationships."

"And *you've* been listening to gossip," he chided.

"So it's not true that you've never dated the same woman for more than three months?" she challenged.

He mentally reviewed his most recent romantic involvements. He'd dated Trinity for about five months altogether, but never for more than a few weeks at a time. Dana? No, that relationship hadn't lasted any more than six weeks. Kristie? About six weeks again. Shayla? Almost three months—until she'd asked him to accompany her to Flagstaff, Arizona, for Thanksgiving to meet the family. He'd taken a hard pass on that invitation.

Brooke was watching him, the hint of a smile tugging at the corners of her mouth.

He wanted to kiss the smile off her face. Or maybe he was just looking for an excuse to kiss her. Because after only one taste, he was addicted to her flavor, craving not just another sample but a feast.

But she was still waiting for a response to her question, so he finally said, "I dated Kimberly Ellis for almost two years."

"High school doesn't count," she told him.

He frowned, once again struck by the certainty that they'd both attended Westmount but unable to grasp any solid memory of her from back then. "How do you know that was high school?"

"Because I was in the same grade as Kimberly's sister, Emily."

Which meant that she would have been a freshman when he was a senior, and definitely not on his radar. "Okay, so I don't have a lot of experience with relationships," he conceded.

"Which is probably one of the few things we have in common," she said.

"You don't date a lot?"

"I've been on a total of three dates since Brendan was born and none at all in the past three years."

"Seriously?"

"I don't know why you sound surprised," she said. "The idea of dating a single mom sends most guys running in the opposite direction." She stared at him pointedly. "Or at least taking a big step back."

As he'd done, when she'd first told him that she had a child. But now that he'd spent some more time with her and met her son, the idea of dating a single mom didn't seem so scary. Instead, the prospect of spending more time with Brooke and Brendan was oddly appealing.

Chapter Seven

Over the next week, Brooke showed up at the ranch daily, if not on any particular schedule, squeezing in visits to the Silver Star around her other commitments. Sometimes she came on her own, and sometimes she brought Brendan with her. On the latter occasions, Patrick tried to make a point of spending some time consulting with his junior consultant.

Brendan really was a great kid, and Patrick had to give full credit to Brooke for raising a well-spoken and confident son on her own. Yeah, the boy was a little outspoken at times, but Patrick quite enjoyed their frank conversations.

Today after their consult, Brendan had asked if he could build a snow fort—a reminder to Patrick that the fresh fall of snow that had been a hassle for him to shovel off the walks that morning was a glorious world of opportunity for a child.

"Since you're here, I wondered if you might have time to check something else," Patrick said, as Brooke returned Ranger to his stall.

"What something else?" she asked.

He gestured to the animal that was curled up in the vacant stall across from Ranger's.

Brooke followed the direction he was pointing, her eyes widening when she spotted the curly-haired dog tucked in the corner. "You got a dog?"

"I didn't get anything," he denied. "It just suddenly appeared."

"When?"

"This morning—or maybe last night. But I didn't see it until this morning."

She cautiously stepped through the open gate. Watching her approach, the dog thumped its tail a few times, even as it ducked its head, as if anticipating a scolding—or maybe worse.

"I'm not going to hurt you," Brooke murmured softly. "I just want to see if you're wearing a collar."

But she paused a few feet away, respecting the animal's space, and lowered herself to her haunches. "Look at you, pretty girl," she said, in the same soothing tone. "Or are you a pretty boy?"

The dog rose to a crouched position and slowly crawled toward her.

"Pretty girl," Brooke decided. "She looks like a labradoodle to me."

She held herself still, letting the animal sniff her, and was rewarded with a swipe of tongue over her knuckles.

"Oh," she said softly, obviously already in love with the animal. She glanced up at Patrick as she stroked the fur beneath the dog's chin, making him wonder what he had to do to get the same kind of attention. "I'll bet she was abandoned and looking for a warm and dry place to sleep." She shook her head. "You wouldn't believe how many pets are dropped off by the side of a road or dumped in an empty field by people who have grown bored with them."

He frowned at that. "Why wouldn't they take them to a local shelter?"

"Because then they'd have to own up to their abandonment rather than pretend the animal just ran away," Brooke explained, as she continued to stroke and soothe the dog. "Although sometimes pets do escape through an open door or window and race off in search of adventure, then can't find their way home again."

"So someone might be looking for her?"

"It's possible. She doesn't have a collar, which means no tags, although she might be microchipped."

"How can you find that out?"

"I have a portable scanner in the truck," she said, giving the dog a last scratch behind the ears and rising to her feet.

She was back in only a few minutes, with the scanner in hand. She set it on the floor so the dog could sniff it and know there was no reason to be afraid.

"How do you know where to look?" Patrick asked, as she scanned the dog's back.

"Microchips are implanted just beneath the skin, right between the shoulder blades," she told him. "Although they can sometimes migrate to other places."

But she finished her check and shook her head as she set the scanner aside again.

"No microchip," he realized. "So what am I supposed to do with her now? Should I put up flyers saying 'Found Dog'?"

"You could," she said. "But if someone was looking for a lost pet, they probably would have called the clinic."

"How about flyers saying 'Dog Looking for a Good Home'?"

"Isn't this a good home?"

"I've got enough other animals to take care of without adding a dog to the mix," he said. Though this one really did seem to be a sweet-natured creature, and he'd often wished for a dog when he was younger.

"She wouldn't be much trouble," Brooke assured him. "Have you given her anything to eat?"

"I opened a can of stew," he admitted. "It was the only thing I could find that seemed suitable."

"Did she like it?"

"Gobbled it up like she was starving," he said. "Though she certainly doesn't look as if she is."

"You think she's overweight?" Brooke asked, a smile tugging at the corners of her mouth.

"You don't?"

"No," she said. "I think she's pregnant."

* * *

"I'm done with my fort!" Brendan announced as he entered the barn.

"Did you leave any snow on the ground?" Brooke asked, noting the amount of white stuff that covered her son.

He grinned, his white teeth a contrast to his red cheeks. "I made snow angels, too."

Then he spotted the dog.

"You got a dog?" he said, looking at Patrick with wide eyes.

"I think it might be more accurate to say that she got me," the rancher replied dryly.

Brendan dropped to his knees, far enough away so that the animal wouldn't feel threatened, and tugged off his snow-covered mittens. "What's his name?"

"Her," Brooke automatically corrected him.

"What's *her* name?" he asked.

"She doesn't have a name," Patrick said. "Or if she does, I don't know what it is."

"How come?"

"Because she's not my dog."

"She should have a name," Brendan said. "Maybe you could call her Chewie."

"Chewie?" Patrick echoed dubiously.

"Because she's furry, like Chewbacca," the boy explained.

"But she's a girl," Brooke said again.

Her son shrugged, clearly unconcerned about the gender implications of the suggested name, as the dog inched closer to the boy. When she was close enough, she nudged his arm with her nose, as if asking to be petted. He lifted his hand to oblige, and she licked his palm, making him giggle.

"Look, Mom. She likes me."

"Well, you are a pretty likable kid," she said.

Brendan flashed her a quick smile before shifting his attention back to the dog, stroking her gently.

"And Chewie's a good dog," he said. "Aren't you, Chewie?"

"How about Princess?" Brooke suggested as an alternative moniker.

"How about we stop trying to give the dog a name?" Patrick countered.

"Why are you afraid of naming her?" she asked.

"Because my grandfather always said that as soon as you name a stray, it becomes yours," he admitted.

"I'm pretty sure she's already yours," Brooke said.

"Princess is almost as good a name as Chewie," Brendan decided, siding with his mother. "If you think it's better for a girl dog."

Patrick's sigh was filled with resignation. "I don't care. You can call her whatever you want, because she's not going to be here very long."

"Want to bet?" Brooke challenged with a smile.

He shook his head. "I'm not keeping the dog and I'm definitely not keeping any puppies."

"She's gonna have *puppies*?" Brendan was clearly thrilled by the idea.

His mom nodded.

"When?" the little boy wanted to know.

"I'd guess in about four to five weeks," she said.

"Can you guess how many?" Patrick asked.

"Sure, I could guess," she told him. "But that's all it would be. If you want an accurate number, you could bring her into the clinic for an X-ray."

"If you aren't gonna keep the puppies, what'll happen to them?" Brendan asked, sounding worried.

"I'll find homes for them," Patrick promised.

"We could take one," her son offered helpfully.

"No, we can't," Brooke said firmly.

Brendan's face fell. "Why not?"

"Because puppies are a lot of work and I don't have the time or the patience to train one."

"I could help," he said.

"I'm sure you'd like to help," she acknowledged. "But who would look after a puppy all day when I'm at work and you're at school?"

"Maybe we could get *two* puppies," he suggested. "Then they could look after each other."

"A creative argument," Patrick said, sounding impressed by the boy's reasoning.

"But not a convincing one," she assured him, before turning to her son again. "Brendan, two puppies would be twice as much work—and twice as much money."

He pouted. "You never let me have anything I want."

She held his gaze for a minute, waiting for him to acknowledge the inaccuracy of his own words.

"You always say no when I ask for a puppy," he clarified.

"For the same reasons I just explained," she agreed.

"But I *really* want a puppy," Brendan told her.

"I know," she said. "But a puppy really wouldn't be

happy trapped inside our apartment for twenty hours every day."

"Your mom's right," Patrick chimed in, surprising Brooke by speaking out in support of her position. "A puppy needs a lot of attention and exercise and training."

She knew Brendan would have folded his arms over his chest if his hands hadn't been busy stroking the dog. Instead his lower lip poked forward to express his unhappiness that the adults were siding against him.

"Of course, the puppies are going to have to stay with their mom for several weeks after they're born," the rancher continued.

"At least six weeks," her son interjected.

Patrick nodded. "At least six weeks," he confirmed. "And during that time, if they're still here, you can visit them anytime you want."

"Anytime?" Brendan echoed hopefully.

"So long as it's okay with your mom," Patrick agreed.

A few days later, when Brooke returned to the Silver Star, she noticed a woman at the paddock fence, feeding treats to the horses. She had long dark hair and was wearing a fleece-lined denim jacket over faded jeans tucked into well-worn cowboy boots. Aware that she'd jumped to conclusions about Patrick's relationship with a female visitor to the ranch once before, Brooke cautioned herself against doing the same thing this time. But considering the rancher's reputation as a player, and the fact that he hadn't made another move on her since the kiss—aside from some casual flirting, which she suspected came as naturally to him as breathing—it wasn't unreasonable to conclude that he was seeing someone.

Brooke grabbed her backpack and the bag of puppy food she'd brought and headed toward the barn.

The brunette quickly moved away from the paddock and headed in the same direction. "Good morning," she said brightly.

Brooke echoed the greeting as the brunette hurried ahead to open the heavy barn door.

"Thanks."

"You must be the new vet," the other woman said, as she followed Brooke down the center aisle to Ranger's stall.

She dropped the bag of dog food just inside the enclosure where the canine had taken up residence, then nodded. "Brooke Langley."

"I'm Sarah," the brunette said.

"It's nice to meet you," Brooke said, as she turned her attention to the stallion. Well accustomed to the routine by now, Ranger patiently complied with her directions as she tied him.

Sarah watched Brooke as she worked. "I feel so guilty that I was out of town when he was injured," she said. "I've been helping Patrick exercise the horses and I can't help but wonder if Ranger escaped the paddock because he needed a good run."

"You spend a lot of time here, then?" Brooke asked, her curiosity piqued by the woman's revelation.

"It's a good excuse to get away from Miners' Pass."

She recognized the most exclusive address in town,

where she knew Patrick's family lived in one of the biggest of the big houses on the street. "Did you grow up near Mr. Stafford?" she asked, deliberately using the rancher's formal title.

"Too close for comfort sometimes," Sarah said wryly.

The girl next door, Brooke guessed.

"He was a complete pain in my ass growing up, and yet I can't help but miss him now that he's gone," she confided. "But I guess most little sisters probably feel that way about their big brothers."

"So you're Patrick's other sister," Brooke realized, as she began wrapping Ranger's hoof again.

"Have you already met Jenna?"

"Not formally, but our paths kind of crossed," she said.

"And since I look nothing like Jenna, you probably thought I was one of Patrick's legions of female admirers," Sarah guessed, sounding amused.

"The possibility crossed my mind."

"He does have a reputation," his sister acknowledged. "Though the trail of broken hearts isn't quite as long or wide as the rumor mill would lead you to believe. In fact, I wouldn't say the hearts were even broken—more likely just a little bit dented.

"Because for all his faults, and I know he has them, Patrick is unflinchingly honest with the women he goes out with to prevent anyone getting hurt. Those who do are the ones who refuse to believe him when he says he isn't looking for any kind of long-term relationship."

"How admirable," Brooke remarked dryly, at the same time wondering if Patrick's sister was trying to send her a message. Of course, the rancher had already relayed that message himself—loud and clear.

Sarah chuckled. "I can see why my brother likes you."

Before she could figure out an appropriate response to that, she heard the barn door opening again, followed by the sound of boots on concrete before Patrick appeared.

"Are you still here?" he asked.

"I'm just finishing up," Brooke told him.

The rancher shook his head. "I wasn't talking to you."

"Apparently I'm the one who's worn out my welcome," Sarah remarked.

"I didn't say that," her brother disagreed. "But when you left the house, almost an hour ago, you told me that you were leaving."

"And I am." Sarah touched her lips to Patrick's cheek, then waved in the vet's direction. "It was nice to meet you, Brooke."

"You, too, Sarah."

"If I'd realized she was still here, I would have come out to rescue you sooner," Patrick said to Brooke, when Ranger had been returned to his stall.

"Did I look like I needed rescuing?"

"No," he admitted. "But Sarah can be nosy at times, especially when she's prying for details about a woman in my life."

"I'm not in your life," she pointed out. "Just on the periphery."

"For now," he said, with a grin that sent a jolt of awareness through her body.

"I brought a bag of special puppy food for Princess," she said. "It will ensure she gets the energy and calcium she needs."

"That was a subtle shift in the conversation," he teased.

Brooke shrugged. "I don't have time for subtlety. I've got a bearded dragon with a possible respiratory infection waiting for me at the clinic."

"You treat lizards?"

"They aren't my specialty, but I'll check it out and refer it to a reptile vet, if necessary."

"Fair enough. But one of these days, when you've got some time, we'll get back to this conversation—and other unfinished business."

It was easy enough to disregard his words, but the intensity of his gaze reminded Brooke of the single kiss they'd shared—and tempted her with the promise of so much more.

Brooke Langley and Lori Banner became best friends in third grade when they realized they shared the same initials in reverse order. They stayed best friends through elementary and high schools before going away to different colleges. Now that Lori worked in the radiology department at Memorial Hospital in San Diego, the friends didn't get to see one another very often, but they did FaceTime once a month and texted whenever there was news to share, or just because.

So when Lori had reached out to say that she was

going to be in town for the weekend, of course Brooke was eager to see her, and they made plans to meet at Diggers' for dinner Saturday night.

"Are you goin' on a date?" Brendan asked, as he watched his mom brush mascara onto her lashes in preparation for a rare girls' night out.

Brooke chuckled at that. "No, honey. I'm having dinner with Aunt Lori tonight."

"Oh," he said, sounding disappointed. "Why don't you ever go on dates?"

She slid the wand back into the tube and twisted it closed.

"Because I've already got a number one guy," she said, playfully ruffling his hair.

"But it'd be kinda cool if you had a boyfriend," he said. "'Cause then you could get married and he'd be my dad."

Aching for her little boy, she turned away from the mirror to give her full attention to him.

"A few dates doesn't necessarily lead to marriage," she cautioned.

"I know," he said. "But you've gotta start somewhere, right?"

"And I know you'd really like a dad," she said. "But you've got an awesome grandpa who's taking you go-karting at Adventure Village tonight."

"Grandpa's the best, but a grandpa's not the same as a dad."

"No, he's not," she agreed.

"So I'm just sayin', I wouldn't mind if you wanted

to go out on dates sometimes," he continued, clearly unwilling to let the subject drop.

"I'll keep that in mind," she promised. "But right now I need to finish getting ready so I'm not late meeting Aunt Lori, okay?"

"Okay," he said.

Half an hour later, after she'd left Brendan with her parents, she was walking toward Diggers' when she saw her friend approaching from the other direction.

"Good timing," they said in unison. Then they both laughed.

After sharing a quick hug, they entered the restaurant, already chatting away as if it had only been days rather than weeks since they were last together.

"I'm so glad you were available tonight," Lori said when they were waiting for their meals.

"I would have canceled any other plans to make myself available," Brooke assured her, although they both knew that the chances of her having plans more elaborate than a bowl of popcorn and a movie with her son were slim to none. "Now tell me what inspired this impulsive trip home."

"I met someone," her friend blurted out, obviously unable to contain the happy news a moment longer.

"Someone from Haven?" Brooke guessed.

Lori shook her head. "No, he lives in California."

"Then why are you here instead of there?"

"Because, as you know, I have a habit of jumping into relationships with both feet and I'm determined to take things slow this time."

"In other words, the only way you could be sure

you wouldn't jump his bones was to leave the state," Brooke teased.

"Something like that," Lori agreed. "And he's a firefighter, with fabulous muscles in addition to great bones, so I think I deserve some credit for holding out this long."

"How long is this long?" she asked.

"I met him three weeks ago," her friend said.

"So why am I only hearing about him now?" Brooke wondered. But she didn't give Lori a chance to answer before continuing, "What's his name? Where did you meet him? What did you do on your first date?"

Her friend was more than willing to share all the details during dinner. Of course, she was interrupted on several occasions by other diners stopping by the table just to say hello or to ask Lori about California or to describe a pet's ailment and request a diagnosis from Dr. Langley—who always suggested they make an appointment because there was no way for her to know what was wrong without examining the animal in question.

But when Lori had finally revealed everything that she knew about hottie firefighter Matthew, it was evident that she was well on her way to falling in love, and Brooke was sincerely happy for her friend.

"It's time for you to get out there, too," Lori said, her tone gentle but firm.

"Have you been talking to my son?"

"Not yet, but I'm not going back to San Diego until I get my fill of Brendan cuddles," her friend promised. "Why?"

"He seemed disappointed that I wasn't going on a date tonight," she confided.

"Obviously your son understands that his mom is an incredible woman who deserves to share her life with an equally incredible man."

Brooke snorted at that. "I think Brendan just wants a dad."

"Well, of course the incredible man would also be a fabulous father," Lori said.

"Of course," she agreed.

"I know you're skeptical," her friend said. "But I promise—one day you're going to meet a man who'll make you forget all about that idiot who contributed to Brendan's DNA."

As an image of Patrick Stafford materialized in her mind, Brooke realized she might already have met that man.

Unfortunately, the sexy rancher had no interest in being anyone's father.

And by the end of the second week, Brooke had stopped worrying—or secretly hoping—that Patrick might make another move. Because the fact was, since the day of that first kiss, they were rarely ever alone together. Frequent visitors to the Silver Star included each of his sisters, various cousins and friends, and on one occasion, she'd even crossed paths with his grandfather. But Brooke never saw, or even heard mention of, his parents visiting.

What she did hear, from his sister Jenna, was that Liz and Derrick Stafford were far too busy to take an interest in their son's "little ranch" and that they were certain he'd be back behind a desk at Blake Mining before the end of the summer. Of course his relationship with his parents was none of her business, but she couldn't help but feel sorry that he couldn't count on their support as he embarked on a new venture—and even more grateful to know that she'd always had the support of her own.

Chapter Eight

On Saturday, Brendan was with his mom at the Silver Star when she got a message from the clinic's after-hours answering service that a local sheep farmer was frantic over the possibility that the new rams he'd introduced to his flock might be infected with a fatal degenerative disease. After Brooke had finished with Ranger, she called the farmer back, asked a few pointed questions about the origins of the suspect animals and their behavior, and agreed that the flock should be quarantined and tested—neither a quick nor easy job.

Tucking her phone back into her pocket, she exited the barn in search of her son. Brendan had gone outside to play fetch with Princess, promising to be careful not to throw too far so the pregnant dog didn't overexert herself.

"Come on, Brendan. We have to go."

"But we just got here," he protested.

"I've got an emergency situation to deal with," she said, knowing the information wouldn't make her son any happier but would compel him to move.

"What? Where?" he asked, already on his feet and handing Princess's slobbery ball to the rancher.

"Just down the road," she said. "But I have to take you to Gramma's first."

"Why can't I go with you?" Brendan asked.

At the same time Patrick said, "Why can't he stay here?"

"Yeah." Brendan immediately latched on to that option. "Why can't I stay here?"

"Because I don't know how long I'm going to be," she responded to both of them.

"I'm sure I can keep him entertained until you get back," Patrick said.

"It could be a couple hours," Brooke warned.

"And the sooner you leave, the sooner you'll get back," he pointed out.

It would certainly be convenient not to have to drive all the way into town and back again. But still she hesitated, suspecting that the rancher didn't have a clue what he was getting himself into. "Are you sure?"

"I'm sure." Patrick put his hands on her shoulders and turned her toward her truck. "Go."

"Okay," she said. "Brendan, I'm going."

He tipped his head back and puckered his lips for a quick kiss, then raced back to Princess.

Patrick puckered his lips, too, the twinkle in his eye challenging her.

Never one to back down from a challenge, Brooke gave him the same perfunctory peck that she'd given to her son.

So why did it feel completely different?

Even several hours later, Patrick didn't regret offering to let Brendan stay at the ranch while Brooke rushed off to deal with the emergency that had called her away. The boy was smart and curious and fun, but he was also a kid without a dad, and Patrick knew he wasn't the right man to step into that role.

Brendan had shared enough details about his day-to-day activities to reveal that his grandparents were very involved in his life. But Brooke's son had never mentioned a father, and it seemed that no one knew anything about the man who'd apparently never set foot in Haven and had no contact with the kid.

His choice? Patrick wondered. Or hers?

If he'd fathered a child—and thank God (or maybe only the diligent and proper use of birth control) that had *not* happened—he wouldn't have walked away from his responsibilities. He might not have been thrilled by the news of an unplanned pregnancy, but he would have done the right thing.

And he sure as hell wouldn't have let anyone keep him away from his child.

So what was the story with Brendan's father? And why did it even matter to Patrick if his only interest was in Brendan's mother?

He was puzzling over that question when Brendan asked, completely out of the blue, "Do you have a girlfriend?"

"Not right now I don't," he said.

"Why not?"

"Oh, um…because I've been busy working to get the ranch ready and haven't really had the time for a relationship."

"My mom's pretty busy, too," the boy confided. "Maybe that's why she doesn't have a boyfriend."

"Maybe," Patrick agreed.

"She says that she doesn't need any man in her life but me, but I'm prob'ly not gonna live with her forever, and then she'll be alone."

"Well, I'm sure she has a few years before she has to worry about an empty nest," he said, trying to lift some of the heavy concern he could see weighing on the boy's slender shoulders.

"But she's never had a boyfriend."

Patrick felt as if he should caution the boy against sharing family confidences with outsiders, but it was obvious Brendan didn't think of him as an outsider, and that made him feel surprisingly good.

"If you wanted a girlfriend, maybe you could talk my mom into being your girlfriend," Brendan suggested now.

"It doesn't really work like that," he said. "A boy and girl both have to want to be together. It's not something they can be talked into."

"But you like my mom, don't you?" he asked, sounding almost desperately hopeful.

"Yes, I like your mom," he confirmed. A whole lot more than he probably should, considering the complicated circumstances of their respective lives.

"And she likes you," Brendan said. "I know she does 'cause she puts that shiny stuff on her lips before we come over here."

"Does she?" he asked, both surprised and pleased by this revelation.

The boy nodded. "And she doesn't do it when we're going to the Rolling Meadows or the Circle G."

"Really?" he mused.

Brendan nodded. Then his brow furrowed as a new thought occurred to him. "Is it me? Am I the reason you don't want to date my mom?"

"What? No," Patrick denied. Because while he'd never before wanted to get involved with a woman tangled up with child-size responsibilities, he couldn't seem to resist Brooke.

And as it turned out, her kid was pretty irresistible, too.

"Where would you get an idea like that?" he asked now.

"My friend Mason said his mom's boyfriend dumped her because he didn't want to be a dad to someone else's kid."

"Then I'd say Mason's mom is better off without him."

"That's what she said," Brendan told him.

"Well, she's right," Patrick said, hating to think that any child would ever feel responsible because a man was selfishly unwilling to step up. As he'd been unwilling to do. But now that he'd had a chance to get to know both Brooke and Brendan a little bit better, he was starting to reconsider his position.

"So what do you think about dating my mom?" the boy pressed, clearly unwilling to give up on the idea.

"I think your mom doesn't need you to play matchmaker," Patrick said gently. "She's a smart, beautiful and amazing woman who wouldn't have any trouble finding someone to go out with if she was interested in dating."

Brendan rolled his eyes. "But I want her to go out with someone I like hanging out with, too."

"You know, you and I can hang out even if I'm not dating your mom," he pointed out.

"Maybe," Brendan said dubiously. "Until she starts dating someone else."

Yeah, Patrick silently agreed. *That would really suck.*

"I'm so sorry," Brooke said, when Patrick opened the door in response to her knock a short while later.

"You can stop apologizing anytime now," he told her, a reference to the multiple text messages she'd sent throughout the afternoon doing just that.

"No, I can't, because I know when you offered to let Brendan hang out, you thought it would only be for an hour or so, and I've been gone—" she glanced at her watch and winced "—more than five hours."

And he could tell, by the weariness in her eyes and the slump of her shoulders, that she'd been working hard for all of those hours.

She sniffed the air. "And it's obviously dinnertime

because you're cooking." She tilted her head, giving him a closer study. "You cook?"

He ignored her question to ask his own. "Are you hungry?"

Her stomach growled an immediate response.

He chuckled.

"Lunch was a long time ago," she confided.

"Then come on in and wash up for dinner," he said.

"Oh, no," she protested. "I wasn't fishing for an invitation."

"I know, but I've been holding dinner for you."

"You cooked for me?" she asked, clearly taken aback by that possibility even more than the fact that he could cook.

"I cooked because I was hungry," he clarified. "I cooked enough so that you and Brendan could eat, too."

"Where is Brendan?"

"Watching TV in the family room. He's already eaten," Patrick told her.

"He has?"

He nodded. "Your son was adamant that six o'clock is dinnertime, so I made sure he had his dinner at six o'clock."

"He gets that from my dad—a definite creature of habit," she acknowledged, making her way to the sink to wash up.

"What can I get you to drink?" he asked. "Beer? Wine?"

"A big glass of water, please," she said, because she was parched. "And maybe half a glass of wine?" Because after the day she'd had, she deserved a little indulgence.

"I've got a Napa Valley merlot or a Finger Lakes pinot noir," he said, as he filled a tall glass with water from the dispenser in the door of the fridge.

"Your choice," she said.

He gave her the water, then uncorked the pinot noir and poured it into two glasses, passing one to Brooke.

"Thank you," she said. "For everything today."

"Not a problem." He opened the oven to retrieve the two plates he'd left warming.

Brooke lifted herself onto one of the stools as he set the plates on the island.

"Dig in," he urged, taking a seat beside her and picking up his own fork.

Brooke didn't need to be told twice.

"Mmm," she said, after chewing and swallowing her third mouthful. "This is really good."

"It's not fancy but it's filling," he agreed.

"My mom makes a good meat loaf," she said. "But I'm not sure it's as good as this."

"Brendan seemed to think mine was better than Gramma's," he told her.

She chuckled. "He'll tell her that, too."

"I get the impression that he spends a lot of time with his grandparents."

"Probably more with them than with me," she confided. "I'm sure it was a nice change of pace for him to spend the day with someone different."

"Does Brendan ever see his dad?" he asked, his tone casual.

She stiffened in response to the question and glanced toward the wide entranceway that led to the family room, as if to ensure that her son was still engrossed in his television program and not within earshot. "Didn't we have this conversation already?"

"We didn't have a conversation. You said Brendan didn't have a father and that was the end of it."

"And nothing has changed since then," she told him.

"You didn't get pregnant by yourself," Patrick pointed out.

"No," she acknowledged. "But that's where his involvement ended."

She set her fork and knife on top of her empty plate. "Thank you for dinner," she said, clearly indicating that she'd said everything she intended to say on the subject of Brendan's father.

And once again, it wasn't much at all.

Unwilling to push and risk her further withdrawal, he said, "I figured you'd be happy to have a hot meal at the end of a long day."

"Truthfully, I would have been happy with a peanut butter sandwich," she said, pushing away from the island to carry her plate and glass to the sink. He followed with his own. "A hot meal pushes me beyond happy all the way to ecstatic."

He chuckled at that as he set his dishes down and drew her into his arms.

"Patrick," she said, sounding wary.

"Brooke," he echoed, amused.

"Ecstatic doesn't mean easy," she told him.

"You mean you're not going to let me have my way

with you while your son is watching *SpongeBob* on TV?" he asked, with feigned disappointment.

She smiled then. "Not this time."

"And now you've given me hope that there's going to be a next time," he warned.

"I didn't mean to," she said. "I'm not trying to string you along."

"I know," he assured her. "I just thought that maybe it was time to finally finish that conversation we started a long time ago."

"I've had a really long day. And so have you," she said.

"Okay, we'll skip the conversation," he decided and lowered his mouth to hers.

It was a casual kiss—teasing, testing—and Brooke knew that if she pulled away, he'd let her go.

She didn't pull away.

Though she still had concerns about acting on the attraction between them, she couldn't object to a kiss.

Sensing her acquiescence, one of his hands settled on her hip while the other slid up her spine to cup the back of her head as he deepened the kiss. She opened for him, not just willing but eager to meet the searching thrust of his tongue with her own.

Did he draw her closer?

Or did she lean into him?

She didn't know. She only knew that suddenly her breasts were pressed against his hard chest, and electricity was sparking through her veins, igniting a deeper desire.

She clung to him, her fingers digging into the soft

flannel that covered his broad shoulders, and briefly fantasized about tearing the fabric open to expose his bare skin, to examine and explore the taut muscles with her hands, with her mouth. To touch and taste him all over.

She was shocked by the explicitness of her own fantasy, and the desire that pulsed through her. A desire that she couldn't give in to. Not here. Not now. Not with this man.

Because Patrick Stafford wasn't just handsome and charming. The way she felt when she was with him was far too reminiscent of the way she'd felt when she was with Xander. And she'd promised herself, long ago, that she would learn from her mistakes.

She eased her lips away from his and drew in a long breath, filling her lungs with air.

"That was definitely a sweet end to the meal," he said. "And dangerously addictive."

He was right on both counts, and the truth only made her more wary. "What are we doing here, Patrick?"

"I thought we were enjoying spending time together," he said.

Which sounded simple and easy, and yet… "I don't want to get used to this."

"Because you don't trust me to stick?" he guessed.

"Because you don't want to stick," she reminded him. "You want to have some fun and move on, and that's fine for you, but I can't do that."

"How do you know without giving it a try?"

She started to dismiss his suggestion out of hand, then realized there might be some merit to it. She was afraid of giving in to the feelings he stirred inside her because she was afraid of getting hurt again.

But what if she could keep things light and casual? What if she could just enjoy being with him?

It was a tantalizing possibility.

"I don't know that I'm capable of having a casual relationship without the expectation of something more," she said. "But I'm sure that Brendan isn't."

"I'm not following."

"He's a seven-year-old boy without a father, and he's already getting attached to you," she explained.

"We're buddies," he said.

"And that's great," she agreed. "Until he starts looking at you as something more than a buddy."

Patrick immediately shook his head. "He's too smart for that."

"You'd think so," she said, as the theme song of her son's favorite cartoon alerted her to the show's conclusion. "But that's not a chance I'm willing to take."

She wasn't surprised that Brendan fell asleep in the truck on the drive home. She *was* surprised that he didn't conk out until they were less than five minutes from their destination. Prior to that, he'd kept himself awake by excitedly recounting every minute of his day with Mr. Patrick.

While she'd been testing potentially infected sheep, she'd barely had a moment to think about her son, but when she did, she'd worried that he might be bored or pestering Patrick with 1001 questions. Based on Brendan's retelling of the day's events, he definitely had *not* suffered from boredom.

In fact, it sounded as if he'd really enjoyed the time he'd spent at the Silver Star. His busy day at the ranch had included a horseback ride (*with a helmet*, he was quick to assure her), helping to groom and feed the horses, "consulting" with Mr. Patrick on his proposed child-friendly ranch activities, playing board games—which usually ranked significantly lower than video games in his estimation but had apparently been a lot of fun with Mr. Patrick—and finally, after dinner, some quiet time in front of the television.

Considering the amount of fresh air and exercise he'd got, it was no wonder exhaustion had finally caught up with him. But not before he'd commented, in a casual tone, that it had almost been like having a dad. The offhand remark confirming that Brooke was right to be worried about her son's growing attachment to the rancher.

Another worry was that, by the time she pulled into her driveway, the earlier threat of snow had turned into the real thing. She suspected the forecasted four to six inches would be blanketing the ground by morning, and though it was just a light dusting right now, she parked in the garage to save herself having to clear snow off her truck later.

Though Brendan was growing fast and getting heavy, she didn't like to wake him just so he could walk upstairs to his bed. Instead, she unbuckled his seat belt and lifted him into her arms, all too aware that her days of being able to carry her not-so-little-anymore boy were already numbered.

She pulled back his covers and lowered him onto the bed, then gently stripped him out of his coat, removed his hat and boots, and pulled the covers up again.

Of course, he hadn't brushed his teeth, but she knew that if she woke him now to perform the task, he'd be wide-awake until the wee hours of the morning—and so would she. So she only touched her lips to his forehead and left him sleeping.

He was the love of her life, but recently she'd started to realize that being a mother wasn't the whole of her identity. Her growing and deepening feelings for Patrick reminded her that she was also a woman, with a woman's wants and needs. And while she had no doubt that the rancher would be able to satisfy her desires, she knew that falling for a man like Patrick Stafford could only end in heartache.

But it was Brendan's tender heart that she worried about even more than her own. After only two weeks, it was obvious that her son had become attached to the rancher. He asked about him every day and was always disappointed to learn that Brooke had gone to the Silver Star without him.

Obviously it had been foolish to believe that the strong and steady presence of Brendan's grandfather could somehow make up for the absence of a father in his life.

But it would be a mistake to count on Patrick Stafford to fill that void for more than a few hours.

* * *

Melissa Stafford didn't believe in signs.

In her opinion, those who waited for signs wasted an awful lot of time waiting, while those who truly wanted something went after it.

So she didn't think it was a sign when she received a text message from her cousin Patrick in Haven only a few hours after she'd been wishing she had somewhere to go to get away from Seattle. But she did recognize it as an opportunity.

"Are you sautéing or snoozing, Stafford?"

She ignored the snarky question and tipped the pan so the browned cremini mushrooms spilled over the freshly grilled striploin plated beside a handful of roasted baby potatoes and a trio of asparagus spears.

"I'm taking a break," she called out, confident that her vacant station would quickly be filled by one of the eager apprentices who hovered around the kitchen at Alessandro's, desperate for the opportunity to do something.

She pulled her phone out of her pocket and reread Patrick's message as she slipped out the back door.

"I thought you'd be working on a Saturday night," he said, when he connected the call.

"You caught me on my smoke break."

She heard the frown in his voice when he asked, "Since when do you smoke?"

"I don't," she admitted. "But the smokers get to skip out of the kitchen for ten minutes every few hours, so I've started carrying a pack of cigarettes in my pocket."

"Is your boss really that much of a tyrant?"

"You have no idea. Anyway, your message said you're looking to hire a cook—is this for your dude ranch?"

"You know about that?"

"Are you kidding?" she asked. "The whole family's taking bets on how long you're going to stick it out."

"Nice to know everyone has such faith in my abilities," he remarked dryly.

"It's not your abilities they doubt but your commitment," she told him. "My dad says you've had five different positions at Blake Mining in the past five years."

"Six years," he said, as if that made a difference. "But I'm going to make this work."

"I believe you," Melissa said. Truthfully, she'd always thought the reason he bounced around from job to job at Blake Mining was that he was never happy there. And while she didn't know if this current venture would make him any happier, she had her own reasons for throwing her support behind him.

"I appreciate your vote of confidence," Patrick said.

"And to show how much I believe in you, I'll take the job."

There was a pause as he took a moment to process her unexpected offer.

"You want to leave your fancy restaurant in Seattle to cook for guests at my vacation ranch in Haven?"

"I do," she confirmed.

"Why?" he asked, sounding just a little bit wary.

"I need a change of scenery," she replied, aiming for a tone that was casual and carefree and not at all desperate.

"Not a lot of people come to northern Nevada for the scenery," he pointed out.

"This is a once-in-a-lifetime opportunity," she told him. "If you were smart, you'd grab hold of it with both hands before I change my mind."

Or started to beg, which would undoubtedly set off all kinds of alarm bells in her cousin's mind.

"What's it going to cost me?" he asked.

"Whatever you had budgeted for a cook's salary, plus a room for me on-site," she impulsively decided, because the salary wasn't nearly as important as the opportunity to get out of Seattle.

"I can manage that."

"Then I'll give my two weeks' notice after the restaurant closes tonight," she said, grateful that she could see not just a road out of her dead-end life but possibilities for a new start in Haven.

Chapter Nine

Brooke was awakened early Sunday morning by fifty-five pounds of jubilant child jumping on her bed.

"Wake up, Mom!"

She pulled the covers up over her head. "It's Sunday," she reminded her son. "The one day of the week that I get to sleep in."

"But it snowed last night and I wanna go tobogganing."

She opened one eye and peeked out from under the covers. "It's not even eight o'clock."

Then her cell phone chimed, and she sighed wearily as she reached for it to check the message.

"Apparently Grandpa's awake, too," she noted. "He says you've got half an hour to get ready or he's going tobogganing without you."

"Yikes! I've gotta get dressed."

"And eat some breakfast," Brooke said, pushing back the covers. "You can't tackle snow-covered hills on an empty stomach."

Of course, Brendan was already gone, racing back to his room in search of something to wear.

She wrapped herself in a plush robe, stuffed her feet into fuzzy slippers and headed to the kitchen to pop some frozen waffles into the toaster. While she was waiting for the pastries to heat, she sent a quick reply to her dad.

He'll be ready. Thank you so much! You've totally made his day. xo

Just then, she heard her son's footsteps coming down the hall. "I'm ready!" Brendan announced, sliding across the tiles in his sock feet.

She gave him a quick once-over. "Do you have a T-shirt on under that hoodie?"

"No, but—"

She lifted an arm and pointed to his bedroom.

He sighed but went to do her bidding.

When he came back again, his breakfast was ready: the OJ poured into his favorite cup and toasted waffles cut into strips to be dunked in the little container of syrup.

While he was eating, she made herself a cup of coffee, using the last pod in the cupboard. She added *coffee* to the grocery list on the fridge, beneath *likrish* and *mashmelos*—obviously her son's additions and proof that he was much better at math than spelling.

She'd just taken a first sip when Brendan pushed away from the island, setting his cup on top of the plate and carefully carrying both to the sink.

"Thanks, Mom." He returned to press sticky lips to her cheek.

"You're welcome," she said. "Now brush your teeth, and make sure you clean every tooth because you didn't brush last night."

"Okay," he agreed.

She finished her coffee while he was occupied with that task, then helped him wriggle into his snow pants and ski jacket. By the time his grandfather knocked on the door, Brendan was ready.

"How is it that you have so much more energy than I do?" Brooke asked her dad.

He grinned. "I don't have to be up with a seven-year-old every morning—and I love tobogganing."

She knew it was true. She had so many memories of racing down the snow-covered hills with her brothers and her dad, then returning home to warm numb hands around steaming mugs of hot chocolate.

"Well, then, be safe and have fun," she said.

"We will," he promised. Then he winked at his grandson. "And we'll let Gramma know when we're on our way back, so she can have the hot chocolate ready, right?"

"Right!" Brendan confirmed with enthusiasm.

Brooke was smiling as they drove away, but she was going to need another cup of coffee to get through a day that had started far too early. Of course, that required getting dressed and heading over to The Daily Grind, where she could grab a doughnut or muffin to go with her coffee. And since she knew her mom was alone this morning, she opted for two of the vanilla lattes Sandra enjoyed—on the rare occasions that she let herself indulge—and two maple pecan Danishes.

"You were late getting home last night," Sandra remarked, when Brooke stopped by with her offerings from the local coffee shop.

She didn't bother to ask how her mother knew. No doubt she hadn't gone to sleep until she'd seen her daughter's vehicle pull into the driveway. Now that Brooke was a parent herself, she understood why her mom had never been able to sleep until she knew her children were safe in their own beds.

"Brendan stayed at the Silver Star when I got called out to Rolling Meadows, and when I got back, Patrick invited me to stay for dinner."

Sandra broke off the corner of her Danish. "What did he make?"

"Meat loaf with mashed potatoes and green beans."

"Was it good?"

"Very good," Brooke admitted.

"A man who can cook… Imagine that," her mother mused.

"Dad can cook."

"Breakfast," Sandra said. "If he ever tackled something like meat loaf, I'd fall off my chair. Then I'd fall head over heels in love—if I wasn't already there."

Brooke rolled her eyes. "Well, my heart is holding

out for something that will hopefully last a little longer than an evening meal."

"But you like Patrick," her mom noted.

"I like him," she admitted.

"Why does that sound like a reluctant admission?"

"Because he's Patrick Stafford."

"And?" Sandra prompted.

"We went to the same high school," she reminded her mother. "And even though he graduated when I finished my freshman year, his reputation lived on."

"Everyone has a past," Sandra noted. "Why are you holding Patrick's against him?"

"Because I don't think he's changed."

"He's been good for Brendan," her mom pointed out. "Since the first time you took him out to the Silver Star, your son hasn't stopped talking about 'Mr. Patrick.'"

"I know." Brooke sighed.

"Or maybe that's the real problem," Sandra suggested.

"I never thought he was missing out, not having a father, because he's got the world's greatest grandfather," she confided.

"But it's not the same thing as having a father," her mom noted. "So maybe it's good for Brendan to spend time with Patrick."

"And maybe it's a shortcut to heartbreak," Brooke said. "Don't forget the way Patrick reacted when I first told him that I had a child."

"It's not unusual for a man to think he isn't ready to be a father—until he is," Sandra remarked. "Anyway, actions speak louder than words, and Patrick has been there for you. *And* for Brendan."

"Maybe he's enjoying the novelty of hanging out with a kid," she allowed. "But when the responsibilities get too real, he's likely to back off again."

"Do you really think so?"

She sighed. "I don't know what to think. And I don't like not knowing what to think, how to feel."

"You've got to stop punishing yourself for falling in love with the wrong man," her mom said gently.

"I'm not," she denied.

"Aren't you?"

"I stopped loving Xander a long time ago."

"So why haven't you let yourself love anyone else?" Sandra asked.

"My life doesn't exactly lend itself to romantic relationships," Brooke reminded her. "Being a single mom with a busy job doesn't leave a lot of time for anything else."

"And yet you've managed to find time to spend with Patrick."

"At the Silver Star, where I treat his injured horse."

"And when Ranger's injury is healed?" her mother asked.

"We'll find out soon enough," Brooke said. "Because I suspect he'll be ready to return to his herd by the end of next week."

"It's healing nicely," Jesse Blake said, with an approving nod as he examined Ranger's injured hoof.

"You've obviously been doing a good job keeping it clean and protected."

"Actually, Dr. Langley's been taking care of the injury," Patrick said, because he believed in giving credit where credit was due.

His grandfather's head shot up. "Are you telling me that the vet's been coming out here every day?"

"The gash was really nasty," he said in his defense. "And coronary band injuries can potentially lead to malformation and permanent hoof defects."

"You think I don't know that?" Gramps bristled. "That's why I told you to call Dr. Langley."

"I'm just trying to explain why I wanted someone with more experience and expertise overseeing Ranger's care," Patrick said.

"I'm surprised Bruce would have the time to trek out here to change a bandage." Then a speculative gleam came into the old man's eyes. "Or is it the other Dr. Langley who's been looking after your stallion?"

"It's the other Dr. Langley," he confirmed.

"Well, the girl knows her stuff," his grandfather acknowledged.

"The girl is a doctor," Patrick pointed out. "She wouldn't have graduated from veterinarian school if she didn't know her stuff."

"Graduated cum laude," Gramps informed him. "An even more impressive feat considering that she studied for her final exams with a baby at home."

"You seem to know an awful lot about Brooke Langley," he remarked.

"Of course I do. Her father and I go way back to his

early days, before that little lady was even a twinkle in his eye. Bruce is mighty proud of his girl—and the grandson who's already decided he wants to be a vet, too."

"Yeah, Brendan did mention that," Patrick said.

"You've met the boy, have you?"

"He's been out here a few times with Brooke."

"A few times?" His grandfather frowned. "I hope she keeps a close eye on him. Even if she's tending to your stock, it's not your job to babysit her kid."

"Brendan knows the rules," Patrick assured him.

"Knowing and following are two different things."

"Brendan does both. He's a good kid."

Gramps shrugged. "If you say so."

The deliberately casual response tripped an alarm in Patrick's brain. "Holy cr—" He quickly censored himself in response to his grandfather's disapproving look. "Sarah was right. You set me up."

"What are you blathering on about?"

"When Ranger was injured and you told me to call the vet, you knew it would be Brooke who came out to the ranch," Patrick accused.

"How could I possibly have known something like that?" Gramps challenged.

"I don't know," he admitted. "But I'm sure that you did."

"My only concern was for the stallion, and I'm glad to see that he's been well taken care of."

Patrick narrowed his gaze. "So you're denying that you deliberately put Brooke in my path to see if sparks would fly?"

"I've learned my lesson about interfering in the personal lives of my grandchildren," his grandfather assured him.

It was, no doubt, a reference to the separation between Patrick's cousin Brielle and Caleb Gilmore, her high school sweetheart, with whom she'd recently reunited and was expecting a child.

But it wasn't really an answer to his question.

Patrick had been looking forward to this day for three weeks, but now that it was here, he couldn't deny there was a little bit of disappointment mixed in with his relief when Brooke proclaimed Ranger's injury healed and gave permission for him to be reunited with his equine companions.

"That's great news," he said.

Except that Ranger's clean bill of health meant that Patrick would no longer get to see Brooke every day, because she'd have no reason to come out to the Silver Star.

Of course, he could ask her out on a date, but he'd tried that once already and been shot down, and he wasn't sure anything had really changed since then. Yeah, they'd shared a couple of sizzling kisses since that first encounter, but she'd firmly put on the brakes after that.

Ordinarily that would have been his cue to move on. Life was too short to waste time chasing a woman who'd clearly communicated her disinterest. Except that Brooke didn't act like she was disinterested when she was in his arms. And the memory of those kisses stirred his blood and nurtured his perhaps futile hope.

"Do you have a minute for a cup of coffee?" he asked, trying to buy some time to figure out his next move—if he was going to make one.

"I don't today," she said, sounding genuinely regretful. "I've got to get home to tackle a mountain of laundry so I can get Brendan packed and ready to go."

"Where's he going?"

"I thought he would have told you—my parents are taking him to Cedar Hills for the weekend."

"No, he didn't mention it," Patrick said. "Where's Cedar Hills and what's going on there?"

"It's a suburb of Salt Lake City where my brother and sister-in-law live with their twin daughters. It's Abbie and Zoe's tenth birthday this weekend."

"You're not going?"

She shook her head. "Someone has to be on call at the clinic. Plus, it's only a half day at school tomorrow, so they'll leave as soon as Brendan gets home and I've got appointments until four thirty."

"Are you going to be working all weekend while your parents and Brendan are away?" Patrick asked, more interested in her plans than her family's.

"Hopefully not *all* weekend," Brooke said.

For a brief moment, he thought she might be hinting that she'd have some free time so that he'd ask her out again, but her follow-up remark disabused him of that notion.

"Though I never know what kind of emergencies might arise," she pointed out.

"That must make it difficult to make plans," he commented.

"I don't make a lot of plans anyway."

Before he could decide if that was a hint, her cell phone rang.

She pulled the device out of her pocket and glanced at the screen. "Sorry, I have to take this—it's the clinic."

He stepped away to give her some privacy.

After a brief conversation, she tucked her phone away again. "And now I have another stop to make before I can get home to tackle that laundry."

He walked beside her to her truck. "Well, thanks again for everything you did for Ranger."

"Thanks for paying your bill," she said.

And then, with a smile and a wave, she was gone.

Brooke could have gone to Cedar Hills with her parents and Brendan. While it was true that someone needed to be at the clinic, there was a vet from Battle Mountain who'd covered for her father in the past—before Brooke had joined the practice—and likely would have done so again if Bruce had asked. In fact, her father had suggested just that, but Brooke wanted to prove that she was capable of caring for his patients so that he would feel comfortable taking a vacation every now and then, and maybe even retire eventually.

Sure, she was a little nervous, being the only vet on call and with her father so far away. But she also knew that she was ready for more independence and bigger challenges. And for the most part, the human clients didn't seem to mind that she was "the other Dr. Langley" so long as she was able to examine and treat their pets or other animals. And those pets, whether they had fur or feathers—or even scales—all loved her.

When she'd said goodbye to her last patient of the day, she checked her phone for a message from her parents, confirming their arrival at Kevin and Vanessa's. She sent a quick reply, adding lots of emojis for Brendan, then noticed she had another unread message—from Patrick.

Her heart skipped a beat, thinking—*hoping*—that he'd finally picked up on the hints she'd dropped about being on her own tonight.

Yeah, she still had some reservations about her ability to indulge in a good time without expectations of anything more, but she thought she was ready to give it a shot. With Patrick.

Unfortunately, his message didn't even hint at a potential good time.

I heard that a horse rolling on the ground is a sign of colic. Is this true?

She ignored the quick spurt of disappointment that he hadn't reached out in a personal capacity, because colic was a potentially serious concern—and the time stamp of the message indicated that it had been sent two hours earlier. She immediately responded.

It can be. Have you noticed any other unusual behavior?

While waiting for his reply, she expanded the cursory notes she'd made in her files earlier.

Shortly after five, Courtney poked her head in the door of Brooke's office. "Do you need me to do anything else before I go?" the vet tech asked.

"No, thanks. As soon as I finish updating this file, I'll be heading out myself."

"I can wait and walk out with you, if you're almost done," Courtney said.

"No, that's fine. It's been a long enough day already and I'm sure you've got plans tonight."

"Lowell made reservations at The Home Station," Courtney confided, naming her boyfriend.

"Special occasion?"

"Our six-month anniversary," Courtney said.

"Congratulations."

"Thanks. How about you—any special plans for the weekend?"

Brooke shook her head. "No plans at all until tomorrow morning, when I'm back here for surgeries."

"The party never stops, does it?" the vet tech teased.

"So it would seem," she agreed, returning Courtney's wave as the other woman headed out.

As Brooke finished with her notes, she found herself wondering if she'd ever been as young and carefree as her coworker. If so, she couldn't really remember because she'd had a six-month-old baby by the time she was Courtney's age. On the other hand, maybe Brendan's existence was proof that she'd not only been young and carefree, but a little bit careless, too.

After she finished her notes, she backed up the computer system and sent Patrick another quick text.

Do you want me to stop by to take a look at your horse?

She was turning into her driveway before he replied.

That would be great.

Though he didn't "sound" overly concerned, it was sometimes difficult to convey tone in a text message. But since she was already home, Brooke decided to freshen up a little before heading out to the Silver Star.

She brushed some mascara onto her lashes and slicked some gloss on her lips—then wiped the gloss off because it seemed too obvious. On second thought, maybe obvious wasn't a bad thing when trying to squeeze through a narrow window of opportunity, she decided. Because the two nights that her son would be out of town were a narrow opportunity for her to focus on being a woman rather than a mom, and one that she might not have again for a very long time. She opened the tube of gloss again, anticipation causing flutters in her tummy.

Because although she was twenty-nine years old, a certified veterinarian and a single mother of a seven-year-old son, the prospect of a romantic interlude with the handsome rancher made her feel like a giddy teenager on prom night. Not just excited but nervous, anticipating how the night would end.

And hoping it was with more than a goodbye kiss.

Was that crazy?

Was *she* crazy?

Patrick had accused her of trying to deny the chemistry between them, and he'd been right. She'd tried to ignore the attraction, but ignoring it hadn't made it go away. So she'd decided to stop pretending and acknowledge that she was ready to take the next step.

Although it was possible she was getting ahead of herself. Because if Patrick's horse was colicky, it could be a very long night for all the wrong reasons.

And worrying about the animal had her chewing the gloss off her lips again as she drove toward the Silver Star.

He must have been watching for her arrival, because the back door opened and Patrick stepped out onto the porch as soon as she pulled up beside the barn.

"Your message didn't mention which horse you're worried about," she said. "Are they stabled for the night or—"

"About that," he interjected. "I have a confession to make."

"A confession?" she echoed.

He nodded. "I sent the text in the hope of luring you out here."

She lifted a brow. "You lied about having a colicky horse?"

"I never said I had a colicky horse," he was quick to point out in his defense. "I simply asked if a horse rolling on the ground was a symptom of colic."

He was right. And it had been a clever ruse. Not that she was willing to give him any credit for it.

"But you let me believe you had a colicky horse," she said instead. "You let me worry that one of your animals was in distress."

He had the decency to look chagrined. "I'm sorry I worried you."

"But you're not sorry you lured me here under false pretenses?" she guessed.

He slid his arms around her and drew her close. "How can I be sorry when you're here?"

"But now that I know you don't have a colicky horse, there's no reason for me to stay."

"I can think of two reasons. One—you want to," Patrick said confidently. "And two—I want you to."

Because he wasn't wrong, at least about the first part, she gave up any pretense that she wasn't exactly where she wanted to be. "As it turns out, I have a confession of my own," she said.

"What's that?"

"I have an overnight bag in my truck."

His lips curved. "Do you?"

"You're surprised," she noted.

"Only because I thought I was going to have to work a lot harder to get you into my bed."

Chapter Ten

"I'm not in your bed yet," Brooke told him.

Patrick dipped his head to brush his lips along the column of her throat, raising goose bumps on her flesh, making her shiver.

"But that's where we're headed," he noted, with a smile as smug as his words.

She could hardly deny it. The fact that she was there, not just at his ranch but in his arms, proved she was committed to taking the next step.

And when he finally kissed her, the skillful mastery of his lips obliterated any lingering traces of uncertainty.

"Okay," she acknowledged, a little breathlessly, when he eased his mouth from hers. "But before we go inside, I think we should set some ground rules."

"Why?"

She would have thought the answer was obvious, but she clarified it for him now. "Because it's important that we both understand what this is and what it isn't."

He narrowed his gaze. "Is this the relationship talk?"

"No," she was quick to reply. "I'm trying to reassure you that I'm not looking for a relationship, that I don't expect one night together to turn into anything more."

"What if, after one night together, one or both of us wants more?" he challenged.

She shook her head. "That's the point in setting the boundaries now—because if one does and the other doesn't, it might lead to awkwardness or hurt feelings. But if we both agree that this one night is the beginning and the end, we can avoid that potential messiness."

"That's really what you want?" he asked, his tone dubious.

Yes.

No.

Truthfully, she wasn't sure what she wanted, but she knew she couldn't risk falling for Patrick, and the only way to be certain that wouldn't happen was to clearly define the parameters of their relationship now.

"That's the only way I can do this," she said. "The only way to ensure that Brendan won't find out."

"We're both consenting adults," he noted.

"One of us is a consenting adult with a child," she reminded him. "And I can't risk my son getting hurt."

"I would never do anything to hurt him."

"I know," she said. "But he's a little boy looking for a dad, and if he even begins to suspect there's something between us, he'll start imagining the three of us together as a family. And when that doesn't happen, he'll be hurt, despite our best intentions."

He shrugged. "Your call."

And yet something in his tone warned her that he wasn't entirely happy, which didn't make any sense to Brooke.

Why would he be annoyed that she'd specified the terms for their involvement? Wasn't no-strings sex what most guys wanted? And wasn't he the one who'd suggested having some fun and moving on?

She really didn't know, though. Her experience with the opposite sex really was limited, and even that limited experience was several years in the past, so it was entirely possible she was misreading the situation.

Deciding to focus on his words rather than his tone, she simply said "thank you" and opened the passenger door of her truck to retrieve her duffel bag.

Patrick automatically took it from her and slid his other arm across her shoulders as he guided her toward the house.

He hung her coat while she took off her boots. She'd been inside several times before, but this time, she knew they wouldn't stop at the kitchen, and the realization had the butterflies in her tummy zooming around as if they were seven-year-old boys high on sugar.

But then he did stop in the kitchen, turning to ask, "Have you had dinner?"

She shook her head. "No, but I had a late lunch."

"So you're not hungry?"

"Not for food," she said, reaching for him.

He chuckled against her lips. “I appreciate your enthusiasm, but I think I should make you something to eat first, because once I get you into bed, I plan to keep you there for a very long time.”

“Promises, promises,” she teased.

“I don’t make a lot of promises, but those I do make, I keep,” he assured her.

“Take me to bed, Patrick. I think we’ve both waited long enough.”

He didn’t make her ask again but lifted her effortlessly into his arms and carried her to the master suite at the back of the house. When he paused in the doorway, she stole a quick glance around the room, noting the neutral-colored walls, dark wood furniture and an enormous—and unmade—bed.

“I forgot to make my bed today,” he admitted, a little sheepishly.

“We’re just going to tangle up the sheets anyway.”

“Good point,” he said and tumbled with her on top of the mattress.

They’d been dancing around and toward this moment for weeks. Now that it was finally going to happen, it couldn’t happen quickly enough for Brooke. She hastily unbuttoned his shirt and pushed it over his shoulders, her hands rushing to trace the taut muscles beneath.

Or maybe she was in a hurry because she was worried that, if she slowed down, she might start to think about how long it had been since she’d been naked with a man. And then she might start to worry about all the ways her body had been stretched out by pregnancy and childbirth.

Especially in comparison to his taut and sculpted body. As she ran her hands over him—happily exploring his pecs, delts and abs—she almost couldn't believe that he'd worked behind a desk for the past several years.

"You didn't build these muscles over the past few months," she said.

"When I wasn't at Blake Mining, I was usually at Crooked Creek helping my grandfather with whatever chores needed to be done," he told her.

"So maybe there's more real cowboy in you than I gave you credit for," she mused, reaching for the buckle of his belt, eager to get some of this real cowboy in her.

"I've always enjoyed working outside," he said. "Though I like to think that I do some of my best work in the bedroom."

"I think I'm going to need a demonstration," she said.

"With pleasure," he murmured.

Then he kissed her again, long and slow and deep, and she was happy to get lost in the sensual onslaught of his mouth moving over hers.

She didn't realize he'd unfastened the buttons of her shirt until he parted the fabric, pushing it over her shoulders and down her arms, trapping her hands in the sleeves behind her back, while he kissed his way down her throat and nibbled along her collarbone. She felt the rasp of the stubble on his cheeks against the soft flesh as he nuzzled the valley between her breasts.

She couldn't think straight when he was kissing her like this. She could barely think at all. And that was before he opened the center clasp of her bra and peeled back the cups, freeing her breasts.

He caught them in his hands, murmuring his approval as his thumbs began to trace circles around the already taut nipples, causing them to draw into tighter points, making her ache and yearn. She felt a similar tightening low in her belly, an almost painful coiling of tension that ached for the pleasure of release.

Then he lowered his head and captured one of those nipples in his mouth, laving the peak with his tongue, causing hot sparks to dance over her skin and liquid heat to pool between her thighs.

She'd forgotten how arousing were the contrasts between a man's body and a woman's, but every pass of his hands reminded her now. His palms were strong and calloused, a testament to the manual labor he'd been doing over the past few months, and she shivered in response to their touch.

Having freed her own hands, she explored him, too. As her fingers glided over his taut and bronzed skin, his muscles tensed and rippled. Intrigued, she leaned closer to press her lips to his chest and felt his groan reverberate through her lips.

She was hardly innocent. She'd lost her virginity almost a decade earlier. She'd carried and birthed a child. And yet she was certain she'd never been touched the way Patrick was touching her. She knew she'd never felt the way she felt in his arms.

Nothing she'd ever known or experienced before had prepared her for the intensity of the heat that pulsed in her veins. Even scarier than that realization was the uncomfortable idea nudging at the back of her mind that she might never feel the same way with anyone else. Certainly she couldn't imagine another man making her want as she wanted him.

After he'd ensured their mutual protection, he settled between her parted thighs. It had been a long time, and she wasn't prepared for his size, wincing a little as he pushed deeper inside.

He captured her mouth with his, kissing her deeply and thoroughly, until her body finally relaxed, accepting and welcoming him. Only then did he begin to move. As pleasure continued to build inside her, she lifted her hips, her heels digging into the mattress. She met him thrust for thrust, tension coiling tight in her belly. Tighter and tighter, until she finally exploded like a firework—a kaleidoscope burst of bright lights and colors—a billion tiny little shards that slowly faded as she drifted back to earth again. Patrick cried out as he found his own release, his body shuddering and then collapsing on top of her.

It was several minutes before her breathing returned to some semblance of normal.

"That was…" She trailed off, not quite sure how to finish.

"Indescribable?" he suggested.

She nodded.

"Although *wow* might also work," he decided, as he summoned the energy to roll off her.

She didn't have a chance to register and regret the loss of his weight pinning her to the mattress before he gathered her close.

"Was it *wow* for you, too?" she asked and immediately cringed at the neediness of her tone.

"Quite possibly beyond *wow*," he said.

She relaxed then, pleased by his response and grateful that she'd packed the overnight bag.

Then her stomach growled.

Audibly.

Patrick chuckled. "Now you're hungry."

"So it would seem," she agreed.

He rolled out of bed and reached for his discarded jeans. "Let's go see what I've got in the fridge."

"Apparently I need to move grocery shopping to the top of my to-do list," he commented, as he whisked eggs in a bowl.

"I don't think I even have the ingredients for an omelet in my fridge," she confided, as she stood beside him, wearing his soft flannel shirt, dicing the pepper and onion.

"That's sad," he said.

"Fortunately, if I'm really desperate, I can walk across the driveway to raid my parents' pantry."

"Is that fortunate?" he wondered.

"When you're trying to feed a growing seven-year-old boy, it's very fortunate."

Patrick poured the egg mixture into the heated pan, then chopped up some leftover ham. When the eggs were set to his satisfaction, he added the onions, peppers and ham, grated some cheese on top, expertly folded the egg in half with a spatula, then slid the omelet out of the frying pan and onto a plate.

"That can't all be for me," she protested when he set the plate in front of her.

"You're the one who didn't have dinner," he reminded her.

"But you just completed a pretty intense workout."

He smiled. "That wasn't work. That was pure pleasure."

She felt her cheeks heat and dropped her gaze to her plate, all too aware that blushing like a schoolgirl was the price of being a redhead. Picking up the fork, she cut off a piece of omelet and popped it into her mouth.

"How is it?" Patrick asked.

"Really good," she said, digging her fork into the fluffy omelet again. "So where did you learn to cook?"

"That's a rather personal question from a woman who made it clear she had no desire to complicate sex with intimacy," he remarked.

"You're annoyed that I wanted to establish some ground rules," she realized.

"I may not have a lot of experience with relationships, but I've always thought it was poor form to plan for the end at the beginning."

"I don't have a lot of experience with relationships, either," she reminded him. "And it may be that, in trying to manage my own expectations, I was a little tactless."

"Apology accepted," he said.

She smiled gratefully. "Good to know you don't hold a grudge."

"I don't want to waste the limited time we have together arguing when we could do much more interesting things."

The promise in his eyes made her insides quiver, but she refused to let him distract her from her original question. "So are you going to tell me who taught you to cook?" she asked, lifting another forkful of egg to her mouth.

"My mother."

"Really?"

"You're surprised she can cook?"

She shrugged. "I would have guessed that your family had a cook in their big house on Miners' Pass."

"My parents do have a cook, but he's only there Monday through Friday—unless they're hosting a weekend event. Otherwise, it's my mom who reigns over the kitchen on Saturdays and Sundays. She says that cooking relaxes her, and I'd agree it's the only thing that does," he confided. "She always seemed more patient in the kitchen, which is probably why I liked hanging out with her there."

"What else did she teach you how to make?"

"In addition to a simple meat loaf—"

"Simple and delicious," she interjected, reminding him that she'd already enjoyed that culinary offering.

"—I do a decent job with an omelet," he continued. "But my grilled cheese is to die for."

"To die for, huh?"

"My sister's words, not mine," he said.

"So why did I get a melt-in-your-mouth omelet instead of a to-die-for grilled cheese?" she wondered.

"They're exclusively offered on the second night," he teased. "So if you wanted to stay again tomorrow..."

"You sure know how to tempt a girl, don't you?"

she said, and she wasn't only referring to the potential sandwich. It was the man more than anything else that tempted her to throw her own rules and guidelines out the window and beg for not just a second night but as many more after that as he'd give her.

"I do my best," he said and leaned over to brush his lips over hers, tempting her even more.

"Mmm." She closed her eyes, savoring the taste of his kiss. "Now I'm craving more of your kisses."

"As it happens, I have an endless supply of those."

"Good to know," she said and drew his mouth down to hers again.

He slid his hands beneath her bottom and lifted her out of the chair. She wrapped her legs around his hips, anchoring herself to him as he made his way back to the bedroom, kissing her the whole way.

Patrick was accustomed to sleeping alone.

Though he enjoyed the pleasurable pursuits that came with sharing his bed, he generally preferred solitude for sleeping. Apparently Brooke was accustomed to sleeping alone, too, because she was sprawled in the middle of the mattress, having somehow managed to push him to the edge.

He considered waking her and nudging her on her way. He knew she wouldn't protest. Considering she was the one who'd set limitations on their relationship, she might even be relieved. But he didn't wake her, because he didn't want her to leave. He wasn't nearly ready to let her go. And that realization was more than a little disconcerting.

Or maybe he was overreacting. Maybe it wasn't surprising that, after three weeks of intense buildup, he needed more than two rounds of exceptional sex to get her out of his system.

She truly was an amazing woman—slim but toned, her muscles firm beneath silky smooth skin. An enticing contrast of softness and strength. Having watched her work with Ranger over the past few weeks, he knew she was as capable as any man, but there was no doubt that she was all woman.

He let his hand skim over her now, from calf to knee, thigh to hip, waist to breast. And, yeah, he got a little distracted there, but how could his attention not be captivated by the way her nipple immediately pebbled against his palm? How could he not be aroused to know that, even in her sleep, she responded to his touch?

He shifted closer and kissed the side of her throat; she exhaled on a sigh and rolled over so that she was facing him. Her eyes, heavy with the remnants of slumber, lifted to his.

"Did I wake you?" he asked.

Her lips curved. "I'm not sure if I'm awake or having an incredibly erotic dream."

"Let's find out," he said and lowered his head to her breast, capturing the taut nipple in his mouth.

She gasped as his tongue swirled around the rigid peak, and again when he suckled the tender flesh. He loved the sensual sounds she made, her throaty murmurs and soft sighs letting him know what she liked. She was so passionate…so incredibly responsive.

He nuzzled the hollow between her breasts, making her squirm, then kissed his way down her torso. He stroked the insides of her thighs, urging them to part, and felt her muscles quiver as she complied with his silent request.

He settled there, his broad shoulders pushing her legs farther apart, opening her to his eager gaze, his avid mouth. He touched her with his tongue, a slow, leisurely stroke. Her breath caught in her throat, then exhaled on a shuddery sigh.

He tasted her again, teasing her with his lips and his tongue until she whimpered, then licking and sucking until he heard her breath catch the way it did when she was oh so close to her release. He held her at the brink for just a moment, glorying in the power he had over her.

But of course that power was only an illusion, because he was equally in her thrall—rock hard and aching for her. He wanted nothing more than to rise up and drive himself into her, driving them both to the finish.

No, there was one thing he wanted more.

He wanted to make her come completely undone, and he wanted to watch it happen.

So he did…and it was the most beautiful thing he'd ever seen.

And when her body finally stopped shuddering with the aftershocks of her climax, he took her to the brink again. Only then did he sheathe himself with a condom and join their bodies together.

Their rhythm was easy and comfortable, as if they'd been lovers for weeks, maybe months, rather than mere hours. There was something about being with Brooke that didn't just feel familiar; it felt…right. And when she lost herself in another climax, he found his own release deep inside her.

The next time Patrick awakened, it was because Brooke was trying to disengage herself from the arm wrapped around her.

He responded by tightening his hold and pulling her closer.

She turned her head to look at him, an apologetic smile curving her lips. "I have to go."

"Why did you bother bringing an overnight bag if you didn't plan on staying overnight?"

"I did stay overnight. It's now morning."

"Not even the cows get up this early," he grumbled.

"How would you know?" she teased. "You're never up with the cows."

"Can't you stay just a little while longer?"

"I've got surgeries this morning, starting at nine o'clock," she said, sounding sincerely regretful.

He glanced at the clock. "I can work fast."

He was true to his word.

And his overnight guest left the Silver Star with a very satisfied smile on her face.

Chapter Eleven

"Someone's in a good mood today," Larissa remarked, when Brooke walked into the clinic a short while later.

"It's a bright, sunny morning," she said, grateful that she had the weather as a ready excuse. Because even if it had been gray and gloomy, she wouldn't have been able to stop smiling, and she didn't know how she would have explained her euphoria then.

She could hardly admit that she was feeling happy and relaxed because Patrick Stafford had given her multiple orgasms multiple times over the span of the ten hours she'd spent with him. Or that she'd been sincerely reluctant to leave his bed.

She wished she could have stayed.

Or that she could go back.

But she was the one who'd made the rules. She was

the one who'd insisted that one night would be enough. It didn't matter that she'd been wrong—she couldn't backtrack now.

And with Ranger's injury healed, she didn't even have the stallion as an excuse to stop by. And if Patrick sent her a vague text message about a potential problem at the ranch, she was going to ask for some specifics before she raced over there again.

Probably.

"How was your dinner at The Home Station last night?" she asked, when she found Courtney prepping the room for their first surgery.

"Amazing," the vet tech immediately replied. "And *so* romantic. The food was unbelievably good, with a different wine pairing for each course. Plus, there was candlelight and soft music."

"It sounds amazing," Brooke agreed. And though there was a part of her that hoped to dine in the fancy restaurant one day, she'd been satisfied with the omelet she'd had for dinner—and more than satisfied with everything before and after.

Thankfully, she managed to put those memories and the man out of her mind to focus on treating her animal patients. She also exchanged pleasantries with and offered reassurances to their human companions.

She had five surgeries scheduled, including two spays, a neuter, repair of a strangulated umbilical hernia in a pet lamb and the extraction of three rotted teeth from a nine-year-old Yorkshire terrier. Everything went according to plan except the second spay surgery, which she had to postpone when the pre-op exam revealed that the owners of the fifteen-month-old French bulldog had waited too long to book the procedure. Little Lulu was already pregnant.

Patrick didn't mind getting an earlier than usual start to his day. Then again, who would complain about waking up with a warm and willing woman in his arms?

In fact, he was in such a good mood, he caught himself whistling as he mucked out stalls and fed the animals. After that, he spent some time playing with the dog and even used the brush Brooke had left for grooming. Princess didn't just accept the attention but seemed to revel in it, and he found himself wondering again how anyone could have let her go.

He returned to the house to answer emails, do some banking and check the updated version of the Silver Star Vacation Ranch website—which Devin had promised would be ready to go live as soon as Patrick gave him the word. He was eager to open for business and for Melissa to arrive so they could test-drive the menu he'd drafted. Of course, Brendan had given him some input on that, too, suggesting kid-friendly additions such as French toast sticks, PB&J, mini corn dogs and a sundae bar.

Thinking of food made him realize that he hadn't eaten since lunch, and even then he'd only opened a tin of chili because he'd been too busy to make anything else. Aware of the limited contents of his refrigerator, he decided to go into town to grab a bite. Maybe he'd even reach out to a couple of friends to get together to share a couple of pizzas and a pitcher of beer.

Or maybe he'd pick up a pizza and take it over to Brooke's house.

The latter was definitely the more appealing option, except that it would be a violation of her rules.

He should be satisfied that he'd had her in his bed and move on. Except that he wasn't ready to move on, and he didn't believe she was, either. His reputation aside, he wasn't really a love-'em-and-leave-'em kind of guy. Maybe he hadn't had many long-term relationships, but he wasn't in the habit of moving directly from one woman to the next, either. Well, not since college, anyway. After his breakup with Kari, he'd perhaps been a little indiscriminate in his effort to forget her betrayal.

But that was a lot of years ago. He'd not only got over Kari, he'd moved on—again and again.

Or maybe he hadn't been as over his cheating ex as he'd wanted to believe, because although he'd dated some really great women since then, he'd never let himself get too attached to anyone. He'd never even been tempted. Until now.

Until Brooke.

It wasn't until Brooke got home and looked in the refrigerator for something to eat that she realized she'd forgotten to stop at The Trading Post. The mostly bare shelves would definitely need to be stocked before her son came home the following day, but she didn't feel up to the task of grocery shopping tonight.

Her stomach growled in protest, as if aware that she didn't have the usual option of going next door to see what her mom was cooking because her parents were out of town with Brendan. She'd been happy enough to send her son off with his grandparents because she knew he'd have a great time in Cedar Hills with his cousins. She hadn't considered how empty the apartment would seem or how lonely she'd be without him.

Of course, she hadn't really missed him the night before, because Patrick had kept her completely and thoroughly distracted. So much so that her body ached all over, and she shivered as she remembered the way he'd touched and kissed her, eliciting shockingly intense responses from her body.

But that was last night.

Tonight, she was on her own. And instead of focusing on how quiet the apartment was without her little boy, she decided to take advantage of the solitude to do the things she didn't usually do when she had a curious seven-year-old underfoot.

She started by indulging in a long bath with mountains of frothy bubbles and scented candles. She even poured herself a glass of her favorite pinot noir—or half a glass, as that was all that was left in the bottle—and savored each sip.

But then the half glass of wine started to give her bad ideas—such as texting Patrick to inquire about his not-at-all colicky horse. Thankfully, she was sober enough to realize that kind of overture might seem like a booty call.

Which, of course, it would be.

Because apparently one passion-filled night after eight years of celibacy wasn't enough for her.

Well, it was going to have to be, she admonished herself as she released the tub stopper. Because she'd made the rules and now she had to play by them.

She reached for a towel and rubbed it briskly over her body, ignoring the way her nipples tingled in response to the brush of the soft cotton, teasing her with memories of a different touch.

As she tugged on a pair of leggings and a shirt, her stomach growled again, reminding her that a half glass of wine was no substitute for dinner. She should probably go out to pick up something from Diggers' or a slice of Jo's pizza, but both options would require her to put on real clothes and leave her warm apartment, neither of which appealed to her. Which meant that she was going to have to be satisfied with frozen pizza tonight.

Brooke had just set the oven to preheat when there was a knock at the door. She didn't often get company, and nine times out of ten, when someone did knock on her door, it was either her mom or her dad. The tenth time it was usually the boy across the street, wanting to know if Brendan could come out and play.

Since she knew it couldn't be either of her parents and it was too late for Russell to be out, she peeked through the peephole before opening the door. Her heart jolted inside her chest when she identified her unexpected visitor as the cowboy of her fantasies.

She lifted a hand to push her hair—still damp from her bath—away from her face and considered pretending that she wasn't home. She definitely wasn't prepared for company. She had no makeup on and hadn't even bothered with a bra because she was alone.

Patrick knocked again, a little louder, making her realize the futility of pretending she wasn't there when her vehicle was in plain sight in the driveway. And truthfully, she really wanted to invite him in.

She unlocked the door and pulled it open.

His gaze skimmed over her, from the thick wool socks on her feet to the damp mass of hair spilling over her shoulders. "You look like you're settled in for the night," he remarked, the corners of his mouth curling with the hint of a smile.

"I wasn't expecting company," she said, hating that he'd caught her so unprepared when he looked so darn good.

"It was an observation, not a criticism," he assured her.

"What are you doing here?" she asked, her gaze shifting from the handsome man to the grocery bag he carried.

"I came into town to grab a bite and it occurred to me that, after a day of surgeries, you might not feel up to cooking."

"I didn't, which is why I was just going to throw a frozen pizza in the oven," she said.

"Or I could make you my to-die-for grilled cheese instead," he suggested.

"I thought that was a second-date meal."

"So we'll consider this our second date," he said.

She opened the door wider to allow him entry, because any kind of grilled cheese shared with the handsome cowboy was better than eating alone—especially if she could have him for dessert.

Except that they'd agreed to one night together and that night was over, she reminded herself.

So why was he here now—offering to cook for her again and calling it a second date? she challenged herself.

Oblivious to her inner struggle, Patrick held up the six-pack in his other hand. "I brought beer, too."

"Good call," she said. "Because the only beverages I could offer are tap water, milk approaching its best-before date or juice boxes."

"What kind of juice boxes?" he asked, making her smile.

"Apple, grape or fruit punch."

"I think I'll start with a beer," he decided, following her into the small kitchen and setting the grocery bag and beverages on the island.

"Do you want a glass?" she asked.

"Bottle's fine for me," he said, twisting the top off one and offering it to her.

She shook her head. "Thanks, but I already had half a glass of wine and I'm on call this weekend."

He put the bottle down and began to unpack the groceries: a loaf of twelve-grain bread, a stick of butter, three different kinds of cheese, a small bottle of honey and a plastic bag with green leaves in it.

She lifted a brow.

"I brought that from home," he said. "Because The Trading Post doesn't usually have fresh basil."

"What's the basil for?" she asked. "And the honey?"

"Why don't you sit down and relax while I make dinner?" he suggested.

"Because now my curiosity is piqued as much as my appetite," she said.

He put his hands on her shoulders and steered her toward the living room. "Go."

"You're bossy," she told him.

"And you're nosy."

Instead of arguing, she retreated to the living room to relax, as he'd suggested.

She could hear drawers and doors opening and closing as he rummaged around for the equipment he needed, but he didn't ask for help, so she didn't offer it. It was a strange experience to have someone else preparing food in her kitchen, but not an unpleasant one. And as the scent of grilled bread made its way to the living room, her stomach growled in anticipation.

A short while later, he carried a tray into the living room with sandwiches and drinks. "Is it okay to eat in here?"

"Sure," she said. "It's a little roomier and definitely more comfortable than the kitchen."

"I like your place," he said, as he set a glass of water and a plate in front of her.

"It's small," she acknowledged. "But it works for me and Brendan."

"It's cozy and warm," he countered. "And—" his gaze narrowed on the antique sideboard her mother had refinished and Brooke was using as a TV stand "—is that a Chippendale?"

She nodded. "One of my mother's flea-market finds. It was painted mint green when she brought it home."

"She's got a good eye," he remarked.

"So do you," Brooke noted. "Not a lot of guys recognize specific furniture styles."

"My parents have a lot of Chippendale furniture at their place," he said.

And not a single piece that had come from a flea market, Brooke surmised, as she lifted half of the grilled cheese to her mouth and took a bite.

"Ohmygod." She closed her eyes as she chewed, savoring the contrasting flavors and textures, with just a hint of sweetness. "This is *sooo* good."

"That's what you said last night," he said.

Her eyes popped open then, and he winked boldly, making her blush.

"I did not," she protested, though she wasn't entirely sure she hadn't.

"Maybe not in those words," he said. "But I read between the lines of your moans and whimpers."

"Then I guess it's a good thing you don't have to worry about listening to a repeat performance," she responded in a prim tone.

He grinned, unrepentant. "What if I said that I love the noises you make when I touch you? That they're an incredible turn-on? And that I've been walking around in a semi-aroused state all day thinking about your body shuddering beneath mine?"

"I'd think that maybe this grilled cheese was just a prelude to a booty call," she said. "Was it?"

"That's entirely up to you," he said. "But since you made it clear that you weren't going to come back out to the Silver Star tonight, I thought I'd come here."

"You have to know it isn't location that's the problem."

"After last night, I'm having a little trouble believing that there *is* a problem."

"I'm not the kind of woman who has affairs, Patrick."

"Yeah, you mentioned that once or twice before," he said.

"And you're not the kind of man who does relationships," she said.

"Not according to the rumor mill in town," he agreed.

"And as a single mom of an impressionable seven-year-old son, I don't want to add any grist to that mill."

"I know how to be discreet, if that's your concern," he assured her.

"Patrick, you can be with any woman you want."

"And I want you," he said.

She sighed, both flattered and frustrated by his obstinacy. "Do you really? Or do you just want to be the one who walks away when a relationship is over?"

"Trust me," he said. "This isn't about ego. It's about attraction. I'm here now because I still want you so much I can't seem to think about anything else."

"Trust doesn't come easily to me," she admitted.

"He really did a number on you, didn't he?"

Brooke knew he was referring again to the man who'd got her pregnant. And though she really didn't want to discuss her romantic history—limited though it was—she realized that telling him at least a little bit about her past might be the easiest way to make him understand why she was so wary.

"He wasn't the only one," she said. "Every time I've let myself rely on a man, I've been let down. And not just in romantic relationships, either."

"Tell me," he said. "I'll take names, track them down and beat them up."

She smiled at that. "Well, first there was Hayden Reed, who, in fourth grade, offered to trade his yogurt tube for my string cheese and then ate both snacks."

"We're going back that far, are we?" he remarked, sounding amused.

"You asked," she reminded him. "Next came Christian Harvick, my lab partner in biology, who didn't bother to do his part of our joint assignment, forcing me to do it so we both didn't get a zero. Then Mr. Olerud, the high school volleyball coach."

"I remember Mr. Olerud," he said.

"He cut me from the team in my junior year in favor of a transfer student, not because Analise was a better player than me but because her father offered to buy new uniforms for the team."

"That sucks," he agreed.

But she wasn't done yet.

"Dr. Etherington was one of my professors at college," she continued. "He docked me five marks for throwing up during a dissection when I was ten weeks pregnant, because if I couldn't stomach the job, I shouldn't be there.

"And then there's my brother Nathan—a plastic surgeon in LA—who changed his mind about coming to Brendan's baptism at the eleventh hour because an A-list celebrity wanted a consult. On a Sunday afternoon."

"I'm sorry," he said sincerely.

"Kevin and Vanessa—my other brother and sister-in-law—were there, though. Proudly standing up as godparents for their nephew, along with my best friend, Lori. And my parents, of course." She set her empty plate on the table. "My dad's the one man who's always been there for me."

"I can see why you have some trust issues," he acknowledged. "But you can count on me, Brooke. Because I won't ever make you any promises I don't intend to keep."

And maybe, for right now, that was enough, Brooke thought, as he dipped his head to touch his mouth to hers.

Because right now, she wanted him as much as he wanted her. More. She parted her lips for the searching thrust of his tongue, her fingers digging into his strong, broad shoulders, holding on to him for balance as the world tilted and spun. And that was before his hands slid under her top, and he groaned against her lips when he found her breasts unfettered. He cupped them in his palms, his thumbs teasing her nipples so that she whimpered.

"If you want me to go, tell me now," he urged.

"I don't want you to go," she admitted. "But you can't leave your truck in my driveway all night."

"I'd ask if you have nosy neighbors, but this is Haven and you have neighbors, so enough said."

She nodded, grateful for his understanding.

"What time do I have to leave to minimize the gossip?" he asked.

"You don't have to leave. You just have to park in the garage."

"I'll be right back," he promised.

* * *

After they made love, Brooke drifted off in his arms. And while Patrick was happy to hold her, his stomach was thinking it wanted another sandwich. Carefully untangling their limbs, he slipped out of her bed, pulling the covers up over her so she wouldn't get cold in his absence.

He was sliding the grilled cheese out of the frying pan and onto a plate when she appeared in the kitchen. Her eyes were sleepy, her hair disheveled, and while he hadn't really expected that she would wander through her apartment naked, he was disappointed to see that she'd pulled an oversize T-shirt on to cover up her sexy body.

"I was hungry," he said, as he sliced the sandwich in half.

"And I was thirsty," she told him.

"Do you want half of this?" he offered.

"No, thanks," she said, reaching into the cupboard for a glass.

As she stretched, the hem of that T-shirt rode enticingly high on her thighs, and he felt his body stir. Was it normal, he wondered, to want a woman the way he wanted her? Or had she somehow entranced him?

He scowled at the thought as he bit into his sandwich.

"Although I meant to tell you that I agree with your sister," she said, as she filled her glass from the pitcher in the fridge. "You do make a to-die-for grilled cheese.

"In fact, I was thinking that if you're not successful in finding a cook for the Silver Star, you could handle the kitchen duties yourself. Omelets for breakfast, grilled cheese for lunch and meat loaf for dinner."

"Lucky for my guests, I did find a cook."

"You did?"

He chewed another bite of sandwich. "And not just any cook, but a graduate of the International Culinary Center in New York currently working at a fancy restaurant in Seattle."

"How'd you snag someone with those credentials?" she wondered.

"Melissa's my cousin."

"Ah." Brooke nodded. "So when's she coming to Haven?"

"She gave her two weeks' notice last week, so I'd guess she'll be here sometime the week after next."

"You *guess*? Most people in business like to firm up those kinds of details."

"I'm not worried," he said. "There's still lots of time before Memorial Day weekend."

"So you've picked the date for your grand opening?"

He nodded.

"That's fabulous news," she said.

"In other news—" he set his empty plate aside and reached for her, drawing her into his arms "—my hunger for food has been satisfied, but not my desire for you."

"Maybe it's a proximity thing," she said.

"You're suggesting that I only want you because you're here and looking sexy as hell in an old T-shirt?"

She glanced down at the T-shirt. "Or maybe you're

under the influence of alcohol," she allowed. "How many beers did you have?"

"Just one."

"You're a cheap date."

"And easy," he promised.

She smiled at that. "You're going to let me have my way with you?"

"You can have me any way you want, anytime," he promised.

Her speculative gleam shifted to something else when a ringing sound emanated from the iPad on the counter.

"It's a FaceTime call," Brooke told him. "Probably Lori calling me back."

She'd reached out to her friend earlier, wanting to tell her about the events of the previous night and seek her advice on what to do next. Since then, Patrick had answered that question for her. Of course, Lori couldn't know that, and Brooke's message had asked her to call whenever she got in, because Brooke had anticipated being home alone all night.

"Don't you want to talk to her?" he asked, when Brooke made no move to answer.

"I do, but…"

"I promise to stay hidden from the camera," he said, anticipating her concern.

So she reached for her iPad and connected the call.

After a brief exchange of pleasantries, she listened for several minutes as her friend told her about the fabulous day she'd spent with Matt, who'd just popped out to pick up pizza for a late snack. Then Lori stopped talking midsentence and narrowed her gaze on the screen. “Oh. My. God,” she said. “You’ve had sex.”

“What?” Brooke tried to feign ignorance, as if she had no idea why her friend had jumped to such a conclusion, but she suspected that her burning cheeks had already confirmed Lori’s suspicion.

“Don’t you dare try to deny it. I’ve seen that sleepy, satisfied look in your eyes in my own mirror to know what puts it there,” Lori said. “Not to mention the redness on your throat that suggests up close and personal attention from a man’s bristly jaw.”

“Okay, yes,” she finally admitted, aware that Patrick was within earshot but not daring to look at him. “I had sex.”

“Really good sex?” her friend asked hopefully.

Brooke felt her cheeks burn hotter.

“Tell me,” Lori urged. “And don’t spare any of the juicy details.”

“I can’t. Not now,” she said.

“Why not?” And then her friend’s eyes grew even wider. “Oh. My. God,” she said again. “He’s still there, isn’t he? Whoever *he* is.”

Brooke closed her eyes on a sigh. “Yes, he’s still here.”

“Who is it? Anyone I know? Can you turn the camera so I can see him?”

“Not telling, maybe and no,” she said, answering each of the questions in turn.

“Okay, don’t tell me,” Lori said. “But don’t be surprised when I come for a visit to meet your new boy toy.”

“He’s not— It’s not—” She huffed out a breath.

Her friend grinned, obviously amused by Brooke's flustration.

"Pizza's here!" Matt called from off-camera.

Lori twisted her head to respond to the summons. "I'm coming." Then she returned her attention to the screen and, with a wink, said to Brooke, "And hopefully you'll be saying the same thing in short order."

Thankfully she cut the connection before her friend heard Patrick choke on a laugh.

Chapter Twelve

"Sneaking out of bed when a man's still sleeping could give him a complex, you know," Patrick said, squinting against the bright light that speared through the gap between Brooke's bedroom curtains.

"Obviously you're not sleeping, or we wouldn't be having this conversation," Brooke responded, as she found her discarded T-shirt on the floor and tugged it over her head.

"I'd like to be sleeping," he said.

She yanked the curtains together to shut out the blinding light.

"With you," he clarified.

She shook her head regretfully. "Brendan's going to be home in a few hours and I have a million errands to run before then, including grocery shopping so I have some food in the house to feed my child."

He sighed. "I've got things to do, too, but nothing that would be nearly as much fun as staying in bed with you."

"I'm sorry," she said and touched her lips to his. "And thank you."

"You're welcome. But why are you thanking me?"

"Because this weekend was the first time I've been away from Brendan for so long, and I thought I'd hate every minute of it. But, thanks to you, I didn't."

"Your flattery is overwhelming," he said dryly.

"I didn't think you needed me to further pump up your already inflated ego."

"I should have stopped with the 'you're welcome,'" he decided.

She brushed her lips against his again. "Thank you, too, for the orgasms."

He grinned. "Anytime."

But she shook her head again.

"That's right—you're done with me now," he said, only half joking.

"I have a child," she reminded him.

"I have no desire or intention to compete with your son for your attention," he assured her. "But in addition to being a veterinarian and a mom, you are an amazing and sensual woman, Brooke. And while I understand that Brendan comes first, that doesn't mean you can't make time for other things or other people who matter. Including yourself."

"Between my job and my son, I don't have a lot of time for anything—or anyone—else," she confided.

"I'm not asking for more than you're willing to give," he said. "Just that you think about me, and when you have some time, you consider spending it with me."

"That sounds rather vague." And, she had to admit, infinitely reasonable.

"Would you prefer that I made irrational demands so that you'd feel better about refusing them?"

"Of course not," she denied. "But what if a couple of weeks go by and I haven't managed to find any time for you?"

"I do have my own life and responsibilities," he reminded her, pushing back the covers and rising out of the bed, completely unconcerned about his nakedness.

"I know that," she said, trying not to stare—and failing happily. "I also know you're accustomed to a…busy social calendar." She flushed a little.

"Not only have you been listening to gossip, it's outdated." He gathered up his clothes and began to dress. "Maybe I've dated a lot of women in the past, but since I bought the Silver Star, I've spent most of my nights there. Alone."

"You had a lot of work to do, updating and renovating the property," she pointed out. "But that's all done now, so you'll have more free time on your hands."

"And how else would I fill that time except by seducing all the single women in town?" he asked dryly.

Now her cheeks flamed. "You're deliberately misunderstanding me."

"I don't think I'm misunderstanding anything, and

I don't know whether to be pissed that you have such a low opinion of me or that you don't think more of yourself to trust I'd want to be with you."

Either way, he sounded pretty pissed.

And maybe he had a right to be.

Maybe she had judged him unfairly.

But this fling or affair or whatever he wanted to call it was outside her realm of experience. She didn't know what to say or do the "morning after" because she didn't *do* mornings after.

"So what do you want me to say? Is this where I'm supposed to apologize?" she asked him now.

"No," he said. "I want you to figure out what you want. When you do, you can let me know."

Brendan was happy to be home and eager to share all the details of his exciting weekend. He'd obviously enjoyed the trip and entertained everyone with his chatter throughout the meal Brooke had prepared for their return.

"So how was your weekend?" Sandra asked, when Brendan had finally tired himself out from talking and gone into the living room to watch TV with Grandpa.

"It was good."

"I hope you didn't spend every minute at the clinic."

She shook her head. "Only Saturday. The rest of the weekend was fairly quiet."

"So what did you do with your time otherwise?"

She could have replied in any number of ways that would have answered her mother's question without telling her the whole truth, but she really needed some womanly advice right now. "I spent some of it at the Silver Star. With Patrick."

"Oh." Her mom considered this revelation for a moment, then nodded. "Well, then. Good for you."

Brooke didn't know what kind of response she'd expected from her mother, but she was a little surprised by her easy acceptance. "You don't think I'm making a mistake?"

"Why? Because you're finally taking steps toward having a life of your own aside from your career and your child?"

"Brendan will always be my number one priority," she was quick to assure her mom.

"And that's okay," Sandra said. "But he shouldn't be the focus of your whole life. That's not healthy for you and not fair to him."

Brooke frowned at the subtle admonishment. "I feel as if I owe him at least that much."

"Why?" her mom asked, then immediately guessed the answer to her own question. "Because he has only one parent?"

She nodded. "I know he lucked out in the grandparent department, but I'm not sure that makes up for the absence of a father in a little boy's life."

"It's not your fault that you fell in love with a man who didn't want the responsibility of being a father," Sandra said gently.

"Maybe not the first time," Brooke agreed, having long ago come to terms with the fact that she'd been too young and naive to know any better when she'd fallen for Xander Davis. "But what if I'm doing the same thing again?"

"Are you telling me that you're in love with Patrick Stafford?" Sandra asked cautiously.

"No," she immediately denied. "But…I do have feelings for him. And the more time I spend with him, the stronger those feelings seem to get, making me worry that I could fall in love with him."

"Falling in love should be cause for celebration, not concern," her mom pointed out.

Maybe. In a perfect world.

But in Brooke's imperfect world, opening up her heart had only led to heartache, and it wasn't an experience she was eager to repeat. Especially if it meant risking her son, too.

Thankfully, with Brendan home, life returned to normal for Brooke. She easily fell back into her usual routines, almost as if the two glorious nights she'd spent with Patrick had never happened.

Monday was her usual full day at the clinic. Tuesday she was occupied with fieldwork in the morning and had surgeries in the afternoon, but she finished early enough that she was actually home by the time Brendan got off the bus from school.

On Wednesday, Brooke spent the better part of the day beside her dad at Ambling Acres, each of them up to their respective elbows in bovine butts, determining which cows were pregnant and which were in heat and ready to be bred. It was hardly a glamorous job, but she always enjoyed being in the field with her father.

Though she'd studied hard and graduated near the top of her class, she knew there were a lot of things that could only be learned from experience, and Bruce Langley had close to forty years' experience.

On Thursday, she visited a local sheep farm to administer routine vaccinations, after which she was invited to share lunch with the farmer and his wife. She considered the personal connection between vet and landowner to be one of the perks of a rural practice and was happy to accept. On her way back to the clinic, she impulsively turned into the drive of the Silver Star, only to discover that Patrick's truck wasn't there. He'd told her to let him know when she'd figured out what she wanted, but she found herself wondering now if he might have already given up on hearing from her.

Friday morning after breakfast, she took Brendan over to her parents' house to wish them a happy anniversary and give them a gift certificate to The Home Station, where she'd made a six o'clock reservation for them to celebrate the occasion. Hugs and kisses were exchanged all around. Then Brooke hustled her son outside again to ensure he didn't miss the school bus.

"But what are we gonna do for dinner for the 'versary?" Brendan asked, apparently having only now realized that his grandparents had plans that didn't include him.

"I thought we could go out to eat tonight, too," she told him. "But probably somewhere a little less fancy."

"Jo's?" he asked hopefully.

"We can go to Jo's," she agreed.

"Yay!" he enthused, with a celebratory fist pump.

"And after dinner, we can go see a movie, if you want."

"The-new-*Star-Wars*-is-playing," he said, rushing the words together in his excitement.

She chuckled. "I guess that's a yes to the movie?"

"I've been waiting to see it *for-ev-er*," he told her.

"The movie only came out before Christmas, so if three months is *for-ev-er*, I marvel over the fact that you survived."

He giggled at that and threw his arms around her to give her a quick hug as the yellow bus came to a stop at the end of the driveway.

She kissed the top of his head—or at least the pom-pom on his hat. "Have a good day, sunshine."

"Love you, Mom."

Though the words had become a part of their morning routine, they never failed to fill her with joy, and she was smiling as she watched him step through the folding door. He made his way down the center aisle of the bus to his usual seat, then turned to the window and offered her a happy wave.

As she drove to the clinic, she found herself reflecting on her parents' marriage. Growing up, she'd taken it for granted that when she was ready to settle down, she'd meet the perfect man, fall in love, get married and start a family. And though her life had taken a different direction, she hadn't entirely given up hope that she might one day meet a man who would love her and her son as much as her father loved her mother and their children.

Or maybe she'd already met him.

She shook her head, immediately dismissing the thought.

Patrick Stafford was definitely *not* the type of man about whom she should be imagining happily-ever-after fantasies. Sexual fantasies, sure. And in the five nights since he'd left her bed, she'd indulged in more than a few of those. But it was time to get her head and her heart out of the clouds and back into the real world.

Because despite his request that she think about him, which she'd done every night when she went to bed alone and more than a few times throughout each day, he'd given no indication that he'd been thinking about her. Not one phone call or even a text message throughout the whole week. And the silence was a little disconcerting.

Was he respecting her boundaries, abiding by her request not to turn their weekend tryst into anything more? Was he waiting for her to make the next move, as he'd encouraged her to do? Or had he already moved on?

And why did the latter possibility leave her feeling so empty inside?

It took every ounce of willpower Patrick possessed not to pick up the phone and call Brooke during the week, but he'd made it clear what he wanted and left the ball in her court. Unfortunately, she'd given no indication that she intended to return to the game, and he was admittedly a little disappointed.

"Why are you in such a grumpy mood?" Jenna asked, when she stopped by the ranch Friday afternoon.

"I'm not grumpy. I'm busy," he told her.

She didn't take the hint.

"Is this about the sexy vet?" she asked instead.

He scowled. "What are you talking about?"

"Sarah told me that you've got the hots for the new vet who was taking care of Ranger," she said. "And now that his injury is healed, there's no reason for her to stop by every day."

"The important part of that is that Ranger's injury is healed," he said.

"I know it's a little old-fashioned," she continued, as if he hadn't spoken, "but if you want to see her, you could call her and invite her to go on a date."

"Is that why you're hanging around here—because you don't have a date tonight?"

"I could have made plans if I'd wanted to," she said, just a little defensively. "And I'll bet, if you bothered to scroll through the contact list in your phone, you could, too."

"I've got things to do around here tonight," he said.

"What kinds of things?" she challenged.

"Are you offering to help?" he asked her.

"No," she said. "I'm calling out your obvious lie."

He scowled at that.

"Look around, Patrick. You've done an incredible job with this ranch. But you're done. Everything is ready. You just need to give Devin the word to make the website live."

"It's not really that simple," he said.

"Of course it is," she said. "But something's holding you back, and I can't figure out if it's a fear of success or failure."

"Why would I be afraid of success?"

"That's a good question," she said and waited for him to come up with an answer.

He sighed. "Maybe I am a little worried that, after spending so much time and money on this ranch, it might turn out that Mom and Dad were right," he acknowledged.

"Does that mean you're ready to throw in the towel and go back to your corner office at Blake Mining, where you can be unhappy for the rest of your life?"

"No," he said. Because she was right. He'd been not only restless but unhappy in the corporate world. But working on the ranch, he felt fulfilled and content. And, yes, happy.

"You've certainly seemed a lot happier since you moved out here—and even more so the past several weeks," she noted.

"It is a relief to know that most of the major work is done."

"Do you really think that's all it is?" she asked.

"Obviously you have a different theory."

"I do," Jenna confirmed. "And her name is Brooke."

Patrick just shook his head, unwilling to discuss his relationship with Brooke—if it could even be called a relationship—with his sister.

"I'm going into town to grab a pizza," he abruptly decided. "Do you want to come with me?"

"No, I think I'll hang out with Princess for a while."

"Okay."

"Hey," she said, as he started to turn away. "If it's okay, I think I'll crash here tonight."

"Sure," he said, because he knew she was only sharing her plans and not really asking permission. Then, because the question had been nudging at the back of his mind for a few weeks now, he asked, "Is everything okay with you and Nate?"

"We're going through a bit of a rough patch," she said.

"Do you want me to stay home tonight?"

That earned him a scowl. "Definitely not. I don't need a babysitter."

"Okay," he relented.

But as he drove into town, it occurred to him that his sister had been spending a lot of time at the ranch lately, making him suspect that the "rough patch" she'd mentioned might be more than that.

It was only a fleeting thought, though, as his mind was more preoccupied with her comment about Brooke. Because whether or not he was willing to admit it, it was true that his happiest days had been the ones he'd spent with the sexy vet—and her son.

On the way to Jo's Friday night, Brooke resolved to put all thoughts of Patrick out of her mind and focus on enjoying her son's company. That resolution lasted only until they walked into the restaurant and she saw the rancher leaning on the counter by the cash register, chatting up the very young and very pretty girl working there.

She ignored the jolt of awareness that surged through her body, leaving high-voltage tingles humming through her veins, even as she cursed herself for the instinctive response.

"Why don't we take one of those tables over there?" she suggested, attempting to steer her son away from the counter before he spotted Patrick.

But she wasn't quick enough.

"Hey, it's Mr. Patrick," Brendan said and immediately began waving. "Hi, Mr. Patrick."

The rancher glanced over and his mouth—the same mouth that had kissed her until they were both breathless and then done other and more interesting things to other parts of her—curved into an easy smile for her son. "Hey, Brendan." Then Patrick's attention shifted to Brooke, and even from across the room, she felt the heat of his gaze as his eyes skimmed over her in what could only be described as a visual caress. "Dr. Langley."

She inclined her head in acknowledgment. "Mr. Stafford," she said, inwardly wincing at the primness of her own tone.

He said something else to the girl behind the counter, then sauntered over to the table where she and Brendan were now seated. He didn't wait for an invitation but straddled an empty chair and flashed another of those bone-melting smiles. "Small world, huh?"

"Small town," she clarified. Though she managed a lighter tone this time, she was helpless to rein in her galloping pulse. Apparently her traitorous body hadn't got the memo from her brain that she was supposed to be over him.

"We're gonna have pizza for dinner," Brendan chimed in, unwilling to be left out of the conversation.

"Then you came to the right place," Patrick said, with a wink for the boy as a server approached the table.

Brooke ordered a diet cola for herself and root beer for Brendan, plus their usual pizza—a medium with cheese and pepperoni, since Brendan didn't really like any other toppings on his pie.

"I'll be right back with your drinks," the server promised. "And your pizza will be ready to go in just a few minutes, Mr. Stafford."

"Can I change it to eat-in rather than take-out?" he asked.

"Of course," she responded.

"Great. And I'll take a root beer, too." He flashed his devastating smile in the server's direction, flustering the poor girl so much that her notepad and pen slipped from her fingers.

He scooped both items off the floor and returned them to her. "You can add the soda and Dr. Langley's order to my tab."

"No," Brooke immediately protested. "Don't add..." Her words trailed off as she realized the server was already hurrying away to do his bidding—and maybe to splash some cold water on her flushed cheeks.

So Brooke directed her attention—and ire—at Patrick. "I'm not letting you buy our dinner."

"I know we're doing things a little out of order," he said. "Usually I buy a woman dinner first, but better late than never, right?"

She frowned in disapproval of his not-so-veiled reference to the nights they'd spent together. Thankfully, her son was oblivious to the implications of Patrick's remark as well as the undercurrents between the adults.

The server returned almost immediately with their drinks and three plates, and then with Patrick's pizza, which she set on an elevated stand in the middle of the table.

Brendan eyed the pie hungrily.

"Go ahead and dig in," Patrick urged.

But Brooke shook her head. "He doesn't like mushrooms."

"It's lucky, then, that they're only on the top and easy to pick off." He lifted a slice from the pan and set it on the boy's plate. "Careful, though. It's pretty hot," he cautioned, as he transferred a second slice to Brooke's plate before taking one for himself.

To her surprise, conversation didn't lag at all while they ate. The even bigger surprise was that it was Patrick and Brendan who mostly kept it going.

Despite his long-ago claim that he had no interest in kids, the rancher spent a lot of time not just talking to her son but actively engaging him on a variety of topics. Of course, he and Brendan had become pretty well acquainted after "consulting" during several visits at the Silver Star, but Brooke was still surprised by the easy flow of their conversation.

In between bites of pizza and sips of root beer, they talked about Ranger and Princess, discussed Brendan's favorite and least favorite subjects at school (phys ed and history, respectively), and somehow ended up in a DC versus Marvel debate, comparing both comic book story lines and movie adaptations. And Brooke noticed that when her son helped himself to a second slice of Patrick's pizza, he didn't even bother to peel the mushrooms off the top.

Of course, two pieces were all he wanted, and he was finished eating before the pie that she'd ordered was delivered to the table.

"Can I go play video games with Russell?" Brendan asked, having spotted his friend by one of the vintage machines at the back of the restaurant. The games were a recent addition to Jo's, introducing *Pac-Man*, *Frogger* and *Tetris* to a whole new generation of kids.

Brooke dug a couple of quarters out of her wallet and handed them to her son.

"Does he ever slow down?" Patrick asked, watching as Brendan raced across the room to the machines.

"Only when he's asleep," she said, a smile touching her lips.

"How long will the games keep him occupied?" he wondered.

"We'll see." She watched the boys slide their coins into the machines and take their positions before shifting her attention back to Patrick. "But there's no reason for you to stick around."

"I'm hoping if I do, I'll get dessert," he said.

Of course, they both knew there weren't any desserts on Jo's menu.

So why was he looking at her as if she was a slice of Twelve-Layer Chocolate Bliss that he wanted to savor?

Chapter Thirteen

Brooke lifted her glass and swallowed a mouthful of soda, hoping the icy beverage would cool that heat that rushed to fill her cheeks. "It's a Friday night," she pointed out. "Don't you have a date or something?"

"There is a woman I'm interested in," Patrick acknowledged. "But she keeps trying to brush me off."

"Maybe you should take the hint."

"I thought about it," he said. "I mean, there are plenty of other single women in this town."

"So why aren't you with one of them?" she pressed, ignoring the stab of something that felt uncomfortably like jealousy.

"Because it occurred to me that maybe I'm being pushed away by this woman not because she doesn't want me but because she's afraid to admit how much she wants me."

"You really do have an impressive...ego."

He grinned. "Yes, she did seem to be impressed by my...ego...last weekend."

She rolled her eyes at that even as her body stirred in response to the memories.

Then his smile faded and his expression turned serious. "I missed you this week."

She swallowed and mentally trampled the blossom of hope that sprang to life inside her. "Did you?"

"You have no idea how many times I picked up the phone to call you."

"And yet my phone never rang," she noted.

"You were supposed to let me know when you'd figured out what you wanted," he reminded her.

"But it's not just about what *I* want," she said. "It can't be."

"Brendan doesn't seem to mind hanging out with me."

"Brendan is a kid desperately looking for a father figure."

"You're trying to scare me off."

"Maybe I am," she conceded. "But I'm also being honest."

"I'm trying to be honest, too," he said. "And I know you said you didn't want to have an affair or a fling or anything else, but since I met you, I haven't wanted to be with anyone else. I haven't thought about anyone else. So maybe we should give the relationship option a shot."

"Oh." She didn't seem to know what else to say.

She hadn't let herself believe that he might want anything more than what they'd already shared together. Because a relationship was somehow a lot more intimate than sex, and a lot more terrifying.

He lifted a brow. "Is that all you're going to say?"

"I don't know what else to say," she admitted. "Except... maybe...do you want to go see a movie with us tonight?"

"I'd love to," he said, as Brendan headed back to the table.

"Aren't you going to ask what movie?"

"Doesn't matter."

But Brendan chimed in again. "We're gonna see the new *Star Wars* movie."

"I didn't know there was a new *Star Wars* movie," Patrick said.

"It's only 'new' in that we haven't yet seen it and it's finally showing at Mann's," Brooke clarified, naming the local second-run theater.

"Have you seen it?" Brendan asked. "Is it totally awesome?"

"I've heard that it is, but, no, I haven't seen it," Patrick admitted.

"You could see it with us," her son immediately offered. "That would be okay, wouldn't it, Mom?"

"I've already invited Mr. Patrick to come with us," she said.

"Did you say 'yes'?" Brendan asked him.

"I said 'yes,'" Patrick confirmed. "I'll even spring for the popcorn."

"You paid for the pizza," Brooke pointed out. "I'll get the popcorn."

"Why don't we compromise?" he suggested. "You can get the tickets and I'll get the snacks, because I want Milk Duds with my popcorn."

"Can we get gummy bears, too?" Brendan asked, when they were in line at the concession stand a short while later.

"How can you want candy after two slices of pizza?" Brooke wondered.

"I'm growing like a weed," he said, quoting her oft-repeated sentiment.

"Which is the only reason I agreed to the popcorn," she told him, as Patrick hid a smile.

"But I like to mix gummy bears in my popcorn."

"Gummy bears *and* Milk Duds are even better," Patrick said.

Brooke made a face. "Please tell me you don't seriously mix candy with your popcorn."

"If I told you that, it would be a lie," he confided.

"Clearly you have the taste buds of a seven-year-old."

"I do have a sweet tooth," he acknowledged, then dipped his head to whisper close to her ear, "That's why I like you."

"Can I get a blue raspberry slushy?" Brendan asked, proving once again that he was paying no attention to their conversation.

Patrick looked at Brooke, seeking her approval before acquiescing to her son's request.

She started to open her mouth to protest that Brendan had already had soda with dinner, but closed it again without saying a word. Though she didn't approve of him overloading on sugar, a night out at the movies was a special occasion and she didn't think it would hurt him too much to indulge a little. But she did caution, "If you want another drink, you better make sure you go to the bathroom before the movie starts."

"I'll go now," Brendan said and dashed off.

She didn't usually let him go off on his own when they were in a crowd, but the entrance and exit of the facilities were visible from where she was standing—and even closer to the condiment bar.

"I'll get straws and napkins," she said, leaving Patrick to wait for their snacks at the counter.

She was occupied for less than a minute, but when she turned back again, she saw that Patrick had both hands on a cardboard tray, a woman hanging off his arm and a smear of peach lipstick beside his mouth. And for one quick moment, she flashed back to college.

She'd felt so lucky to be with Xander, who was so incredibly handsome and charming and popular. And she hadn't worried about the other girls who were always flirting with him, because he'd chosen to be with her and only her. It was what he'd always told her. And what she'd believed—until she'd found him in bed with her roommate.

But Patrick wasn't Xander, and she had no reason to resent the attention he was getting from the other woman or want to yank him away from the female who was now leaning close to whisper in his ear.

To his credit, Patrick didn't look at the cleavage on display by the woman's V-neck sweater. In fact, he seemed to be looking everywhere else and exhaled visibly with relief when his gaze connected with Brooke's.

The pouting brunette, clearly unhappy with the lack of attention she was getting, tugged on his arm to draw his focus back to her again.

Patrick shook his head in response to whatever she'd said, and she finally released his arm and turned to rejoin a group of friends waiting for concessions.

As he approached, Brooke plucked another paper napkin from the dispenser and offered it to him. "You might want to wipe off the lipstick. That shade doesn't really work with your skin tone."

He set the tray down on the edge of the counter to take the napkin from her. "That was Nikki," he said, as he scrubbed his cheek. "We went out a few times, a couple of years ago."

"You don't owe me any explanations," she assured him.

"I think I'd want an explanation if I saw one of your ex-boyfriends kissing you when we were out on a date together."

"An unlikely scenario considering that the number of my ex-boyfriends can be counted on one hand," she said. "And also, this isn't a date."

"Enjoying a movie and sharing popcorn counts as a date in my books," he said.

"I can guarantee I won't be sharing that popcorn if you put gummy bears and Milk Duds in it," she said.

"It's still a date."

"With a seven-year-old chaperone?"

He shrugged. "Dating a single mom is a new experience for me, but I'd guess child-age chaperones are fairly common."

"Which is another reason you might prefer to watch the movie with Nikki."

"I already told her I wasn't interested or available because I was seeing somebody else."

"Inviting you to join me and Brendan at the movies doesn't mean we're seeing each other," she said.

"How about more than eighteen hours naked together?" he challenged. "What does that mean?"

Before she could figure out an answer to his question, Brendan was back, wiping his damp hands down the front of his jeans.

"There are dryers in the bathroom," she pointed out to her son.

"They take too long and I don't want to miss any previews," Brendan said.

"And on the plus side, at least you know he washed," Patrick said.

Since she couldn't deny the truth of that, she only said, "Let's go find some seats."

It wasn't a date.

Patrick's claims to the contrary aside, Brooke was certain of that.

And yet, when their fingers touched inside the bucket of popcorn (because, yes, she couldn't resist the salty treat, despite the candy he'd tossed inside—to her son's delight), tingles ran up her arm and memories of his strong hands moving over her flooded her brain and heated her body. And when he leaned close to whisper to her, he let his lips skim the outer shell of her ear, making her shiver. And when the theater was dark and the popcorn was gone, he linked their fingers together and held her hand.

It was both an unexpected and sweet gesture, and it made her realize how much she'd missed out on by not dating in high school and then falling for the wrong guy in college. Maybe it was her inexperience that made her susceptible to Xander's seduction, or maybe he'd been every bit as charming as she'd imagined, but she'd fallen hard and fast, and then she'd fallen into his bed.

Looking back, it was hard to pinpoint the reasons for her infatuation with Xander. During their whirlwind courtship, he'd never shown up at her door with food just because he thought she might have had a difficult day or cooked for her when she'd had to work late on an assignment. He'd never even taken her to a movie. And while those were all little things, they added up to a lot.

The fact that Xander had never done any of those things proved that she'd devoted far too much time and energy to a relationship that was a lot of nothing. But of course Xander's biggest failing was that he'd never shown any interest in his child, instead choosing to drop out of her life before their baby was even born.

She'd been holding herself back from Patrick because she'd thought he was like Xander, but she realized now that any similarities were only on the surface. Yes, both men were handsome and charming and had turned her inside out with their kisses, but that was where the similarities ended.

Determined not to be a prisoner of her past mistakes

any longer, Brooke shifted in her chair and let her cheek rest against Patrick's shoulder. He turned his head and touched his lips to her temple, and she felt herself teetering precariously on the edge of something scary and unknown.

Maybe she was walking a dangerous path, but with Patrick at her side, she couldn't help but want to take the next step.

"That was *totally awesome*," Brendan declared, as they were exiting the theater. "What did you think, Mr. Patrick?"

"I think you're right," he agreed.

"Mom?" Brendan prompted.

"Totally awesome," she echoed.

But her tone lacked the enthusiasm of her words, making Patrick suspect that something was bothering her. And he thought he had an idea what it might be.

For more than seven years, Brooke had been a single mom. During that time, it had been just her and Brendan—and her parents, but Sandra and Bruce Langley had defined roles in their grandson's life. Patrick was a new factor in the equation, and it was going to take some time to balance things out.

Until then, he suspected there would be a lot of one steps forward and two steps back, because Brooke was going to need some time to get used to sharing her son's attention and affection.

Though he was parked on the opposite side of the parking lot, Patrick walked with Brooke and Brendan to her truck.

"Thanks, Mom," Brendan said, as she buckled him into his booster seat. "I had a great 'versary tonight."

She kissed the tip of his nose. "You're welcome."

"I had a great time, too," Patrick said, when she'd closed Brendan's door.

She managed a weary smile. "Good night, Patrick."

"That's it?" he asked. "You're not going to invite me to come over for a cup of coffee?"

"It's late."

"It's not that late. And I'm wired from all the sugar I had during the movie."

"That's what happens when you add gummy bears and Milk Duds to your popcorn," she said.

"But it was good, wasn't it?"

"It was...interesting," she said, her tone softening a little.

"Coffee?" he prompted again.

She sighed. "One cup."

He followed her home and pulled into the driveway behind her. As he got out of his truck, she was opening the back door of her vehicle.

"What are you doing?" he asked, as she started to lift her son.

"He's asleep," she said in a whisper.

"I can see that. But you can't be planning to carry him up all those stairs," he said incredulously.

"I do it all the time," she told him.

"Not tonight," Patrick said. "I'll take him."

"I can manage," she protested, then huffed out a breath as he easily lifted the slumbering child into his arms.

"You might want to go ahead and unlock the door," he suggested.

So she did, and turned on the hall light so Patrick could find his way to the boy's bedroom, where she folded back the covers on her son's bed.

Patrick gently laid Brendan down on the mattress, then stood back as Brooke removed his coat and boots, pulled up the covers and kissed his forehead. The effortlessness of the routine confirmed that it was indeed something she did all the time, and reminded him that, despite his growing feelings for the single mom and her son, they shared a bond that he couldn't compete with or—thanks to his dysfunctional upbringing—even understand.

"Regular or decaf?" Brooke asked, as he followed her into the kitchen.

"Regular," he said, making an effort to shake off his melancholy.

She selected a pod from the basket beside the brewer and popped it into the machine.

"So what did Brendan mean when he said he had a great anniversary tonight?" he asked, as she passed the mug of coffee to him.

"Oh, we went out tonight because my parents were out celebrating their thirty-eighth anniversary."

"Thirty-eight years—that's impressive," he noted.

She nodded. "And even after all those years of marriage, and more than four decades together, they still enjoy hanging out," she said, sounding just a little bit wistful.

"You want the same thing," he realized.

"Someday," she agreed.

He wondered why the admission didn't make him panic. Of course, "someday" suggested a future event, and she'd given no indication that she was thinking about a future with *him*. Heck, she'd even hesitated before inviting him to a two-and-a-half-hour movie.

"You were lucky to live with their example," he said. "My parents wouldn't inspire anyone to matrimony. More than once, I've heard my mom remark that she only ever planned to have two kids—Jenna only happened because she and my dad were more focused on their reconciliation than birth control.

"Considering how many times my parents separated and got back together over the years, I'd probably have a dozen more siblings except my dad had a vasectomy before Jenna was born."

"But your parents are still together?" she asked.

"They're together *again*," he said. "They were married for sixteen years. Then they divorced and lived apart for nine years. During that time, they each had several other relationships before reconciling and remarrying ten years ago."

"Still, it must say something about their feelings for one another that they found their way back together," she ventured.

"Maybe," he said, sounding dubious. But then his thoughts moved on to something else, and he smiled. "Their anniversary is in the fall, and my mom wanted a big celebration this past year. Somehow she convinced Jenna to plan the party—or maybe Jenna volunteered." He shrugged. "Either way, my parents gave her the guest list and told her what they wanted in the way of food and drink, and left Jenna in charge of the rest."

"What went wrong?" Brooke asked.

"That depends on who tells the story," he said. "From Jenna's perspective, everything went according to plan. From my parents' perspective, she ruined their thirty-fifth anniversary.

"Because they were expecting a thirty-fifth anniversary party, counting from their first wedding, but all the banners and balloons and table decorations Jenna ordered had the number ten on them, which was the actual number of years since their second marriage. As much as our parents might want to pretend that they've been happy together since the beginning, the rest of us haven't forgotten the nasty fights inevitably followed by days—or sometimes weeks—of icy silence."

"Note to self—don't ever mess with Jenna Stafford," Brooke remarked.

He grinned. "Nobody ever does more than once."

Though he was tempted to linger, he swallowed the last mouthful of the one cup of coffee she'd promised him, set down the empty mug and stood up.

"I really did have a good time with you and Brendan tonight," he told her.

"I did, too," she said, walking him to the door.

"So...can I call you sometime?"

That earned him a smile. "Absolutely."

"Good."

"You can even kiss me good-night, if you want."

So he kissed her good-night.

And it was a really long, really great kiss, after which

he drove back to the ranch with his window down in a futile effort to cool the heat in his blood.

There, finally, was the sign Melissa had been looking for.

Not a figurative signal from the universe, but an actual painted-on-wood, secured-in-the-ground sign announcing Silver Star Vacation Ranch.

She turned into the long drive, grateful and relieved to know that she'd arrived. And after more than twelve hours on the road, she was eager to park her car and stretch her legs.

Or maybe stretch her whole body, preferably on a soft bed.

"I didn't think you were going to be here until tomorrow," Patrick said, opening his arms to her.

Though she hadn't seen her cousin in almost two years, he hadn't changed a bit. Well, except for the fact that he'd traded his designer suits for cowboy boots. But when his familiar arms wrapped around her, she felt the unexpected sting of tears behind her eyes as she hugged him back, grateful for his warmth and his strength and especially his welcome.

"I decided to drive right through," she told him.

"That's a long drive," he remarked, a hint of concern in his voice.

"I was eager to get here."

"Well, welcome to the Silver Star," he said, spreading his arms wide to encompass the land and buildings around him.

She turned in a slow circle to survey every direction.

"Toto, I have a feeling we're not in Seattle anymore," she murmured, paraphrasing Dorothy.

"There's no yellow brick road, but that flagstone path leads to the house and a fresh pot of coffee."

"That sounds great," she said, popping the trunk of her car. "Let me just grab my bags and—"

"I've got 'em," he said, effortlessly lifting them out.

"Not that I don't appreciate the help, but aren't I supposed to be working for you?"

He grinned. "I'll show you around the ranch today and shackle you in the kitchen tomorrow."

"Seems fair," she said and followed him to the house.

"It's pretty isolated out here," he said, sounding almost apologetic. "Town isn't too far, but there's not a lot to do there, either."

"It's great," she said. "Really. I meant what I said about wanting a change."

She tried to sound positive and upbeat, but apparently she didn't quite succeed because Patrick's next question was "Anything you want to talk about?"

"Nope."

He held her gaze for a long moment, as if trying to decide if he should press for more details. But he finally shrugged, and she let out the breath she'd been holding.

"In that case, I'll show you to your room."

Chapter Fourteen

Since Brendan had discovered that Patrick had a dog—despite the rancher's repeated denials of ownership—he wanted to visit the Silver Star every day to play with Princess. Brooke frequently gave in to his requests because it gave her an excuse to see Patrick and occasionally sneak away with him to steal a few kisses. And while she was enjoying spending time with the rancher, she was careful to keep the nature of their relationship a secret from her son for fear that it would lead to expectations of the three of them becoming a family.

When they arrived at the ranch Thursday afternoon, Patrick wasn't anywhere to be found and Stormy was absent from the paddock, so she assumed he'd taken the animal out for some exercise. Princess was outside today, too, exploring in the sunshine. But as soon as

Brendan called to her, she came running—or waddling, considering the girth of her swollen belly.

Though Princess was moving more slowly these days, she still loved playing catch or tug-of-war, but she seemed just as happy snuggling up with Brendan and would let him pet her for hours. And it seemed like hours had passed when a pretty brunette with deep green eyes came out of the house and asked, "Does anybody here like peanut butter cookies?"

Brendan's hand shot up in the air. "I do!"

"That's lucky," she said. "Because I just took a tray out of the oven and I don't want to eat them all by myself."

"You must be Melissa," Brooke said.

"And you're Brooke," she said, shaking the proffered hand.

"And I'm Brendan," he chimed in.

"I would have guessed that, if you'd given me a chance," Melissa said, with an indulgent smile.

"I'm impatient," he said.

The cook chuckled at that. "So what do you say to cookies and milk, Brendan the Impatient?"

"Can I say 'yes,' Mom?" he asked hopefully.

"You can say 'yes, please,'" she told him. "But make sure you wash your hands."

"I will," he promised. Then to Melissa he said, "Yes, please."

"I've got coffee, too," Patrick's cousin said to Brooke. "If that's your preference."

"I'd love a cup," Brooke said. "Just let me give Princess a quick check first."

She didn't think she stayed with the dog for very long after Brendan had gone inside with Melissa, but by the time she made it to the house, there was nothing left of the cookies but a few crumbs and her son was in the family room watching TV.

"So when did you get into town?" Brooke asked Melissa, as she sat at the island with her mug of coffee.

"Three days ago, and I'm leaving tomorrow for a three-day culinary expo in Vegas."

"So culture shock hasn't set in yet?"

Melissa smiled as she shook her head. "I know it's going to be an adjustment, but I think I'm going to like it. Especially with Jenna living here, too."

"Does Patrick know she's living here?" Brooke wondered.

Melissa grinned. "She thinks he might, but so far, he hasn't said anything about it."

Then the door opened and Patrick came in, stomping snow off his boots.

"Actually, I just remembered that I've got something I have to do," Melissa said, and with a quick wave she was gone.

"That was weird," Brooke said.

"What was?" Patrick asked, glancing around to ensure they were alone before bending down to press a quick kiss to her lips.

She shook her head, deciding it didn't really matter why the other woman had made a hasty escape, because it meant that she could steal another of the rancher's delicious kisses.

Patrick looked pointedly at the empty plate as he

poured himself a mug of coffee. "Did I miss out on cookies?"

Brooke nodded. "Freshly baked peanut butter," she said. "I didn't get any, either, because by the time I came in, they were gone."

"Melissa knows her way around the kitchen," Patrick said.

"That's why you hired her, isn't it?"

"Of course," he admitted.

"So why does it sound as if you're second-guessing your decision?" Brooke prompted.

"Because I can't shake the feeling that there's something going on with her that she's not telling me."

"If there is, it might be because it's none of your business," she pointed out gently.

"I bet she'll tell Sarah," he mused. "No one can keep a secret from Sarah."

Brooke shook her head. "Are you even listening to me?"

"Of course I'm listening. But she's my cousin, and if—"

"No," she interjected. "I mean, I know she's your cousin, and that makes the lines a little blurry, but she's here to cook for your guests."

And though the ranch wasn't yet officially open for business, within days of the website going live, he'd received dozens of inquiries and even a handful of bookings for the weekend of his grand opening.

"Would you be prying into the details of her life if she was a stranger you'd hired?" Brooke asked, returning to her original point.

"No," he admitted.

"Then let it be," she advised.

"Okay," he said. "I'll let it be *if* you take a walk out to the barn with me so we can make out in the tack room."

She lifted a brow. "You seem to be under the illusion that you're negotiating from a position of power here, when it really doesn't matter all that much to me whether you let it go or you don't."

"Does that mean you won't take a walk with me?" he asked, sounding disappointed.

"No, I'll take the walk," she said. "But only because I really want to make out with you."

He grinned. "That's a good enough reason for me."

Brooke was taking a short break between appointments at the clinic the next day when Larissa handed her a stack of messages. While there didn't seem to be anything urgent, she noticed that Patrick had called three times, so she picked up the phone and dialed his number.

"I think Princess is in labor. What should I do?" he asked, sounding like an adorably flustered expectant father.

"You've already done everything you can to help her," Brooke reminded him. "She's comfortable in the whelping box, and she's got a heat lamp to keep her warm. The rest is up to her."

"There's nothing else?"

"Keep me posted," she said.

After that, she put Princess out of her mind while she

dealt with other patients—at least until Patrick called again two hours later.

"Any puppies yet?" Brooke asked him.

"No. And she seems absolutely miserable. I know I'm probably overreacting," he admitted, "but is there any chance you can come out to check on her?"

"I really can't," Brooke said apologetically. "I've still got three patients in the waiting room. But if you're concerned, you can bring her into the clinic."

He was there in less than thirty minutes.

"You must have left the ranch as soon as I hung up the phone," Brooke remarked, as she entered the exam room where he waited with Princess.

"Pretty much," he agreed.

She gently stroked the dog's swollen belly. "How are you doing, Princess?"

The dog looked at her with pleading eyes, a low whine sounding deep in her throat.

"You're having a rough go of it, are you?" She kept her hands in place as the animal's belly tightened with a contraction. "Yeah, I've been there," she murmured soothingly. "Giving birth can be a scary process, but you're not alone."

Princess's tail thumped against the table, making Brooke smile.

Then she saw the bloody discharge.

Patrick paced the waiting room, waiting and hating every minute of it. When Brooke had told him that a cesarean would give her the best chance to save Princess and her pups, he'd immediately consented to the surgery. But now that he was on the other side of the wall, her words echoing in his head, he was forced to accept that "best chance" meant there was still a chance the dog could lose her pups—and that he could lose Princess.

He hadn't chosen the dog, but she'd apparently chosen him. In the beginning she might only have been looking for a warm, dry place to sleep, but over the past several weeks she'd been his constant companion. Except when Brendan was at the Silver Star—then Princess readily abandoned Patrick in favor of the boy's attention and affection.

He didn't mind. In fact, he enjoyed watching them together. There was something both simple and sweet about the bond between the child and the dog. And if he was being completely honest, Princess wasn't the only one who looked forward to Brendan's visits to the ranch. Patrick was growing attached to the boy, too.

And Brendan's mother, who was scrubbing up to perform emergency surgery on Princess, bringing Patrick's thoughts full circle again. Weary and worried, he dropped into one of the hard plastic chairs just as the bell chimed over the door.

"Hey, Mr. Patrick!" Brendan said, as he crossed the room to stand in front of him. "Gramma dropped me off 'cause she had to go to a 'pointment and Mom said we could get pizza for dinner when she's done work," he explained. "What are you doing here?"

"Your mom's helping Princess have her babies."

"Cool." Brendan sat down beside him. "Have you been waiting very long?"

Forever.

Patrick glanced at his watch. "Half an hour."

"A lot of people think that it's easy for animals to have babies," Brendan said, perhaps trying to reassure him. "But sometimes they need help."

He nodded.

"And sometimes a mom doesn't survive having babies," the boy continued. "And sometimes the babies don't survive being born. Then there are creatures—like spiders—that actually eat their own babies." He made a face, then hastened to assure Patrick, "But you don't have to worry about Princess. Dogs don't do that."

"Good to know," Patrick said, both impressed and a little unnerved by the child's matter-of-fact accounting of the harsh realities of nature. Because the last thing he wanted to think about right now was the possibility that he might lose Princess or any of her pups.

And what if it was his fault?

What if he'd waited too long to bring Princess to the clinic?

"Do you wanna play cards while we're waiting?" Brendan asked, as if aware that Patrick was in desperate need of a distraction.

"Do you have any cards?" he asked.

"No, but Larissa keeps some in her desk," Brendan said, heading to the counter to talk to the receptionist.

Sure enough, he returned a few minutes later with a deck of cards in hand.

"Crazy Eights or Go Fish?" he asked.

"Crazy Eights," Patrick decided. "But you'll have to remind me how it's played."

It turned out the kid was pretty good at Crazy Eights. In fact, Brendan won five straight games.

"You suck at this," he said. "Maybe we should try Go Fish."

But Patrick sucked at that, too, and Brendan won several rounds before he gathered the cards up and stuffed them back in the box.

"Are you worried about Princess?" the boy asked.

"A little," he admitted.

"You don't have to worry. My mom will take real good care of her."

Then Brendan put his hand on Patrick's, as if to offer comfort.

And looking at the child's small fingers curled around his much larger hand, he was comforted—and grateful not to be alone.

To Brooke, there was no greater joy than the miracle of new life. Whether it was the hatching of an egg, the foaling of a horse or the birth of a human baby. Each and every time, it was beautiful and amazing. Sure, it could be messy and complicated, but in the end, when there was new life, it was all worthwhile.

Today, it had been very worthwhile.

Stripping off her gloves and gown, she went out to the waiting area to share the good news.

Brendan saw her first and immediately bounced up from his chair and raced over. "Did you help Princess have her puppies? Can I see them?"

"Let me talk to Mr. Patrick first," she said, as the rancher rose slowly from his chair, worry etched in the tiny lines beside his eyes and in the set of his jaw. "Princess is his dog."

Of course, Brendan stayed right by her side, determined to hear all the details.

"Congratulations," she said to the rancher and watched the weight of worry visibly lift from his shoulders.

"They made it?"

She nodded, smiling. "They made it. Three boys and three girls."

"How's Princess?"

"Right now she's still a little groggy from the sedation, but she's already showing an interest in her babies. I'd suggest giving her another half hour before you take them home."

"Take them home?" he echoed, sounding panicked. "Wouldn't it be better if they stayed here?"

She chuckled softly. "No, it would be better for mom, and her babies, to be in familiar surroundings."

"But—I don't have the first clue what to do with them."

"I could help," Brendan was quick to offer. "I know a lot about puppies."

"You're hired," Patrick immediately replied.

"Except that child labor laws—and this mom—prohibit working on school nights," Brooke said.

Brendan pouted. "But I wanna see the puppies."

"You can go back and see the puppies in a few minutes," she promised.

"I really don't know what to do with them when I get them home," Patrick said to Brooke.

"Just put them in the whelping box and make sure Princess has access to food and water. She'll take care of her puppies."

He did as Brooke had instructed, and then he stood there for a long while, watching them and feeling helpless. The puppies were so tiny and Princess so wiped out from the unsuccessful labor followed by the surgery that he didn't want to leave them alone in the barn overnight. Thankfully there was a cot in the tack room.

But the next morning, he wasn't feeling so thankful.

Because while the narrow bed might have been okay for a short nap—or a short child—it wasn't built for the overnight comfort of a full-grown man. After six hours on that narrow bed, Patrick didn't feel any more rested than when he'd first lain down on it, and his bones creaked and groaned in protest when he stood up.

He made a quick trip to the house to take a hot shower and brush his teeth before returning to the barn. Glancing at the bowl of dog food, he thought Princess might have eaten a few bites. He was sure she'd at least drunk some of the water.

The puppies were clearly hungry now, too, rooting around in search of their breakfast. Though their eyes were still closed, they didn't seem to have any difficulty finding the source of their sustenance, and they suckled hungrily. Patrick winced in sympathy with Princess as the tiny mouths tugged and pulled on their mother's nipples, though she didn't seem at all bothered by their feeding.

Clearly Brooke had been right—the new mama had

everything under control and would have been just fine if he'd spent the night in his own bed.

Never again, he promised his aching muscles.

He didn't realize he'd spoken aloud until an amused female voice asked, "Never again what?"

"Never again am I pretending to sleep on that cot," he admitted to Brooke.

"You spent the night out here," she said.

It wasn't a question, but he nodded anyway.

"Maybe this will help."

She handed him a foil-wrapped—

"Breakfast burrito."

"What did I do to deserve this?" he wondered, eagerly unwrapping it.

"You spent the night pretending to sleep on a cot so that you could keep an eye on your dog and her babies."

"She's not—" He sighed. "Damn, she is my dog, isn't she?"

"Without a doubt," Brooke said.

He bit into the burrito. "Mmm," he said, around a mouthful of egg and cheese. And then, "But how did you guess I'd spend the night out here?"

"I'm a vet, and I know things." She smiled then. "I also remembered Melissa mentioning that she'd be away at a culinary expo this week, so I guessed you wouldn't get a hot breakfast and probably wouldn't leave Princess long enough to even pour a bowl of cereal."

"I would have. Eventually," he said. "But this is better."

"Breakfast burritos are a favorite of Brendan's, so I made one for him and one for you, and that gave me an excuse to come out and take another peek at the puppies."

"Just the puppies?"

She shrugged. "Maybe I didn't think it would be so bad to see you, too."

He popped the last bite into his mouth. "Did I tell you how amazing you were yesterday?"

"I'm flattered you think so," she said.

"You saved Princess and her puppies."

"I only did what any vet would have done."

"Maybe," he acknowledged. "But I've never known another vet to make competent performance of duties look so sexy."

"Yeah, I've been told scrubs are a good look for me," she said dryly.

"You look good in anything," he assured her. Then he winked. "And even better in nothing."

"That's my cue to head out," she decided.

"Busy day today?"

"Always."

"Well, thank you again for breakfast."

"You're welcome." She lifted a hand to his cheek, rubbed her palm against the raspy stubble, then dropped her arm and stepped back. "You should try and get some sleep."

He caught her wrist and drew her close again, dipping his head to touch his mouth to hers. "I'd go to bed right now if you'd go with me."

She shook her head. "You know I can't."

"But are you at least a little bit tempted?"

"More than a little," she admitted.

"It's not much of a consolation, but I'll take it," he said. And he took another kiss for good measure, too.

Brooke continued on her way to Rolling Meadows, but instead of thinking of the day ahead, she found herself thinking about Patrick. And not just the kiss—though her lips were still tingling from the brief but potent brush of his lips—but his obvious attachment to the dog he'd foolishly tried to deny was his. This even after he'd paced the floor of the reception area while Princess was in surgery, paid the bill for the procedure and stayed up with her through the night to look after her while she looked after her babies.

For all his claims about not being ready to be a father, he had impressive paternal instincts. And though she knew it was crazy, she couldn't help but feel a little envious of the canine mom.

When she'd given birth to Brendan, she hadn't had a partner to share the joy and excitement of the moment. Yes, she'd been fortunate to have her mother as her birthing coach and her father in the waiting room. But it wasn't the same as having a partner to share all the exciting and terrifying moments along the way.

And though she'd told herself she didn't need a man to hold her hand, there were times when it would have been nice not to be alone. Such as when she'd heard her baby's heartbeat for the first time; when she'd seen the grainy image on the ultrasound monitor; when she'd felt him move inside her the first time, a gentle flutter, or, five months later, an impatient kick. And especially when her water broke in the middle of the night.

She sometimes wondered what it would be like to share those special moments with someone—and the wondering inevitably led to yearning. Not just because she really did hope to give Brendan a brother or sister someday, but because she wanted a partner to share all the trials and triumphs of parenthood and of life, someone to grow old with, someone she could always count on.

But Patrick wasn't that person. Just because he was doting on his dog and half a dozen adorable puppies didn't mean he was ready to make a personal commitment. And based on what he'd told her about his parents' relationship, she could understand why he wasn't looking for a happily-ever-after.

Still, it made her sad that he didn't believe happy endings were possible. And it made her wonder if anything—or anyone—might ever be able to change his mind.

Chapter Fifteen

"Something smells good," Patrick said, sniffing the air as he walked into the kitchen the day after Melissa's return.

"It's Grandma Stafford's chili recipe," she said. "With an extra dash of Tabasco and a few chili peppers."

"When can we eat? I'm starving."

"You wouldn't be starving if you'd come in for lunch," she pointed out.

"I was out with Dean, marking the riding trails."

"Well, I'm starving, too," she confided. "So have a seat and I'll dish this up."

He sat, and she served him a bowl of piping hot chili topped with shredded cheese and a sprinkling of green onions.

He dug into the meal with enthusiasm.

"This is really good," he told her. "A little spicy, but good."

"I can dial back the heat for your guests, if you think it's too much."

He nodded. "I have to admit, when I saw the menu from your restaurant in Seattle, I was a little worried that you were going to make stuff with edible flowers and fancy sauces that weekend cowboys weren't going to want to eat."

"I can do edible flowers and fancy sauces, but I understand comfort food, too," she assured him.

"I'm convinced," he said, dipping his spoon into his bowl again.

And though Melissa had claimed she was starving only a few minutes earlier, she abruptly pushed her bowl away and reached for her water.

As she lifted the glass to her lips, Patrick noticed that her hand wasn't quite steady and her face was suddenly pale.

"Are you okay?" he asked, concerned.

She sipped her water, then nodded as she set the glass down again.

"Are you sure? You look—"

She shoved her stool away from the island and bolted to the bathroom. Only a few seconds later, he heard the unmistakable sound of retching.

He pushed his own bowl away with the fleeting thought that he might have to reconsider their professional association if she'd given him food poisoning. But his speculation was quickly supplanted by concern for his cousin. Should he take her a glass of water? Get her a cool cloth for her face?

He was still debating whether to give her privacy or offer assistance when he heard the toilet flush, then the tap run. A moment later, she returned to the kitchen.

"Sorry about that," she said, sounding both embarrassed and remorseful. "I didn't mean to put a damper on your appetite."

"Yeah, I think I'll make a sandwich," he said, though his appetite had definitely been dampened.

"There's nothing wrong with the chili," she insisted indignantly.

He lifted his brows. "Then why were you puking your guts out?"

"Because apparently my morning sickness prefers to make an appearance during the latter part of the day."

Patrick stared at her, as if he didn't quite understand what Melissa was saying. Apparently some people couldn't even recognize a sign when they were hit over the head with it—a thought that might have made her smile at another time. But she didn't feel much like smiling now.

"I'm pregnant," she said bluntly.

"But..." he sputtered, clearly taken aback by her announcement. "You didn't say anything about being pregnant when you offered to take the job."

"Because being pregnant won't interfere with my ability to do the job."

"Of course it will," he said. "Because a pregnancy leads to a baby."

She opened her eyes wide, feigning surprise. "Is that how it works?"

He scowled, clearly not appreciating her sarcasm. "And a baby is a big responsibility."

It was his tone more than his words that made her understand the cause of his panic. "You don't have to worry, Patrick. My baby won't be *your* responsibility."

"Except that you and your baby will be living here, won't you?" And then his gaze narrowed as another thought occurred to him. "That's why you were so eager to get away from Seattle."

"One of the reasons," she acknowledged. But she refused to feel guilty about her deception and she wasn't going to apologize for doing what she needed to do.

"Does the father know about the baby?" he asked.

"Of course," she said.

"Your parents?"

"Not yet." And maybe she did feel a little guilty about that, but Melissa needed some time to decide what she wanted to do before she shared the news.

"So I'm harboring a fugitive," he concluded.

"They know I'm here," she said. "They just don't know that they're going to be grandparents in less than seven months."

"You have to tell them, Melissa."

"I know. I just need to figure some things out first." Such as how to convince her parents that she was capable of raising a child on her own without their support or interference, and that wouldn't happen until she'd managed to convince herself.

"Anything I can help with?" he asked.

She smiled at that and gave him a quick hug. "You already have. You gave me a job and a place to live."

"I'm still going to have to hire someone else," he realized.

"What? No," she protested.

"I don't mean to replace you, but to help you," he hastened to clarify.

"Maybe just for a few weeks, before and after the baby is born," she said.

"Whatever you need," he told her.

And her eyes filled with grateful tears.

By the time Brooke finished at the clinic, she was exhausted. It hadn't just been a long day but a difficult one, as she'd had to break the news that Marmalade, Peggy Bartlett's beloved feline companion of seventeen years, had tested positive for lymphoma—again.

Two years earlier, the orange tabby had successfully undergone chemotherapy treatments and gained a new lease on life. When the cat was first diagnosed, only six months after Peggy had buried her husband, the woman was determined to do everything she could to keep the cat alive—so that she wouldn't lose someone else she loved. Brooke had completely understood and supported her choice, though Peggy was still making monthly payments to the clinic for those treatments.

This time, the woman made the difficult decision to end Marmalade's suffering. As Brooke administered the injection—every vet's least favorite part of the job—she cried right along with Peggy. Thankfully, Marmalade was her last patient of the day, so she was able to take some time to sit with the older woman and offer condolences that she knew didn't make anyone feel any better.

When she finally left the clinic, she wanted only to go home, put her feet up and watch something mindless on TV. But of course she couldn't, because she'd promised Brendan that she'd take him to the Silver Star to see Princess and her puppies.

"Have you named the puppies yet?"

It was the first question Brendan asked Patrick upon their arrival at the ranch.

"No," he said. "I thought I should let their new owners give them names."

"You've found homes for them already?" Brooke asked.

"I've had a couple phone calls, thanks to the notice you put up at the clinic, but I haven't met any prospective owners yet or made any promises."

"You should at least keep one," Brendan said. "Princess might be sad and lonely if she has to give up all her babies."

"I wasn't even planning to keep Princess," Patrick reminded him.

Brooke smiled at that. "And now she's wearing a collar with her name and your phone number on it."

"A collar *you* bought for her," he reminded her.

"You put it on her."

"You should keep Leia," Brendan suggested.

"Who's Leia?" Patrick asked warily.

"The one that looks most like Princess."

He sighed. "You've come up with names for all the puppies, haven't you?"

Brendan nodded. "The other girls are Rey and Rose," he said, pointing to each one in turn. "And the boys are Luke, Han and Finn."

"It's possible the new owners won't be *Star Wars* fans, you know," Patrick told him.

The boy frowned, as if he couldn't imagine such a possibility. "But they might let them keep the names anyway."

"They might," he agreed, before turning his attention to Brooke. "Everything okay? You got quiet all of a sudden."

"Just a really long day," she said.

"Anything you want to talk about?"

She glanced in Brendan's direction. Though her son seemed preoccupied with the puppies, he had an uncanny knack for absorbing every word of a conversation not intended for his ears. So while it might have been nice to share the details of her crappy day with Patrick and lean into the strength of his embrace, she only shook her head.

Understanding, he didn't push for details. Instead he asked, "Anything I can do to help?"

Though she appreciated the offer, she shook her head again.

He wrapped his arms around her anyway and held her close for a long moment, and it helped a lot.

Friday night, Patrick picked up takeout from Diggers' and took it to Brooke's apartment to share with her and Brendan. He'd wanted to take them out to the restaurant, but Brooke preferred to dine in. She claimed she was wiped out after a long week at work, and while that was probably true, he suspected it was more true that she wasn't ready to make a public statement about their relationship. Or even a private statement, as evidenced by her determination to keep Brendan in the dark.

"Melissa told me her news," she said, after Brendan had gone to bed and they could talk more freely.

"So you know I wasn't wrong when I suspected that she was holding something back," he said.

"She's still qualified for the job."

"Overqualified," he admitted. "And she deliberately manipulated me into giving her the job."

"You wanted a cook. She wanted a job. That sounds more like a mutually beneficial arrangement than manipulation to me," Brooke remarked.

"She wanted out of Seattle and jumped at the first opportunity that presented itself."

"Maybe she did need a place to go and some distance from the father of her child," she allowed.

He frowned at that. "What do you know that I don't? Did the father threaten her in some way? Did he—"

She held up a hand to halt his tirade. "I don't know the details of her situation, but I know he made it clear that if she insisted on having the baby, she was on her own."

"Apparently I need to go to Seattle and kick someone's worthless—"

"No, you don't," she said, cutting him off again. "What you need to do is trust Melissa to make her own choices."

"Because clearly that's worked out for her so far," he said dryly.

"Maybe a pregnancy isn't something she would have chosen at this time in her life," Brooke acknowledged coolly. "But it might turn out that this baby is the best thing that could have happened to her."

"I'm sorry. I wasn't thinking about the fact that..." He trailed off, as if uncertain how to finish the thought.

"That eight years ago, I was in the same position your cousin is in right now?" she finished for him.

"Yeah," he admitted.

"But I had my parents to support me. Melissa came here because she doesn't believe hers will. And because she trusts you." She pinned him with her gaze. "Don't disappoint her."

"Is that what you're waiting for?" he wondered. "Me to disappoint you?"

"I thought we were talking about your cousin."

"And now we're talking about us," he said. "Or maybe about the fact that you don't want anyone to know that there even is an 'us.'"

"That's not true," she denied. "There are plenty of people who know."

"If 'plenty' translates to 'a select few who won't slip up and say something in front of Brendan,'" he remarked dryly.

"I'm not going to apologize for wanting to protect my son from gossip."

"Is that all you're protecting him from?" Patrick challenged.

"History teaches a hard lesson," she said. "And I don't want to be the fool who didn't learn from her mistakes."

"I hope you're not comparing me to your ex, because I would never have let a woman I'd been involved with raise our child alone."

"Let me guess… You would have offered to marry her."

"Of course," he immediately replied.

"Well, for your information, Xander did offer to marry me. And I said yes, because I was twenty-two years old and terrified by the idea of having a baby on my own."

He was clearly taken aback by this revelation. "You were married to Brendan's father?"

"No. I wasn't foolish enough to go through with it after I found him in bed with my roommate," she confided reluctantly. Because eight years later, she was still embarrassed to admit that she'd fallen for a guy who'd obviously thought so little of her.

"He didn't even apologize," she continued. "That's when I realized he'd wanted to get caught. That he probably chose her so he would get caught, so I wouldn't marry him."

"He was an asshole." Patrick's blunt response soothed some of the residual sting from Xander's cruel actions.

"He was," she agreed readily.

He frowned. "And you think I'm like him?"

"No, I don't think you're anything like him," she said.

"Then what's the problem?" he asked.

"The problem is that I don't really trust my own judgment anymore," she admitted. "And it's not only my heart I have to worry about this time."

Now that he knew a little bit more about Brooke's situation with her ex, in addition to the previous history she'd shared, Patrick wasn't surprised that she had trust issues. And while he wished she would show a little more faith in him, he wasn't entirely sure he deserved it.

He would never cheat on her—or any woman, but he'd never been able to make a commitment to a woman, either. The closest he'd ever come was shopping for an engagement ring. But he'd held off buying one in favor of taking Kari to the store so that she could pick out what she wanted. It turned out to be a good call, because she hadn't wanted to plan a future with him.

Unhappy with the trek down memory lane, Patrick was grateful to be distracted by his grandfather's arrival at the ranch.

"You're a long way from Crooked Creek," he remarked, greeting him with a hug.

"I'm on my way to Helen's for dinner," Gramps said, referring to the woman that he'd been dating for more than two years now.

It had been a surprise to the whole family to discover that Jesse Blake had opened up his heart again after mourning the loss of his wife so deeply and for so long. But in one of those odd twists of fate, Gramps had met his lady friend at a birthday party for Spencer's daughter, Dani.

And while it was strange for Patrick to see his grandfather flirting and cuddling with a woman who wasn't his grandmother—or really, any woman at his age—Sarah was right. There was a definite spring in the old guy's step since he'd started spending time with Helen.

"And since I was passing by, I thought I'd stop by to see the pups Dani's been talking about." Gramps continued his explanation.

"They're pretty darn adorable," Patrick told him, leading the way to the barn.

"Are you planning on keeping any?" his grandfather asked.

"I wasn't even planning on keeping Princess," Patrick confided. "But somehow she's wearing a pink collar with my contact information on the tag."

"Princess?" Gramps echoed, sounding amused.

He shrugged, unwilling to admit it was the vet's son who'd named the dog—or that Brendan's attachment to the animal had undoubtedly been a factor in Patrick's decision to keep her.

"Well, every ranch should have a dog," his grandfather said, surveying the area where the canine mama was in residence with her pups. "So maybe it's lucky that she found you."

"I would have preferred to be found by a shepherd or Lab mix."

"A labradoodle is part Lab," Gramps pointed out.

"And part fluff ball."

"Which might explain why the puppies are so darn adorable." His grandfather's usually stern expression softened as he watched the little ones snuggle close to their mama.

"If you believe every ranch should have a dog, is that

why you're here?" Patrick asked, picking up the thread of their earlier conversation. "Do you want to take one of the pups home to Crooked Creek?"

"I'm thinking about it," Gramps said.

"Have you talked to Spencer and Kenzie about this?"

"Why would I? I don't need their permission to get a dog just because we all live at Crooked Creek."

"You do if you plan on giving that dog to Dani," Patrick said.

"I thought you'd be anxious to get rid of the pups, not try to talk potential adopters out of taking one off your hands."

"I want to see them go to good homes," he acknowledged. "I don't want them to be the cause of friction in a good home, and Spencer and Kenzie have their hands full enough right now with an almost seven-year-old and a new baby."

"Sounds like you might know something about the demands of a seven-year-old," his grandfather mused thoughtfully. "Makes me think there might be some truth to the rumors I've heard about you hanging out with the pretty vet and her son."

"It sounds to me like you didn't come here to see the puppies as much as to go on a fishing expedition."

As if to prove him wrong, Gramps shifted his attention back to the puppies. "Do they have names?"

"Apparently they do," Patrick said.

"Who's that one, with the lighter-colored fur?"

"Luke."

"Strange name for a dog," Gramps said.

Patrick just shrugged.

"Has anyone else asked about him?"

"Not specifically."

"Then you can reserve him for me."

Chapter Sixteen

"Five minutes," Brooke said, giving her son the usual warning so that he'd be ready and waiting when the school bus pulled up at the end of their driveway. "Did you brush your teeth?"

Brendan nodded and tugged his knit cap onto his head.

She slid his lunch box into the front pouch of his backpack and zipped it up.

He shoved his feet into his boots. "Can we go to the Silver Star after school today?"

Brooke shook her head. "Not today. I've got a full day at the clinic and then I've got to go check on Mr. Wallace's goats."

"You could drop me off at the Silver Star on your way," he said, as he fumbled with the zipper on his coat.

"No, I can't." She shook her head again as she helped him zip up. "But you can either come with me to see the goats or you can stay with Grandma."

Her son pouted. "Why can't I go to the Silver Star?"

"Because it's not on my way, and because you weren't invited." She put on her own coat and boots to wait outside with him.

"Patrick said I could visit the ranch anytime," he pointed out.

"Any time when you're with me," she acknowledged, wondering when her son had dropped the *Mister* and how that detail had escaped her notice until now. "He didn't offer to babysit you."

"I'm not a baby," Brendan said, slinging his backpack over his shoulder.

"No, you're not," she agreed. "But you're also not old enough to be left on your own, and Mr. Patrick might have other plans."

"But I want to help with the puppies."

"And that's a nice idea," Brooke said, as she steered him out the door. "But you wanting to help with the puppies would require me to drive fifteen miles out of my way and I don't have time for that today."

"I want to help with the puppies," he insisted, adopting the mutinous tone she knew only too well.

"And I told you not today," she reminded him, maintaining a level tone.

He folded his arms across his chest. "You're not the boss of me."

"Actually, being your mom pretty much means that

I *am* the boss of you," she said, giving up on any effort to de-escalate the situation.

"I wish I had a dad," Brendan shot back. "I bet a dad would let me go to the ranch."

She might have been less shocked if he'd slapped her, because his words stung more than a physical blow. And while her mind understood that he was lashing out because he wasn't getting his way, the heart that had only ever wanted what was best for her little boy was bruised and aching.

But there was nothing to be gained from letting him know how much his words had hurt her, so she drew in a slow, steadying breath and tried to respond calmly and rationally.

"Well, you've got me instead," she finally replied. "And I've already said you're not going today, so that's the end of the discussion. And if I hear one more word about the Silver Star or those puppies, you won't be going tomorrow, either."

"You're so mean!" Brendan protested, his eyes shiny with unshed tears.

She had no response to that, because she didn't doubt that, from his perspective, she was being mean. Because he couldn't possibly understand everything that she had to cram into a twenty-four-hour day. And in addition to all the usual duties and responsibilities, she was also trying to protect her little boy's heart.

Over the past couple of months, it had become apparent to Brooke that Brendan was growing far too attached to not just the ranch but the rancher. Patrick had been great with her son and genuinely seemed to enjoy hanging out with him, but what would happen when her relationship with Patrick ran its course? When he started dating someone else, would he still have time for Brendan? She wanted to believe that he would, but how could she expect Patrick to make her son a priority when the child's own father hadn't done so?

Of course, there was no way to explain any of this to a sensitive seven-year-old boy, so all she said was "There's your bus, honey."

She reached out to give him a quick hug, as she did every morning, but Brendan pulled away from her—for the first time ever—and made his way down the driveway.

The bus driver lifted his hand in greeting and Brooke waved back, managing a smile despite the heavy weight of her heart in her chest. Then she watched as Brendan made his way down the center aisle to take his usual seat by the window, but he kept his gaze focused forward instead of turning to wave, as he was accustomed to doing.

Brooke exhaled a weary sigh as the bus finally pulled away. With tears in her eyes, she turned toward her parents' house.

"Do you have coffee on?" she asked, walking into the kitchen after a perfunctory knock on the door.

"Always," her mom said.

Brooke sat at the table, wanting her mother's wise counsel more than another hit of caffeine.

Sandra poured two cups of coffee, and Brooke recapped the highlights of the conversation with her son as she sipped the hot drink.

“Did I overreact?” she wondered.

“Do you think you overreacted?”

“I don’t know,” she admitted. “I know he’s excited about the puppies, but even before they were born, he was *always* asking to go to the Silver Star, so maybe I’m afraid that Patrick is the real draw, and—” emotion choked her voice “—I don’t want Brendan to get hurt.”

“Why are you so certain that he will?” Then, after a moment’s hesitation, Sandra asked, “Or are you more worried that *you* will, Brooke?”

“I’m not certain,” she admitted, wiping away a tear. “But Patrick told me at the beginning that he wasn’t ready to be a father.”

“And yet he’s been spending an awful lot of time with you *and* your son over the past few weeks,” her mom remarked. “He wouldn’t be doing that if he didn’t care about both of you.”

Brooke sighed, because it was true. It was also true that she’d been holding back. Not because she didn’t trust him, but because she was afraid to trust her own heart. A heart that was already more than halfway in love with him.

“Don’t you think it’s time to let go of the past and look to the future?” Sandra asked gently. “To take a chance and finally let yourself be happy?”

Maybe it was, she mused. “Being at the Silver Star certainly makes Brendan happy.”

“And that’s great, but what about you?” her mom prompted.

“I like being there, too,” she confided. “Being with Patrick makes me happy. And gives me hope that the family I once dreamed of having might not be beyond my reach after all."

Sandra smiled, even as her eyes got misty. "Then give him a chance. Give *yourself* a chance."

Brooke decided that was good advice.

After hugging her mom and thanking her for the coffee, she headed toward the clinic. And she promised herself that the next time she saw Patrick, she would be honest about her feelings and her hopes for their future together.

Brooke felt so much better after talking to her mom that she managed to put the argument with Brendan out of her mind for most of the day. In fact, she even considered softening her stance and taking him to the Silver Star after dinner, but only if he didn't have any homework to do. Because how could she object to her son wanting to see Patrick when she wanted to see him, too?

Of course, that was before her dad walked into the exam room just as her four-legged patient walked out. Her quick smile immediately faded when she saw the expression on his face.

"What's wrong?"

Her father had never been one to tiptoe around bad news and he didn't do so now. "Brendan didn't get off the school bus today."

"What do you mean? Did Mom have to pick him up at school?" she asked, unable or unwilling to make sense of what he was saying.

"Your mom called the school, and the teacher on duty insisted she saw him in line for the bus. But when she called the bus company and they patched her through to the driver, he said Brendan never got on the bus."

"Then where is he?" Brooke demanded.

"Right now, no one seems to know."

Her father's words struck terror in her heart, and she had to grip the exam table with both hands for support.

"But we'll find him," Bruce promised.

"I know he was mad at me this morning," she admitted. "But I never thought he was the type of kid who would run away..." And then another, even more horrific, thought occurred to her. "But what if he didn't run away...? What if someone took him?"

"No one took him," Bruce said firmly, though he'd gone a little pale, obviously shaken by the thought.

"We should call the police," Brooke said.

"I already did. Sheriff Davidson was going to the school to talk to his teacher. And your mom's at home, because we thought someone should be there in case—*for when*—Brendan comes back."

Brooke nodded, needing to believe that her son would find his way home. Or that someone would find him. Until then, however, she had no idea where he was, and it terrified her to think of him wandering the streets alone.

"I've asked Larissa to reschedule the rest of your appointments so we can go out and start looking for Brendan right away. Your mom wanted to start organizing the neighbors into search parties, but the sheriff suggested we check out his favorite places around town first."

"Okay," she agreed, already making a mental list: the

playground by the school, Ridgemount Park, Jo's—for the video games. And then another possibility occurred to her. "The Silver Star."

"You think he'd head out to the ranch?" Bruce sounded dubious—and looked even more worried.

And Brooke understood why. The ranch was a nearly impossible distance from town on foot and the rural roads saw a fair amount of traffic traveling at highway speeds.

"I'll call Patrick." While she couldn't imagine that her son might have actually made his way out to the Silver Star, it was suddenly obvious to Brooke that the ranch was his ultimate destination.

"You can call from the car," her father said. "I'll drive."

Patrick was feeling pretty good about his life as he sat in front of his computer, double-checking reservation requests with room assignments for the grand opening of the Silver Star Vacation Ranch. With only a few weeks to go, everything was on track and on schedule. But the icing on the cake was his relationship with Brooke and Brendan. And, yeah, that had been a surprise to him, too. Not only that he would enter into a relationship with a single mom, but that he'd fall head over heels for her kid.

He wasn't ready to get down on one knee, but he wasn't freaked out by the idea that they might one day be a family, either. Okay, he was maybe a little freaked out—and worried about his ability to be a good husband and father, considering his own hadn't been much of a role model—but he wasn't completely freaked out. And that, he decided, was a definite step forward for him.

So when his phone rang and a quick glance at the screen identified Brooke as the caller, his lips curved automatically and he swiped to connect the call. "I was just think—"

"Brendan's missing."

Those two words not only stole his breath but his ability to form a coherent thought. "What—how—where—"

"I don't know," she said, interrupting him again. "But I think he might be on his way to the Silver Star."

He could hear the desperation and panic in her voice and the same emotions began to take root inside him. Questions continued to swirl in his mind, but he managed to keep them in his head this time, understanding that she didn't need him to add to her concerns.

"My dad and I are on our way there now," Brooke continued, "but if you could keep an eye out for him..."

"Of course," he immediately responded, pushing his chair away from the desk.

"Thanks."

Patrick heard the tremor in her voice and knew she was hanging on by a thread. He wanted to say something to reassure her, but he knew nothing would make her feel better until Brendan was found safe.

"I'll see you soon," he said instead.

Then he disconnected the call and shoved the phone into his back pocket. He felt as if there was a weight on his chest, making it difficult to draw air into his lungs.

"Patrick?"

He hadn't heard Melissa come into the room and he started now at the sound of her voice.

"Is something wrong?" she asked, sounding concerned.

He wasn't the type to panic. At least, he'd never been so before. But he was starting to feel panicky now as Brooke's words replayed in his head, an endless ominous loop. "Brendan's missing."

"Missing?" his cousin echoed. "Oh, no…the poor boy. And Brooke. She must be beside herself."

He nodded, because of course she was. Any parent would be frantic to discover that a child was missing, and he'd heard not just worry but fear for her son in Brooke's voice.

Patrick hadn't anticipated that he'd feel the same way. After all, he wasn't Brendan's father or stepfather—he wasn't even officially dating the boy's mother. He had absolutely no rights or responsibilities with respect to the child, and yet those words—*Brendan's missing*—had cut him off at the knees.

Because over the past couple of months, as he'd spent time with and got to know the little boy, he'd grown to care for him. A lot. And he couldn't bear to think of him lost or alone.

"What can I do to help?" Melissa asked now.

"I don't even know what I'm supposed to be doing," he confided, as he shoved his feet into his boots and reached for his coat. "But Brooke thinks Brendan might be on his way here."

"Here?" Worry etched a frown in Melissa's brow. "How would he find his way from town?"

"I don't know." Although there was a school bus that passed by every day, to pick up and drop off at the Carson place, just down the road. "But if Brendan's here, I'll find him."

"I'll put on a fresh pot of coffee."

He nodded and headed out the door.

Though he'd tried to sound confident when he'd said he'd find Brooke's son, he didn't expect it would be easy. Even if Brendan had known to get off the bus at the Carson residence, it was nearly a quarter mile from there to the Silver Star—assuming the kid knew east from west and didn't start walking in the wrong direction.

And apparently he did, because as soon as Patrick started down the driveway, he spotted a familiar pint-size figure in a blue ski jacket and red pom-pom hat wrestling with the heavy door of the barn before squeezing through the narrow gap.

The relief was both immediate and overwhelming, so much so that his fingers were trembling as he sent a quick text message to Brooke:

He's here.

Then he took a minute to allow his erratically beating heart to settle back inside his chest—and forward the brief message to Melissa—before he followed Brendan into the barn.

He caught up with him by the stall where Princess and her puppies had taken up residence. Although the gate was open, the boy remained outside, respecting the animals' space while mama nursed her babies.

"Hi, Mr. Patrick." Brendan greeted him as if there was nothing unusual about his presence at the ranch. "I came to see the puppies."

Patrick shoved his hands deep into the pockets of his jeans so that he wouldn't haul the boy into his arms and hug him tight, because he didn't want to freak Brendan out with such an unexpected display of emotion.

"Where's your mom?" he asked instead, wondering how Brooke's son would explain the current situation.

"She had to work late at the clinic."

"So how'd you get here?"

"I took the number three bus," Brendan told him.

Beneath the pride in his voice, there were hints of both defiance and worry. Yeah, the kid knew he was in trouble, but he had no idea how much.

"Does your mom know you're here?" Patrick asked.

The boy's gaze slid away, a telltale sign that he wasn't being entirely truthful when he said, "I told her I wanted to see the puppies."

"Did you tell your grandma, too?"

Now he shook his head.

"Do you think she might be worried, not knowing where you are?"

Brendan shrugged, but the way he hung his head confirmed that he was finally starting to realize the consequences of his actions.

Of course, neither of them could know the true extent of those consequences until Brooke arrived, and as Patrick directed the boy to the tack room to wait for his mom, he didn't envy her the worries and responsibilities of parenthood.

But maybe there was a tiny part of him that wished he could share them with her.

He's here.

The message on Brooke's screen blurred as the tears she'd been fighting to hold back finally broke through on a sob and spilled onto her cheeks.

"What is it?" her father asked, lifting one hand from the wheel to reach for hers.

She clutched it gratefully. "Brendan's at the Silver Star."

Bruce exhaled a breath. "That's a relief."

Her phone pinged with another message. "Mom's on her way, too. She found out from Russell that Brendan got on a different bus to go see the puppies." She swiped at the tears on her cheeks with the back of her free hand. "I'm so glad he's safe. And I'm so..."

"Furious," her dad suggested.

She nodded. "And hurt and disappointed and so many other emotions I can't even begin to decipher them all."

"The joys of parenting," Bruce remarked, squeezing her hand.

"How did you survive raising three kids?" she wondered aloud.

"I didn't do it on my own," her dad reminded her. "And you don't have to, either."

"Believe me, I know how lucky I am to have the support of you and Mom."

"Always," he said. "But I wasn't referring to us."

Did he mean…Patrick?

Did he know about her personal relationship with the rancher?

Of course he did, because she'd told her mom and her mom and dad had no secrets from one another.

But Brooke shoved those thoughts aside for now to focus on the only thing that really mattered: Brendan.

It seemed to take forever to get to the ranch, and Brooke had her seat belt unlatched before the vehicle was at a complete stop. She threw open the door and nearly tumbled to the ground, but Patrick was there. He caught her in his arms, and she was tempted, for just a moment, to lean into him and take strength from his strength.

Instead, she pulled away from him and squared her shoulders. "Where's Brendan?"

"He's in the tack room." Patrick stepped in front of her again, deliberately blocking her path.

"I need to see him," she said, hating that her voice hitched.

"I know." He set his hands on her shoulders, stroked them down her arms. "But I think it would be a good idea if we talked first about how you want to handle this, what you plan to say, so that I can back you up."

"I've barely had a chance to catch my breath, so I don't know what I'm going to say," she admitted, a hint of irritation in her tone. "But I know that I don't need you to back me up. This is between me and my son. It doesn't have anything to do with you."

Chapter Seventeen

Patrick dropped his hands from Brooke's arms and stepped back so that she could pass. She made an immediate beeline for the barn, swiping at the errant tears that spilled onto her cheeks along the way. He knew her emotions were running high and that he should probably cut her some slack, but he couldn't help feeling both hurt and frustrated by her determination to keep him on the periphery of her life.

"I guess that put me in my place."

"She didn't mean to lash out at you," Brooke's dad said, his tone gruff but sympathetic.

"Are you sure about that?" Patrick asked him.

"She was scared. We all were. When Brendan didn't get off the school bus, Sandra was frantic. And when she told me, I was frantic."

Patrick nodded his understanding, because he'd been frantic, too, when Brooke called to tell him.

"And I know it was a thousand times worse for Brooke," Bruce continued. "She's always tried so hard to be a good mom, and when something like this happens, a parent can't help but question every decision they've ever made.

"Add to that the fact that she has no one to share the responsibilities of parenting with, and she's carrying a hefty burden. Sure, she can take all the credit for raising a pretty terrific kid, but she also shoulders all the blame when something goes wrong."

"Good thing she has strong shoulders," Patrick remarked.

"They're strong because they've had to be. Because there haven't been many people in her life that she can count on."

Patrick got the message, loud and clear. If he wasn't ready to be the kind of man that Brooke—and Brendan—needed, then he had no business indulging in a romance with the single mom.

It was time for him to step up or step back.

Brooke tried to hold it together. She really did. But when she saw her little boy sitting on the edge of the bench in the tack room as if he'd been put in a time-out—and maybe he had—she couldn't hold it together anymore. And though Brendan likely didn't have a clue why his mother was crying as she hugged him so tight against her chest, he was soon crying, too.

"I'm sorry, Mommy," he said, when she'd finally managed to pull herself together again.

"I know," she said, still teary-eyed. "You're also grounded."

"What? Why?"

"Because this is one of those times when an apology doesn't make everything okay," she told him.

"But—"

"No buts," she interjected. "You know the rules, and you deliberately broke them."

"I didn't think not going to the Silver Star was a rule," Brendan protested.

"The rule is that you never go anywhere without asking permission and especially not without telling me where you're going," she reminded him.

"I didn't ask because I knew you'd say no," he admitted.

Brooke sighed, struggling to find the right words. "You might find this hard to believe, but I don't say no just for fun. When I tell you that you can't do something, there's usually a good reason. When I want to know where you are and who you're with at all times, it's because I need to know that you're safe."

"I *was* safe," he said. "I was *here*."

"But I didn't know that when Grandpa came to the clinic to tell me you didn't get off the bus," she pointed out. "And Gramma and Grandpa didn't know it, either. Which is why we've all been worried sick about you."

Fresh tears welled up in his eyes and he wrapped his arms around her, pressing his wet face against the front of her shirt. "I'm sorry," he said again.

And somehow the squeeze of his skinny arms managed to obliterate the last vestiges of terror that lingered in the corners of her heart.

And now that the fear had finally subsided, the questions pushed to the front of her mind, prompting her to ask, "How did you even get here?"

"I came on the number three bus."

Brooke frowned. "The bus drivers aren't supposed to let you get on any bus but your own," she said, uneasy to learn that he'd been able to walk onto the wrong vehicle.

He dropped his gaze to stare at his boots. "The usual bus driver wasn't driving today."

"But how did you even know what bus to take?"

"I asked Daniel Carson what was his bus."

Daniel was a grade ahead of Brendan at school, but they'd been in the same class when Daniel was in SK and Brendan was in JK. They'd had similar-looking backpacks that year and somehow mixed them up one day. Brendan had been inconsolable when he'd realized what happened, certain his mom wouldn't be able to pack his lunch for the next day if he didn't have his lunch box. So Brooke had driven out to Daniel's house to let the boys exchange bags.

Although that had been almost three years ago, she knew her son remembered the incident—and where Daniel lived, because he'd pointed out the house on various occasions when they'd driven past, wanting to know if she remembered "the boy who took my backpack."

"So you walked over here from Daniel's house?" she asked, still trying to put the pieces together—and not completely lose it again to realize that her son had crossed a major road between the two properties.

He nodded.

Even now, knowing he was safe, she felt sick to think of her seven-year-old child walking the rural road on his own. Because although he'd obviously reached his intended destination without mishap, there were so many things that could have gone wrong.

"I'm really glad that you're safe," Brooke said, aware that Patrick had returned to the barn and stood in the open doorway of the tack room, listening. "I'm also really mad that you disobeyed me after I said you couldn't come to the Silver Star today."

Brendan's lower lip trembled. "I just really wanted to see the puppies." Then he looked at Patrick, as if pleading for his help. "And you said I could come to the ranch anytime I wanted."

"With your mother's permission," the rancher reminded him. "What you did wasn't just against her rules, it was inconsiderate and potentially dangerous." He paused. "You also lied to *me*, Brendan, and that hurt my feelings. I thought we were friends. And friends should be honest with each other."

Patrick glanced at Brooke, then back at her son, and said regretfully, "So until you prove, to your mom's satisfaction—and mine, too—that you can follow her rules, you're not allowed at the Silver Star."

The boy's jaw dropped and his eyes filled with fresh tears before he spun on his heel and raced out of the room.

Brooke sighed and moved closer to the window,

through which she could watch Brendan run into the open arms of his grandmother, who'd obviously arrived while they were in the barn. Then Bruce folded his arms around both his wife and grandchild.

"You know, I always thought that whole 'punishing you hurts me more than it hurts you' thing parents tell their kids was a load of garbage," Patrick said. "But, damn, that was hard."

"Doing the right thing usually *is* hard," she agreed.

"How long is he grounded for?"

"I don't know yet. But thank you," she said. "For backing me up with Brendan."

"Always," he promised.

And in that moment, she caught a glimpse of what life might look like with a partner to share all the joys and sorrows, and she believed that Patrick Stafford just might be a man she could count on.

He didn't see Brooke at all over the next few days, and he thought that was probably a good thing. After the incident with Brendan and his conversation with the boy's grandfather, Patrick realized he had a lot of things he needed to figure out.

He'd told Bruce the truth when he said he couldn't imagine the roller-coaster emotions Brooke had gone through when her son was missing. Before he'd started spending time with Brooke and Brendan, Patrick hadn't appreciated the tremendous responsibilities that went hand in hand with raising a child—especially for a single parent.

Brooke deserved to be with someone who could take

some of that weight off her shoulders. A partner who was willing to share both the credit and the blame, the good times and bad times and scary-as-hell times. And as much as he might wish he could be that person, he knew that if he tried, he would only end up disappointing her.

The example that her parents had set in their relationship had given her something to aspire to, but he didn't know how to be a husband or a father. Certainly Derrick Stafford had never been a model of either. And while Patrick had learned a lot of what not to do, Brooke deserved better than that.

Now he was faced with the task of having to tell her the truth: that he was just one more guy she couldn't count on.

But he wasn't prepared to do it just yet, and he wasn't sure what to say when she drove up as he was cooling Pongo down after a ride.

Hopping out of her truck, she offered him a smile that squeezed his heart.

"I didn't expect to see you today," he said.

"I was passing by on my way back to town and thought I'd stop to invite you to dinner tomorrow night. It's my day off, which means that I'll actually have some time to cook," she said. "And hopefully figure out how to apologize for the way I reacted the other day when Brendan was missing. Or after he was found."

"Please don't apologize," he said, aware that he was going to do something worse than bruise her feelings and with less justification.

"So...dinner?" she prompted.

"Actually, Melissa's trying out a new chicken-fried steak and gravy recipe tomorrow."

"Oh. Okay." She looked at him then, as if waiting for him to say something more.

He remained silent.

"This would be a good time for you to invite me to have dinner with you here instead," she said, with a hopeful smile.

He was more than a little tempted to do just that, and to put off what needed to be done. But that wouldn't be fair to either of them.

"You grounded Brendan," he reminded her.

"I'm sure my parents would be happy to have Brendan stay with them. And since I'm not grounded, I could even stay for dessert," she said.

It was obvious what she was offering, and it seemed like forever since they'd made love…

But since when did he think of sex as making love?

And since when did he think about a woman every minute of every day that they were apart?

Only since Brooke.

She was always on his mind and in his heart.

The terrifying truth was that she meant more to him than any woman he'd dated in a very long time, maybe ever. And he could easily imagine a life with her and Brendan, but he wasn't ready to be a husband and father, to be tied down with a family.

"Actually, I don't think that's a good idea," he said.

The teasing smile on her face faded, and the light in her eyes dimmed. "Why not?"

He could tell by the flatness of her tone that she

already knew what he was going to say. But she was going to make him say it. She was going to make him prove he was every bit the callous jerk he'd promised her he wouldn't be.

"I just think…it's been a crazy week with everyone's emotions running high and maybe— I think maybe it's time to take a step back."

"A step back." She nodded. "I guess that puts us right back where we started, doesn't it?"

"I'm sorry, Brooke."

"No, I'm the one who's sorry," she said. "Sorry that I let myself believe you might be different. That I believed *you* when you said you cared about me and Brendan, that we mattered."

"I *do* care about you and Brendan," he told her. "I'm just not ready to take on the responsibilities of a wife and child."

"Whoa!" She held up both hands. "I invited you to dinner. I didn't ask you to marry me."

"But isn't that where you thought our relationship was eventually headed?" he challenged.

"Eventually is a rather vague timeline," she pointed out. "And even if it did cross my mind that we might *eventually* move in that direction, I can assure you that I'm in no rush to tie myself to a cowboy with a reputation for bailing at the first sign of a relationship getting real."

"That's not what's happening here," he protested, though the denial sounded hollow even to his own ears.

"That's exactly what's happening," she said. "And truthfully, I'm not surprised. Maybe this relationship charade lasted a little longer than I expected, but we both knew this was where we'd end up, didn't we?"

And without giving him a chance to respond, she got back in her truck and drove away.

Brooke had told him that she wasn't surprised, but she was.

Not only surprised but hurt.

Just when she'd started to think that she'd been wrong about him, that there was more to Patrick Stafford than his reputation, he'd proved her not just a fool but a lousy judge of character.

Thankfully, she didn't have to come up with any excuses to justify to Brendan why they weren't going out to the Silver Star, because he was grounded. And maybe by the time his grounding was lifted, he would have forgotten about Patrick and the Silver Star.

But as angry as she was with Patrick, she couldn't deny that there had been some truth to his accusation. She'd agreed to an affair, and then she'd started to imagine the physical intimacy might lead to something more. Because she wanted more, not just for herself, but for her son, too.

She wanted a man who wanted to be a father to Brendan, but now she knew Patrick wasn't ever going to be that man. And if she'd been hurt by the realization, it was her own fault. Because he'd told her right from the beginning that he wasn't looking to take on that kind of responsibility.

Of course, he'd then spent a couple of months doing a pretty good imitation of a man taking on that responsibility. But that was all it had been—an imitation. She deserved the real thing. And so did Brendan.

Jenna and Melissa were in the kitchen, eating caramel apple coffee cake and drinking herbal tea, when Patrick walked into the house. He usually couldn't wait to sample whatever his cousin had whipped up, but he wasn't the least bit tempted by the freshly baked treat today, his belly filled with a hard, heavy ball of guilt and regrets.

Jenna glanced past him, as if looking for someone else. "I thought I saw Brooke's truck in the driveway."

"Yeah, she was here," he confirmed.

"She usually pops in to say hi," Melissa remarked.

"She had to get home."

Though he'd attempted to keep his tone neutral, the look exchanged by the two women warned that he hadn't quite succeeded.

"Oh, Patrick. What did you do?" Jenna asked him.

"What do you mean?" he hedged.

"You broke up with her, didn't you?" His sister's tone was accusing.

"How do you break up with someone you aren't really dating?" he challenged, unnerved by the eerily accurate insights of the women.

"He didn't break up with her," Melissa said, speaking to Jenna now. "He did something worse—he broke her heart."

"I did not," he denied.

His sister folded her arms over her chest. "Did you make her cry?"

"No."

"She wouldn't cry in front of him," Melissa decided. "She's stronger than that."

"Or maybe because she agreed that it was time to go our separate ways," he offered.

"I don't understand," Jenna said, sounding sincerely baffled and maybe a little disappointed. "I thought she was different. I thought you really cared about her."

"I did. I do," he admitted. "But the longer we let things continue, the more everyone was going to be hurt when it was over."

"Why did it ever have to be over?" his sister demanded. "Why couldn't you, for once, let yourself actually be happy?"

"I am happy," he said. "I like my life the way it is. I'm not looking for a ready-made family and I definitely don't need the complication or the responsibility of a child."

Jenna shook her head. "You really don't see it, do you?"

"See what?"

"You only *think* you don't want a family, because you don't want a family like the screwed-up one we grew up in—and no one can blame you for that," she said. "But while you've been renovating buildings and fixing fences over the past several months, you've also been creating a family here."

"Is there alcohol in that cake?" he asked Melissa, suggesting that might be the cause of his sister's nonsensical rambling.

"Pregnant," she reminded him. "And your sister isn't just sober, she's insightful, and you should listen to her."

"You might not realize you're doing it, but you instinctively care for and nurture everyone under your roof," Jenna continued. "Melissa, me and even Princess."

"I'm letting you stay—*temporarily*—in an empty room, and Melissa works here," he pointed out.

The women exchanged another glance.

"Denial," they said in unison.

He just shook his head.

"Whether you want one or not, you've got a family right here," Jenna continued. "But until you fix things with Brooke, it's going to be incomplete."

Of course, it took Patrick a few days to come around to the realization that his sister was right.

For a guy who claimed to not want complications, his life was full of them: he had a dog and six puppies in his barn, a runaway sister in his guest cottage and a pregnant woman in his attic.

But what he didn't have—and the only things he really wanted—were Brooke and Brendan.

He picked up the phone to invite her to come out to the Silver Star, then put it down again, suspecting his request would be refused. He considered calling the clinic to ask her to come out to the ranch to check on his animals, but knew she'd see right through that ruse and probably send the other Dr. B. Langley in her stead. Which left him with only one option: to grovel on her turf.

Maybe it had taken him a while to come around

to the realization that they were meant to be together, but he had to hope that he wasn't too late to convince Brooke to give him—to give them—a second chance.

Brooke saw the appointment on her schedule when she arrived at the clinic Wednesday morning.

2:00 Patrick Stafford—puppy exams/shots

She'd known it was inevitable that their paths would eventually cross—after all, her father wouldn't always be available to take every appointment she wanted to avoid—but she'd expected to have more time to put the broken pieces of her heart back together first.

But two o'clock was manageable, she decided. Maybe a few hours wouldn't be enough time to fix her heart, but it would be enough to put up her shields and a professional smile on her face.

"Good afternoon, Mr. Stafford," she said, greeting him as she would any other pet owner—polite and professional.

"Hello, Brooke."

She didn't respond to his familiar address, but her cool reserve began to melt when he opened the door of the crate and the puppies tumbled out onto the floor, climbing over one another in their excitement to escape the confined space.

"Oh…they've gotten so big," she said, automatically crouching to give them the adoration they craved. Because while she might want to hold herself aloof from the rancher, she was helpless to resist these babies.

"They're six weeks old now," he said, as if she might have forgotten that she'd not only been there but played a key role in bringing them into the world.

"Time for their first shots," she confirmed. She scooped up the nearest puppy, her fingers sinking into the soft fur as she lifted it to read the name on its tag. "Hello, Han."

The pup answered by swiping his tiny tongue over her chin, making her smile even as her heart was breaking all over again.

"I also want to be sure they're in good health before I let them go to their adoptive families," Patrick said.

"Have you found homes for all of them?" She gently lowered the puppy to the scale to check his weight.

"All except Leia."

"No one wanted her?" she asked, surprised.

"There was interest," he said. "But I thought about what Brendan said and decided to let her stay with her mom."

"So you'll have Princess and Leia," she realized.

He nodded.

She refused to believe it meant anything that he'd chosen to keep the puppy her son had wanted as his own.

"And my grandfather's taking Luke, and Sarah has claimed Han, so the original trilogy are all going to be close to home."

"That's nice," she said, as she continued to examine the puppies—taking temperatures, listening to their hearts, checking their eyes and ears.

"Finn looks like he might find a permanent home

next door, Rey was claimed by my cousin Ashley, and your vet tech has dibs on Rose."

"Courtney's been talking about getting a puppy for almost a year," Brooke noted. "Being the first one to hold Rose after she was born must have convinced her it was time."

"Are you sure you haven't changed your mind about wanting one?" he asked.

"I've changed my mind at least a hundred times," she admitted. "But my reasons for not taking one haven't.

"There you go," she said, setting the last pup back in the crate he'd used to transport them to the clinic.

"Thanks." He latched the door.

"You can settle up with Larissa at reception," she said, prodding him to move along.

"I will," he promised, but still made no move to leave.

"Was there something else you wanted?" she finally asked.

"Yeah, I want you to come over for dinner this weekend. You and Brendan," he hastened to clarify. "Assuming he's over being grounded by then."

"Why?" she asked, not just surprised by the invitation but a little wary, too.

"Because I've missed you," he confessed. "Both of you."

She wasn't going to let herself be swayed by the sincerity in his voice. And she certainly wasn't going to set her son—or herself—up for more disappointment.

"I screwed up in a big way, and I just want a chance to explain…and maybe to make it up to you. What do you say?" he cajoled. "Friday or Saturday—your choice."

She wanted to rant and scream in frustration that he couldn't shove them away one minute and expect them to come back the next. But she didn't want him to know how much his rejection had hurt her, so she only shook her head and said, "I'm going to be out of town this weekend."

"Where are you going?"

"A veterinarian conference in San Diego."

"This is the conference you mentioned a few weeks back—the one you weren't sure would be worth your time?" he guessed.

She nodded. It was also the one she'd considered inviting him to attend with her, so she wouldn't have to sleep alone. But of course she wasn't going to mention that now.

"Why'd you change your mind about going?" he asked.

"I found out that a friend from college is presenting the findings from a new study on bovine respiratory syncytial virus," she said.

"I have to wonder if you really want to learn more about BRSV or if you just want to put some distance between us."

"I think you've already done that," she pointed out.

"I was an idiot," he said.

But she shook her head. "No, you were right. Things were getting too intense. Too real."

"I want it to be real," he told her. "I want you, me and Brendan to be together. A family."

It was everything she'd dreamed of—and everything he'd said he didn't want. "Where is this coming from all of a sudden?"

"It's not all of a sudden," he denied. "I know it probably seems like it is, but that's only because I refused to recognize what was in my heart."

"Barely a week ago, you told me that you wanted to take a step back," she reminded him.

"A week ago, I was scared and stupid. Now I'm just scared, because what I feel for you and for Brendan is strong and real, and it terrifies me to imagine my life without both of you in it.

"And I'm screwing this up again," he realized. "Because I skipped over the most important part. That I love you, Brooke."

"No," she said, looking away so he wouldn't see the tears that filled her eyes. So he wouldn't guess the desperate longing in her heart that wanted to propel her into his arms. "You can't do this. You can't come in here and tell me that you love me and expect it to make everything okay."

"Then tell me what I can do," he urged. "Tell me what you want."

"I want you to go so Larissa can bring the next patient into this room."

Chapter Eighteen

"Melissa—hi. Come on in."

"I apologize for stopping by unannounced," Patrick's cousin said. "But I made peanut butter cookies today, and I wanted to drop some off for you before they all disappeared."

"That was really thoughtful," Brooke said. "And now that I've got cookies, I think a cup of tea is in order. Care to join me?"

"A cup of tea sounds wonderful," Melissa agreed.

Brooke led her into the apartment and turned on the kettle. "What kind do you like?"

"Do you have anything without caffeine?"

"Peppermint, lemon and decaffeinated Earl Grey," she offered.

"Hmm…the Earl Grey sounds good," Melissa decided.

Brooke made the tea, then opened the container of cookies and set half a dozen on a plate in the middle of the table.

"So how are you doing?" Melissa asked, when Brooke sat down across from her.

"I'm okay," she said. It wasn't exactly the truth—between the drama of Brendan's bus adventure, being dumped by Patrick and then his visit to the clinic, she felt as if she'd been strapped into an emotional roller coaster—but she thought she was doing a pretty good job of faking it.

"I can't imagine anything more terrifying for a parent than not knowing where her child is," the other woman confided.

"It's definitely not an experience I ever want to repeat," Brooke told her.

"So how long is Brendan grounded for?"

"I'm still trying to figure that out. My gut instinct was to say until he's sixteen, but even in the heat of the moment I realized that was a little extreme."

"But understandable," Melissa said.

Brooke smiled, grateful for the expectant mom's support. "But now I think my memories of the terror might subside enough that I'll be willing to let him out of my sight in about six months."

"Does that mean you're taking him to San Diego with you?"

"Obviously Patrick told you about my trip?"

Melissa nodded.

"I wish I could take Brendan with me, but he'd be bored to tears—or he'd convince his aunt Lori to take him to Disneyland, which would hardly fit the definition of a grounding," she said, with a shake of her head. "So he'll stay here with my parents."

"I met your mom and dad at the ranch that day," Melissa said. "They were amazing—so calm and cool despite everything going on."

"They are great," she acknowledged. "I definitely lucked out there."

"Patrick wasn't nearly as lucky."

"And now we get to the real reason for your visit?" Brooke guessed.

"I really did come to see you—and to bring you cookies. But maybe I also wanted to plead my cousin's case a little," Melissa admitted.

"There's no case and, therefore, no pleading required. He's the one who decided that everything was getting a little too real."

"If you knew about his relationship with his parents, you'd understand why Patrick tries not to get too attached," his cousin told her.

"I know they split up a few times but always got back together," Brooke said.

"It might have been better for their kids if they didn't always get back together," Melissa confided. "My family moved to Seattle when I was ten, but before then, I spent a lot of time with my cousins. And in the years that followed, I'd often come to Haven for a week in the summer and Sarah and Jenna would come to Seattle for a week after Christmas, or vice versa."

"It's nice that you were able to stay close," Brooke said.

"It was," the other woman agreed. "But one time when I was there, Uncle Derrick and Aunt Liz got into a big fight. I don't remember what it was about, or if I even knew what it was about, because it seemed that an argument about one thing inevitably turned into something else.

"Anyway, later that night, when I thought the fighting was over, I went down to the kitchen to get a drink and I heard Uncle Derrick grumbling about something 'his son' had done, and Aunt Liz shot back saying 'maybe he's not your son.'"

Brooke sucked in a breath.

"That was my reaction, too," Melissa said. "And not wanting to hear any more of what they were saying, I turned around to tiptoe back up the stairs—and almost ran right into Patrick."

"He heard?"

Melissa nodded. "A few months later, Derrick and Liz split up. When Jenna and Sarah came to Washington over the Christmas break, they told me that their dad had demanded a paternity test."

Now Brooke winced.

"No one believed Liz had ever cheated on her husband—except maybe Derrick, and probably only to ease his guilty conscience. But even if there was a possibility Patrick wasn't Derrick's biological child, he'd raised him since birth, so you'd think DNA wouldn't matter as much as the bond they shared."

And Brooke didn't doubt that his father's willingness to disregard that bond would have struck a harsh blow to their relationship.

"His parents each used him as a weapon in their efforts to hurt one another, never considering that their son would be the one to carry the deepest scars."

"I had no idea," Brooke said. "I mean, I know he isn't particularly close to either of his parents..."

"And now you know why."

And knowing, she couldn't help but hurt for the rejected boy, but that didn't mean she was willing to forgive the man who'd rejected her and her son.

"I think Patrick didn't want to get involved with you because he worried that he wouldn't be able to love a child who wasn't his. Because that's the message he got from his father's demand for a paternity test. But then when Brendan was missing, he panicked because he realized that he already did love him, and the prospect of losing him was more than he could bear."

"Instead, he pushed him—pushed both of us—away," Brooke pointed out.

"And immediately regretted it," Melissa said.

She sighed. "So what am I supposed to do now?"

"What do you want to do?"

"I don't know," Brooke confided. "I was so hurt when he walked away, even if it only proved that he was exactly the type of guy he always claimed to be. But then he came into the clinic and asked for another chance, and now... I don't know what I'm supposed to feel."

"There is no 'supposed to' about feelings," the other woman said wisely. "So I'd suggest you stop trying to reason this out in your head and listen to your heart."

"But how many chances am I supposed to give him?" she asked. "How many times am I supposed to put my heart—and my son's—on the line?"

"I'm hardly an expert, but I'd say that depends."

"On what?" Brooke wondered.

"Whether or not you're in love with him."

He'd screwed up.

If he'd had any doubts that he was 100 percent at fault, both of Patrick's sisters and his cousin were only too happy to reassure him on that point. And to offer all kinds of unsolicited advice. But while he appreciated their interest and concern, he decided that what he really needed was a junior consultant.

He knew he was taking a big risk. Brooke had been clear from the beginning that she didn't want Brendan to know about his mom's relationship with "Mr. Patrick." She didn't want to raise her son's hopes that a few dates might lead to something more.

And he'd gone along, because he figured she knew her kid a lot better than he did—which of course she did. But as a result of this effort to manage Brendan's expectations, she'd succeeded in keeping her own little world intact—and Patrick on the outside looking in.

He didn't want to be on the outside anymore.

So, yeah, he was about to take a big risk, but he was looking for a big reward.

And Saturday afternoon, after Brendan's grounding had been lifted and he was allowed to visit the ranch, the boy played with Princess and her puppies until they were all played out and ready for a nap. Patrick then invited him into the house for milk and cookies and what he hoped he might someday look back on as his first father-son chat with the boy.

Not entirely sure where to begin, he said, "Do you remember when we talked before about your mom not having a boyfriend?"

Brendan, his mouth full of cookie, nodded.

Patrick tucked his sweaty palms into the front pockets of his jeans. "Well, I was thinking about what you said…and I've decided I'd like to ask her to be my girlfriend. If it's still okay with you."

"It's more than okay," the boy said. "It's awesome!"

"I'm glad you think so," he said, aware that he was manipulating the situation—and possibly Brooke's son—to get the boy on his side. But considering how spectacularly Patrick had struck out on his own, he knew it was time to bring in new talent. "But I think it might take some work to convince your mom."

"You could try giving her flowers," Brendan suggested.

It was solid advice, he acknowledged, and a little embarrassing to realize the kid had pointed out a basic courtship ritual he'd completely overlooked.

"Girls get all mushy when you give them flowers," the boy added sagely.

"How many girls have you given flowers to?" Patrick asked him.

Brendan rolled his eyes at the question. "None, but Grandpa gives them to Gramma all the time, and even if she's mad at him, she stops being mad and they kiss."

"Flowers are a good idea," Patrick agreed, smothering a laugh. "Kissing is even better."

Brendan made a face.

"Don't knock it until you try it," he said, then hastily revised his advice. "But don't be in any rush to try it."

"I've tried it," the boy told him. "Ruby asked me to push her on the swings at school, and 'cause I did, she kissed me and said I was her boyfriend."

"Where did she kiss you?" he wondered.

"By the swings," Brendan said again.

"I mean— Never mind," he said, deciding he wasn't ready to tackle the various issues involved with girls and dating, but also making a mental note to keep Ruby away from the boy he hoped would soon be his son. "Back to the flowers. Do you know if there's any particular kind of flowers your mom would like?"

"Yellow ones."

Patrick nodded. "Okay, then, let's go do some shopping."

When Brooke FaceTimed with Brendan Saturday night from her hotel room, her son was full of excitement as a result of his visit to the Silver Star—his first return to the ranch since his grounding was lifted.

The previous night, when Sandra told her Patrick had invited Brendan to visit, Brooke had considered not letting him go. But she knew it wasn't fair to punish her son again because she was hurting, so she gave permission but left it up to her mom to decide if she wanted to take him. Of course, Sandra had never been able to refuse her grandson anything.

And as Brendan regaled her with puppy tales, Brooke could tell he was overjoyed to learn that Patrick had decided to keep Leia, and also sad to know that most of the other puppies would soon be going to different homes.

"But at least I'll get to see Princess and Leia whenever we visit the Silver Star," he said.

Damn, maybe she should have let him have a puppy. If she had, he'd be less likely to notice when he didn't get invited back to the ranch that had almost become a second home to him over the past couple of months. But right now, she didn't have the heart to tell him that there were unlikely to be many visits to the ranch in their future.

"And you might find Rose at the clinic sometimes," she said instead. "Because her new home is going to be with Courtney."

"Yay!" he said.

They chatted for a few more minutes, and though Brooke purposely didn't ask her son about Patrick, that didn't stop her from thinking about him. And wondering if he'd really meant it when he said he wanted a second chance.

If it was possible that he really did love her.

She'd hoped that getting out of town—and away from Patrick—for a few days might help her clear her head and sort out her emotions so that she could start to get over him. But after his visit to the clinic earlier in the week, a tiny blossom of hope had begun to unfurl inside her heart. Hope that she wouldn't have to get over him but might instead be able to look toward a future for them together.

You, me and Brendan... A family.

She pushed the enticing thought to the back of her mind and made her way to the restaurant where she was meeting Lori and Matt for dinner.

But the whole time she was seated across the table from her friend and her new beau, Brooke couldn't forget the question Melissa had asked. She'd pretended she didn't know the answer, because she didn't want to be in love with Patrick. Because being in love required openness and vulnerability, which, experience had taught her, could result in hurt.

Except that being with the happy couple also reminded Brooke that love could result in healing. Lori and Matt had each been in relationships with other people before, but those unsuccessful experiences hadn't held them back from taking another chance and finding a true connection together.

By the time she went back to her empty hotel room alone, she'd made a decision. Not about whether or not she was in love with Patrick, because that had never really been in question, but to finally tell him the truth about her feelings.

It was almost dinnertime when Brooke finally arrived home from San Diego on Sunday. She'd texted her mom with her ETA when her plane landed, only to learn that her parents were going out to eat and wouldn't be there when she arrived. After two and a half days away, she was disappointed to have to wait even longer still to see Brendan and give him the bag of saltwater taffy she'd brought back from Ocean Beach.

Preoccupied by these thoughts, it took her a moment to realize that the lights were on inside her apartment when she opened the door, and another to register the scent of…toast?

"Hello?" she said cautiously.

"It's Mom!"

Brendan raced out of the kitchen and threw his arms around her. Patrick followed at a more measured pace and paused a few feet away, as if uncertain of his reception. That made two of them.

"Welcome home," he said.

"I…didn't expect anyone to be here," she said.

"We wanted to surprise you," Brendan said, squeezing tight.

She hugged him back, happy to see him…and not quite sure what to read into Patrick's presence, though her hopeful heart was leaning in a very specific direction.

Stop trying to reason this out in your head and listen to your heart.

"Are you surprised?" Brendan asked now.

"Very," she confirmed, realizing that her mother had obviously been in on whatever this plan was.

"Are you happy surprised or mad surprised?" Patrick asked cautiously. "Because if you're mad, I take full responsibility."

"I'm…still-evaluating surprised," she said.

"We got you flowers," Brendan said, drawing her attention to the beautiful arrangement of yellow roses, gerberas and tulips set in the middle of the table. "Do you like them?"

"Oh." She felt a flutter in her belly. "Yes, I do. They're beautiful."

Her gaze shifted back to Patrick, who was watching her with such focus and intensity, she felt that flutter again.

"Brendan, why don't you take your mom's bag to her room?" he suggested.

"Okay," her son agreed, pulling out the handle and wheeling it away.

"If you wanted to get him out of the room, you just bought yourself about twelve seconds because my bedroom isn't very far."

"I remember where your bedroom is. And, yes, I thought you'd probably want him out of the room when I did this," he said, sliding his arms around her.

Though she thought they should talk before they moved on to other things, she didn't balk at being drawn closer. And when he lowered his mouth to kiss her, she couldn't help but respond—her lips softening, her body melting.

Conscious of the twelve seconds she'd allotted, he reluctantly eased his mouth from hers. "Welcome home."

"You said that already," she told him.

"Did I tell you that I missed you?"

She shook her head. "No."

"Well, I did. And not just this weekend, but every day of the week before that, when I was foolish enough to think I could ever live without you."

"I missed you, too, but—"

"Are you hungry?" he asked.

She wasn't sure if he'd cut her off because Brendan had returned to the room or if he didn't want to hear how she might finish that thought.

Either way, there was only one answer to his question. "Starved."

"Good, because dinner is ready."

"I thought something smelled good when I walked in."

"And I thought it was you that smelled good enough to eat," he said, lowering his head to nibble her throat.

She took a step back, her cheeks flushing with heat as Brendan giggled.

It made her happy to hear her son happy, and while Brendan had never been a shy child, he'd positively blossomed under Patrick's attention. But why should she be surprised that her little boy had fallen in love with the rancher when she'd done the same thing?

Yes, she'd been hurt and angry when he'd brushed her off, but the residue of those feelings couldn't dim the brightness of the love that filled her heart.

And maybe it was scary to think about giving him another chance, but it was a lot scarier to think about living the rest of her life without the man she loved.

So they sat on their knees at the coffee table and ate to-die-for grilled cheese—which Brendan helped make—followed by Sweet Caroline's Twelve-Layer Chocolate Bliss for dessert.

When Brendan had licked the last remnants of icing off his fork, he leaned over and stage-whispered to Patrick, "When are you gonna ask her?"

"Apparently right now," Patrick said.

"Well, *do* it," her son urged.

Brooke watched the interaction between them—one a little impatient, the other a little bit nervous.

"Ask me what?" she asked warily, thinking her son might have somehow finagled the promise of a puppy from the rancher.

"If you'll be my girlfriend, and maybe go out on a date with me sometime," Patrick replied.

Not a puppy, but something much bigger, she realized.

And she understood the significance of him making the request in front of her son. He wasn't just asking her to go out for dinner or to a movie, but to acknowledge that they were in a relationship together. He was asking her to take a chance—to give their relationship a chance.

Don't you think it's time...to take a chance and finally let yourself be happy?

"I will," she agreed.

"Yay!" Brendan cheered and pumped his chocolate-smeared fist in the air, prompting Brooke to send her son to wash up and get ready for bed.

When Patrick gathered the dessert plates to take them to the kitchen, she followed to help tidy up. But he had other ideas.

Better ideas, she decided, when he kissed her, long and slow and deep.

And then he said, "I love you, Brooke. I know those words don't make everything okay but—"

She touched her fingers to his lips to halt the flow of words and replied simply, "I love you, too."

When the kitchen was tidied, Patrick and Brooke returned to the living room. Brendan, having brushed his teeth and changed into his pj's, snuggled up on the sofa with them.

Together. A family.

"I've been thinking about something," Brendan suddenly announced.

And Patrick had a sneaking suspicion he knew what that "something" was.

"What have you been thinking about?" Brooke asked her son.

"I don't wanna be the third Dr. Langley."

"That's okay." Brooke ruffled his hair affectionately. "You've got lots of time to figure out what you want to do with your life."

"I wanna be a vet," he said. "But I wanna be the *second* Dr. Stafford."

"You can't just change your name, Brendan."

"I can change mine if you change yours," he said.

Patrick sighed. "You really don't understand what 'later' means, do you?" he said to Brendan.

"I'm impatient," the boy reminded him.

"I know," he admitted.

Brooke looked at Patrick then, a slight furrow between her brows. "I think I'm missing something here."

"That's because your son skipped a few steps ahead. What Brendan was supposed to say—but not until you'd had some time to get used to dating me," he said, with a pointed look at the child, "is that you could be the first Dr. Stafford…if you agreed to marry me."

Then he pulled the ring box out of his pocket and opened it to reveal a three-and-a-half-carat diamond solitaire set in a platinum band.

"Ohmygod." The words were a whispered prayer as hope bloomed inside her more abundantly than the flowers on the table.

"Do you like it? I picked it out," her son said proudly. "It's a princess cut." He looked up at Patrick. "Did I get that right?"

She had to laugh. "Of course it's a princess cut. And of course I like it, but…" She looked helplessly at Patrick, stunned and overwhelmed. "Don't you think this is happening a little fast?"

He shook his head. "I think I've been waiting for you my whole life."

"But are you sure you're ready to get married?" she asked. "It's a pretty big step from girlfriend to fiancée in one night."

"And I can't wait for you to be my wife, so that you and Brendan can come to live with me at the Silver Star."

"And I want to live at the Silver Star and finally have a dad," Brendan chimed in.

"So what do you say, Brooke? Will you marry me so that we can all live together and Brendan can call me 'Dad' instead of 'Mr. Patrick'?"

"Say 'yes,' Mom."

"You better be sure about this," she warned Patrick. "Because if I say 'yes,' it's forever."

"Well, that's good," he said, holding her gaze so that

she could see the truth and depth of his feelings in his eyes. "Because I want you—both of you—forever."

"In that case, my answer is yes," she told him.

"Yay!" Brendan cheered.

Brooke suspected he'd also pumped his fist in the air, but she didn't see it because Patrick was kissing her.

"I told you she'd kiss you if you gave her flowers," the boy said smugly.

"You did indeed," Patrick agreed.

"And how is it that my son is an expert on kissing and flowers?" Brooke wondered.

"It's a long story that starts with his grandparents and leads to a girl named Ruby."

She decided the story could wait till another time.

After all, they were going to have a lifetime together.

* * * * *

MILLS & BOON

Coming next month

THE PRINCE AND THE WEDDING PLANNER
Jennifer Faye

Bianca shook her head. With him gazing into her eyes, her heart had leapt into her throat. Was that desire reflected in his eyes? The prince desired her? Her heart tumbled in her chest.

She didn't know how long they stood there staring into each other's eyes. It was like Leo had a gravitational force around him and she was being drawn in. Though she knew letting anything happen between them would be a mistake—compounding all of the other uncertainties in her life—she remained rooted to the spot in front of him.

Her heart raced as she found herself getting lost in his dark gaze. Her fingers tingled with the urge to reach out to him—

Someone cleared their throat. Loudly. Annoyingly.

And in that second, the connection dissipated. Bianca blinked and glanced away. Heat rushed to her face. She was grateful she didn't have to speak because she didn't trust her tongue to work correctly.

Leo cleared his throat. "Yes, Michael. What is it?"

"You are needed, sir. The call from Canada."

Leo sighed. "I'll be right there." Once the man moved on, Leo turned his full attention to her. "I'm sorry. I've been expecting this call all day."

"I understand. You have important business to attend to."

Reality had come crashing in on them. And none too soon. He was a royal prince. She was a wedding planner with an uncertain heritage. They did not belong together.

"About this…" As his voice trailed off, he looked at her with confusion reflected in his eyes.

He wasn't the only one to be confused. Her heart had betrayed her mind in wanting what it could not have. And now that her feet were once again planted firmly on the ground, she couldn't forget that she was here to do a job. That needed to be her focus. Not getting swept up in some fairytale.

"It's okay," she said. "You have important work to do."

"You're not upset about ending the evening so soon?"

She shook her head. "Not at all. I understand that business must come first."

As he escorted her back to the palace, he didn't offer her his arm. And she made sure to keep a reasonable distance between them. Because as much as nothing had happened between them, something most definitely had almost happened.

Continue reading
THE PRINCE AND THE WEDDING PLANNER
Jennifer Faye

Available next month
www.millsandboon.co.uk

COMING SOON!

We really hope you enjoyed reading this book. If you're looking for more romance, be sure to head to the shops when new books are available on

Thursday 20th March

To see which titles are coming soon, please visit

millsandboon.co.uk/nextmonth